THE CUBAN

by

KIM RODRIGUEZ

Omnific Publishing
2355 Westwood Blvd, #506
Los Angeles, CA 90064
www.omnificpublishing.com

First Omnific ebook edition, April 2018
First Omnific trade paperback edition, April 2018

Library of Congress Cataloguing-in-Publication Data

Rodriguez, Kim
The Cuban / Kim Rodriguez – 1st ed. isbn: 978-1-623422-55-4
1. Miami—Fiction. 2. Cuba—Fiction.
3. Romance—Fiction. 4. Rich woman —Fiction. I. Title

10 9 8 7 6 5 4 3 2 1

Book Cover Design by Micha Stone and Amy Brokaw

Printed In the United States of America

To Rafa, for coming to life.

CHAPTER ONE

On the penultimate night of my cruise to Panama, I opened the wardrobe and found my new favorite dress, a black, long-sleeved, off the shoulder ball gown that had been a present from my older brother. The couture Valentino had shipped directly from the new flagship boutique in Rome, a museum-like space so opulent it could've been carved from Michelangelo's Tuscan marble quarries. I knew it well.

The card read, "Dear Amanda, I saw this dress at a fashion show last month and thought it would look fantastic on you. Happy Birthday, Kieran." The gown was magnificent, a romantic tapestry of nude-colored silk beneath black Italian lace, featuring a tight corseted bodice that masterfully counterbalanced the full, floor length skirt. It fit like a glove, and as I turned to admire myself from the back, I let my hands glide down the lace over my breasts to my waist, appreciating its provocative architecture. Knowing the dress didn't need much else, I ran my fingers through my long honey-blonde hair and applied a bit of makeup, then grabbed a simple black clutch and slipped into matching Gucci stilettos, silently thanking my thoughtful, albeit mostly absent brother, even though my gut told me he hadn't chosen it. *The man who bought this dress is in love.*

I made my way to the formal dining room and found it alight with sound and activity, pausing a moment to read the sign beside the oversized mahogany double doors: "Caribbean Night on the *Ruby* Welcomes *Conjunto Matanzas*, a Celia Cruz Tribute Ensemble." I snaked through a crowd of beautifully dressed passengers, all the way down the dark corridor to the threshold of the main salon, an already opulent space artfully decorated for tonight's celebration as a technicolor tropical paradise.

My palms sweat and my heart fluttered as the beat of the drums pounded, my body awakened by the drama of wailing horns and the grandeur of a live Cuban orchestra. I smiled as I passed by the large stage overflowing with tuxedoed musicians, all of them focused on a short, round woman in a beaded cocktail dress and blond pageboy wig, a shameless vixen who shook every part of her voluptuous body while belting out sultry foreign lyrics into the microphone. At the close of the final verse, she held an impossible note, veins in her neck straining until her last breath, then threw her arms up in the air and cried out ¡azucar! The crowd went wild.

The singer's crimson gown exploded around her knees as she was possessed by the music, and out of nowhere, a dark, sexy musician emerged from the shadows and pulled her across the stage, his tight, violent grip forcing her up against him. They exchanged a knowing look as his hand dropped to pull her pelvis into his, both of them swirling their hips together to the rhythm, eyes bewitched. Hypnotized by the energy in the room, at least a dozen couples rose from their tables to join the crowd of flushed, panting dancers already on their feet, every man and woman seduced by the carnival atmosphere and sensual Cuban music.

Our head waiter Ernesto spotted me before I approached the table. Smiling and beckoning me closer, he edged his way between the crowded tables, asking for my hand by extending his own. I reached out, glad to see a welcoming face. Although Ernesto had to have been close to seventy years old, it was clear he'd once been a very handsome man, with kind eyes and the whitest, fullest head of hair I'd ever seen.

"Good Evening, Ms. Rose," he said. "You look ravishing—just like a movie star." His eyes shined as he took in my appearance and then, with a slight bow and a grand flourish, he produced a single-long stemmed pink rose. I couldn't tell where he'd kept it hidden, but I imagine the trick must have been one of the many skills the dashing Ernesto had perfected over the years.

"A rose for Miss Rose," he poeticized, clearly amused by his own wit.

"Thank you, Ernesto," I said. Pleased, he pulled a black velvet chair out from beneath the medium-sized table for six. I inhaled the scent of the rose as I lowered myself into the plush seat, and even though we both knew I'd pay for the rose a hundred times over in the tip envelope at the end of the week, it was still nice to pretend. I set the flower down beside my clutch on the crisp white tablecloth and offered my tablemates a polite hello.

Ernesto had been kind enough to seat me preferentially, facing the stage, so my attention went back to the band. The singer, breathless from dancing, returned to the microphone as the lively music came to an end and the room thundered with applause.

"Ladies and gentlemen," she began in a thick Spanish accent, "as Celia Cruz says, 'please excuse me, you know my English is not very good-looking!'" She paused, knowing exactly where her joke would get the big laugh. Right on cue, the audience erupted, and in appreciation she blew a kiss to the crowd. "Please enjoy your food with the romantic music of *Trio Palmera* and I come back later and we dance again!" Backing away with a coquettish wave and more kisses, she held her dress up and descended the backstage steps.

"Rafa, double Russian Standard Gold, neat!" Ernesto barked out the order somewhere over my shoulder, clapping his hands. "Quickly, for the lady with the rose. *Rápido, muchacho! Pa' la señora que tiene la rosa.*" I'd only had to ask Ernesto for my drink once the very first night, and after that, he kept my double vodkas coming. He was just doing his job, yet his attentiveness still resonated somewhere deep inside me.

I reluctantly turned my attention to the others, now knowing them well enough to be certain we had nothing in common. Every night this week I'd struggled to make conversation with the mismatched group, an adult mother and daughter from Boston, a cute retired California couple, and a wealthy red-headed divorcée in her sixties from Miami. The divorcée, Sharon, zoned in on me right away, desperate for conversation.

"So, Amanda, how did you like the jungle today?" she asked, fingering the dainty Harry Winston Sunflower bracelet on her wrist. I'd seen it just last month in New York, quite beautifully displayed in a window, but now it struck me as gaudy and cheap-looking on her wrist.

"I didn't feel well," I said. "I had to come back to the ship early and rest."

"The heat," said Sharon, with a certainly that led me to believe she knew her way around much more than I realized. "My—friend—told me the crew never gets off the ship here." At the mention of a new acquaintance, I braced myself for what was coming and took another little sniff of my rose.

"Well, I stayed in," she said, bringing her martini glass up to her glossy red lips, "but I had a great time. Four great times, to be exact." She gave me a wink and took a sip.

"Ah. You had company."

Past any formalities on this topic, I'd been hearing about Sharon's romantic interludes all week. She must have felt some sort of single woman camaraderie with me, because she hadn't hesitated to share the details about all the men she'd slept with on her vacation, mostly members of the ship's crew. I began to feel awkward, and shifted in my seat, wishing for my drink, beyond happy to cut the conversation short when *Trio Palmera* took the stage.

As the first few notes of the Cuban son washed over me, a translucent veil fell upon the room like a memory, softening my vision and disbanding reality. It was a lovely sensation, and without any real reason, something shifted. Everything became more colorful, musical notes sounded sweeter, and for the first time in so long, I was at peace. I questioned why I'd ever tortured myself with frantic trips to European castles and museums when everything I needed was here on the water, in the air of the open ocean.

"Su bebida, señora." *Your drink, ma'am.*

A man's deep voice came from behind, unbearably close. His breath lingered on the sensitive skin of my neck, his words crashing against me, two hands without a body. No one had ever spoken to me in my ear, not even a lover, and I came alive. Anticipating the brush of his jacket against my shoulder, I froze, fighting the instinct to move toward him.

He leaned in from the left to place the cocktail on the table. First, I saw the black of his jacket, then the white of his shirt, and finally a

Roman nose far more beautiful than any artist had ever sculpted. My body softened and my pupils dilated, my brain instantly high from whatever wicked chemicals rushed my body, his light blue eyes probing mine as he set the glass down beside my flower. I took in as much of him as I could, marveling at his chiseled face, the dark unruly hair framing it, and the bit of stubble above and below his perfect mouth. Digging my fingers into the flesh of my thighs under the table, my body turned rigid as a board, and when his lips parted ever so slightly, it seemed for a moment he might lean in to kiss me right there, without so much as a hello first.

Unable to withstand his gaze for more than a second, I found the spot on the glass where his hand had just been and drank deeply, and though the alcohol hugged me from the inside, for the first time its effect seemed pale in comparison to what I was already feeling. By then he was gone and I was glad, because one of us had to retreat or surely I would combust. I had just stared into the sun.

"Holy shit!" said Sharon, mouth agape, barely able to contain herself. She leaned in, her generous cleavage spilling onto the table. "Did you see him? He was gorgeous!"

Even though it was the truth, it bothered me that she was so worked up. In just a split second I'd sensed the vulnerability in him, the same kind of weariness carried by an animal that isn't sure if you're going to pet or kick it. I didn't like to think of anyone being stalked by a sex-crazed woman all night, forced to put up with her antics for fear of losing his job. However, with that face it couldn't possibly be the first time a woman fell apart at the mere sight of him. He would know what to do with her.

"What did Ernesto call him? Rafa?" asked Sharon, giddy with excitement. "He sounded Cuban, and goddamn if those Cuban men aren't something else in bed," she purred, her chin resting against perfectly manicured talons. "I'd like to take him home with me." Her big diamond rings glistened in the soft light of the dining room as she allowed her mind to conjure images of undulating, intertwined flesh.

"That's funny," I said, actually thinking it was disgusting. Sharon's unbridled lust of course reminded me of Plato's charioteer analogy, and as the vodka kicked in I let my mind wander to happy places. In the *Phaedrus,* Plato compares the human soul to a charioteer and two horses, the charioteer representing reason, the white horse intellectual passion, and the black horse physical lust. Across the table I could almost see Sharon's soul splintering into pieces, the white horse and charioteer half dead from being dragged straight into hell by a black stallion in heat.

"Sweetie, I'm not joking," she said, misinterpreting the smile that had crept across my face. "What do you think these young men are here for? They all want to meet a sugar mama." She cocked her head to the side and batted her eyes in disbelief. "Not one single crew member has approached you this week?"

"God no." I'd never been propositioned by anyone, and I doubted it would ever happen. Men had a tendency to ignore me.

"Well, they probably think you're still too young and pretty," she said, scanning the room for her prey. "And you don't say much, either." Her comment stung because I knew she meant I wasn't very interesting, but by that time she was barely aware of me or our conversation anyway, so I ignored it.

"Too young for what?"

"To be single *and* rich."

Tired of waiting, Sharon grabbed her clutch and stood up like a woman possessed, pausing only to discreetly adjust the V-neck of her evening gown. There was no doubt she was a very attractive woman regardless of her age, and unlike me, Sharon would get exactly what she wanted.

"Excuse me," she said to the table.

"Where are you going?" I asked. It was none of my business, but I had a good idea.

"The ladies' room, of course," she answered, with mock exasperation. I wasn't sure who she thought she was fooling, because there was no doubt she was going to roam around the kitchen until she found her next meal in the form of a gorgeous waiter named Rafa.

With that, Sharon was off, and since the rest of my tablemates appeared lost in their own banal conversations, after the generous appetizer I decided I'd had enough. I just couldn't relax knowing that at any moment he might come back, so I thought it wise to leave early. My delicate state of mind was already barely hanging by a thread, and the last thing I needed was something to upset my equilibrium and throw me into a mood that would be difficult to come back from. I'd had enough of that to last a lifetime.

The night was lovely but cold, so I decided to stay inside and take the long way back to my cabin, passing the casino, the auditorium and the now closed shops. Walking the distance of the ship made me aware of the weight of my gown, and it struck me as a shame to waste such a beautiful dress on a failure of an evening. Unlike other people I knew, I judged success not by my possessions or wealth, but by the time spent enjoying the company of people I love. In that respect, I was very poor and had been all my life. I envied people who had large extended families to share holidays and life events with, and even when our parents were alive, they always traveled without us, leaving my brother and me with the nanny of the month. We had no real family left because my mother had been the only child of an only child, and my father's only brother had died in his late teens. I can say that my parents were in love, but their affection for each other was often at the exclusion of other people, including their children. When they died together overseas, Kieran and I barely noticed.

Since then, it had mostly been just us, my workaholic brother, and me, his shy, intellectual little sister. In later years, my one chance at a family had gone horribly wrong, and I made it my mission to pretend it had all been a bad dream. I longed for the day Kieran would find the right girl and start a family of his own, because now our only comforts were the vast wealth we'd inherited, the family business that Kieran ran for us both, Boxwood Paint, and each other.

It was almost midnight and I began to feel sleepy, so I entered the darkened library and cut across the deck to my suite. The sounds of laugher and noise gradually faded as I made my way deeper into the ship, nearing the sanctuary of quiet, secluded cabins. Looking down into my clutch for the room key, I turned the corner slowly, eyes down, and stood in front of my door fumbling, annoyed at the possibility I might have to go all the way back to the front of the ship for assistance.

"Damn," I muttered, trying to find the card.

Just then, I heard a man clear his throat. I looked up to see him—Rafa—leaning against the handrail about ten feet away. He had a slight smile on his beautiful face, and he stood in a way that was so cool and leisurely, I thought perhaps he had mistaken me for someone else.

"Hello," he said in a Spanish accent so thick I could barely understand even the single word. He wore the elegant tuxedo from earlier but looked nothing like a waiter; he was absolutely chic, like a model straight out of an Italian fashion magazine. He remained in his spot by the rail, about ten feet away from me, and even though I should have been scared of him, I had to admit it was the opposite.

"Have you lost your … key?" It took him some effort to come up with each word, clearly struggling to translate the ideas in his head as he spoke to me. He was working hard on all fronts, and despite the obvious language barrier, his warmth poured through me as it had earlier at the table. There was no fear, only the same incredible pull toward him again, and this time I wasn't sure I even wanted to resist.

"No, I found it," I said softly, feeling the slick card between my fingers. He remained perfectly still, and it was then I realized he wouldn't move until I either went to him or told him to leave. We both stood in the quiet hallway of the ship, Rafa in his tuxedo and me in my designer gown, in awe of how two complete strangers could fall into such immediate intimacy. There was nothing around us, no music, no people, and no distractions, only the clarity of the bright lights above and the subtle hum of the ship's engine. We saw each other plainly in the light, each of us thoroughly lucid, yet absolutely intoxicated and not pretending otherwise. It was as if the universe gave us a quiet moment to recognize one another, so as we lazily took each other in, unrushed, I came to the conclusion that he was the most beautiful man I had ever seen. Perhaps not perfect, but perfectly assembled.

A million scenarios ran through my mind. Maybe I'd inadvertently made him think I was looking for casual sex, or Sharon had said something to suggest I was alone and desperate. But even if he only wanted me in bed for an hour, I didn't think I'd have the will power to turn him away. When a man looks like he was sculpted in Heaven's atelier, a woman can only spend the rest of her life regretting all the things she didn't do with him. The little smile on his face turned into a wonderfully sexy scowl, and sensing my indecision, he took his hand from his pocket and held it out to me.

"Come here," he said in the same deep, unmistakably masculine voice I'd heard in my ear earlier. I took the three or four steps toward him and placed my fingertips on his, and smiling to himself, he pulled me in.

I became lost in the smell of his hair and a cologne that reminded me of a Guerlain fragrance I remembered from long ago. The fabric of his tuxedo brushed noisily against the tulle under my own lace gown as I came closer, and while I desperately craved his skin on mine, I was only brave enough to put my cheek against his. I closed my eyes and heard him sigh as he shifted his weight from one foot to the other.

"You're so beautiful," he murmured.

I didn't want to pull back, afraid of an awkward moment. It was too delicious standing here just as we were. How can two strangers simply fall into an embrace without even knowing each other's names? We danced without moving, a pure leap of faith off a tall cliff into a dense fog. Purring with satisfaction, he lost a little of the control he'd been trying so hard to maintain. His hands moved up my back as his soft lips found my neck, sweet kisses so tender that my legs buckled, but when he felt my body go limp in his, he grasped me so tightly by the waist that I let out a cry.

My clutch and everything in it hit the floor as his mouth came down on mine, the whole of my being opening fully, allowing him access without qualification. We parted our lips, his tongue searching my mouth feverishly, demanding entry. He pulled my body into his own and let me feel his growing need. *You do this to me*, he said without words.

After a few moments, he stopped and scanned me again, differently this time. He paid no attention to the black curl that fell out of place onto his lightly tanned forehead, and it was so charming I resisted the urge to push it back. With both hands snugly on my narrow waist, he then gave me a sweet, chaste kiss as if we hadn't just been about to swallow each other whole.

"Do you want me—" Again, he tried to find the right word. He glanced down the long empty hall. "To leave?" I marveled at his expression, taking in his lips, now delightfully swollen and red from kissing me. Youthful eyes the color of the sea begged me to stay. For him, the entire encounter had been nothing but an exercise in self-control.

"No." Still in his embrace, I whispered, "Speak to me in Spanish. I understand you." *No. Háblame en español. Te entiendo.*

"Really?" he asked in Spanish. His face lit up when I nodded, as if I had just opened up a door he assumed would always be closed between us, and with that simple arrangement, the power between us shifted. For once, I wasn't responsible for the conversation and the amusing observations. By promising to speak to him in his own language, the esteemed Dr. Amanda Rose, former professor of English, was now the student rather than the teacher.

"Can you understand me?" I asked, speaking to him in Spanish. The way I spoke was basic and unrefined, but I knew it was good enough, and as I expected he grinned from ear to ear, affording me my first glimpse of his ultra-sexy smile.

"Of course. Perfectly."

Rafa picked my evening bag up off the floor and used the key to open the door, and as we crossed the threshold of the cabin, all pretense and fear fell away. I walked ahead of him, my heart racing and my body attuned to his presence. I stopped at the bed and waited, facing away. The door shut and I knew he was close, but there was only silence.

When I was ready, I turned to face him and began, "So, what—"

Before I could finish, he caught me off guard and kissed me. I almost fell backward onto the bed, but his arms, rock-hard across my back, cradled me as I leaned against him with all my weight. He pressed us together, my body responding to his proximity in a way that was unthinking and automatic, my physical state of arousal now completely under his control. A rush of moisture pooled between my legs as he again dipped to kiss my neck and the curve of my shoulder, his grip at my back relaxing and guiding me into a seated position on the bed.

Dropping to his knees, Rafa looked into my eyes, his angelic face lit from the side by a single fixture above the mirror. He was a vision of shadows and light, and though I lacked the eye of an artist, I was certain Rafa must be at the peak of his exquisite beauty, one so rare it would be criminal not to capture it and preserve it forever. *Rafael, the angel, waiting tables on a cruise ship. Rafael, the Adonis, using his beauty to romance sad, rich, old women.* It made me sad, yet I knew he must be here for reasons that made sense to him, and I wouldn't condemn him for it.

"Please get up," I said, troubled by the idea that he could be interested in trading a night of passion for money. I brought my knees together. Simply put, I knew I couldn't possibly take advantage of anyone in need.

"Why?" he asked sharply. "Do you think you should kneel between the man's legs first?"

I was surprised he would risk angering me when he had already put so much into my seduction, but I knew he'd sensed my pity, and rather than allow me to feel superior, his instinct was to challenge me. I'd presumed he could only be offering me pleasure in exchange for what was in my wallet. It might be true, but how little did I think of myself to assume it *must* be true?

"You don't even know my name," I shot back.

"Your name is *Amada*," he said, as he moved his hungry gaze up and down my body and then squeezed my ankles. The muscles in my thighs relaxed and my legs inched apart again.

"It's Amanda," I replied. His hands moved up the back of my legs, pushing the lace skirt of my gown up as he went. Responding to him, my thighs opened a little more.

"No, you're my *Amada*," said Rafa, squeezing my knees. *No, tú eres mi Amada.* With each long stroke he claimed my body from the bottom up, relaxing me, eroding my control, attuning me to him. Amada, I finally remembered, is Spanish for *my love.*

"But you don't know my name," he countered. He blinked slowly, hypnotically, then rubbed the side of his face against the inside of my thigh, expertly using his coarse whiskers and soft skin to create delightful, unexpected sensations. I was coming apart already and he'd barely touched me.

"I heard Ernesto call you Rafa. Your name is Rafael." I struggled to get the words out, finding it difficult to catch my breath with Rafa's head between my legs. He maintained eye contact with me as he nodded yes, then turned his gaze downward so that he could gently kiss each of my knees and then lick the inside of my naked thigh.

"Nice to meet you," he murmured, his soft, wet tongue making its way higher and higher, each stroke melting me inch by inch until I found myself flat on the bed with his handsome face fully in my core. He pulled my silk panties to the side and spread me with his fingers, one too many moments passing before he let his tongue explore me with abandon. I expected him to start thrashing away, but instead he surprised me with a series of torturously slow, precise movements right at my entrance, and when he finally made his way inside, he lapped my walls for a long time. The way he used his mouth was unlike anything I'd ever felt before, his soft tongue ebbing and flowing as he gently rubbed my breasts over my dress. I squirmed and clenched, willing him to go a little higher, but he only gave me more of the same silky kisses. His stubble grazed the delicate skin of my inner thighs again, and the rough sensation coupled with the almost unbearable softness between my legs caused me to come up off the bed. I brought my most sensitive spot to his mouth, silently begging for release.

"Not yet," said Rafa, as he made his way back up. I tried to hide my disappointment by studying his lips, gloriously shiny and plump from his work. We lay together side by side now, and although I was incredibly aroused, I still didn't reach out. He noticed, and I watched his blue eyes go down the length of my body and then stop somewhere I couldn't tell. "Touch me," he urged. His face softened as he smiled and kissed me.

Before long I was on my stomach in the center of the bed. I arched my back as he positioned himself astride me, and it took him no time at all to find the zipper of my gown and pull it all the way down until the cool air of the room swept against my skin. I shifted a little so that he could slide it off and drape it across the wing chair, and now, almost fully nude beneath this stranger, I noted that my lack of abandon, so out of character, didn't bother me at all. I was simply going to let him have me. So this is what a one night stand is. Strip. Have meaningless sex. Get out.

"The dress is exquisite," he said, "but not nearly as *fina* as you." He let his hands roam over my back, my ass, and my legs, and I cursed myself, because even in a moment like this, I couldn't help but notice the nuances of his language.

"Fine?" I asked, momentarily switching back to English.

Rafa paused for a moment to think, then resumed the delicious massage, slowly increasing pressure until he was sure I liked a firm touch. His precise, measured rhythm turned me to complete putty in his hands, and he worked my body as if intimately familiar with every fiber under my skin. Still kneading, he said, "*Fina* means elegant or delicate."

"Like when you say, 'fine china,'" I murmured, understanding, but lost in his touch.

"Yes. Just. Like. That."

His voice was pure velvet in any language, and as he spoke, he pulled my panties down my legs and over my stilettos, leaving me completely naked while he himself remained fully dressed. He punctuated the last word by inserting one finger inside me, precisely where his soft tongue had just been. He rested his other hand on my lower back as my backside rose up to meet the finger massaging me from the inside. I was ass up, chest down, no doubt a pleasant view from his angle.

Knowing that he couldn't see my face if I didn't want him to allowed me to think only about what I was feeling, so I instinctively rotated my hips in unison with the finger inside me. He pushed downward into my soft passage, in the direction of the bed below, and when he slipped a second finger inside, I experienced the strangest sensations of warmth, happiness and well-being. It was amazing, and as he expertly rubbed just the right spot, he called forth something stronger than an orgasm. It was so intense, in fact, that I was fearful of what exactly my body might do if he continued.

"Your curves are so beautiful," he said. "I wish you could see yourself."

"Tell me," I whispered. Brazen and blissfully lost in whatever he was doing to me, I turned my head in the other direction and shut my eyes, anticipating the explicit, base words he would no doubt use to describe my form, that of a shameless woman who'd allowed a complete stranger to violate her in less than thirty minutes. Whatever he said, I deserved. But even so, I just wanted to hear him speak. I cried out in protest when he slid off my legs and slipped his fingers out, never having been so close to something so wonderful.

"Turn over," he said. Now fully under his spell, I did as he asked and once again we locked eyes. I didn't want to his physical beauty to hypnotize me, but it was impossible. What could it be like for a man to be so unnaturally handsome that women instantly lost all sense of morality, I wondered. I pitied him for all the disgusting, hungry women who had used money and influence to lure him into their beds. "Had he been born a prince, he undoubtedly would have been an arrogant playboy with the world at his feet, but as an uneducated pauper from a third-world country, he surely had been forced to exchange his only currency to satisfy the most basic of needs." Sadly, he of all people should have been born an aristocrat like so many of the utterly worthless men I had known, but he hadn't been. Rafael was just a waiter, made even more vulnerable to the corruption of the world by his magnificent beauty. Even though every inch of my skin was fully bared to him, he seemed far more exposed than I.

From my supine position, I became aware of the rise and fall of my pale breasts, my nipples two swollen blossoms directly in our line of sight. Rafa held my legs apart and looked thoughtfully. I was a ball of need and didn't care about anything except feeling him inside me again.

"I see *The Origin of the World.*"

He knew the painting. I blushed, recalling the model's anatomy, her abundant pubic hair and generous curves. I could picture it in my mind's eye perfectly, as I had just viewed it last spring in Paris at the Musée d'Orsay. He had been with me then, and I hadn't even known it.

My pelvis still humming, I sat up and kissed him, overcome by the instinct to possess and ravish. I was out of my mind with desire for him now, and whether it made sense or not, I knew our bodies were meant for one another. I slid my hands under his jacket and felt his sculpted body beneath the fabric, he every bit as hard as I was soft. I lost any sense of self-doubt and set about consuming him because I knew I wanted him everywhere: in my mouth, in my hair, between my legs, upon me as a blanket. Devouring his lips, I unfastened his tie, his vest and then his shirt. I pushed the heavy garments off and took a moment to examine the naked torso I could feel afire beneath my own skin. He remained still and let me admire him as I traced my fingers along a narrow waist that widened into tanned, broad shoulders and muscular arms that looked as if they had carried the weight of the universe. Irrational and wild, I tugged clumsily at his belt buckle, but he took my wrist and held me still. *Oh, no more of this*, I thought. *Just give me what I want.*

"Amada," he said breathlessly, resting his forehead on mine, "I can please you in other ways. I don't want you to remember me and feel empty. You're too delicate for that." Again the word *fina*. I was china to Rafa: pretty and easily broken.

For possibly the first time in my life I was at a loss for words, so I gladly let my body take over. Rafa still had me by the wrist, so I used my other hand to caress between his legs. He was so hard and beckoning that I was drawn instinctively to that part of him, and without thinking I leaned down and nipped at him through the fabric of his pants. He moaned with pleasure and slightly released his grip so that I was able to pull away and have full use of my hands. Both on our knees now, we kissed and swayed together, still on the precipice of nothing and everything. I burned for him, my body yearning to coil itself around him in the most indelicate of ways. I rubbed against Rafa like an animal in heat, completely unashamed of my neediness, and with that, any sense of chivalry finally left him. Once he decided to take me, any concerns he might have had for being sensible were promptly abandoned, and I saw it in his eyes the moment it happened.

Rafa took my forearms and pushed me down, as I had been before, then got off the bed. He stared at my body as he finished undressing and I returned his gaze, enraptured just as much by his muscular thighs and his broad shoulders as I was by his large, erect penis. Just before dropping his pants to the floor, he removed his wallet from a pocket and pulled out a condom, and I watched with pleasure as he held himself away from his body and rolled it down his shaft. He was so beautiful everywhere, especially there, and because he was so turned on, I don't know if he even realized he gave himself a quick stroke before getting back into bed on top of me.

"Rafa," I breathed, face to face with him. He kissed me savagely and pushed his whole weight and rock hardness onto me. Feeling unbearably empty, I writhed and ran my fingernails down his back, trying to control his movements and line him up at my entrance, but he wouldn't allow it.

"What, Amada?" he asked, looking right into my eyes. "I don't understand."

"I—" I gasped, choking on my own words.

"I can't help you, then. I'm leaving," he said, actually sitting up as if to get out of bed. I don't know what came over me, but I went crazy. I threw my leg over his to keep him from standing up, grabbed him by the hair and bit his shoulder from behind, hard. I know I startled him, but he rewarded me with a little smile anyway.

"Please," I begged. Still wrapped around him from behind, I peppered his shoulder blades and the back of his neck with delicate kisses.

"Wrong answer," he said, and stood up again. It didn't matter that I tried to stop him, as he only had to use a bit of his considerable strength to free himself and walk across the room. He stood defiantly by the dressing table and crossed his arms over his chest as he spread his legs a little and gave me a good view of the body we both knew could bring me so much pleasure. I practically salivated watching his muscles undulate under his tight, tanned skin. His jaw, tight and angry looking, betrayed him, clear evidence of his intense arousal. On the bed without him I felt cold and alone, desperate to figure out whatever it was he wanted to hear.

"I want you inside me," I said, switching to English, only because I wasn't quite sure what those particular words would be. Instinctively I knew he would understand, and as I predicted, he smiled and waited for more.

"It's your fault," I said in my sexiest voice, catching on. "You used your fingers and tongue but stopped before I could finish. Twice. You made me ache way up here where I can't reach." I placed my hand over my belly for emphasis.

His composure broke a little, and I saw him close his eyes and clench his jaw again. Hm. He liked that. I started to feel brave, but it lasted only a second.

"You think I have sex for money," he said. "Do you really think I give myself to anyone who asks?"

"No, I don't," I stammered back in Spanish, "Not like that." I went to him and was pleasantly surprised when he opened his arms and embraced me even though he assumed I was silently judging him.

"I think you're doing exactly whatever you need to do, nothing more and nothing less."

"You're correct," he agreed, bringing his strong hands down around my backside. He kneaded my ass as he kissed me and then, without warning, hiked me effortlessly up onto himself. I gasped with pleasure as I wrapped my arms around his neck and felt him fill me to the brim, then still.

"All I need is to feel you around me, tight and warm," he whispered in my ear. It wasn't enough that he was inside my body, he made it his business to be inside my head, too. "I've been hard all night because I haven't been able to stop thinking about us together just like this." He slowly began to move his hips, balancing me on his angled pelvis. "I knew you would feel good," he groaned, moving faster, "but I never imagined I could enjoy you this much." *Nunca me imaginé que iba a gozar tanto de tí.*

I tightened my grip around his shoulders, and like the inarticulate beast I had become, I bit him again, this time on the back of the neck. He responded by grunting and grinding me down onto him even harder, generating exquisite little stabs of pain at the opening of my sex. Fully impaled and suspended in midair, we defied gravity as I rode his hard body. Rafa thrust into me again and again, effortlessly pressing me into him as we made love in our own perfect cocoon.

"You like to bite," he mused, licking the side of my face from my collar bone all the way up to my temple. "It drives me crazy." He probed my mouth with his tongue as if searching for his own body somewhere deep inside me, arched and stiff all over, like a famished tiger attacking its prey.

"Only you," I gasped, not really understanding why I was compelled to be rough with him.

"That's exactly right, only me," said Rafa, still working us both into a frenzy with his powerful thrusts. He was all the way inside, farther than I knew was possible, pushing in and in and in. Beads of sweat rolled down his back but he just wouldn't stop, and I shut my eyes tight when the feeling from earlier came again, an approaching wave I was certain would pull me under. Fear washed over me and I tried to push him away.

"No, I can't," I cried.

Ignoring my protests, Rafa turned us and backed me up against the wall, compounding the already extreme sensations deep within me. My emotions ran wild and my thoughts made no sense—one moment I wanted to hurt him, and then the next it was something approaching love. It didn't take long before my body started to tingle in a way that worried me, a sure sign that something raw and uncontrollable and completely unknown was approaching. Because he'd braced his forearm arm above my head, it was the first thing I saw when I had the same overwhelming urge to bite him. Holding nothing back, I clamped down hard on his biceps, but this time he let me know how much it hurt.

"Amada!" He glanced at his arm and then stared at me in disbelief. Overwrought with desire and near the edge himself, he put his

hand over my mouth and grappled us down to the floor, positioning me on all fours in front of him. I arched my back, and without
missing a beat, he dug his fingers into my hips and kept up the same
punishing rhythm until the room filled with his deep groans and my
own cries. Seeking reassurance, I turned and looked into eyes already
fixed on me.

"I love you," said Rafa. His face softened while his body remained
hard and unyielding. "Don't be afraid."

The euphoria rolled in quickly, and before I knew it the room
changed color, my vision pixelated, and I hallucinated that the stars
had come up above us like fireworks and bathed the room in a bright
cascade of light. His virile body had stirred some sort of mystical
energy in me, and as he worked my hips back and forth, side to side,
he drove it out and set it free. My entire being quaked and turned
inside out for Rafa, and his did the same for mine.

CHAPTER TWO

After we'd crawled to the bed and slept for an hour, Rafa awakened at 4:25 am. He went to the bathroom and tried to get back into bed quietly, but I heard him. We lay on the bed facing each other now, under the covers in the deepest hour of the night, when on impulse I asked him to tell me about himself. Most men would have hated the question, but to my delight, Rafa was a natural storyteller who didn't hesitate to tell me all about his childhood.

Rafael De Leon was born in the little seaside town of Playa Larga, Cuba, in December of 1980. His mother had been widowed while still pregnant, and by the time Rafa was twelve, she attempted to escape crushing poverty by moving to the city. There they lived in a decrepit walk up behind the Cathedral of Havana, where an entire floor of tiny apartments shared one small, filthy washroom that his mother wouldn't let him use without slippers. Though she was very talented, she made very little money as a professional seamstress and they both suffered because of it. Rafa grew up terribly poor, but he had good friends, and they played on the streets of Havana at all hours of the day and night.

Sometimes, when his mother was desperate for coffee, she would send her son out to beg for it, and more often than not he would return with a little sack of espresso beans. He was known affectionately as 'Ojos Azules,' or '*Blue Eyes,*' in the neighborhood, and if the neighbors had anything to spare, they would let him have it. They didn't care very much for Rafa's mother Carmen, but they adored her smart, sweet boy and treated him like one of their own. His good looks earned him lots of perks, like the quarter pound of Serrano ham he could often charm out of the waitresses at *La Bodeguita del Medio*. I asked him if he knew that the bar was internationally famous because of Ernest Hemingway, and he said no, all he knew about it was that he could get his ham there. He was a well-mannered boy who made good grades, and when his mother died during his senior year of high school, he moved in with one of the elderly widows in the neighborhood who let him live there for free as long as he did most of the chores around the house.

"What happened to your father?" I asked. He stared up at the ceiling, lost in thought. He had to be thinking about his father now, and I silently cursed myself for bringing it up. I certainly didn't like to talk about my own parents, so I don't know why I would ask about his. But I was consumed with curiosity about Rafa, whom I had come to realize would be leaving me very soon, forever.

Rafa shifted onto his back and tucked an arm under his head. I came face to face with the bite mark I'd made, and before he could answer my question, I ran my fingers along the already darkening bruise.

"I'm sorry. I've never done that before," I said, full of remorse. I pulled the sheet up all the way to my chin, embarrassed.

"Don't worry, you were just having a little fun." He gave me a little peck on the lips and a nice, earnest smile. While my side of the sheet was practically over my face, his side had worked its way dangerously low on his hips, and I flashed back to being crushed between him and the wall. My belly did a little somersault from the inside. Without looking at me, he spoke softly. "I don't know why I said that."

Of course I knew what he meant, but I told myself it had been a figure of speech that I didn't quite understand, and I'd put it out of my mind right away knowing better than to take it seriously. Nothing was static, or wholly true or wholly untrue, and I liked to think of language as fluid and musical, full of ephemeral meaning. It was nothing but a song that had disappeared into the ether.

"I know. You were just having a little fun." I smiled as he turned onto his side again and observed me for what felt like a long time.

"In that moment, I did mean it. I don't know why, but I did. I've never done *that* before." Rafa's blue eyes disarmed me as they had from the moment we met, and any earlier inclination I might have had to censor myself went right out the window. I didn't just lust for him, I decided I liked him.

"You are so handsome," I mused, inspecting his chiseled cheekbones, aquiline nose, and angular jaw, all wonderfully masculine features which perfectly complemented soft skin and long, almost feminine eyelashes.

"How long does it take for people to get past this?" I asked, gliding a finger across each of his eyelids. He didn't answer, but he came closer and kissed me again, so very sweetly. He caressed the back of my head and gently ran his fingers through my tangled hair.

"So, tell me about you," said Rafa, genuinely curious. It was as if he wanted me to tell him a story. He was undoubtedly sexy as hell, but he could also be quite charming.

"I'm a lonely woman who goes on vacations to find attractive men to sleep with. That's all there is." I winked and gave him an innocent smile.

He and I clearly had the same sense of humor, because he laughed right along with me. In the quiet and darkness of the cabin, I couldn't imagine a more welcome sound. Even though it wasn't the most forthcoming answer I could have given considering everything he told me about himself, he accepted it for now and didn't press any further.

"Ugh, no, that's your friend, Sharon," he said with obvious distaste.

"Sharon!" I exclaimed, remembering the night before. "What did she do to you? She's not my friend, by the way," I said, rolling my eyes.

"She showed up in the kitchen and offered me five hundred dollars to go back to her cabin." He found this funny for some reason and smiled to himself, although I suspected he tried to find the humor in everything, perhaps out of necessity.

"Unbelievable," I said. I couldn't imagine the indignity of being on the receiving end of that offer. "She's been with different men all week, but I didn't know she was paying them for it. That's awful."

"Hm." He lightly scratched his bare belly, diverting my attention to the line of dark hair that began beneath his belly button and disappeared beneath the sheet. "I've only been here a short time, but I've heard about that. It's pretty common."

I took a chance and asked, "Have you ever?" He considered the question, and I didn't think he would lie, so I instinctively I braced myself for something I might not want to hear.

"Well, I can't say I never would if I were desperate. I would do it to survive, or if my family was hungry. You do what you have to. I think most people would. But I haven't been there yet." I admired his honesty. "It would have to be a pretty bad situation to risk catching a disease." I thought back to the condom he carried in his wallet. He was careful.

"How are you so sure I don't have any diseases?" I challenged, somewhat indignant. Rafa cocked an eyebrow.

"You are not the kind of woman who propositions men, you are the kind men chase and never catch." He lowered his voice suggestively and added, "I can tell you're a good girl."

"That's a big assumption," I said.

"It is, but I'd call it an educated guess," he said. "How many partners have you had?"

"One."

"How long ago was that?"

"About ten years ago," I said. "The last five years of my relationship were lonely, and I haven't been with anyone since then."

He didn't openly react, but I think he was stunned, and I began to get the feeling we wouldn't be talking for much longer, so I pressed for as much information as I could get. I tried to ignore his bedroom eyes for now.

"What about you?"

"Amada, regardless of what you might expect, I've had very few partners, and because of my last job, I've had every vaccination and blood test under the sun many times, and so did they. I haven't been with anyone new in a long time."

"What was your last job? How long have you been working here on the ship?" He didn't really want to answer, so when he noticed me shiver, he took his time drawing the comforter up over us a little higher.

"OK now?" he asked. I nodded, but kept my eyes on him expectantly.

"Just a few months." He sighed, as if already very tired of it. "I only left Cuba six months ago. That's why my English is so bad, but I make up for it in other ways, don't I?" He reached under the blankets and used his thumb and forefinger to lightly stimulate one of my nipples. *Oh, God.*

"Were you a waiter in Cuba?" I don't know how I got the words out, considering what he was doing to my chest. He ran his fingertips over my skin ever so lightly, in random patterns from my nipple to the side of my breast near my arm as if drawing in the sand. An exquisite sensation, all the thinking parts of my brain began to shut off one by one, like switches on a circuit breaker.

"No," said Rafa as he moved on top of me. He kissed me deeply as his deliciously hard body blanketed mine, and we opened and closed our mouths in unison, tasting one another with no inhibitions. He positioned himself between my legs, and although I knew he must be right at my entrance, I couldn't feel him there yet.

"You are so very lovely, and that's why I'm here with you. The only reason," he said. "I saw you and for a second thought you were my favorite actress. But you're even more beautiful."

"Who's that?" I asked dreamily.

"Oh, come on," he teased. "As if you haven't heard it a million times."

I had no idea who he was talking about, but I did believe he thought I was beautiful, and when I looked up at him and into his eyes, I saw love. I was not naïve enough to think it was for me, but I did know that I was seeing the kindness in him, the integrity, as well as his love of life and pleasure.

"I don't have another condom," he said, "and I have to leave in a few minutes. What would you like me to do for you? Tell me. Anything you want." He moved down my body, took my nipple in his mouth and licked gently. I considered asking him to have sex with me anyway, but given his strong feelings about diseases, I thought I'd better not.

"Rafa," I purred, "that feels so good."

He continued to suck on my breast, then after a while moved to the other. I writhed beneath him as he paused every so often to let his warm breath tease my wet skin. He would stop and then start, give and then take away, a master of the erotic arts. He drove me mad by offering and then withholding precisely what he knew I most craved. Even though he said he had to leave, his drive to arouse me beyond all reason was alarming, and I began to suspect he might leave me like this. I ran my hands through his thick black hair and let my mind wander to happy places. One of my favorite poems came to mind, and I couldn't help but recall the first few words as I often do when I am completely relaxed. Plato, Milton and random lines of poetry would often float through my mind at the strangest of times, and over the years I had learned to just let it happen, because like most things, it was for a reason.

"Had we but world enough, and time," I said in English, "this coyness, *sir*, were no crime!" I playfully tugged on a handful of his hair as I said the word 'sir.' It caught Rafa's attention, and he completely stopped what he was doing, which was not what I wanted at all.

"Don't stop," I whispered, meeting his gaze.

"I'm thirsty," he said, sitting up on top of the sheet, completely immodest and unaware of his beauty. He ran his hand through his already mussed hair as he leaned toward the nightstand and took a big gulp from an open bottle, then offered it to me. It was impossible not to admire his graceful body as his torso extended and flexed.

"Go on," he prompted, swallowing an enormous mouthful of water. "What was that?"

I was learning how obstinate he could be, and his body language informed me that he wouldn't be doing anything else until I satisfied his curiosity.

"What time do you have to leave?" I asked.

"At five. I'm so sorry." He caressed my cheek with real affection. *Con cariño*, I thought.

I sat up with him, allowing the sheet to pool at my waist. Ten minutes. I leaned back against the headboard and closed my eyes, hoping I could recall the poem I once knew word for word. It had been years, and thinking of it again was bittersweet, but I couldn't deny how fitting it was. I thought of the antique round oak table in my old classroom at the college and how it had been my habit to walk the perimeter of the room as I read out loud while my students followed along in their books.

"The speaker wants to seduce a virgin, so he tries to persuade her by reminding her that as mortals, we're all short on time." I kept my eyes closed and recited the parts I remembered.

> *Had we but world enough, and time,*
> *This coyness, lady, were no crime.*
> *We would sit down and think which way*
> *To walk, and pass our long love's day;*
> *Thou by the Indian Ganges' side*
> *Shouldst rubies find; I by the tide*
> *Of Humber would complain...*
> *An hundred years should go to praise*
> *Thine eyes, and on thy forehead gaze;*
> *Two hundred to adore each breast,*
> *But thirty thousand to the rest;*

Rafa's hands went to my eyelids, my forehead and my breasts. He wanted me to show me he understood, and although I knew the poem well, I'd never experienced it precisely in this way, not just because he was touching me, but also because for the first time I identified more with the speaker than the virgin. I continued as Rafa's hands roamed my body.

> *An age at least to every part,*
> *And the last age should show your heart.*
> *For, lady, you deserve this state,*
> *Nor would I love at lower rate.*

But at my back I always hear
Time's winged chariot hurrying near…
Thy beauty shall no more be found,
Nor, in thy marble vault, shall sound
My echoing song; then worms shall try
That long preserv'd virginity,

He moved the sheet aside and began to stroke between my legs, but I had to put my hand over his to still it because I knew I wouldn't be able to go on if he continued. We remained this way, his hand on me and mine on his, until I finished the poem.

And your quaint honour turn to dust,
And into ashes all my lust.
The grave's a fine and private place,
But none I think do there embrace.
Now therefore, while the youthful hue
Sits on thy skin like morning dew,
And while thy willing soul transpires
At every pore with instant fires,
Now let us sport us while we may;
And now, like am'rous birds of prey,
Rather at once our time devour,
Than languish in his slow-chapp'd power.
Let us roll all our strength, and all
Our sweetness, up into one ball;
And tear our pleasures with rough strife
Thorough the iron gates of life.
Thus, though we cannot make our sun
Stand still, yet we will make him run.

I opened my eyes to find Rafa studying me. It took a moment, but my brain switched gears and I was able to go back into Spanish. I squeezed the hand that was still between my legs and smiled, quite curious to know what he thought.

"Andrew Marvell. *To His Coy Mistress*. 1681. It's my favorite poem." I smiled and waited, hoping he would share his thoughts with me. He intertwined his fingers with mine, then did the same with the other hand.

"Lie down," he said, pulling me toward the foot of the bed. *Acuéstate.* Now beneath him, he kissed me with a gentle pressure that fully awakened my body, then, still clasping my hands, he nuzzled my jaw and my neck, gradually using more of his mouth until he was sucking and licking as if he would eat me alive. He wasn't shy about letting me know how much he was enjoying himself, and as he crushed his hips into mine, this time I did feel the smooth skin of his penis against my inner thigh, but he stilled just before reaching my sex.

"Amada," he panted, "I want you again. I know you have no reason to believe me, but I swear to you it's safe."

"I do believe you, but how do you know I won't get pregnant?" I asked, curious to see what he would say. His expression changed into one I had difficulty reading, but the question did seem to sober him up a little.

"Is your IUD out of date yet?" He asked so matter of fact, it took me off guard. As far as I knew, no one was supposed to be able to feel it. Had he actually been looking for the string?

"No. How—"

"I felt it, sweetheart." As he waited for my permission, his breath hitched as he briefly closed his eyes and rubbed himself against my skin. "It's alright either way. Even this feels so good."

"Yes, please." I said, and wrapped my legs around his waist. I wanted him just as much as he wanted me, maybe more.

"Please what?" he teased, looking down.

Momentarily popping out of my sex trance, I found his blue eyes and said, "If you know I'm a nice girl, then why do I have to say it?"

He pushed all the way in, then withdrew until he was about an inch inside me and remained completely still.

"It feels like Heaven inside you," he said, looking down at me, his eyes soft.

"No," I moaned. "Please, no." I couldn't withstand the agony of having him right there when I craved him so badly. Fully aware of what he was doing, he put his weight on his elbows, leaving a considerable amount of space between us.

"I love it when you tell me exactly what you want," he said. "It turns me on more than you'll ever know." He leaned into the crook of my neck and took a deep, satisfied whiff of what I presume was my own natural scent.

"I don't usually talk like that," I said, trying to get closer. I squeezed my thighs together and attempted to pull him further into me, but he was as immovable as a brick wall.

"That's not going to work," he laughed, then dropped his voice. "I like knowing my elegant lady turns into a provocative seductress in bed, just for me. Where did you learn that poem?"

"Rafa, please move. I can't take it another second," I pleaded.

"I'll just stop if you don't answer my question. Three … two …"

"No, no, don't!" I begged, clenching my thighs around him. "I used to be an English professor, alright?"

"Well done," he said, thrusting in, then pulling out almost the whole way again. The friction between our bodies was wonderful, but when I noticed he was looking away from me toward the wall, I realized it was because he was laughing.

"You're so evil!" I yelled, infuriated. I tried to squirm away from him, but his powerful arms might as well have been an iron cage. I wasn't going anywhere, and we both knew I really didn't want to. He fully released the fit of laugher he had been holding in, and then I think he felt sympathy for me, because he shifted so that he was about halfway inside me.

"Sh, sweetheart," he said, moving a little now. I was grateful he decided to have a little mercy on us both. He kissed and nuzzled my forehead as I relished the sensation of skin on skin, his torturously slow movements as bad as they were good. I relaxed my hips and settled in, mistakenly assuming full, deep penetration was forthcoming. Wrong. He felt me open for him and made a sound that reminded me of someone enjoying the taste of good wine, yet he still remained in total control.

"Why don't you teach anymore? How many languages do you speak?"

"More, Rafa." I moaned and dug my nails into his ass, hoping he felt even a fraction of my agony.

"Like this?" he asked, all the way inside me again. We made crude sounds of satisfaction as he skillfully aroused us both with a few short but rhythmic pelvic thrusts and a firm love bite to my neck. Satisfied for the moment, he paused.

"There," I panted. "Don't stop." I squirmed beneath him, silently cursing his incredible self-control.

"French?" he asked, completely ignoring my pleas. I nodded, weak.

"So what did you do in Cuba? You never answered," I asked, clawing his lean, muscular back. My efforts fruitless, I continued to probe. "Well, we've established you weren't a prostitute—"

"Although I would have been a damn good one." He pressed into me once more, the feeling of relief immense, and out of sheer gratitude I found myself kissing his face, his chin, his broad chest, worshipping him as if he had just bestowed upon me the last drops of sustenance in the entire world. My body broke out in a cold sweat, so hot for him that I would have done absolutely anything to have more.

"So?" I demanded, underestimating how ruthless he could be with his body and mine.

"Questions will cost you," he murmured, retreating again. "And look, it's already five. I've got to go." He shook his head and made a little *tsk tsk* sound, as if to say I had only brought it upon myself.

"No!" I screamed. Feeling as if I might cry, the unexpected sense of loss alarmed me.

I should have listened when he warned I would feel empty inside after he left. My freedom, my liberty was slowly slipping away as this man pierced my being. His eyes went to the other parts of the room, a playful performance meant to suggest that my questions might cause him to become bored and leave at any second. Immune to my pleas, he remained deadpan and unsympathetic until I broke down and gave him the extreme reaction he so fancied.

"Goddamn it," I said, grabbing his expressionless face firmly between my hands. "Stop teasing me." I'd gone positively mad and didn't care how much I was forced to humiliate myself.

"Or what?" A wolfish smile crept across his beautiful face. "You can't even say it. Beg for my—"

"How about I just kick you out and you go finish in your own bed?"

"You won't do that," he said, still smiling. "I just gave you your first vaginal orgasm. I have you now."

"What?" I panted, searching his eyes. How could he possibly know?

"You heard me," he smirked. I thought of how he'd made my body feel and swallowed hard. It had been beyond imagination, but I was certain there was no way he could do it again.

As if reading my thoughts, his light blue eyes opened up into storms and anguish, probably from punishing us both for way too long. He reached behind his back and forcefully disentangled my legs from around himself, and just as I was about to cry with frustration, he threw my legs over his shoulders and thrust inside me farther than anyone had ever gone before, using his power to show me he was there, deep inside me where I needed him. Something ignited deep in my core near my cervix causing every nerve ending to resonate, and wanting more, he rocked forward and pressed his tongue into my mouth so that I was bent in half, completely open and vulnerable to him.

"Will this do?" Rafa demanded, disengaging roughly as his angelic face twisted in pain or ecstasy, or both. "I would never dream of leaving you dissatisfied, Amada. I will always give you what you need. Do you have enough of me now?"

He kept us just like that for a moment then went wild, and as the bed started to bang against the wall I gasped, wondering if the passengers next door would report us to the concierge. His savage, relentless thrusting went on for so long I thought I might break into pieces, but when he reached between us and pressed the palm of his hand deep into my belly, I erupted. The same sense of angst washed over me as it had earlier, but instead of trying to escape, this time I correctly recognized it as nothing but a concentrated affirmation of life itself. I allowed to myself to engage without fear, and the light inside my closed eyes came again, just as it had before. I sobbed and contracted around him in a state of pure bliss, and as soon as he felt my internal muscles spasm, he surrendered all control and made a low, indecent sound as his entire body stiffened and emptied into me.

Rafa let me bring my legs down but remained nestled inside me until he was completely soft again, holding me as I dabbed at the corner of my eyes. For the first time in my life, I had literally cried in ecstasy.

"I don't know what's wrong," I said, hiding my face.

"Hormones. Perfectly normal," he whispered. He kissed the top of my head and positioned himself so that we were both comfortable but still intertwined. We lay together in blissful silence, and just when I thought I might fall asleep, I realized he was already off the bed and dressing. I wanted us to hold each other longer, but to my dismay, he already had his shirt and pants on.

"Rafa, no," I said reaching out, desperately missing him already. He looked so adorable rushing around trying to find all his clothes, while I lay in the bed absolutely spent and satisfied beyond all imagination. If I didn't know any better, I would think this man possessed some sort of magical power that enabled him to astrally project us to other planes. His body transported me, and I couldn't imagine how he could recover so quickly when I would surely be worthless for hours.

"*Mi amor,*" he said, "look at the clock. It's almost six. I'll be fired." He squeezed my foot through the blanket and continued the hunt for his belongings. He was back to his sweet, tender self, obviously regretful of leaving me alone so soon after our mind-blowing sex. I suddenly remembered that it was the last day of the cruise and went into a tailspin.

"Wait, when will I see you again?" I asked sitting up anxiously. "We disembark tomorrow. Will you be at dinner tonight?"

He shoved his feet into his shoes and looked around for his jacket and tie with visible impatience. He furrowed his brow and scowled a little as he dropped to his knees when he spied the tie under the bed. Even as he crawled around the floor, Rafa managed to look distinguished and graceful. He wasn't a common man, and nothing about his circumstances would ever change that. It was his birthright to be extraordinary in body and mind.

"No, baby. I'll be cooking in the kitchen. I was only in the dining room because someone else was out sick." Now fully dressed, he smiled at me but glanced furtively at the door. I hated to delay him but couldn't help but panic.

"So ... when?"

"I'll come back tonight around two, alright?" He leaned over and gave me a peck on the lips, then held up my room key so that I would see him slip it in his pocket.

He went to the door and glanced down the hallway before stepping outside, presumably to make sure he wasn't seen by any of the crew. Before he shut the door, he leaned back into the room and whispered something I couldn't quite make out.

"What did you say?" I asked, still in bed, feeling terrible about the long day he had ahead.

"A doctor," he said, just a little louder. "In Cuba, I was a doctor."

CHAPTER THREE

I awoke around three in the afternoon, more refreshed and alert than I had been in a long time. It was a marked contrast to my mood yesterday, so tired and ill from the heat, unsure of how or why I still managed to be. Tomorrow might be different, but today I was alive, and the reasons for it didn't matter. I stood in front of the full-length mirror, still naked the way he left me, to see if I looked any different. Physically, no, but yesterday I would not have dared look at myself at all, preferring to ignore my own existence as much as possible. For the time being, as long as this lasted, I would not be haunted.

I dressed in a tank top and shorts, still feeling echoes of him across my body. He had left himself all over me, my bed and my mind, not to mention the sinister-looking purple souvenir on my neck. I put concealer on it, grabbed my sun hat and went out onto the deck of the ship, unusually open to interaction with other people.

I went to the pool and stretched out on a lounge chair, enjoying the abundant sunshine and the warm air of the Caribbean. I wondered how close we would come to the shores of Cuba and whether Rafa would even notice. The ship was scheduled to disembark in Miami in less than twenty hours, and he would stay here, toiling away in a cruise ship kitchen while I went back to Boxwood and a life that consisted of nothing but reading, traveling and the occasional evening at home with my brother when he was between business trips.

As the pool filled up with passengers and screaming children, I didn't feel my usual urge to retreat to a quiet corner, remaining in place as the reggae music blasted and the lounge chairs filled up around me. A family of four piled up beside me, and still I stayed put, feeling good. It was a mood that was welcome, yet so unlike me.

A young waiter approached with a tray of drinks. Dark and attractive like all the young men on the ship, he was nowhere near as handsome and rugged as Rafa, who was in a league of his own.

"Good afternoon, madam," said the waiter in an unmistakable Spanish accent. "Cocktail?" I was rather skilled at identifying even the most subtle inflections, often surprising people when I could tell not only what country, but also what state they were from. Still, I tended to err on the side of caution, because some people confused my legitimate interest with cultural bias.

I lifted the brim of my hat a little and leaned forward to scan the sugary, fruity drinks on his tray, none of which were the least bit appealing. "Do you think you could bring me a double Russian Standard Gold vodka, neat?" I asked.

"Right away," he said. As the waiter turned to leave, I realized he would be able to properly translate for me. I took a chance that he wouldn't be offended if I asked.

"Wait—"

"Yes, ma'am?"

"Do you speak Spanish?"

"Yes, ma'am," he said proudly.

"What does the word *médico* mean?"

"It means doctor." He looked around, concerned. "Is someone sick?"

"No, no," I said. "I'm just writing a letter. Are you sure? Could it mean paramedic, or nurse or something else?"

He cocked his head to the side and said, "No, ma'am, those are other things. *Enfermera* is nurse, *paramédico* is paramedic. *Médico* is doctor," he said, with the absolute certainty only a native speaker can have. "Does that help you?"

"Yes, definitely," I said, leaning back. "Thank you very much."

"My pleasure." Looking down at my legs he added, "Ma'am, forgive me, but please be careful of the sun. It's very strong here."

That evening, as the ship made its way home closer to Miami, I took a few minutes to enjoy the Caribbean sunset from the balcony in my cabin. The sky was a palette of pinks and blues, and the water was unusually calm, almost glassy. I had seen beautiful sunsets in my native Florida many times, but tonight I was more than a passive bystander. I thought of all the other people watching this same light at this precise moment in time, some just born and some about to die. No matter who we are, or where we are in our journey, some things always remain the same, and it is we who change and see it differently. Copernicus was wrong, the Earth is the center of the universe—our universe—and human souls are nothing but satellites.

Back inside, I chose a more demure dress for the final evening of the cruise, but it was no less beautiful than the black lace gown still draped over the side of the chair. I couldn't bear to disturb it, and it gave me great pleasure just to see it there as a reminder of what had transpired the night before. Tonight I wore a high-necked, backless floral Givenchy tulle dress I'd bought just four months ago in Paris. The salesgirl had called it the "Printemps" gown, and when it was all wrapped up in yards of paper and fabric, she presented it to me in a satin box the size of a small desk. As I struggled to carry the package out, I almost bumped into a very elegant woman who appeared to be in her eighties or nineties. She'd watched me make my purchase with great interest, so I asked the salesgirl who she was.

"The Viscountess Romilly," she whispered with awe.

The Viscountess glanced at me out of the corner of her eye again, and I thought it was because she might have thought me too plain to be deserving of such a gown. Unlike her, I wore no makeup, no jewelry and very simple clothing. Bejeweled and powdered as finely as any woman in Paris, clearly she had once been a very beautiful woman. Even now, the Viscountess Romilly was the epitome of refinement and sophistication, the reward for a life fully lived. On my way out, she met my eyes and said, "Profitez-en pendant que vous le pouvez, mon cher." *Enjoy it while you can, my dear.*

I glanced at myself in the mirror after dressing and found that I did enjoy the gown very much. It was a work of art, created by hand over many thousands of hours, exemplary of an artistry that could make even the most ordinary woman remarkable. I didn't pay much attention to the fact that I had allowed myself to overdo it in the sun this afternoon and was getting redder by the minute; my only concern was that Rafa's plum-colored bite wasn't covered by the neckline of the dress. I searched for the tube of concealer everywhere, but even though I opened every drawer and cabinet, I still couldn't find it. I tried to arrange my hair so that it was covered, but I knew it wouldn't stay in place longer than five minutes, so I boldly put it up in a French twist. Let the world see what my lover had done.

Finally ready for dinner, as I was about to leave the cabin, I caught sight of something shiny at the foot of the bed. I came closer and saw that it was Rafa's watch, and as I admired the simple rectangular face, I rubbed the strap between my fingers, keenly aware of how close the leather had been to his skin. I slipped it on my wrist and went to him.

The final night of the cruise was markedly quieter than the raucous theme nights earlier in the week. Instead of a lively orchestra or band, tonight the only entertainment was a pianist at a baby grand piano, but the music was no less pleasing. Late again, I missed the appetizers and arrived just in time for the first course, but Ernesto attended to me right away and made sure I was comfortable and happy.

"Antonio, double Russian Standard Gold, neat! *¡Rápido muchacho!*" he snapped from somewhere behind me. I smiled even though I knew it wouldn't be Rafa over my shoulder tonight, and I wondered if he was thinking of me as well. My cocktail appeared at once and was replaced by a fresh one as soon as I finished it.

I made small talk with my remaining tablemates and learned of their plans after disembarkation. Serena and her quiet daughter Jennifer would return home to Boston and then go to Palm Beach for Christmas. Serena was confident the girl would be engaged to her hedge fund baker boyfriend by then.

"He's not much to look at," she snorted crudely, "but he's so rich!"

Sam and Judy told us about their plans to return home to New York for a few days and then continue on to Egypt. It had been Sam's lifelong dream to visit the pyramids, and although Judy confided she wasn't in perfect health, they would make the trip anyway. Serena told us how she'd dated a man from Cairo a few years ago and highly recommended the Four Seasons, which I had to say sounded wonderfully exotic. I made a mental note to ask Kieran if he would go with me.

Finally Sharon arrived, and if Ernesto minded her tardiness, he of course didn't show it. He seated her across from me in the usual place and made the hand signal for service to begin. Not wanting to interrupt the conversation, she looked over and waved hello. Her expression completely changed, however, when she noticed the mark on my neck and gave me a smug, knowing look. I'd completely forgotten about it, and clearly everyone else had been too polite to say anything. Sharon, however, had very little tact, and I wasn't going to discuss it with her or anyone. If it made her feel better to assume I had been up to something, then let her. I simply ignored all her smirks and remained engaged in the discussion at the table.

We were all deep in conversation about which ruins we had visited—Chichén Itzá, Stonehenge, the Parthenon—when the food arrived. A trio of waiters set the plates down in front of us simultaneously, as is the custom in formal dinner service, but rather than look down at my own plate first, I saw Sharon's plate across from me. The filet mignon looked heavy and unappetizing, and I was about to ask the waiter to take my plate away when I noticed what I'd been served, a beautiful arrangement of oysters and caviar. I looked up at Antonio, the middle-aged waiter who'd been bringing my drinks all night. "Compliments of the chef," he whispered.

With a lump in my throat, I studied the food prepared just for me by my Rafa. He'd placed a spoonful of the plumpest, blackest, caviar I'd ever seen beside two perfectly cooked oysters in sabayon sauce. I took a moment to admire the dish, then put a forkful of the glossy orbs in my mouth. They exploded on my tongue, salty and mellow, and the room fell away as I went adrift amidst images of hands on bodies, breath on skin, legs and tongues, experiencing it all again. I marveled at Rafa's ability to sense what I wanted even from afar.

Antonio brought out plate after plate of unique dishes just for me. During the fish course my tablemates ate salmon, but Rafa sent me seared abalone, and for the pasta course, I had truffles over tagliatelle instead of puttanesca. For dessert, it was coconut flan instead of bananas foster.

"Oysters and pearls," cooed Judy, grasping her husband's hand. "Remember we had that at The French Laundry in Napa?"

"I do," said Sam, kissing his wife's cheek.

"What does a girl have to do to get caviar like that?" Sharon, visibly drunk and barely able to contain her resentment, popped an olive into her mouth and glared at me as she chewed.

"Request it ahead of time," I snapped, now sickened by her. I imagined how she must have propositioned Rafa, repulsed by the fact that she'd offered him money. Going by her attitude now, I knew she must have been difficult to deal with when he'd said no, and I wondered how he'd softened the blow. I made a mental note to ask Rafa how one nicely rejects a person like Sharon.

Fortunately, her change in mood did not spoil what had been a lovely dinner. By the end of the evening we all said our goodbyes and everyone passed along thick envelopes of cash to a very appreciative Ernesto. I had given him about a thousand dollars, and I supposed he would receive similar amounts from the others. Even though he would split it with his crew, it would still be a very nice amount for each person. No doubt there was money to be made here, one way or another. On my way out, I caught hold of Antonio's arm.

"Would you give this to him?" I asked, placing Rafa's watch discreetly in his hand.

"Of course, Madam," said Antonio, not bothering to ask who.

I stopped for a few hands of blackjack and surprisingly broke even, but it was after midnight now, so I thought it best to just go to bed and wait. Back in the cabin I kicked off my Prada stilettos and took off my dress, placing it on top of the one from the night before. I turned off all but one small light in the bathroom and slipped under the covers in nothing but a pair of lace panties.

That night I dreamed of Egypt. In my dream I rode a camel across a wide desert, and as I traveled I could see the pyramids in the distance. It was windy and sandy, but the colorful scarf across my face offered enough protection for me to breathe. My hearty camel trudged on, tired, but we finally made it to the Great Pyramid. I dismounted and led him by the harness to the base, and as I was about to enter, a mob noticed me and wouldn't allow me to pass. The men spoke a sharp, ancient tongue that was neither Egyptian nor English and angrily held out their hands demanding coins. I had nothing of value, so I became afraid and looked among the men for a kind face. I saw a young man too proud to beg like the others, and he wore so many scarves I could only see his bright blue eyes. My fear turned to anger as I tried to push past the others to reach him, but the closer I came, the further away he appeared to be until he disappeared. Heartbroken, I sat down in the sand and fed my greedy camel a pomegranate from the palm of my hand.

I awoke to the sensation of my lover's lips on my fingertips, and although I was still half asleep, I could make out every feature of his striking face in the darkness. While he was on his knees beside the bed, the scent of Ivory soap and vetiver washed over me, and whatever he had been wearing earlier had been replaced by a crisp white shirt and dark jeans. I ran my hand through his soaking wet hair and then turned on my side toward the balcony, inviting him into the bed. He didn't bother to take off his clothes, only his shoes, and slipped in behind me under the covers.

Rafa promptly adjusted himself to fit around my curves, and then wrapped his arms around me, burying his face in my hair and positioning his broad, hard chest against my back. After a minute or two, I assumed he had fallen asleep, and I didn't mind one bit because just being with him was so lovely.

"You're hot," he said, running his hand along my thigh. My skin felt raw, but I didn't pay much attention to anything except the exquisite feeling of Rafa in bed with me. I'd waited all day in a state of suspended arousal, and nothing mattered except his body next to mine. In spite of our proximity, sensing something was wrong, he set aside any other intentions he might have had and repositioned his open hand from my leg to my forehead.

"Hm, thank you," I said.

"I mean the temperature of your skin, sweetheart." I winced as he switched on the lamp and the room flooded in light, but it was delightful to get a good look at him. He was exhausted, but even so, I couldn't help but admire that perfect face and chiseled body. I didn't think I would ever get tired of the sexy way he moved, especially during moments when he was least self-aware. I noticed the watch I sent back to him on his wrist, and distracted by the masculine shape of his hand, I stroked his long fingers. He paid no attention to what I was doing, and though his expression had changed into a little frown during sex last night, I was amused to note that it was probably indicative of any attempt at concentration. Maybe it was all the time I'd spent in the sun earlier, or the three or four double vodkas, but I was lethargic and silly. I smiled at him, but he didn't return it.

"Let me see," he said. He got out of bed and dramatically pulled back the covers. To his credit, he kept his composure, but I was horrified. Over the course of the evening, my skin had turned fire engine red. I didn't look anything like this earlier, but now my arms, chest and legs were ablaze, and pretty much all my exposed skin had fried in the Caribbean sun. Thankfully, my face had been covered by the hat and there was no blistering, but he glared at me in utter disbelief.

"My God, didn't you wear any sunscreen today?" he asked, a little more harshly than necessary. I didn't know him well enough yet to be able to figure out whether his outburst was really anger or simply concern.

"Well, no," I stammered, sitting up to look at myself, "I usually don't go out in the sun, so I didn't have any. It was just such a nice day that I—"

"Turn over," he interrupted. Though he used the same words, it was nothing like when he said the same thing to me the night before. He took at least a minute to examine me everywhere, visibly displeased.

"Did you bring any Advil or lotion with you?" he asked, frowning again.

"No," I said. He pushed a few buttons on the phone and passed me the receiver when they answered. "Ask for ibuprofen and aloe vera."

"Are you upset?" I asked, sipping from the Evian bottle he'd given me. I didn't really like room temperature water on a good day, so trying to get it down now was pretty unpleasant. Large amounts of water tended to make me sick, and I certainly didn't want to do that with him around, but he insisted I drink it all.

"No, of course not," he said, now sitting on the chair beside the bed, "but you have a serious sunburn and you're dehydrated." Even as he spoke to me, he never really stopped looking me over, as if he were putting together the pieces of a puzzle. "Were you drinking this afternoon?"

"I had a few drinks," I admitted. He unbuttoned his shirt halfway and rolled up his sleeves.

"Double vodkas, I presume. And then you fell asleep in the sun?"

"I guess so."

"Does 'a few' mean two or four?"

"Four-ish," I said sheepishly.

"We're going to have a talk about that when you feel better," he said. Without any further conversation, he got up, went to the bathroom, turned on the water and then came back to the bed for me.

"I want you to soak in the tub for a little while, but never mind about the Advil tonight. You can start taking it tomorrow."

"Why?" I asked, knowing I had a tendency to take Tylenol or whatever I had on hand without giving it a second thought.

"The alcohol."

As the tub filled, I started to feel a little more alert even though it was about three in the morning, but I knew Rafa had to be tired and I regretted he had to take care of me instead of getting some sleep. He went in to check the tub, and satisfied there was enough water, came back to get me. "Come," he said patiently. "Let's have a nice bath."

In the bathroom, Rafa remained expressionless as he watched me step out of my underwear, though I saw a flicker of something wild in his eyes that went away as fast as it came.

"I'll take them," he said, reaching out.

"Is that so?" I dropped the scrap of blush colored lace in the palm of his hand.

"To the laundry bag," he said, his mood still indecipherable.

He left and quickly returned, but instead of getting in with me, he pulled a chair into the bathroom and sat down beside the tub. The cool bath felt good on my inflamed skin, and it also had the temporary effect of waking me up a little.

"It's cold."

"It's cool, and it's supposed to be," he said, stretching his legs and intertwining his fingers behind his head. It was as comfortable he could get sitting in a hard chair in a bathroom when he surely would have rather been in bed.

"Get in with me," I said, positioning myself suggestively so that my breasts came up above the water line.

"Uh uh," he scolded. "You should have thought of that before you baked your lovely skin in the sun." He gave me a gentle little push back down into the water so that I was fully submerged up to my neck again. It was clear that for the moment I had absolutely no chance of seducing him, so I gave up and settled back to soak. It was different between us tonight, but no less intimate. He closed his eyes, so I closed mine and let my mind wander. I thought of the beautiful plate of oysters and pearls.

"I loved everything you prepared for me tonight at dinner. You made me feel very special. Thank you." I meant it.

"I thought of you all day," he confessed, a hint of longing in his voice.

A good minute or two of silence passed between us, but then I just went ahead and asked. It seemed to be a delicate subject, so I tread carefully.

"Why are you cooking on a ship if you're a doctor?" I took a peek at him, but he still had his eyes closed and hadn't moved a muscle.

"I *was* a doctor. I'm not a licensed physician anywhere in the world but Cuba, and I won't be going back, so technically I'm not a doctor anymore and never will be again." He spoke so methodically, as if it were perfectly normal for a person to switch careers after a decade of specialized education and work. I tried not to be insistent, but I wasn't understanding this at all. The water sloshed dangerously close to the rim of the tub as I sat forward and turned toward him.

"So, let me get this straight, you—"

"Please don't get excited," he said. I wasn't sure if he was talking about my growing physical restlessness or my questions, but when the concierge knocked, he shot me a look that said *sit back*. Reluctantly, I obeyed.

"I'll get it when we're done," said Rafa. "I want you to stay in there a while." He pushed his sleeves up a little further and shifted position. He couldn't be comfortable, yet he wouldn't leave my side. His hair was almost dry now, but I noticed that he hadn't shaved. The stubble was very attractive on him, just like everything else.

"What happened? What kind of doctor are you?"

"I'm—I was—an *Internacionalista*. I specialized in internal medicine in Cuba, then I volunteered when they asked for doctors to go abroad. Cuba sends medical teams to poor countries affected by disasters like hurricanes and earthquakes. I'm surprised you've never read about it in the news—Castro is famous for it. I worked in Venezuela a long time, but last year they sent me to Haiti to help after a hurricane, and I had a very bad experience. I had to leave. That was six months ago."

"You mean you had a ... breakdown?" I asked, not really understanding the word he used. *Me emocioné*, he'd said.

"Something like that. We were alright in Venezuela because we mostly made house calls in poor villages and helped with very basic care, but when we got to Haiti, things changed. The energy was strange. A lot of the other doctors became unhappy and started talking about leaving, but they couldn't because they still had loved ones in Cuba and they knew the consequences if they tried. That wasn't a concern for me, so one night I snuck out of the camp, requested asylum at the American Embassy in Port Au Prince, and told them I wanted to go to the United States."

"Did you go alone?"

"Yes, but only because everyone else had family they couldn't abandon. During the interview process, the government makes sure all the traveling doctors have plenty of family and children that will stay behind as insurance, but the director of the program liked me and didn't hold it against me, so I was allowed to go. I told her I wanted to have an adventure, and she believed me. Her instincts were correct because I had no intention of ever leaving, but it just happened one day."

"A woman?"

"Yes."

"Do you think a man would have made the exception for you?"

"No," he sighed. "I didn't take her to bed, but I flirted with her for weeks. It was the only way, and if I hadn't, I wouldn't be here today. You do what you have to, Amada."

"What if the embassy had said no and sent you back?" I asked, horrified at the thought.

"The US government has a special program for doctors and nurses who defect from Cuba called the Cuban Medical Professional Parole Program. Everyone knows about it, especially the Cuban government, and that's why we're watched so carefully. The program doesn't offer any kind of assistance, but you're allowed to enter the country legally and stay. I ended up working at a restaurant in Miami for a few months until I sorted some things out, and then someone I trust told me I should take a job on a ship. It's worked out. Room and board are taken care of, and I don't have any expenses here, so I've been able to save quite a lot of money."

"How could you have no money if you were working as a doctor?" I asked, astonished. "They get quite rich here."

"Doctors in Cuba make about twenty-five dollars a month, Amada. Taxi drivers and tour guides make far more. There's no financial incentive at all."

I was awed by what he was telling me, my entire frame of reference reshifting now that it was clear he'd become a doctor for completely selfless reasons. I thought about what I'd paid for the Givenchy gown draped across the chair in the stateroom and cringed. Thank goodness he'd never know.

"Anyway, even if I'd had any money, they never would have let us travel with access to it. We're not allowed to bring too many belongings, and they take away our passports as soon as we get to any foreign country. I had to leave everything I owned behind, which wasn't much anyway."

"Who takes your passport away?" I asked, fascinated.

"Our minders."

The more he told me about himself, the more I realized there was far more to his story than he could possibly tell me in one night, but I had to ask if he was sorry he left. Above all else, there was a great deal of regret in his voice.

"Don't you miss it?"

"Well," he said, shifting in the chair, "it was a very unplanned, emotional decision, which is never good." I saw the pain in his eyes as he added, "Yes, it does make me sad that I can't help people anymore. If that's it for me, I'll miss it very much."

"Rafa, if there's anyone who should be a doctor, it's you. All you need to do is get your license here—" He didn't let me finish. He'd shut down and was done talking about it, which I accepted. For now.

"It's time to get out of the water." He stood and helped me step out carefully, then patted me dry with a fluffy towel and guided me in the direction of the big mirror over the sink so that he could take a close look under the light.

"I wish I had my glasses, but you seem better." I was dying for him to give me a kiss, but instead he just told me to go to the bathroom and meet him in bed.

Rafa was waiting for me with aloe vera gel in his hand and rubbed it into my tender areas until I was sticky as honey.

"Where are your clothes?" he asked. I pointed to the closed suitcase beside the dresser. He found a pair of simple cotton panties and held them out for me to step in to, so I balanced myself on his shoulders as he slipped them on and up over my hips.

"Nightgown?" he asked.

"No," I purred, trying to get a rise out of him. I came a little closer, but he simply turned me around to face the bed.

"Get in."

Rafa turned out the light and curled up beside me. "Sleep on your back," he instructed, draping an arm just below my breasts where I wasn't red.

"You're keeping your clothes on?" Unable to hide my disappointment, I rubbed him through the fabric of his pants, and in spite of his cool demeanor, I was reassured by the fact that at least he was rock hard.

"They're clean. I just changed." He took my hand and dropped it on his thigh with a cute little smack, as if to say *and keep it there.*

"That's not what I mean."

"Your skin is raw. It's not going to happen, so settle down," he said, a trace of a smile in his voice. "Think about baseball."

"Fine," I said, laughing with him. "Rafa, what happened that day to make you want to leave?" I didn't want to upset him, but I was dying to know more. He wouldn't occupy me in other ways, so my mind was still at work.

"You don't want to know," he said quietly. "I'll tell you about it another time, but for now, just imagine how bad it gets in a poor country like Haiti when there's no clean water, no shelter, no food and no medicine. People become angry and irrational, and you can only be around that for so long before it gets in your head. You eventually become ill yourself." Then a pause. "Alright?"

"Alright," I said.

"We're very lucky," he said, drifting off to sleep. "No matter what, remember that."

* * *

Later, the sun woke me up as it shined through the open balcony curtains. The lovely ocean panorama I had enjoyed all week had been replaced by a view of the dingy Miami cruise terminal, and instead of the soothing movement of the ocean, there was only the rough vibration of an idling ship engine. It had been a rough night, and although Rafa had been there to take care of me, I was still happy to awaken in the bright, clean light of the morning. I thought of all the things I missed about home and felt happy to be getting back to Boxwood and my familiar surroundings. Yet, something was wrong. I looked down at Rafa, who was still sleeping, and I knew. I couldn't bear the thought of leaving without him.

I took the opportunity to really study him now in the early morning light, wondering if perhaps I could find a flaw or something unpleasant that would make me want to go on with my life as if he had never existed, but I saw nothing but beauty on the outside and the inside. He was utter perfection, and I bitterly questioned how such a selfless man could end up so alone in the world. He'd been a virtual prisoner most of his life, whether of poverty, a communist government, or simply his own loneliness, like me. Now, once again he was adrift with no security and no family. In fact, in the US he would be considered illiterate. A man who had once saved lives every day was now reduced to the most basic existence with no clear path in sight. He made my heart ache, and I was full of need and compassion for him.

"Good morning," he said, opening his blue eyes. *Ojos azules.*

"Good morning to you," I replied, caressing his face. He held my hand to his cheek and kissed it gently as he sat up.

"How do you feel?" Rafa squinted uncomfortably in the bright sun, covering his eyes so that he could get a better look at me. His clothes were wrinkled and twisted around his body in odd ways, as if he'd tossed and turned all night. I hadn't felt him move, but then again, I'd slept very deeply.

"Much better," I said coming closer. I draped a leg across his body and hugged him tight.

"Careful," he said, lightly caressing my ribs and belly. "It's not a good idea yet."

"I think it's a great idea." Totally disregarding his objections, I placed his hand on my breast, but he only looked me up and down, still unwilling.

"Please don't make it any harder on me, Amada. It was torture last night."

"But I want you," I said, nuzzling my nose against his. I carefully unbuttoned his Oxford shirt all the way down to his belt buckle and ran my hands all over his torso, pushing the shirt off his shoulders as I leaned down to flick one of his nipples with my tongue and then the other. I felt myself getting wet as I struggled to find a position that would satisfy my increasing need to grind my body against his, and he watched with fascination as I slipped out of my own underwear and opened his pants, exhaling when I released his bulging erection from its confinement. I took it in my mouth, sucking from base to tip, and made a point of looking up at him as I put pressure on the underside with my tongue. It turned him on so much I thought his chest might explode from inhaling so deeply.

"I've been wanting to do that since the moment I saw you," I said, wiping the saliva off my mouth with an exaggerated swipe of my hand. The idea that a good girl like me had been fantasizing about having him in her mouth must have made him lose it a little, because it took him a second to shake off whatever sensations had taken over his brain, but once he did, he reacted swiftly. When he realized what I was up to, he sat up from his reclining position.

"Now you're toying with me, Amada, and if you really won't take no for an answer, then I'm going to have you any way I like. Maybe on the balcony," he said thoughtfully. "But it'll be just for me this time."

I giggled at the absurdity of it, knowing he wouldn't dare with so many cruise ship passengers disembarking down below, but to my horror he took my amusement as a challenge. Releasing me, he sprung from the bed and found a white bathrobe in the closet.

"Put this on," he said, still wearing his unbuttoned, open jeans. His engorged cock glistened with moisture from my mouth, an impressive sight indeed.

"You're joking," I said, tying the robe around my waist.

"Nope. All of Miami is going to hear you call out my name."

He took my hand and led me out to the balcony, impatiently positioning me between the rail and his body, and while I was occupied by the movement of the people only a few stories below, Rafa snaked his arm around my waist and pulled me into him, his swollen penis barely concealed by the thin, silky fabric between us.

"Rafa!" I exclaimed. "What if someone notices?"

"Oh, are you feeling shy now?" he asked tersely. "A minute ago you were very brave."

"It's not necessary to be so dramatic to make a point," I said.

"I disagree," he snapped. "Bend over."

Pleased he'd finally given in, I leaned forward enough to see the people down below, expecting to feel him inside me at any moment. I rested my head on my arms, acutely aware of everything around me as he lifted the back of my robe.

"So pretty," he said.

He inserted two fingers deep into my vagina and swirled them around. The sensation was divine, so I arched my back and opened for him, but when his fingers were wet enough, he used one hand to hold me open and the other to spread my own moisture from front to back. The sensation of him in a new place was exquisite, but I froze when he paused there, in the one place he hadn't touched me before. It was without a doubt the most unexpectedly erotic moment of my life.

"I'm having some very nasty thoughts, Amada," he rasped, "but that's the point, isn't it? To push me?"

"I've never done that before," I said, looking over my shoulder. He had a sweet little half smile on his face that was sexy but also infuriatingly smug. "I don't think I'm ready."

"You look ready," he said, running his finger up and down. I moaned with pleasure never realizing just how good a simple caress in the right spot could feel.

"I like to make you lose control," I muttered, my eyes closed as my lips parted to take in more air. His touch was literally taking my breath away.

"I know you do," he said, moving the tip of his finger in small circles. "You were supposed to be waiting for me last night, but I couldn't even touch you. Then you tried to seduce me while I was caring for you, which is not allowed. You know I won't cross the line, no matter how excruciating it is. But that doesn't keep you from trying. You're doing it right now."

My backside tingled with sensations that were unfamiliar yet so very delicious, and I focused on the people below as he shamelessly continued to rub me there, alternating between hard and soft pressure. I thought about how I must look from his perspective, spread wide open, yet completely trusting of him and sure of my own power. He was right. I knew he'd never do anything I didn't want, no matter how I behaved. The breeze coming in from the ocean blew over us both and under my robe, exposing me and what he was doing to anyone who happened to glance up from the pier below. For the first time, I wanted to both control and surrender to a man.

"When I say no, it's for your own good. You're not going to get what you want from me by dangling a sweet little carrot in front of my face and then pulling it away. I'm not dumb, and I'm not easily manipulated. Who knows every inch of your body?" he asked, changing to a maddeningly light touch, though I'd lost track of exactly what he was doing because every nerve ending below my waist was on fire.

"You do," I gasped.

"Who else can make you feel this good?" He licked my back with his soft tongue, sweeping upward with his fingers at the same time as if to imply he was thinking about putting his mouth on me, too. The thought of it both excited and frightened me, and he knew it.

"No one," I purred.

"Then why do you try to dominate me? You'd be disappointed if I were weak. Admit it."

"You're right," I whispered after a long pause, unable to lie. I couldn't believe he'd expertly coaxed such an unsavory confession out of me. His touch was a hypnotic truth serum.

I was melting from the sensation of his body and his voice, not to mention his very skillful caress, but above all else he was such an incredible mindfuck that I didn't know whether I was coming or going. Yet, in spite of my euphoria, or perhaps because of it, he chose that exact moment to move his hand away.

"Keep going," I demanded, breathless and on the brink of release.

"I'm in charge, sweetheart," he said, letting go and pulling my robe back down with a flourish.

"Rafa!" I exclaimed, my body still screaming. "You wouldn't."

"I might."

Desperate for his hands on me again, I leaned into him and tried to turn around, but he held me still. Unlike me, he had a will of steel, and even at moments like this when it was at my expense, I admired it.

"Listen," he snapped, roughly grabbing my hips. "Pay attention, Amada. In the future, don't make it difficult for a man to do the right thing. You're safe with me, but it makes me sick to think of you in a situation you couldn't get out of. Don't tease men you barely know no matter how harmless you think it is. Promise me."

His voice was softer, but his words hung heavy in the air, the implication being that this between us was finite and there would be others, men who were not worthy of my trust. I nodded, then felt him rest his chin on top of my head. It was a surprisingly warm, unguarded gesture, but it didn't take long before he was back in the moment.

"Now that we've had this little talk, I'll oblige you. Tell me what you want, and be specific, or I might change my mind." Now that he was in total control he was more at ease, and when he put his arms on either side of my body and gripped the balcony rail, his thick erection pressed against me, a reminder of all the wonderful things within his power to give.

"I'm so wet. I want to feel you inside me," I begged, still bent over. I couldn't wait much longer. I writhed against his bulk with increasing impatience, but still he didn't move.

"Something I don't know," he said mercilessly. I have no idea where it came from, but I replied with the first thing that came to mind. If I'd had a chance to think about it, I probably wouldn't have said it.

"I want your smell all over me when I'm touching myself in bed tonight, thinking of you."

"Mm," he moaned, his breathing erratic now. His fingers grazed my thighs as he reached for the hem of my robe again.

"Not out here," I said, looking back at him then down at all the people below. Earlier it had seemed possible to be discreet, but now I was certain I'd scream his name, just as he'd promised.

"I want everyone to see what I'm going to do to you," hummed Rafa, grinding his hips into mine.

"No, Rafa. It's only for us," I begged.

"Then get on the bed, naked," he said, now struggling to maintain his composure. "On your hands and knees facing the balcony, and stay that way."

I stood up straight and tried to go, but he wouldn't move. I turned to him, wondering what I was doing wrong.

"Take the robe off *here*," he said, gliding a finger between my breasts.

I shrugged it off, and with a nod he let me pass. His gaze followed as I went inside and positioned myself exactly as instructed, summoning him to me by arching my back and parting my legs. He walked past me into the bathroom, turned on the faucet for a minute, then came back out drying his hands. When he was finally ready, he placed the towel beside me, guided me back a few inches to where he was standing at the side of the bed, and licked my thigh with his flat, wet tongue.

"Look at those curves," he rasped, his voice thick. "As if I ever had a chance."

Steadying my hips with his now ice-cold hands, I felt instant relief as he sank deep into my drenched core, followed by waves of intense pleasure throughout my body. I lost myself in the feeling of him inside me, and as he moved in a perfect, steady rhythm, I could think of nothing but how right it was to be joined with him. It approached too fast this time, our sexual energy already at a head because whether we'd realized it or not, every minute since he'd walked in the door last night had been part of our foreplay. It seemed that every minute we spent together, in fact, was nothing but a precursor to *this*.

"Oh my God, Rafa," I sighed, "you feel so good."

In response he placed his hand on the back of my head and gently turned me toward the mirror to our right. There we were, wildly grinding against each other, our reflection even more lewd than anything I could ever imagine. I was completely stripped for him, legs spread, mouth open wide, his muscled arms and large hands roaming possessively over my lower back and hips as he guided me back and forth with skilled ease.

Rafa stilled as he met my eyes in the mirror, then bent down and hastily pulled out of me, quickly replacing his penis with two clever fingers. He pushed my shoulders down so that my sex elevated and opened for him, and from that perfect angle he massaged me from the inside and licked me as I startled at the unexpected pleasure. When my legs gave way, he easily held me up by the hips with his own strength, and as I caught sight of his profile in the mirror, his face completely buried between my legs, neck and back straining, wildly devouring me from behind, I exploded without warning. I saw our past, present and future as my muscles clenched around him, and to my amazement he was mindful enough to stop what he was doing and watch me, too. Rafa gazed intently at my sex as I climaxed, and as he studied me with curiosity, whatever he observed triggered his own release. While still outside my body, he pulled me close and let go.

Immediately after my orgasm subsided my legs began to shake, so Rafa slipped his arm under my pelvis and held me up, mindfully avoiding the places on the front of my body where my skin was still hot and inflamed. He took a moment to trace a finger through his own warm essence as it dripped down the back of my thighs before using the towel to wipe most of it away, leaving a small amount that he gently rubbed into my skin there and between my legs.

"Are you cleaning me or fingerpainting?" I giggled, looking back at him.

"I don't know," he said, smiling back. "Both."

When he was done, I crawled forward and attempted to collapse on my stomach, but before he let go he turned me so that I ended up on my back. He tumbled onto the bed beside me, spent but obviously satisfied. We lay together side by side until it became easy to talk again.

"You're kind of complicated," I said, propping myself on my side as I caressed his hard, flat stomach.

"The world is complicated. I'm simple." He fondled the outside of my sticky thigh as if it were the most intriguing thing in the world.

"You have a very strong sense of right and wrong, don't you?"

"God knows I tried, but you do not respond well to delayed gratification, Amada. Look what kind of debauchery you drove me to," he said, absently rubbing his thumb and forefingers together.

"So is my lover an altruist or a libertine?" I asked him, again in English. The duality of his nature intrigued me. One minute he could be the most caring, nurturing man in the world, then in bed he turned into a complete animal. I ran my fingers through his jet-black hair, appreciating how the stark white pillowcase under his head framed his face beautifully. It illuminated his chiseled features from behind, like a halo in a Renaissance painting.

"I think I know what you said, and I assure you I'm not *un libertino*. I would never tie you up or enjoy your pain, and I sincerely hope you would never allow anyone else to do that to you, either. That shit needs to be worked out with a psychiatrist. Always remember that a man must respect you in and out of bedroom and give you nothing but pleasure."

"But all the women's magazines say I'm responsible for my own orgasms, not you," I joked. Once again, I saw a flicker of desire in his eyes, then something else.

"No, that's my job."

I loved his face, not just because of his disarming beauty, but also because he was so expressive. I noted that now he looked particularly somber as his eyes fixed vacantly on the ceiling.

"Amada, it's time for you to disembark," he sighed. The chaos on the dock had reached its crescendo, the din reminding us that the outside world was waiting and our small slice of Heaven in this little room was gone forever.

"I don't want to," I said, staring straight ahead at the wall. There we were, side by side, unable to look at one another. Finally he sat up and buttoned his pants.

"Almost every passenger is off the ship by now. You have to pack up." He turned his back to me and acted as if he hadn't heard a word.

It hurt to see him do it, and I knew I didn't want to remember him that way. I touched him, fascinated by the way his strong muscles undulated beneath his golden, baby-soft skin.

"What muscle is this?" I asked.

"*El músculo trapecio*," he said, putting on one of his shoes.

"Trapezius in English?"

"I don't know." He shot me a look over his shoulder.

"And this one?" I moved my hand lower.

"*El músculo dorsal ancho*. What do you think you're doing?"

"What is it called in English?"

"I told you, I don't know." There was an edge to his voice now.

"Then I'll be your teacher. You can get your medical license here while you work for me."

He spun around and looked at me like I was mad. I'd struck a nerve, so I braced myself for whatever was coming.

"You're crazy." He rolled his eyes at me and continued to dress himself.

"What do you mean?" I demanded. He still didn't answer, so I poked him in the back. "Why aren't you taking me seriously?"

"Because you haven't thought it through," he said, eyeing me as he stood to pull on his shirt. "You can't just pick me up and take me home like a stray dog you found on the street."

"Let me help you, Rafa. I'll pay more than what you're making here. I need a driver, and no one cooks in my house, so you can cook, too. And at the same time, I'll help you with your English and we'll get you ready for your exams." It was more than that, although I was still too afraid to let him know just how much I needed him as a lover and a friend.

"I'm all alone in that big house. I'd love your company. You mean to tell me you'd rather stay here, when I can offer so much more?" I spat it all out quickly so that I could make my case before he cut me off again, but all he heard was help, driver, and cook.

"So, I would be your employee? Hm. Well, that sounds like a very balanced relationship. What were those duties again? I think you left one out." He kept his eyes down as he buttoned his shirt from bottom to top.

"Your problem is that you wouldn't be able to bend me over a balcony and show me who's boss anymore," I said, tugging on his belt buckle to get his attention.

"Your little arrangement wouldn't stop me from bending you over anything." He met my gaze, but I looked away before he could see me blush. To my chagrin, I thought I heard him laugh a little under his breath.

"I know how much that dress costs, Amada." He walked over to the Valentino gown. "That's *haute couture*. How much did you pay for that?" He'd called it *alta costura*, which took me a second to translate from Spanish to French, and then into English.

"How do you know what it is if you were so poor?" I knew it was a horribly elitist thing to say, and I had to admit I was surprised by my own arrogance.

"Because my mother worked as a seamstress her whole life for pennies a day, and she almost went blind from sewing little pearls and sequins on evening dresses by hand until three in the morning." He waited, his eyes daring me to admit the cost of the dress.

"I don't remember how much." A lie, yes, but I wasn't going to help him make his point.

"Bullshit. I bet it cost twenty thousand dollars." *Mierda. Te apuesto que costó veinte mil dólares.*

"It was thirty-five thousand dollars." His mouth dropped open, but then he nodded his head, vindicated. I couldn't even begin to imagine what he thought of it.

"And this one?" he asked, gesturing to the black lace gown from the night we met.

"I have no idea. It was a gift from my brother."

"Your *brother*?" His voice dripped with sarcasm, but it was still deep and sexy, and now that he was angry, he seemed to take up even more of the room. "I doubt it. The man who bought that dress was madly in love."

"You have quite an imagination," I said, but inwardly I couldn't believe we'd both gotten the same incredibly specific impression.

"I will never be able to buy you a dress like that, Amada."

"I don't need any more dresses!" I leaped off the bed and threw on my robe. Feeling exposed, I searched for the tie in vain, so I reluctantly held the robe closed with my fist.

"It would never work between us," he said, looking at me, then the dress, then back again. "Let this be a wonderful memory. It will be for me."

"Am I really just a one-night stand to you?" Tears welled up and my throat burned, a clear sign that this was not going to turn out as I'd hoped. He put his hand on my cheek and looked at me as if I were the most heartbreaking thing he'd ever seen. He moved as if to embrace me, then stopped himself.

"God, you're killing me. I warned you," he said softly. "I knew you were going to have a hard time with this part."

"You were right," I said sniffling. "I'm disgusted I let you have me so easily last night. I'm ashamed of myself."

"No, sweetheart, don't be," he said, going back to the buttons on his shirt. "It felt right. We just knew."

"Then come with me." *Come live with me and be my love*, I thought, remembering the Marlowe poem. I searched his eyes for anything that revealed his true feelings, but he'd gone completely blank. Overcome with emotion, I stifled a sob and tried to undo the buttons he'd just fastened, but he simply moved my hands away, kissed them, then took a few steps back.

"Use your common sense," he said, getting upset. "I could be a con-artist or a serial killer for all you know." A horrified look flashed across his face. "My God, I hope you haven't done this before. You can't just invite men you barely know to your home, Amada. You have no clue how the world really works, do you?"

"No, I guess I don't. I can't imagine how I've lived to be this old as stupid as I am."

"Amada! Don't talk that way about yourself," he snapped. "I don't like it."

"Then don't call yourself a stranger. You know there's something between us."

"It's the sex," he sighed. He ran his hand through his hair, the metal on his watch reflecting the harsh light gradually angling its way into the cabin. "It's easy to get confused when it's so good. Of course I'm feeling it, but the difference is I know I can't have everything I want."

"The difference is you don't think you deserve it," I countered sharply.

"Jesus, I told you I loved you," he hissed, grabbing me by the elbow. "Now you want me to go home with you after two days? We're obviously not thinking straight!" He let go and went back to wrestling with the damned shirt, still shaking his head in disbelief.

"Well, I have to accept that this is nothing new to you. I know they chase you left and right, Casanova. I'm under no illusion that I'm any different." I crossed my arms and thought of Sharon and her nauseating comments. At first, I thought he was going to continue to ignore me, but then he gave up on the buttons and slammed his hand down on the dresser.

"How could you go to bed with a waiter on a seven-day cruise and think it could end any differently!" he shouted, finally showing the emotion I craved. "I'm not good enough for you!"

"You're not a waiter, you're a doctor! You're an educated, hard-working, brave man who just has to acclimate to new surroundings, and I want to help you. You're not the first person in the world to start over!" I took a step toward him, but he held up his hand for me to stop.

"You're not getting what you want this time. When you get home and think about it, far away from that bed, you'll see I'm right." We turned toward it at the same time, the disheveled sheets and strewn pillows clear, tangible evidence of how much we'd enjoyed each other.

"Rafa—"

"Amada, enough. I'm trying to rebuild my life. I can't drop everything on a rich woman's whim." He paused, suddenly realizing how cruel he'd been, but didn't take it back.

Humiliated, I let go of my robe and started to throw clothes haphazardly into the open suitcase on the floor. Most of it hit the carpet, but I continued to toss my belongings in that general direction, looking away so that he wouldn't see the tears streaming down my face. He made a feeble attempt to hug me, but I pushed him away. I didn't want him to see me weak and exposed. He'd cut me to the quick, and I hurt.

"Give me your number," he begged. "We can get together when I'm in Miami. Let's keep in touch."

"Are you kidding?" I was dumbfounded. "You want to be fuck buddies? Get out!"

I took one last look at him, standing by the door with his rumpled white shirt still open at the top, the most devastatingly handsome man I'd ever seen. I offered him everything I had, and he still didn't want me. I went into the bathroom and slammed the door shut, and outside I heard him do the same.

CHAPTER FOUR

I know shouldn't have told her to keep in touch. I have no clue what came over me, and she was right for screaming at me to get out. All she wanted was for me to be with her. I thought about following her into the bathroom, but I couldn't in good conscience do what she wanted, and now that I had completely insulted her, she was done. I'd accused her of only wanting me for sex, of trying to control me with money, put down her clothes and basically criticized her entire existence. Oh, but sweet Jesus, the sex had been so fucking hot. I can't believe I'd never have her again. Still, there must have been some part of me that knew I couldn't walk away forever, because before I left her stateroom I glanced at her luggage tags. *Amanda Rose, 331 Gablesworth Boulevard, Coral Gables, FL.*

I ended up on the crew deck because I didn't want to run into her again before she left. Jose, Eduardo and Edgardo were already at the little bar getting hammered, so I sat down on a stool and watched them down shot after shot. They were usually together and pretty much always making a spectacle if they were off the clock. Jose and Edgardo were around my age and not too bad to be around. Edgardo was single, but Jose had a wife in Miami that he cheated on constantly. More than once he'd discreetly come to me to ask if this bump or that red spot was VD. It was.

"Hey, Paul Newman, what's going on?" Eduardo was Mexican and had a strange sense of humor. We got along most of the time, but sometimes he rubbed me the wrong way because he was in his forties and still acted like a horny teenager. They all gave me a couple of friendly swats on the back. "Nah, I'm just joking," said Eduardo, not knowing when to stop. "I meant Brad Pitt!" The three of them erupted in such ferocious laughter that Eduardo began to choke. These idiots were already three sheets to the wind, but apparently that wasn't good enough because they ordered another round of tequila.

"Hey, bartender, get our friend here a drink." Jose waved to Salvador at the other end of the bar, a nice kid from Colombia who sometimes worked with me in the kitchen. Sal wanted to become an architect and liked to talk to me about college and his future career.

"What's up, buddy?" said Sal, coming over to my side. The crew bar was small and dark, just an ugly hole in the wall, but it was the only bar we were allowed to use on the ship. He poured a shot for me, then one for himself. "Bacardi Black," he said, out of earshot. "Fuck that tequila shit."

We did our shots and watched Eduardo and his friends make complete fools of themselves every time a female crew member walked by. I was really surprised none of them had been fired or even arrested for their behavior toward women. Eduardo was not above grabbing a woman's ass or breasts when he was intoxicated, and the other two weren't much better. For some reason the female crew tended not to be Hispanic, which for them was a good thing, because any self-respecting Latin woman would kick those guys right in the balls. Oh, how I would love to see that. No, they mostly directed their disgusting antics toward the European women, who were way too quiet and demure to dish it right back.

Lisa, a polite, young Swedish crew member walked by and said hello to Eduardo and his pals, and then to me and Sal. She was obviously shy, but over the past few months she'd made it clear that she found me attractive and had even tried to kiss me at a party once. Lisa was very sweet, but she was way too young. She also had a tendency to turn up wherever I happened to be lately, which was fine, but I knew it was because she was hoping for something to happen between us. I didn't feel a connection with her, but mostly I wished she'd stop following me around because the company I was forced to keep on this ship wasn't the best. Every time she came looking for me, she usually had to cross paths with Jose and Eduardo, too, so I worried she was on their radar a bit too much.

"Girl, you are fine! When are you gonna be the meat in our sandwich, baby?" slurred Eduardo in broken English, turning so sharply to look at her he almost fell off the stool. I was so tempted to tell him to shut the fuck up, but I knew it would be impossible to work with him after that. Just in case, I looked around to see what I could use as a weapon if things got ugly, and I made note of the paring knife Sal had been using to cut limes at the end of the bar.

"Hello, Lisa," said Sal politely. I said nothing but waved to her as well. I was still so self-conscious of my English that I went out of my way not to speak it under any circumstance. I'd broken that rule for my Amada, but she was the only exception.

"Just look at those three imbeciles," I said to Sal. I really couldn't stand them anymore, and he nodded in agreement.

"Yeah, but we don't all have mad game like you, man. Some of us actually have to *work* to get some pussy." He gave me a high-five, but unlike Eduardo, I knew he really was just being a smartass. He'd never talk that way to woman and was a very decent guy, so I didn't hold it against him. Sal was just a college kid, but the other three were old enough to know better.

"Yo, man, you look like shit," said Sal. "What have you been up to?"

"Nothing," I said, thinking of my Amada's soft lips. I traced the rim of the shot glass with my finger, remembering the curve of her hips.

"You going into Miami today?"

"No. I need to sleep." I was exhausted and had to be back on duty by five o'clock. I had a long night ahead of me, but it was nothing compared to the hours I had worked in the sanitariums in Havana or in the Haitian countryside, because at least here everyone had basic necessities. Women weren't raped every day and babies didn't die of malnutrition and cholera. No matter how hard I worked in a kitchen, it would never be like that, and that's all that mattered.

I noticed Lisa still watching me from across the bar, and Eduardo and his buddies watching her. I got a bad feeling about it, so I asked Sal to come to the table with me where she was sitting alone.

His English was almost perfect, unlike mine, and it was time for me to have a talk with this girl. I didn't want to embarrass her, but she needed to hear some things. Her face lit up when I sat down, and I knew that the conversation would be a disappointment for her, but it was the right thing to do.

"Hey, guys," she said. "What's going on?" She had a heavy Swedish accent, but her English was good enough for me to understand. Over my shoulder I heard Eduardo making jokes in Spanish at my expense. "Oh look, Marlon Brando is gonna go get that ass. Show us how it's done, pretty boy. Why don't you share for once, man?"

Ignoring what was going on in the background, I focused on her. She really was a nice young lady, so I gave her a sincere smile and kept my eyes on her while I spoke to Sal in Spanish. She played with her long, blond ponytail in girlish anticipation of what I might say.

I hated to hurt her feelings, but enough was enough.

"Translate for me, partner." I slapped Sal on the shoulder and took a deep breath.

"Go." Sal waited for me to begin, and after every few words or so I paused to give him time to interpret. I was so tired, but I wanted to get this right, unlike the complete mess I'd made with my Amada.

"Tell her that I know she comes around down here to see me, and I enjoy seeing her, too. Tell her that I respect her and like her very much as a friend. However, I'm at least fifteen years older, and that means I cannot take advantage of her crush on me—"

"Yo, are you sure you want to say that last part? She's cute."

"Yes, I do. Jesus, just say it." I waited for him to repeat what I'd said word for word and continued, undaunted by her now crestfallen expression. "Explain to her that I don't want to see her in this crew bar alone anymore, and if I do, I am going to be very upset. She is too pretty to be wandering around by herself when all the men down here are drunk and rowdy. I want her to watch her drinks and stay with her roommates when she's not working." I let him finish and waited with interest to see what her reaction would be.

"Rafa, I get it. You mean them, right?" Lisa rolled her eyes in the direction of Eduardo and friends, who were still being complete jerks.

"Yes," I said in English. I didn't want to overstep my bounds, but I was really uncomfortable with the vibe I was getting, and I'd never forgive myself if something happened because I didn't warn her.

"Sal, tell her that after a woman is sexually assaulted, she's never the same again. It haunts her for the rest of her life and can have serious health implications. She has to be careful and take her safety very seriously."

"Yo, that's fucked up. You're gonna scare her."

"Tell her. And stop saying 'yo' all the time. That's not how an architect speaks."

* * *

I was back in my cabin by noon ready to sleep. Thankfully my roommate, Eric, was nowhere to be found, which gave me the quiet and privacy I craved. I took a quick shower, turned off the lights and slid into the lower bunk to get some rest. My cabin was no larger than a small closet, and in truth, I was beginning to hate it, not because of its small size or how utterly basic it was, but mostly because the little metal box I lived in now reminded me of the sparse, depressing hospital rooms in Cuba that held nothing but bad memories. I wondered how long it would take before I started to feel like a mental patient myself.

I hadn't had any family for a long time, but I did take comfort in my friendships. I missed the other doctors I'd studied and worked with throughout my career, and I hoped one day I'd see them again when Cuba was no longer the prison it had been for so long. The types of conditions we worked in forced us to become close, and no longer having that connection was strange. Irina was probably still in Haiti, and I wondered if she resented me for leaving without even saying goodbye. We'd broken up a long time ago, but she'd remained a loyal friend in spite of my refusal to marry her after five years together. I knew I didn't want children, so I couldn't see the point of having a wife.

My mother, long gone, used to tell me that women were going to fall in love with me very easily, and never to be so cruel as to play with their fragile emotions. "Be clear with your intentions, or you'll be the kind of man who makes women miserable, like your father. You look just like him. God help them," she'd said.

I still hadn't fallen asleep by one o'clock, and I knew I was going to be exhausted later if I didn't rest. Tired of fighting it, I rearranged my pillows and allowed myself to think about her. My Amada would be on her way home now, maybe already there if she lived in Coral Gables. I remember that area. It was very fancy and just a few miles away from Little Havana. She had to hate me for turning her down, but there was nothing else I could do. Only a gigolo lives off a woman. She'd offered me a job, but it was certainly just out of pity. I didn't believe she really wanted someone to cook for her every day. My Amada was light as a feather in my arms. What could a woman like her need from me besides the obvious? There was nothing wrong with that, but where would that leave me when she found someone more suitable? I'd just have to start all over again, but with a broken heart, too.

Damn, I'd forgotten to tell her to keep putting aloe on that sunburn. She was so goddamned sexy in spite of being redder than a lobster today, but people that fair-skinned can't be in the sun for hours. Four double vodkas. Ridiculous. That's got to stop. My God, how rich she must be to wear clothes like that. Why had she ever given me the time of day? Such a beautiful, elegant woman must have men falling at her feet. Her Spanish had been very good for an American, but then again, she probably had to learn multiple languages in school. There's so much more I'd like to know about her, but it's too late now. She's so smart. I wonder if she's ever had Cuban coffee. Oh, the sex. Those perfect breasts. I'll never be inside her again. What the hell was wrong with me, fucking her without a rubber and coming all over her like an animal? *I want her to read to me in bed naked again.*

The alarm went off at quarter to five, and I shot out of bed hot and disoriented. I was supposed to be in the kitchen by now. Shit. I rubbed my face and felt more stubble than I knew I could get away with. If I rushed, I could shower and shave and still make it on time, and if Sal was up there, he'd make sure things got started for me.

As I approached the miniscule bathroom, the door to the hall swung open and blocked my path, as it had many times in the past.

No two doors could be open at once in a room this size, so when Eric and I were both in here it was very difficult to move around. Eric was just as tall as me, 6' 3," but not nearly as nimble. He reminded me of a Viking: tall, square and blond. He plowed into me again for probably the third time this week.

"Sorry, friend" he said, "but I have to use the bathroom."

I tapped my watch to let him know I was late. It would have been so much easier if they'd given me a Spanish speaking roommate, but for whatever reason I ended up with Eric.

I liked him, but after a few months I was getting very tired of being unable to communicate with just about everyone I came across. I longed to be around my people and my language again.

"No, don't worry," he said, squeezing past me into the bathroom. "We're delayed until six. Some luggage truck isn't here yet."

I called up to the kitchen and thankfully Sal answered, but it was noisy and he could barely hear me. His speech was almost indiscernible from the clatter of pots and pans and frantic kitchen chaos.

"Hello? Who is it?" he yelled into the phone.

"Partner, I'm on my way up."

"Good, it's getting busy. Behind you!" he said to someone else.

"See you in ten." The receiver was almost in its cradle when I heard him bellow into the phone on his end.

"Rafa!"

"What?" I brought the phone back up to my ear, expecting him to warn me that the chef was on the rampage again. They were like generals in the kitchen and loved to keep everyone in a perpetual state of fear. I was sure that this particular German man we worked with now was suffering from some kind of psychiatric disorder.

"Ernesto left an envelope here for you. It's thick, man, maybe a fat tip. Come get it before someone takes it. I don't have a safe place to put it."

"I'm on my way. And stop saying 'man'."

I made it to the kitchen in record time to see about twenty men racing back and forth across the greasy, slippery floor I'd just mopped last night right before I'd gone to see my Amada. It was filthy again, and it never ceased to amaze me how dirty commercial kitchens were. Yes, there were rules that were supposed to be followed, but there was always someone washing lettuce in a dirty sink, peeling fresh vegetables over a putrid garbage can or serving salad in an unwashed bowl. The chefs encouraged this carelessness through their often unreasonable demand for expediency and mass production. It took a while to adjust my thinking to that mentality, because in a hospital a mistake can cost someone their life, but here it was just about getting the food out, no matter what. I was terribly concerned every time a passenger came in with a food allergy, because I knew most of the guys in the kitchen didn't understand or really care. One day there would be a tragedy in the dining room, and I'd either have to stand by and let it happen or face the consequences for trying to intervene. I hoped I'd be gone before then, because no matter what, I knew I could never let someone die if I could prevent it.

I found Sal tossing vegetables at record speed into an enormous pot of stock. He pulled the envelope from his apron, tossed it over and gave me a shove with his elbow. "Open it. I've got this."

I slapped him on the back and stepped to the back corner of the kitchen. The only thing on the outside of the white envelope was my name in a bold, feminine script. I opened it and removed an engraved card folded around a stack of cash. There had to be at least a thousand dollars in hundred-dollar bills, plus a check made out to me for thirty-five thousand dollars. I opened the card and read the note, starting with her phone number and address at the top.

> Rafa,
>
> I'm sorry. I have no idea what you've been through, and I have to respect your choices. You're my friend and I want to keep in touch. Please call if you need anything. I'll miss you so much, but I understand. I believe in you. The best is yet to come.
>
> Your Amada xo

Her words unraveled me like a punch to the gut. Why had I been so unkind? What had I done? An enormous wave of regret washed over me and the realization came that I had abandoned her the way I'd been abandoned all my life, and still she forgave me and wanted to make sure I was alright. I knew she'd written the check for that exact amount to show me it was nothing to her and that I should take it. I'd been so wrong. She was giving of herself freely because she wanted to, not because she wanted to control me.

Out of the corner of my eye I saw Sal watching me with interest. He put a lid on the pot and jogged over, placing his hand on my shoulder with concern.

"What's wrong? Bad news?"

"No, but I need to take the week off."

* * *

I made it ashore just before the ship departed at six, and I was in a taxi by quarter after. It had been several weeks since I'd been in Miami at all, and about six months since I'd first arrived. I'd had no reason to come into town, so I stayed on the ship mostly to save money and rest, but it was no doubt good to be back. Miami is the best city in the world because it's everything Cuba would be if we were free. It's a place where people of every color and nationality come together, and every culture is celebrated. In an international city like this, you never know who you're going to meet, and for me, that was the pinnacle of excitement. With every mile we drove into the city my mood lifted. My Amada must have so much fun living in a gorgeous city like this.

A few minutes into the trip, my ill-humored Haitian taxi driver turned down the radio and asked for an address. "Where in Coral Gables?" His accent brought me back to that terrible day in Haiti and reminded me of the precautions one has to take there, so I gave him the name of my Amada's street but withheld the house number. Rule number one is that you don't give out any information unless you have to. I hoped he wouldn't try to speak to me any more until we were closer, but no such luck. His interest was piqued. "Shit, that's a billionaire neighborhood. Guard gated. You on a list?"

"Gated?" I asked. I wasn't sure what he meant. There were very few gated places in Havana, and mostly they were for the tourists not allowed to see the realities of the country.

"Yeah, bro, guards. You can't get in unless the resident puts you on a list. *Gated communauté.*" I saw his eyes in the mirror change from annoyed to suspicious. "Damn, you fresh off the boat, huh?" This kid was getting a little rude, and I hoped for his sake he wasn't thinking about trying to take advantage of me.

I considered my options. I wanted to surprise her, but if I couldn't reach her, then I'd be better off going to a restaurant in Little Havana and waiting there.

"Take me to *Varadero.* You know where that is?"

In the mirror I saw my driver roll his eyes. "Yeah, mon, I been there once or twice."

I met his gaze in the mirror and gave him my best *don't fuck with me* look until he turned away first, a self-preservation measure I'd adopted while traveling overseas in rough places. I watched the road carefully to make sure he was actually going to Varadero and not some abandoned building where a gang would hold me up. I was carrying my Amada's cash and they'd have to kill me to get it.

On the way there, I called her number and got no answer, so I texted her that it was me, on the way to her house for a visit if she still wanted to see me. I put the phone away and waited for a reply.

We arrived at the world famous *Varadero Restaurant* about five minutes later, and when my Haitian friend asked if I wanted him to wait, I said no. Even if I was headed to my Amada's house soon, I didn't feel comfortable with him any more and would rather get there in another cab. Traveling to dirt poor countries on a regular basis teaches you to always be critical of every stranger you meet. I was horrified when she invited me to her home so quickly, but she lives in a different world. I made sure the cab driver left and then went inside.

Inside that small, shabby little mirrored restaurant, I'd died and gone to Heaven. It's hard to explain how it feels to be homesick for your country if you've never felt that way, but I'd been living with it for so long that it became a regular part of my existence I didn't even notice anymore. It took weeks to get used to the strange food on the ship, and one of the few things I could stomach now was peanut butter and jelly sandwiches. At the beginning, every time I ate that damn peanut butter and jelly I wished like hell it was Cuban black beans and rice. But after a while, I just stopped wishing for it. Walking in here now, my heart hurt, because every food I saw, everything I smelled, and every face I greeted was like coming home. It was so comforting to hear everyone speak with a Cuban accent, a sound so distinct from any other in Latin America. Not that it was any better, it was just the most familiar to me, so it was beautiful.

A short, heavy-set Cuban lady in her sixties came to the counter and greeted me enthusiastically. She had a motherly air about her that radiated warmth. "Hello! Look at this young man! So good-looking! What are you going to eat? You're too skinny." I had to laugh because that was such a Cuban thing to say. She wasn't flirting at all, it really was just a way of being friendly. She was serious about the skinny part, though. For a Cuban mom, there is nothing worse than a skinny kid, especially a boy. Skinny means sick or poor in Cuba, and a Cuban woman won't let up on you until you are at least twenty pounds over-weight by medical standards.

"Yes, I'm hungry," I said, just to make her happy. I ordered big portions of *picadillo*, a Cuban beef hash, fried sweet plantains that we call *platanos maduros, Arroz Imperial*, a dish I'd never seen in Cuba but was some sort of delicious Miami chicken and rice casserole, and of course my beloved black beans and rice. I asked her to put an assort-ment of pastries in a box for me, too.

"Please make sure you put in at least six guava pastries," I said politely. "They're my favorite."

She immediately yelled across to another woman filling the box, "Don't forget the *pasteles de guayaba,* Mirta. That's what he likes! Put six—no, put a dozen in there!"

"Here," said the Cuban lady, "drink this and wait over there. I'll bring it all out to you in a few minutes." She handed me a Cuban coffee that I hadn't even asked for and sent me to wait at a table. I sat down to enjoy all the hustle around me, especially the old men at the take out window arguing politics. I had to laugh out loud when I heard a female voice in the back yell out to ask me whether I was single. These ladies were cracking me up, but it was still so much nicer than being chased around by sex fiends like Sharon on the cruise ship who only had one thing on their minds. Here I was regarded as prime husband material, not a toy to be used like Kleenex and then thrown away. It didn't even matter what I did for a living. I was young, tall, healthy and Cuban, and that's all there was to know.

The Cuban lady peeked around the corner and asked me with no shame whatsoever. This was need to know information, and the older women didn't mess around when trying to find their daughters a husband.

"Are you single? I have a very pretty daughter studying to become a lawyer."

"No, I'm sorry," I said with a wink.

"What a shame," she said, unable to hide her disappointment. Going back into the kitchen she said to someone, "No, he's not. And, boy, does he have beautiful eyes." *Que pena. No, no es soltero. Y mira que tiene unos ojos preciosos.* It was just so amusing, because if I'd said yes, I'd be interviewed and then set up on a date with her daughter right away. She no doubt was already imagining blue-eyed grandchildren. Well, that's just how it works: husband, children and family are priority number one to Cuban women, and they make no bones about it. I don't know how I'd managed to keep my single status for so long. It had to be all the traveling. I relaxed, took a sip of my delicious Cuban coffee and enjoyed how good it was to be around people I understood.

Just before the food came out, the phone vibrated in my pocket. Already in a fantastic mood, I couldn't wait to hear her voice. It had only been a few hours, but I missed her already.

"Rafa?" said a small voice on the other end of the line. I thought it was her, but I wasn't sure. I covered my other ear and leaned down a little to see if I could hear her better.

"Amada?" I asked. She didn't sound like herself.

"Yes, it's me. I'm so glad you called. Where are you?"

"I'm at a restaurant in Little Havana, very close. I took the week off to spend it with you." A pause. "Do you still want me to come? If you changed your mind—"

Without warning, she erupted in sobs. I was floored. What could be wrong with her?

"Sweetheart, calm down. What's wrong? You're scaring me. What happened?" Now I was really concerned. What if she never made it home? I glanced up at the takeout bags on the counter. The nice Cuban lady was putting all sorts of things in the bags I hadn't ordered, like fresh bread and a bag of crackers.

"Rafa, I'm OK. I had a bad day." I heard her sniffle a few times. "Just come over, please." I understood now. It was about us. Once I realized I could make it better, I stopped worrying.

"Look, I just bought enough food for an army. We'll relax, have dinner, and everything will be fine."

"That sounds perfect." Amada gave me the code to her gate and I told her I would see her in fifteen minutes. The Cuban lady had been watching me and came around the counter with the food when I put the phone down, so I stood up and met her halfway. I took the bags and gave her a generous tip, but not before she patted me on the arm as if to check and see how solid I was. She was pleased, but it was also her way of letting me know she liked me, and I had to say I liked her, too.

"Come back soon, young man," she said mischievously, "especially if you break up with that girlfriend."

There happened to be several taxis in the parking lot, so it took less than ten minutes to get to Amada's house. This time my driver was a middle-aged man from Caracas, so we chatted the whole way. "How are things in Venezuela these days?" I offered him some Cuban crackers and listened to him talk about how the country had been in complete chaos since Chavez died. As we traveled south down 42nd Ave, it was interesting note how the landscape changed from small, industrial buildings with iron bars on the windows to statelier, Spanish tile roofed houses and large, palm tree lined streets. I counted three Bentleys and countless Mercedes as the driver told me how people in his country were sneaking across the border to Colombia looking for food. I remembered Venezuela well because it was one of the places in the world Cuban doctors maintained a permanent presence, but I hadn't been there for about five years. Hugo Chavez and Castro had been like-minded friends, so I'd been to South America many times.

The driver turned down a small side street called Old Cutler Road, and for a moment I thought he might be lost or up to something because it seemed like we were going into the woods or somewhere very remote.

"Are you sure this is the way?" I asked, ready to react if I didn't like his answer.

"Definitely. I've been down here many times. I used to drive for a car service and lots of celebrities live here. Heh, wait until you see these mansions. They're palaces."

Soon there were no more houses, just the small two lane road we were on and what seemed like endless concrete block walls and thick hedges. I rolled the window down to get a better look and was surprised by the strong smell and sound of the ocean, which had to be very close even though I couldn't see it.

We took a left turn at a rather plain, nondescript sign that read "Gablesworth, North Entrance" and rather abruptly arrived at a little house that reminded me of a police checkpoint. "Don't worry," said the driver, sensing my anxiety. "It's nothing like that." Apparently I wasn't the only one in the car who knew what it was like to be stopped by the military at gunpoint.

An aloof guard asked for both our driver's licenses and took them back into the booth. I had no idea what he was doing with them, but as he handed mine back, he looked at me carefully as if to remember my face and then waved us through. At first, I saw nothing. It was like driving through an expansive, manicured park, but the only people we saw were armies of landscapers on either side of the road. They were everywhere, trimming bushes and branches, blowing grass off the road, and mowing grass that looked perfect already. There was even more activity outside a series of buildings set back least a quarter mile on the right.

"That's the Gablesworth Club. It costs over one hundred thousand dollars to become a member. Can you imagine?" We passed two SUVs parked on the side of the road leading to the club, and my driver looked in the mirror and gave me a warning. "This neighborhood has 24 hour armed security, night vision cameras, and constant surveillance, so keep that in mind. The Coral Gables Police practically lives here. Don't go one mile over the speed limit or they'll be all over you."

As we made our way through the neighborhood, we drove past a dozen houses, each one larger and more impressive than the one before. Each mansion had something unique about it beyond its size, whether it was a statue in the front yard, an eye catching water feature, or just a perfect lawn the size of a soccer field.

"Incredible," I said to myself out loud.

"Hah, this is nothing. You need to see all these houses from the back. Every single one has a yacht parked right behind it." Just before he took a hairpin turn to the right, he pointed to another concrete wall directly ahead of us and said, "The ocean is five hundred feet that way."

He passed another four houses and stopped in front of a massive gate, the last one at the very end of the street. The little call box was barely visible from between the ivy covering yet another block wall.

"Here it is, partner. We going in the front or the back?"

"I don't know," I said, looking around, surprised there was more than one entrance.

"Well, if you have a code, punch it in, but if not, we need to go to the service entrance."

I leaned out the window and punched in the code Amada had given me. The gates made a whirring sound and opened slowly, revealing a long, winding driveway of blush-colored concrete pavers, leading up like a lazy river to an ivy-covered Mediterranean style house so vast I could see one side but not the other. Amada's house was set on a peninsula, so that the property, at least an acre, was framed by

Biscayne Bay on all but one side. It was utterly breathtaking, a setting so fantastic and absurdly romantic, especially now at sunset, that it didn't seem real. The driver guided the cab around the massive fountain in the center of the circle drive and came as close as he could to the front entrance. I grabbed my bag and the food and stepped out onto the driveway, bowled over. After I paid the fare and the tip, the driver shook my hand and gave me his card, instructing me to call him directly if I ever needed another ride. "Ask for Octavio. Everyone at Varadero knows me. Good luck."

It was at least twenty feet to the loggia, and overwhelmed by the sheer size of everything around me, I approached gingerly, wondering how I could possibly knock on the fifteen foot tall wooden doors without hurting my hand. *What a strange day this has been.*

Luckily, I didn't have to hunt around for the doorbell because one of the doors swung open and there stood my Amada, tiny and even more beautiful than when I left her this morning. It had only been a few hours, but it felt like weeks since I'd seen her.

My first impulse was to go to her and give her a kiss, but I noticed she wasn't smiling, and her demeanor was so odd that I didn't move. Her eyes were puffy and bloodshot, and she looked so sad that I set the bags down as carefully as I could and then opened my arms for her. The contrast between her beautiful home and her dark mood made me sad for her, too. She threw herself into my embrace and hugged me tight, burying her face in my chest.

"Rafa," she said sorrowfully. "You came."

"Baby, why are you crying?" Stroking her hair, I let her sob into my chest for a few seconds, then took her face in my hands and made her look at me. "Tell me," I pleaded, wiping away her tears with my thumbs. God, she was going to break me.

"I thought I'd never see you again," she said. "When you said it was over, I believed you." Her big eyes and delicate, heart shaped face reminded me of a porcelain doll, making it impossible to look at her and not feel intensely. The same thing happened the night we met, which is why I ignored all common sense and showed up at her stateroom. Something about her stirred my emotions, and it pained me beyond words to see her this way.

I'd missed her terribly, but I always knew I could choose to see her, and deep down, I knew I would. She, on the other hand, had no idea if I would sail off, never to be heard from again. I thought about how I would have felt if the tables had been turned, and I realized that I would have been just as panicked, if not more. I hadn't considered her feelings at all, only my own sense of pride, and if she'd run away from me, I would have fallen apart, too. The reality of what I'd done hit me like a ton of bricks. I didn't know what to do other than use my body to soothe her, so I took her face in my hands again, but this time I kissed her the way I'd wanted to when she first opened the door, and because it was that way between us, she opened up for me like a flower.

CHAPTER FIVE

"My love, stop crying." *Mi amor, ya deja de llorar.* He whispered in my ear the way he did the first night, knowing instinctively that he had to get that close for me to really hear him. We were still out front and I realized I hadn't even invited him inside. I had to stop this insane crying or he would think I was a basket case, so I wiped away my tears with the back of my hand and kissed him on the cheek again to let him know I was alright.

"It's fine now," I said. Rafa was so handsome that I didn't know what to do sometimes when I looked at him. It was so easy to get lost in those blue eyes and forget there was a real person inside. I was just as guilty as every other woman who had been hypnotized by his physical beauty, but there was so much more to him than that. There he stood, in a simple black t-shirt and jeans, tearing my heart apart. As a doctor and as a man, those blue eyes had seen so much. He had witnessed the beginning of life, the end of life, he had left his home, endured war, disaster, poverty, and abject loneliness, yet he had remained strong and helped so many, including me. And instead of admiring him for his capabilities, all day I had cried because I craved his lips, his hands, and his beautiful body on mine. I was a shallow woman driven only by my own carnal desires, and if I had ever been an intellectual, two days ago I ceased to be. I'd been humanized by the feverish need for his touch, and I hated myself for being so affected.

"I don't think you're fine, but you will be. I'll fix it." He took my hand and kissed it, then my forehead.

"Come on," I said, leading him inside. I'd been home since ten thirty this morning, and almost eight hours later I hadn't made it past the foyer and the front room. My bags from the trip were still piled up where the driver had left them, large cruise line tags still attached, and it was pretty clear that I hadn't even turned on a light or opened a curtain anywhere in the house. Now that the sun was setting, the timed landscape lights had gone on, but the interior of the house was still dark. I turned on the majority of the first floor lights as I led him through the marbled entry and great room. I set the food and his overnight bag down in the kitchen, moving past the living room quickly so that he wouldn't notice the open bottle of vodka next to the couch.

"Should we eat now?" I asked. "What did you bring?" He was strangely quiet, so I stopped rifling through the bags and looked up at him. "Rafa?"

"I can't believe this is where you live," he said. "I've never seen anything like it. I've never dreamed of anything like it." He stood in place and looked around in every direction, amazed by the size and fittings of the house. It was over the top, unnecessarily so, but it was how my parents wanted it. Money had been no object, and Kieran and I hadn't bothered to change anything. My mother had loved Carrara marble and glass chandeliers, so they were everywhere, and the main house alone was over twenty thousand square feet.

"Here, let me give you a tour," I said. I took his hand and we walked through the entire house, flipping lights on and off as we went through each wing. We went down a level and started in the cellar, where I showed him Kieran's extensive collection of Bordeaux, and from there we took the elevator up and walked through the dining room, the library, the unfurnished art gallery and the formal dining room. Upstairs, I showed him each of the nine guest bedrooms and ten bathrooms, ending the tour in the cavernous cream and white French provincial bedroom that many years ago had belonged to my parents.

"Tomorrow morning I'll show you the grounds and the boat," I said, pointing at the bay through the large window. Rafa looked uncomfortable as he stood in the center of the room, taking everything in. He still hadn't said very much.

"You live here by yourself?" he asked quietly.

I rarely ever brought anyone back to the house, but when I did, they were usually awestruck. I wasn't getting that from him now, though. He didn't like it at all. In fact, I sensed a strong dislike.

"Yes, my brother has another wing, but he's almost never here. Most of the time I'm alone."

"This is your room? Your bed?" he asked, as if he was afraid to touch anything.

"Yes," I said, reaching out. "You can sleep here or in any room you like. Sit down."

"No, I'm in street clothes," he said, looking around. "It doesn't feel like you."

"Why are you acting strangely now? You seemed so happy to see me." My words snapped him out of whatever trance he was in, because for the first time since I brought him inside, he focused on me instead of the house.

"Amada, I don't know where to begin. I'm thrilled to be with you, but there are no words for this place. The house is beautiful, but it's a museum. You really live here all alone?" *La casa es una belleza, pero es un museo. De verdad que vives aquí solita?* He regarded me with such sympathy that the tears came again.

"It's been in my family for generations. I don't think about it." I put my hand on his arm, seeking his touch, but clearly he was picking up on something that made him uncomfortable.

"How old is this house?"

"It was built in 1928." He nodded, as if I had confirmed something.

"Amada, I don't want to offend you, but I can't stay."

"Why not? You're not leaving again, are you?" I prepared to unravel.

"No, baby, I meant *we* can't stay. You're coming with me." He caressed my face and kissed me on the tip of my nose.

"Where?"

"All I know is we're not sleeping here tonight." I didn't know what to make of his behavior, so I said nothing. I could see his mind working, and finally he spoke again, choosing his words carefully. "You were sitting in this house all day by yourself, drinking, without even opening a curtain or a window. All those suitcases are still packed, and I'm sure you haven't even thought about eating. Of course you were hysterical by the time I got here. This is a palace for a hundred people, not one woman. That's why you take so many trips."

He looked around again decisively, as if he'd just had an epiphany, and walked the twenty feet or so across the carpet to my closet. I heard him fumbling for the light switch.

"It's a chain right above you," I called out. He found it and the room flooded with light.

"Pack a bag," he said, still deep in the other room. "Tonight we're staying at a hotel, and then we'll figure everything else out tomorrow." He stepped back out into the bedroom, holding one of my oldest Versace dresses, a barely there scrap of scarlet red fabric. "Wear this, and put on some red lipstick, *mamita*. We have to go out."

Even though he wasn't thrilled about the house, it delighted me to see him here in my environment, among my personal things. My heart swelled with affection for him.

"I have to take a shower first," I said. "I'm still sticky."

"If you must." He looked at my thighs and smiled, remembering why.

* * *

Rafa told me we were going to a Latin club in Little Havana called *The Copper Crown*. Before we left, Rafa ate and changed into a fresh shirt and dress pants, while I showered and put on the red dress he chose for me. I never wore red lipstick, but I found some in my vanity drawer, and I had to say it looked nice. I pinned my hair back on one side and slipped into my sexiest high-heeled sandals.

Downstairs in the kitchen, I found Rafa bent over with his back to me, filling the refrigerator with food. My heels clicked on the marble floors as I walked slowly across the kitchen, and as I came closer, he straightened up but didn't turn around. "Stop right there," he said, "or that dress is going to end up on the floor."

Rafa went to call a cab, but I told him that would be silly considering we had five cars at our disposal. He regarded me with a mixture of exasperation and disbelief when I told him to go down to the garage and choose the car he liked best. To my surprise, he passed up the two Jaguars, the Ferrari and my Lexus and picked me up at the front door in the black Range Rover, and when I got in I noticed that he'd tossed our bags, a few bottles of Evian and a box of pastries in the back, all the essentials we'd need to stay out for the night. In the car, Rafa visibly relaxed and turned on the radio, settling on a classic rock station. It was almost nine and the city lights glittered all around us, but I noticed them only because I was with Rafa. I closed my eyes and let the music of my beloved Led Zeppelin wash over me.

"I love Miami," he said thoughtfully. I enjoyed watching him scan the road and control the Rover with ease, and it only made me wish we'd taken out the Ferrari instead. "That reminds me. I kept your letter, but I left the check and the cash in your dresser drawer. I love that you want to help me, but that is never, ever going to happen."

"Rafa—"

"No, listen to me, sweetheart. We have lot to talk about, but at the top of the list is the following: I am not taking any money from you, and I am not going to be your employee. My money is ours, and your money is yours. That's the way it will always be. Always. Do you understand?"

"No, I really don't because—"

"Do you like the way I make love to you?" He took his eyes off the road for a second and shot me a stern look. His usually sweet blue eyes narrowed considerably, revealing a few deep lines between his brows.

"Excuse me?" This was certainly not a topic I expected to discuss in the car, but he was full of surprises.

"Answer the question."

I thought for a second. "You make love like Led Zeppelin sounds, Rafa."

"Judging by the way you look listening to that song, I'll take that as a yes." He put the blinker on and sped ahead of another car to take the next exit, then turned his attention back to me once we merged onto the highway.

"Most definitely yes. Isn't it obvious?" I crossed my legs suggestively and turned my body in his direction.

"Good. Let me tell you why you like it so much. It's because I put you first. Sexually, physically and emotionally. I hold myself responsible for your happiness, and accepting money from you goes completely against that philosophy. I don't care what other people think of my opinion. Even if it's archaic, that's just how it is for me. It's not negotiable."

He ran his hand up my bare thigh, and I let him touch me all over as he drove toward Little Havana. He licked his lips and looked at me suggestively as if running different scenarios through his head.

"You're driving me crazy with that tight little body and those red lips, Amada. Always wear red for me." He gave my hair a tug and pulled me in for a quick kiss, making me aware of the wetness accumulating between my legs again. God help me, I was perpetually ready for this man.

"I will." I took his free hand off my hip and brought it to my mouth. "I'll do anything for you," I said, as I gently bit down on each of his fingertips.

* * *

The Copper Crown was alive with activity, through from the outside the place didn't look like much. From the car it was difficult to see the entrance, a small, blacked out door on the side of the building. Rafa tossed the keys to a valet and we walked up hand in hand, my dress so restrictive I could barely keep up with Rafa's long strides. As we came closer, I heard salsa music coming from inside every time the door opened. Rafa shook the young man's hand at the door, a big fellow who welcomed Rafa by name.

Inside the club, it was another world. There were wall to wall beautiful people everywhere, all milling around in groups with a drink or dancing near the front. We made our way through the crowd and ended up at the bar, where Rafa stopped to ask if I wanted a drink.

I remembered his comment earlier about the open vodka bottle, so I declined. I really had no desire to drink now, anyway.

"Not yet," I said, struggling to speak over the loud music. "What's that smell?" There was a faint but peculiar odor in the air, not bad, but definitely pungent. Earthy and masculine, it reminded me of burning leaves.

"People smoking cigars on the patio." He inhaled deeply. "I like it. It reminds me of my grandfather." It was the first time he'd mentioned anyone other than his mother, so I hoped that later, maybe after a few drinks, he'd loosen up and tell me more.

Rafa walked ahead of us through the dimly lit club, gripping my hand tightly as he made his way past a small section of tables where people were drinking and eating. It must have brought to mind the Cuban takeout we still had back at my place. "I can't believe you didn't try any of the food I brought you," he said over his shoulder. "Don't worry, I'm cooking for us now, and you're going to start eating."

I didn't realize we weren't here to drink or dance until we got to the very back of the club behind the stage. It was a little secluded for my taste, so I checked out our surroundings, hoping there weren't any unsavory characters lurking in the shadows. He put his arm protectively around my waist and kissed my cheek, and I had to say that in this setting Rafa was visibly happy. Gone was the quiet, guarded waiter I'd met on the ship, and in his place there was a strong, confident man comfortable in his natural environment. Miami did bring out the best in him, and I enjoyed seeing it.

"You're safe here. It's not fancy, but everyone is very respectable." *Decente* was the word he'd used, but I knew what he meant. He knocked on the door, and in a moment we were face to face with another club employee who appeared to be about 6'5' and as wide as refrigerator. The dark man's face lit up when he saw Rafa, who greeted him enthusiastically.

"Sandro! Good to see you!" he said, hugging his friend. I stood by quietly until Rafa was ready to introduce me, and though it was odd meeting people in such a revealing dress, I tried to forget about it and act like myself. Still, it was a far cry from my typically conservative clothing, so I couldn't help but feel strange and exposed.

"Rafa, you bastard! We've been wondering when you'd be back!" He leaned in as Rafa said something I couldn't quite make out." Sure, man, she's with someone now, but I'll tell her you're here." Looking down at me he said, "Oh, excuse me—"

"Sandro, this is my girlfriend, Dr. Amanda Rose," he said with pride.

"Oh, wow, good to meet you," he said, pumping my hand. Once I'd walked past him, Sandro gave Rafa a high five and whistled under his breath.

Sandro stood aside so that we could pass, and inside there were about fifteen men playing cards and dominoes at three different tables. Rafa went around the small, plain little room and greeted them all, introducing each man by his title, all of whom of whom greeted me affectionately and stood up to shake my hand. One man was a judge, and several were police officers and attorneys. It really was a distinguished crowd, but you'd never know it. All the men were in Bermuda shorts smoking cigars and joking with one other like a bunch of teenagers in a pool hall, and they all wanted to hear about Rafa's adventures on the ship.

"Rafa! Come over here and play Brisca with us while you wait!" The man introduced to me as a judge waved him back over and and pulled out the chair next to him. "Come, sit!" Clearly he wasn't going to take no for an answer, but it seemed like Rafa wanted to anyway.

We went to the table, and to my surprise Rafa sat down and patted his knee.

"On your lap?" I'd never sat on anyone in public before, and Rafa knew why I was hesitating and of course found it very funny. He regarded me with a mix of amusement and tenderness, and because the cute little smile on his face was impossible to resist, I did as he asked. As I put my arm around his neck, he leaned in my ear and whispered, "Don't worry, *profesora*. Cuban men like their women smart and sexy."

One of the three men at the table, Carlos, looked up from his hand and took the cigar out of his mouth. He had to be in his late sixties but was still quite attractive, and I liked the big beauty mark right in the center of his cheek. "She speaks Spanish?"

"Yes," said Rafa. "Very well, don't you agree?"

"Where did you learn to speak Spanish, Amanda?" Carlos tucked a card under the stack of cards in the center of the table and took the one that was already there. They were playing with a deck of cards I'd never seen before.

"In school."

"Getting her Ph.D. Amanda is a Professor of English," said Rafa.

"Oh, she's a doctor. Excellent," said Carlos.

"I'm not—"

"*Doctora* is also a woman who has a doctorate in an academic subject. *Médico* is strictly a medical doctor," Rafa explained, patting me on the thigh. I loved his touch, but the highbrow, academic part of me was cringing at the way I was dressed and how I was draped all over Rafa, yet no one at the table acted as if it was the least bit out of the ordinary.

"Amanda," said the judge named Oscar, "teach him so he can get his license. Force him to speak to you in English. He knows we'll get him a residency as soon as he passes the tests. Then, in three years, he's done." He waved his hand in the air as if he were chopping off an imaginary head. "He's still not even forty years old by then."

"That's exactly what I plan to do," I said, rubbing Rafa's shoulder.

"You know, he can become a nurse in a year," said the third man at the table, who I think had been introduced to me as Javier. "They have that program at FIU."

The room erupted in a chorus of *No*s and *Oh my God*'s, which was hilarious, because I hadn't realized everyone had been listening to the conversation at our table. It certainly was an intimate group.

"He did not go to medical school in Cuba for how many years and save lives all over the world, dealing with Ebola and malaria and God knows what else every day to end up a nurse here," ranted Carlos. "We all know what Castro puts those poor traveling doctors through. Please."

He took a sip of an amber colored drink and puffed on his cigar again. I noticed that Rafa didn't interject a word, respectfully allowing them to carry on the conversation without interruption, and they all spoke so fast and loud I had to concentrate to be able to follow everything they said. Here Rafa sounded just like them, making me realize that he'd altered his natural way of speaking just for me.

"Hey, nurses make good money," said Javier, waving his hand in the air. "Every hospital in Miami has twenty nurses who were doctors in Cuba. So what?"

"They only do that because they have families to support right away and can't get a residency," said Carlos. "Rafa doesn't have those problems. He's stuck working a crap job for a while until he learns how to speak the language and gets his professional license, just like we all were. Big deal. You know what I had to do to get through law school again here? Clean out rat cages in a laboratory!" Everyone nodded their heads as if it was indeed the worst job they'd ever heard of.

"Rafa's just fine, don't try to talk him out of what he needs to do. Damn!" *¡Coño!* He banged his hand on the table and that was it. Carlos had spoken, and no one else was going to say another word about it.

"Remember," he said to Rafa, "you can't give out medical advice or assistance to anyone here. It doesn't matter if they're bleeding to death in the middle of the street. It's illegal, and you'll get sued, too. You don't have a license, so you don't have that responsibility anymore." He took another puff from his cigar.

"I know." said Rafa. "So, I guess I also shouldn't—"

"Hey!" said Carlos with a chuckle, meeting Rafa's eyes. "You know what I mean."

"You deal," said Javier to Rafa, passing him the deck. Happy to change the subject, Rafa turned his attention to me.

"This is a Spanish deck." He tapped the stack of cards on the table and fanned them out. While I was looking at all the colorful images, he very lightly bit my breast through my dress. Mortified, I turned beet red and silently mouthed for him to stop. "No one saw me," he said with a wink. It was true. A waitress had just set down a huge platter of fried appetizers and little sandwiches, so everyone was very focused on the food and passing plates around.

Javier popped a little fried ball in his mouth and wiped with a napkin. "Come on, deal," he said impatiently. Rafa scooped up the cards, shuffled, and dealt. He showed me his hand and explained that the object was to get the points for as many hands as possible. They'd been playing as singles before, but now that there were four people, he would be playing as Carlos' partner. He pointed to the card he'd placed right side up under the deck.

"That one decides what the trump suit is for the game. If it's a high card, worth ten points or better, any of us can exchange it for a seven of the same suit after a winning hand. The suits are called *bastón*, *espada*, *oro* and *copas*. Get me a croquette, mamita."

"These?" I asked, holding up a little fried cylinder. I fed Rafa *croquetas, bocaditos, papas rellenas* and *mariquitas* as he won round after round of Brisca, giving him a little peck on the lips every few minutes. The finger sandwiches they called bocaditos contained a delicious pickle and ham spread I really liked, and to Rafa's great satisfaction, I ate two myself. We were all having so much fun that time flew by, and at least an hour had passed when Sandro called out to Rafa.

"She's ready for you, partner."

I hopped off Rafa's lap after he gave me a little pat on the thigh, but when I went to sit back down in his chair, he grabbed me by the elbow.

"No, sweetheart, come with me."

"Why?"

He answered by pulling me by the hand to yet another room off the game area. It was quiet and dark, and I could barely see a thing, but we walked to the center of the space and took it all in. The only light came from about a dozen candles placed strategically around the room, and there were lots of bottles and knick knacks everywhere, as well as all sorts of interesting scents I couldn't place. It wasn't necessarily a messy space, but it wasn't neat either.

"Rafael, my son." To our left stood a tiny white-haired woman no taller than five feet, and because he towered over her, Rafa had to bend considerably to give her a hug and kiss. She wore a long, white dress with a bright shawl around her shoulders and colorful, beaded necklaces that tapped against each other as she moved. Though she was frail looking and had to be at least ninety years old, she was sharp and observant, her relatively unlined face an exotic mix of Asian, Latin and African cultures.

"Madrina," he said reverently, as he leaned forward to let her make a gesture over his head.

"It makes me so happy to see you again. How was your trip?" she asked, smiling now at me.

"It went very well. Here, I had this made for you in Panama." Rafa reached into his pocket and produced a beautiful gold bracelet, channel set with shiny white and black stones. She looked at it closely and was obviously very pleased, but instead of slipping it on her wrist, she shuffled to a little table in the back of the room and set it up against a statute of a Catholic saint.

"She likes it," she said, when she came back over to us. *Le gusta.*

"Good. Madrina, I want to introduce someone to you." Rafa motioned for me to come over, so with some hesitation I stepped toward them and extended my hand.

"Hello," I said. "Nice to meet you."

To my surprise they both laughed, and instead of shaking my hand, the old woman held out her arms for an embrace. Strangely, it wasn't awkward, because I sensed that Rafa had some sort of special connection with her.

"Doña Delfina, this is my friend, Dr. Amanda Rose," said Rafa.

"She's lovely, but she's not your friend, Rafael," she said sweetly. "She's your lover." *Ella es tu amante.*

"Yes, Madrina," he answered, although it wasn't a question. Rafael held out his hand and escorted her back to a rocking chair I hadn't seen when we walked into the room. There were two more chairs and a little glass coffee table next to her. "Sit down," she said. *Sientense.*

We sat across from her, and I couldn't help but notice the assortment of objects on the table. There was a lit, smoking cigar resting in a large glass ashtray, more unlit candles of various colors and heights, a dish of what appeared to be honey, scattered pieces of hard candy and a small egg cup containing a shiny liquid metal. Intrigued, I reached out to touch it, but Rafa saw what I was going to do and stopped me.

"No, that's liquid mercury. It's toxic."

Doña Delfina positioned her hands on her belly and intertwined her fingers. She sat quietly and watched us, and because Rafa didn't seem to be in any hurry to talk, I did the same.

I wished he had explained more to me about what we were doing tonight, because I hadn't a clue how to behave. The candlelight cast moving shadows in the room, an interesting counterbalance to the otherwise still and quiet space. Finally, after about two or three minutes, she began.

"This is her. The other thing is gone, but there are still some matters that need resolution. For you, for her, and for the both of you." She took the cigar from the ashtray, puffed on it, and set it back down. Then she leaned back, closed her eyes, and kept talking. "You think something is in her house."

"Yes, Madrina," said Rafa. "It was there."

"You're right. The space has to be cleaned, and so does she. Something has attached itself, and for her to have peace, it must leave."

I was about to interrupt when Rafa squeezed my hand. I understood that he wanted me to keep quiet, but I was dying of curiosity. It was clear she was some sort of fortune teller, and Rafa believed in it.

"Then, when that's done, I want to bind you together. There will be children." I almost fell off my chair, because if there was one thing I knew for certain, it is that I would never have another child.

"Madrina—"

"I know what you fear. Don't." She lifted a finger and pointed at him. "You must accept what is meant for you." And with that, she stood, clearly indicating our meeting was over. "Give Sandro the address. We'll be over at eleven o'clock tomorrow morning. I need a white dove, a coconut, a bouquet of white flowers and three gallons of coconut water. I'll bring the herbs." And with that, she dismissed us.

"Thank you," said Rafa, giving her a kiss on the cheek.

"You're welcome, Godson. Now go make love before you're too old, like me," she said with a giggle.

After saying goodbye to Doña Delfina and his friends, Rafa and I headed to the Ritz-Carlton Coconut Grove for the night. In the car, I had a million questions.

"Children?" I choked out, in tears. "Something is *attached* to me?"

"I know, sweetheart," said Rafa, his hand on my cheek. "It's a lot to take in at once. Maybe I should have prepared you better, but once we get in bed and talk, and you'll understand.

I promise."

"Rafa—"

"Wait until we get there," he said, with a pained look. "Just let me hold you."

Unable to find a tissue anywhere in the car, I dabbed at my eye with my finger and tried to stay quiet, but I couldn't help myself.

"Is she a medium or something? I mean, everybody knows they're fake! You can't really believe any of that!"

"Please, let's get to the room and I'll explain everything." Rafa took a deep breath, his expression hardening. "She's not a fraud. She saved my life."

Because it was already so late, the staff got us into our accommodations quickly, and it was a good thing because I really didn't want to lose my composure in public. It was a beautiful room that otherwise would have been very romantic, but I was so shaken up by what I'd heard, I barely noticed anything other than the chair I fell into the minute we walked in. We didn't even bother to turn on the lights, but Rafa went in the bathroom, washed his hands, then came right back out.

He dropped to his knees in front of me just like the night we met, and looking at him through my tears, I was moved by his physical beauty as always, but this time there was more.

I was learning that Rafa was a complex man whose good looks were actually the least complicated thing about him.

"Amada," he said, rubbing his whiskered face across the soft skin of my thighs, "let's get undressed. You'll feel better if you lie down and relax with me."

"You have no idea," I said. For the second time in one day I was bordering on hysterical, and when I went to get out of the chair, he held me down by the hips and kept me there.

"Calm down, please." He was firm but way too in control of himself, which made me even angrier. I had every right to be upset, and I had to make him understand that. I considered telling him about my son, just so he'd make sure it never came up again.

"I will not calm down! I can't talk about children. I don't want to hear that kind of thing anymore." I buried my face in my hands and sobbed. It was the one subject that could tear me down to nothing in an instant, and here it was again. Rafa pulled me into his arms and hugged me tight, but at that moment all I wanted was to make my mind go blank.

"Can you please make me a drink?" I asked. My eyes fixed on the minibar across the room. I couldn't think about these things anymore, and I'd do anything to make them all go away.

"Baby, no" he whispered, kissing my tears. "Look at me, that's not the best way." He held the back of my neck with his left hand, and without any of the customary preamble, met my gaze as he licked two fingers and skillfully inserted them inside me. It wasn't something I was expecting, yet it didn't startle me, either, and in spite of my deteriorating emotional state, his touch had the intended effect. A flood of relief washed over me as my mind gave way to my body.

"Sh," he said, his lips on mine. Rafa caressed my face and continued massaging me for a minute or two, but he didn't bring me anywhere near an orgasm, and because it wasn't his usual caress, I don't think he was trying. He did, however, get me back in to a frame of mind in which it was possible to communicate.

"Better?" he asked. I didn't answer, but satisfied that my mood had improved, Rafa slipped out of me and kissed me again, this time on the cheek. Normally at this point I'd be halfway through a double vodka, but I had to give him credit. He'd known how to diminish my stress level faster and more efficiently with something far simpler. I was thinking so clearly, in fact, that it occurred to me to hand him a tissue from the box beside me on the end table. He took it, wiped his hand discreetly, then put the tissue in his pocket.

"Do you want me to take off your dress?" He undid the ankle straps on my shoes and slid them off my feet. I moaned when he pressed his thumbs into my arches, a sensation so intensely pleasurable that it reverberated deep in my sex.

"You certainly know how to handle a woman," I complimented, purring as he rubbed my soles. There are the kind of people who make a bad situation worse, and the kind who make it better, and he was obviously the latter. I couldn't imagine what it would take for him to lose his temper, and I never wanted to find out.

"My woman, yes," he said.

"Do you use your hands to fix every problem?" Oh, that felt good. His grip was so strong, and I'd always preferred a firm touch.

"Well, you'd be surprised how much of our mental state can be transformed simply through physical manipulation. Massage is one way, but did you know there are painkillers in the chemicals released during orgasm? Some people say they can effectively treat their migraines by having sex." He smiled and glanced up quickly to make sure I hadn't lost interest, but I was listening.

"And it works the other way around, too. When you're suffering physically, it takes a tremendous toll on the mind. You really can drive yourself crazy by wallowing in negative thoughts." He continued to rub, putting more pressure on my feet than I had ever experienced. I closed my eyes and started to melt in to the chair.

"You're smart," I said, but he just laughed.

"It's not like I invented it, mamita. I learned from books like everyone else."

"It's not just books. You're clever." This reminded of something, and I peered at him through heavy lids. "Rafa, how did you know I could have a vaginal orgasm? I didn't think I could."

"That actually comes from a book, too," he said, still rubbing my feet. "There's published research dating back to the 1920s that suggests a woman's C-V distance determines whether or not it's possible for her to have an orgasm from intercourse alone."

"What's that?"

"Clitoral-vaginal distance. If it's less than two and a half centimeters, scientists think you can have one."

"And I fall in that category?" I asked, sitting up.

"Lucky us," he said with a smile.

"When did you pull out the yard stick and check?"

"The first night. Even though it was annoyingly dark, I managed."

"What if my C-V distance had been more than that?"

"Then I would have changed my strategy. One way or the other, you know I take care of business." He gave me a little wink and started to rub my calves, which was surprisingly wonderful.

"Strategy, huh? Now I remember everything," I said. "You went straight to oral sex because you wanted a good look, then you felt around for an IUD string, and that's why you were so confident about not needing a condom with me. That's really kind of sneaky! It's like having the answers to a test ahead of time!"

"Don't be mad," he said, dissolving into laughter. "It wasn't as calculated as you just made it sound. Anyway, sometimes STDs are visible and sometimes they're not. You need blood work to be sure. The condom—I have no excuse. We took a chance and trusted each other."

"I'm not mad," I sighed, still complete putty in his hands. "It's actually fascinating."

"Believe me, all I could think about was kissing and touching you all over. I was delirious with lust."

"What else did you notice?"

"Nothing," he said after a pause. "You have a right to your privacy, no matter how intimate we are."

"Rafa," I said, sitting forward with interest, "how did you know it was my *first* vaginal orgasm?"

"Because you were so afraid of it," he said, kissing my knee. "You still are."

"Why do you think it's never happened before?"

"Your anatomy makes it possible, but it's all about whether you're in the moment. The mind is the greatest erogenous zone. Without that part, nothing's going to happen."

"That makes sense," I said, considering everything he'd said. "You know, I really do enjoy talking to you. Even if we'd met under other circumstances, I'm sure we would have at least been good friends."

"What do you mean by other circumstances?" he asked, glancing up.

"I don't know. In school. Or if one of us were already married to someone else." He gave me a funny look that I couldn't decipher.

"Well," he said, putting aside whatever he was thinking, "if you think I'm so smart, then listen to me when I make suggestions. Let's start exercising together."

"Sorry, handsome," I quipped. "I never work out."

"I think you should start running. You'll see." He stopped rubbing and then gave my thighs a squeeze. "I also want you to stop drinking for a while, if you can. Give your body a break. If you can't, we'll deal with it."

"Of course I can. I don't know why I overdo it. It's a bad habit." I hoped he would believe me, because it was true. If it were more serious than that, I would have told him.

"For what it's worth, I don't think you have a problem. I think you drink because you're lonely and preoccupied with the past, but you're not going to be any of those things now that I'm around." He pulled playfully on my pinkie toe. "So, can we try it?"

I put my foot on his groin and found that he was already erect. I traced his impressive length up one side and down the other, enjoying the feeling of his firm shaft through the fabric. "Sure, but you'll have to keep me entertained."

He watched my painted toes dance over his erection with obvious delight. "My pleasure," he said.

After he finished in the bathroom, I washed my face and put on a satin nightie. I thought about leaving the makeup on, but I didn't feel the need to hide behind anything with Rafa, so I came out of the bathroom barefaced. He wore nothing but his glasses and a pair of boxers, looking sexier than ever as he read a local magazine. I curled around his body, reveling in our closeness and in how good his skin felt on mine. He opened his arms and pulled me toward him, effortlessly rolling me on my back.

"Nice glasses," I said.

Rafa pulled down the straps of my chemise and checked the pink skin on my chest and on my legs. "It's peeling now. Don't ever do that again, mamita. It's so bad for you."

I heard everything he said, yet all I could do was touch his lips with my fingertips. I adored his face, probably for the same superficial reasons every other woman did, yet the more I knew him, the more meaningful his features became. I noticed little things now, like the barely discernible chicken pox scar between his eyebrows, and it made me wonder how old he'd been when he was sick and who took care of him, if anyone. It was nice that he let me stare at him as long as I wanted, and he liked doing it, too. It was never awkward between us when we took the time to really contemplate each other.

"You are so sweet," he whispered, kissing my lips. "And there it is again."

"What?" I kissed him back and flicked my tongue in the little groove between his lip and chin. He took off his glasses and set them on the nightstand.

"The look that tells me it's time." He climbed on top of me, slithered out of his boxers and put both knees between my legs. Spreading me open with ease, he reached down and positioned himself so that it would only take one thrust to fully seat himself inside me.

He tasted me deeply as always, our tongues moving together in a cadence unique to us. I'd never enjoyed kissing as much as I did now with Rafa, probably because it felt like the most natural thing in the world, and he never tired of putting his lips on me in a million different ways, whether it was to kiss me or lick me all over. He caressed me for a long while, eventually making his way down to my sex, where he used a feather light touch that drove me wild. Of course, it didn't take long before I was close to the edge, but then he stopped. Somehow he always knew exactly when to hold back, and though he might not always be able to read my thoughts, he certainly could read my body.

"I am going to teach you how to wait." he said. "It's even better that way." I looked into those endless blue eyes for reassurance. "It's a gift, not a punishment," he promised.

He brought his mouth down on mine again, tongues resuming the same tempo. As lovely as it was when took me from behind, this was far more intimate. I adored seeing his face, feeling his weight on top of me, and being able to touch him all over with ease.

I reached down between us and began to caress his penis. I stroked him with my fingertips at first, feeling the suppleness of his skin and then the hard valleys and ridges created by the pattern of the vein underneath. I enjoyed learning about him this way, virtually blind, relying only on my sense of touch. Enticed by the texture of his skin, I couldn't stop stroking it, the way you can't stop petting soft fur or cashmere.

Cradling his testicles in my hand, he moaned as I gently handled one and then the other. I pressed between them, feeling the base of his erection underneath his skin where it joined his body and enjoying his soft sighs as I massaged him there and then in the space behind his scrotum. I had no idea what I was doing other than slowly exploring his beautiful body, but it no doubt felt very good to him, because he'd stopped kissing me and for the first time gave me absolute control.

"Amada," he sighed, letting his head drop in the bend of my neck. He tightened up, and guessing it had something to do with imminent ejaculation, I gave his testicles a very gentle tug to see if I could help him last longer. I waited for a complaint, but Rafa said nothing and let me continue to stroke him in the same spot while he moaned and licked my collarbone like it was the most delicious thing he'd ever had in his mouth. It was amazing to see him so aroused and uninhibited, and for the first time I understood why he liked pleasing me so much.

I thought of the chapter in *Moby Dick* titled "The Whiteness of the Whale," a lengthy discourse on the symbolism of color. If Melville's great opus could be so preoccupied with a single color, I wondered how it was possible that in all of Western literature no one had ever written an ode to the male form. Perhaps they had, and it was hidden somewhere among the Greek classics or in the banned books of French erotic literature. The glory of a man's body, especially his phallus, was just as profound as female beauty in its own way, fully deserving of contemplation and admiration. Lost in my own peculiar mix of thoughts, I wondered what Rafa was thinking about, and while I wouldn't have asked any other man, the rules were different with him. I was glad to know, because it was in marked contrast to my own erudite meditations.

"You're velvet, Rafa." I whispered, still caressing him. "What does it feel like?" He looked up regarded me with a combination of need and exhilaration, and after taking a moment to think about my question, he put his hand on mine to still it.

"Like pure joy."

"*Jouissance*," I smiled. "So let me keep going."

"I'm too close. I have to finish inside you tonight."

"Why?"

"I just do." *Porque sí.*

We switched positions, but instead of straddling him I hovered above his swollen penis. I lingered there to build his anticipation, then slid down his erection like melting caramel, relishing every inch. He was hot and thick, and he filled all of my empty space to the hilt. I sighed with contentment when he was completely inside me, knowing instinctively that our connection went beyond our bodies to the metaphysical. There was no question that we were one, and although we might not be able say how or why, I saw it in his eyes too. Wanting nothing between us, he found the hem of my nightgown and pulled it off, watching with fascination as my nipples tightened in the cool air of the room. He used his hands to support and weigh each of my breasts as if trying to commit everything in his sight to memory.

I couldn't hold still any longer, so he let me experiment until I found the perfect angle on my own, and seeing that I wanted to be somewhere between flat and upright, helped by propping himself up on a pillow. With that small adjustment, we hit the perfect spot. I kissed him deeply as I rode him, delighting in the incomparable pleasure of every thrust. For the first time, he let me lead our dance, and I finally knew what it was like for him when he became possessed. The more I took from him, the more I wanted, and as we embraced, he let me feast on him, my carnivore pelvis wanting nothing less than to eat him alive. The room filled with our grunts and whimpers, but as we both neared our climax we became blind and mute, each of us aware of nothing but the freefall of our own body into the other's as Rafa satisfied his instinct to fill me up.

CHAPTER SIX

I held my Amada in my arms, and having just experienced the most intense orgasm of my life, I was overcome by a sense of serenity and happiness unlike any other. I couldn't kid myself, I did feel love for her in and out of bed, but more so at this moment than ever. I knew very well that my body had released oxytocin during my orgasm, and as the supposed love chemical, my mind was under the influence of a powerful drug. But deep down I knew it was more than that. I'd had a lot of sex in my life, but never like this. When she asked why I wanted to be inside her, I should have told her then, but I couldn't bring myself to confess that after thirty-six years of bachelorhood, I'd fallen in love so fast. I'd barely accepted it myself.

When we were done making love, I stayed inside her for as long as possible and didn't let go until our bodies came undone. We ended up on our sides, facing each other in silence, and she looked peaceful, so unlike her mood when we got to the hotel. I looked in her green eyes and noticed gold flecks in a starburst pattern, a little universe right there, just for me. My brave lover had been so giving and uninhibited tonight that I was delighted to let her have me any way she liked. I would have given her anything, allowed anything, just to see what her preferences revealed about her.

I took her palm and kissed it, loving her taste and her bare skin. Hypnotized by her scent, my lips traveled to her nipple, and she let out a gasp when I drew it in my mouth and sucked it like a piece of hard candy.

"Oh, I love when you do that," she purred, running her fingers through my hair.

"I haven't tasted you nearly enough tonight." I moved to the other nipple and made a mental note to wake her in the morning with a nice long kiss between her legs.

"Hold that thought," she said. "I'll be right back."

While she was in the bathroom, I turned on my back and stretched out, feeling happy. I realized I'd worked up a little appetite, so I went to the table where we'd set down our belongings and found a bottle of Evian, and to my delight, the forgotten box of pastries.

"Jesus, Rafa. How do you have such a fantastic body? You look like someone who spends all day in the gym." On her way back, she gave me a little kiss between my shoulder blades, but before I could return the favor she was back in the bed, reclining seductively just like the courtesan in Manet's *Olympia*. God, she was beautiful.

"I'm glad you like it, because I certainly can't keep it off you."

"Seriously. Tell me."

I peeked inside the box and let her have another good look. The pastries smelled delicious. "I just try to exercise when I can and eat healthy," I said absentmindedly, poking around all the sweets. I turned around and held up the box triumphantly. "But not tonight!"

After I washed my hands, I pulled a chair up, placed the box between us and showed her everything I'd bought earlier.

"Here," I said, handing her a glass of spring water. "Have you ever tried Cuban pastries before?"

"Never."

"Oh, then this is going to be fun. You're taking a bite of every single one."

"No way," she said, "I won't be able fit into those tight little dresses you like."

I scanned her naked body. "Well, I like you better out of them, anyway. Eat up. Doctor's orders."

I pulled a pastry out of the box but then noticed her expression darken.

"What's wrong, mamita?"

"I—" She looked down and then back at me, hesitant.

"You can tell me."

"I don't like doctors. You're the obvious exception, of course."

"Why not?" I asked, but she turned her head in a way that made it clear she didn't want to elaborate, so I let it go.

"You're like a cat, Amada. There is something very feline and aloof about you." I kept the word unapproachable to myself. "Who do you like then?"

She smiled at me, her beautiful face blossoming into a lovely expression. "I like you. A lot."

"I like you, too, sexy." Once again I held back the urge to tell her I loved her. It was too soon.

"So, what's this?" She gestured to the pastry in my hand.

"This," I said, regaining my composure, "is your introduction to Cuban culture."

"Is it? I think I've already had quite an introduction by my Cuban lover."

"True. Then it's your introduction to Cuban *food*." I offered her the horn-shaped pastry filled with Bavarian cream and dusted with powdered sugar. "My mother called these *caracoles*. They were my favorite when I was little." I watched Amada take a dainty nibble off the end. "No, sweetheart, this is how you eat them." I ate half the pastry in one bite and put it down. We laughed and moved on to the next one, the syrupy Capuchino.

"Oh, what are these little cones?" she said, dipping her finger in the pool of liquid. She sucked her forefinger and opened her eyes wide. "Yum."

"They're named after the hats worn by the Capuchin monks. You need a special pan, but otherwise they're easy to make. It's sponge cake soaked in a ridiculous amount of simple syrup, but when I make them I add rum."

"They smell divine."

Because of the syrup, the bakery had packed them in their own special container. I took a plastic spoon and fed her a bite. "If you're me, you just pick one up and drop it in your mouth, but since you're a lady, I'll feed you in a civilized manner."

"Rafa, this is delicious." She rolled her eyes and licked all but a bit of syrup off her lips, which I was happy to do for her.

"I can see this one has a lot of possibilities for us. Good to know." We continued to giggle together as I fed us both pastry after pastry. I made her try the slice of Cuban cake, the *quesito*, the *torticas de Morón* cookies, which she called dry, and finally, we came to my favorite of all time.

"This is the king of all Cuban sweets, the *pastel de guayaba*. A lot of people think they can make guava pastries at home with frozen dough, but it's not the same. You can only get the real thing from a bakery because it's so hard to make. We eat these for breakfast, as a snack, and as a dessert, and you can't call yourself Cuban if you don't like guava. This is a good one." I pointed to the thick ribbon of filling. "See, plenty of fruit." She bit into the corner and, like any decent *pastel*, crumbs went everywhere.

"It's so sweet." she said, wiping her lips with a napkin. "It's good."

I let her take as many bites as she wanted and then I finished it. "Simple pleasures, Amada." Feeling stuffed, I moved the box off the bed and laid down beside her again. Nothing could be as good as this.

"You didn't get to go to a bakery very often as a kid, did you?" she asked.

"No," I said. I didn't want to bring down our mood, but I always wanted to be honest with her. Maybe I didn't have to share everything, but I wouldn't lie. "I've had an interesting life, I guess."

"Tell me about it." She pulled the covers over us and draped her arm over my hip. "And I'd like to know why Delfina is so important to you."

"I wasn't always so alone. Until I was twelve, I lived in Playa Larga and had my mother, my grandmother, my grandfather, and a brother." She raised her eyebrows at the word 'brother.' "Yes, a twin. His name was Miguel. We were very poor, Amada. So poor that we sometimes went to bed hungry. My mother wasn't a bad woman, but as life became harder, it broke her. She never smiled."

"What did she look like?"

I closed my eyes and tried to remember her face. "She looked like me. Light eyes, dark hair, fair skin like you. She was beautiful, but she had lines on her face and she was always so tired. Her name was Carmen Rodriguez De Leon, and she was only thirty-eight when she died. My father was named Lázaro De Leon Mendoza, and he was murdered at the age of twenty-two."

"Rafa! How did it happen?'

"They told my mother he'd been seeing a woman in another town and when the woman's husband walked in on them one day, he shot my father in the back of the head. I don't know if that's true, because my mother never talked about it, but that was the gossip. She was so angry she destroyed every photograph of him she had, so I have no idea what he looked like.

"My father's parents lived next door to us, and my grandfather's best friend was a man named Anselmo. He was such an interesting guy, always at my grandfather's house. I remember he would read to us from *Don Quijote* from time to time, and because of him I've always wanted to read that book. Anyway, Anselmo never wore anything but white from head to toe. I found out later it was because he was a *santero*. Do you know what that is?"

"No." My Amada drew a little closer to me, her interest clearly piqued.

"It means he was a Santería priest. Santería came to Cuba from Africa, and it's a very mystical faith that many Cubans believe in."

"Like Voodoo?"

"Sort of, but Santería evolved specifically in Cuba. It's a very secretive religion, and it's not monotheistic like Christianity. Offerings are made to the deities or *Orishas* using different rituals and initiations. Everyone in Cuba knows what it is and respects it, whether they choose to believe in it or not. We all grew up around it.

"The problems started when Anselmo became convinced that his spirit guide wanted my brother and I to be initiated as practitioners. My grandfather was honored, and my mother allowed it because she thought eventually people would pay us money to help them. When we were babies, she'd also been told by a fortune teller that she should always listen to us because we were special and had great vision."

"Didn't he have any children of his own to teach?"

"That doesn't matter. You have to be selected by the spirits, and if they don't want you, you can't be initiated no matter who you are. We learned everything from Anselmo, and after he felt we were ready, he had us dress in white clothing for a year."

"Why white?"

"It represents clarity and purity, and some say it repels negative spirits. If you pay attention, you'll occasionally see people walking around Miami dressed all in white. They're being initiated as santeros and santeras." The next part was difficult for me, but I continued because I could see she was taking it well.

"When we were at the end of the year, and Anselmo was about to conduct the final initiation rite, my brother began to act strangely. Miguel had always been different and very difficult to be around, but at that time he confessed to me that he'd heard voices his whole life, and now they were getting louder and saying terrible, frightening things to him. He became paranoid that people were trying to kill him, and that final week he was completely out of his mind. My mother wanted to take him to a hospital, but Anselmo said that a bad spirit was trying to prevent him from becoming a priest, so he asked her to give him one more day to see if he could get rid of it. But that night my brother managed to sneak away without anyone noticing, and two days later, he washed up on the shore. His death was ruled an accidental drowning, but I know he killed himself."

"Rafa, I'm so sorry." Amada kissed me on the cheek and wrapped her legs around me, hugging me tight. "You don't have to go on." Her green eyes met mine, soft and sweet as every other part of her.

"It's fine. I want you to know." I gave her a peck on the lips and continued. "Many years later, after I became a physician, I realized he had to have been schizophrenic. He would have been fine on the right medications, but they had no clue. I also think he might have ingested something toxic, perhaps an herb that triggered the hallucinations. Remember that liquid mercury you were going to touch? It's basically illegal because of how poisonous it is, but it's considered a very powerful ingredient in Santería spells. Many people have it out in a little dish in their homes without realizing the poison they're breathing in when it evaporates. If consumed, it doesn't take much to kill you. There are lots of things in Santería you have to be very careful with because it's an old, primitive religion. It has to be updated to reflect what we know now about health and medicine, but so few people understand both sides of it.

"Naturally there were no words for how grief-stricken we were, especially my mother. Anselmo and my grandfather insisted that I should take the final step and go through with the initiation, but she refused. She would have nothing to do with it anymore, and she just wanted me away from it. That was the day we packed up what little we had and moved to Havana. I never saw my grandparents or Anselmo again."

"The fear she had of losing you is understandable," said Amada. I detected a peculiar tone in her voice, and I was pretty sure I knew why.

"Yes, now I do understand it, but at the time it was very hard for me to adjust to losing almost everyone I loved at once. My mother was more depressed than ever, and I had to learn to fend for myself in a big city. People liked me, though, and they mostly helped me."

"Because of how handsome you are," she said.

"To be honest, probably. Blue eyes are rare in Cuba, and my appearance was the only bit of luck I had in my young life. Women have always been attracted to something about me, so I flirted with a lot of waitresses to get a free meal here and there." I rubbed my nose against hers, trying to keep the mood light. "It works on you, doesn't it?"

"It does. I can't resist you. I'm as weak as all the rest." Her hand slipped along my backside under the covers. "But what about Delfina? You said she saved your life."

"She did, but that was very recently. I told you that I was an *Internacionalista*—"

"I looked it up today when I got home. When I was missing you."

"Oh, baby." I kissed her sweet lips. "I don't know what I was thinking."

"Forget it. Go on," she said.

"I've worked all around the world, but this tour in Haiti was different. Every one of us was miserable from day one, and the morale was very low."

"Why?"

"I don't know, but I have my theories now. None of us really knew, we just all felt the same thing. We worked in the countryside and Amada, the things we saw, I just don't want to tell you. Our group was sent to contain a cholera epidemic, and it was Hell on Earth from the moment we arrived. To make things even worse, there was a young Haitian woman in the village who developed a crush on me. Her name was Martine, and at first I believed her when she said she was sick. But pretty soon I figured out what she really wanted."

"Sex?"

"Definitely sex, but I also think she was looking for a husband. She tried everything, and I wanted to let her down easy, but when her advances became too much, I had no choice but to ban her from my clinic. It enraged her, so she attacked me and started screaming obscenities in French. She had to be escorted out by two of our officers, and people told me later she'd threatened my life and said I would be sorry."

I noticed that Amada's mood had changed, so I asked what she was thinking about. I assumed she was displeased about the idea of me with another woman because she suddenly seemed distant, but I was wrong. I should have known her reflections would be far more sophisticated.

""It was inevitable: the scent of bitter almonds always reminded him of the fate of unrequited love,'" she said.

"What's that? Another poem?" I loved it when she read to me. I was awed by her knowledge, but I also loved how she pronounced every letter as she spoke, something that was so difficult for me to do. It was a pleasure to listen to her.

"It's the beginning of *El amor en los tiempos del cólera* by Gabriel García Márquez. I actually read that book in Spanish," she recalled. "I read so slowly in Spanish though, so it took forever, but it was worth it. Your language is so beautiful."

"Everything is poetic to you, isn't it? Love and death, pleasure and pain. Even though you don't like people, it's the human condition that moves you." My cultured, elegant Amada, so unlike me. I touched her pale face, unable to find a single imperfection in her porcelain skin.

"Maybe so." She took my hand in hers and gave it a squeeze. "So what happened with the girl?"

"I never saw her again. But the next day I started to feel off. I couldn't concentrate and I couldn't remember important things. Every day it got worse, and then after about a week I started to get very depressed. I couldn't stop thinking about my brother, and one night I had a dream that he came to visit me there at the foot of my bed in Haiti. Miguel appeared exactly how I remembered him, just twelve years old, dressed all in white. He told me I'd been cursed and that I should leave right away. After he told me he loved me, I woke up at three in the morning, sick with a high fever, and I knew if I didn't leave that one way or another I would die. Regardless of what was making me ill, I had to go find help. By the time I got to Miami a few days later, I had a fever of 105. In the hospital, they assumed I'd contracted a bacteria or virus in Haiti, so they gave me strong antibiotics, but it didn't help.

"I was on the verge of death, in and out of consciousness, and that's when I remember seeing Doña Delfina over my bed. She said to someone, 'They did something very powerful to him in Haiti.'" *Le hecharon algo muy fuerte en Haiti.* "She rubbed something on my chest and gave me a sponge bath with herbs I remembered from my childhood, something like what Anselmo had used when he tried to save my brother. In fact, I can't smell lemongrass without thinking of that time. And she also gave me something to drink—it was vile—and prayed over me all night. I slowly recovered, and the doctors were very proud of themselves, but no one knew Doña Delfina had been there."

"Who brought her?" Amada drummed her fingers on my thigh, impatient to hear the rest.

"She'd been visiting Sandro's new baby two floors below, when one of her guides spoke to her and told her she would become a mother that night, too. She went into a trance and ended up in my room, although she doesn't remember how."

Amada arched an eyebrow, but I continued, still amazed by the story myself.

"When I was discharged, Doña Delfina and Sandro were there to pick me up, and she insisted I stay with her to recuperate. Every day she gave me a special bath, fed me, and prayed over my bed. By the end of the week, I'd made a full recovery."

"Rafa, is it possible that it was a physical illness and the antibiotics did eventually work?"

"It is, yes." Anything was possible, that much I knew.

"But you don't think so."

"No, even though I'm a scientist, in this case I honestly believe it was Voodoo. The mind is a very powerful thing, more than we know."

"So how did you end up on the ship?" she asked.

"After I recovered, I told Doña Delfina about my childhood and how I understood what she did. She asked that I stay and work for her, and after the way she took care of me, there was no way I could refuse her anything. I cooked and tended bar—"

"She owns everything? The bar, the restaurant?"

"Oh yes. But very few people get to go to the back room and have a consultation with her. It's by personal invitation only."

"So you worked for her as a cook?" Amada absentmindedly ran her fingers up and down my lower back, which turned me on. It was terrible that I couldn't feel her touch or sometimes even look at her without getting excited, but it happened every time.

"Yes, a cook. Other things, too. Sometimes when someone came in, she asked me to check them and see if their illness could be physical. If I thought it was, she would send them away and tell them to go to a doctor. If I couldn't immediately find a physical cause, then she would proceed. So far, I haven't been involved in that part, although she does want to initiate me. She says she became my godmother the day she brought me back from the other side, so I should let her if that's what the Orishas want."

"So that's why you call her *Madrina*. But ... Orishas, Rafa?" I could see that Amada still didn't believe in the supernatural part of my story, and I completely understood. It was unbelievable.

"I know what it sounds like, sweetheart, but you have to remember I grew up around it. Most Cubans have. I don't question it, but you have every reason to. I'm just telling you what happened. I respect your right to choose what you believe, and I won't be offended."

"But didn't that judge warn you not to give medical advice to anyone?"

"He meant outside of our trusted circle. They all see Doña Delfina on a regular basis and are indebted to her one way or another. They would protect her by any means necessary. Most of those men were around during my recovery, and they saw what I went through, so they trust me as much as they trust her. I can help them and the people they bring to her without fear of repercussion. Besides, I don't perform any procedures and I can't prescribe anything. All I do is give my opinion and recommend they see a licensed doctor if that's what's necessary."

"And the ship?" She moved up and started to trace my shoulder and tricep with her fingertip.

"Sweetheart, you have to stop that or there will be no more talking for a while," I warned, taking her hand in mine to keep it still. "One day, after a couple of months, Doña Delfina called me in to tell me her spirit guide said I should go out on a big ship. He told her that on this trip I would find something very important, and when I did, I should bring it back with me. I didn't want to go, but she insisted, saying I would make plenty of money in the meantime, and when I returned home, my future would be settled. Again, I couldn't say no to her, and it seemed like a reasonable way to save money, which I knew I should do, so I went. Three days later I was on the *Ruby*, and three months later I met you."

"You think I'm what you were supposed to find?"

"You heard her. She said so. Anyway, when I read your letter, I knew." I pushed a few locks of hair away from her face and then made a decision on the spot. "I won't go back. I'll live and work in Miami again."

"Rafa, I'm so happy!" said Amada, hugging me. It delighted me to see her this way because I knew I never wanted to disappoint her again like I had this morning.

"Good. Do you feel better about everything now?" I asked.

"Yes, of course, I'm thrilled," she said, "but I don't understand what she said about children, Rafa—" Her voice began to tremble as pain clouded her eyes. She'd fall apart again if she tried to talk about it, and that was the last thing I wanted.

"Sh, Amada," I said. "I saw your scar, too." Her C-section incision was small and had faded to almost nothing, but I'd noticed it.

"The first night," she sighed.

"Just because I know it's there doesn't mean it's any of my business. We'll talk about it when the time is right." She let me touch the bump of slightly raised skin, which was a good sign. "We have no idea what she meant, so let's not make assumptions. Just put it out of your mind for now."

"What does Delfina think you're afraid of?" She flipped her hair back and readjusted herself on the pillow, a clear signal she was ready to change the subject.

"She knows I think my brother was schizophrenic and that I don't want to have children because of it. I couldn't bear to see my child suffer like that." I stroked her hair, and we both were silent for a while. "It's not just you, Amada. I feel the same way, so there's nothing more to discuss. When you're ready to share the details, you can. Or don't. All that matters is that's we're together now."

"Rafa," she sighed. I wasn't sure what she meant, but she looked exhausted, so I checked the clock.

"It's after three. We talked all night. Let's go to sleep, baby," I said.

"What does Delfina want to do at my house?" she asked, heavy-lidded.

"She just wants to cleanse the house of any bad energy. It's very simple to do. Are you alright with that? It can't hurt anything."

"Fine. I just wish we could sleep in a little longer." She rolled over and curled up. She looked tiny, and every protective instinct I had went into overdrive.

"Me too. I'll be right back."

"Say it in English," she murmured.

"Why?"

"You're supposed to start speaking to me in English." I could barely make out her words now. She was half asleep already.

"I'll start tomorrow, *profesora*."

When I came back from the bathroom, she was out. I turned off the lights and took my sweet Amada in my arms, her back to my front. It was crazy to think how both of our lives had changed in less than a week, and now I couldn't imagine another day without this woman. She reminded me of the type of medieval fair-haired beauty men went to war over. Or was it the Greeks? My Amada would know. I might be able to stitch a wound, but she could debate the significance of great literature, speak multiple languages and carry on an intelligent conversation on any conceivable subject. She'd traveled the greatest European capitals and worn the finest clothes money could buy. I couldn't imagine where in the world my sophisticated lover could go and not charm every man in the room, and here she was with me. I wasn't good enough for her and I'd told her so, but if she wanted me, I was hers. My delicate queen, alone by her own design. Not anymore.

CHAPTER SEVEN

I was awakened by Rafa's head between my legs, and though it was only nine in the morning, true to form he was already hard at work trying to make me happy in one way or another.

"Amada, you taste so good. I want you for breakfast every day." He flicked his tongue every place but where I wanted it most, creating a sensation that was both maddening and delicious. I knew all about his waiting philosophy, but sometimes a woman just can't.

"Higher." I begged, tilting my pelvis down. I really had become so brazen with him. It was hard to believe he put up with it, but he did. The first thing out of my mouth this morning was a command for him to service me exactly how I wanted. There was no 'good morning,' or 'how did you sleep' from me, just 'tongue here.' I had to laugh at my own behavior, but it was his indulgence that was turning me into a complete brat.

"Where?" he asked.

"You know where."

"I have no idea. You first." He wiped his mouth and looked up at me, propping his chin on his hand, hoping for some kind of show.

"Sorry, ladies don't do that," I said.

"I don't believe it for a second. Come on," he said, squinting.

"Rafa, you know exactly what to do, and if you can't see, put on your glasses," I said, giving his head a gentle nudge back down.

Rafa bowed his head between my legs to conceal his laughter, but then granted all of my very specific requests until I had an outstanding morning orgasm, after which he climbed on top of me and made love with such passion it took my breath away.

"You make me so hard it hurts, Amada," he gasped, pounding me into the bed. "Being inside you is all I think about anymore. I swear I dream about it."

* * *

By eleven o'clock we were back at my house, unloading the Rover in the driveway when a taxi pulled up. It was a typical hot fall day in Miami, and though the water was a little choppy, it was absolutely gorgeous outside. The inside of the house was another story, specifically the rows of unpacked luggage, empty cupboards and miles of windows to open, but maybe we could just enjoy the outdoors together today.

"Rafa, is that them?" My sexy man came around from the back of the car and gave me a little pat on the butt as he walked past me toward the cab.

"No, it's Octavio with the supplies I ordered."

He looked so good walking away that I impulsively yanked him back toward me, put my hand between his legs and gave him a big kiss.

"You are very feisty this morning, missy," he said, giving me a playful swat on the rear as he disentangled himself from my grabby hands and made his way down the driveway.

"Hope you can handle it," I called out.

"Baby, you know what happens when you talk like that," he warned, glancing over his shoulder. On second thought, it was a gross understatement to call Rafa sexy; he was just pure sex.

It looked like the same cab from yesterday, and when the driver got out, Rafa smiled and put his hand on the man's shoulder. People really did take to him right away, and he liked them back, which was certainly a good quality in a healer and in a man. While they chatted for a few minutes, I brought a few things inside the house, and by the time I was back outside, the cab was gone and Rafa had a large shopping bag in one arm and a birdcage in the other. As he came closer, I could make out a small white bird sitting peacefully on one of the perches. For a moment I thought Rafa had bought a pet, but then I remembered Doña Delfina's request for a dove.

"What exactly is she going to do with it?" Not long ago I'd read an article in the Herald about the increasing incidence of animal sacrifice around Miami. If that's what was planned, I wouldn't allow it. Reading my mind, Rafa assured me it was nothing of that nature.

"She's just going to say a few prayers and then let it fly away."

We set the cage on the loggia and continued to unload the car until Sandro and Doña Delfina pulled in through the open gate. To my surprise, they arrived in a black S-class Mercedes with jet black tinted windows, a highly illegal vehicle modification in Miami. Then again, if she was under the protection of very powerful people, she probably didn't have to worry about it.

"Nice car," I said to Rafa.

"She's very rich. Anyway, look who's talking."

Rafa went to greet Sandro and help Delfina out of the shiny, dark sedan. He beamed with affection for her, which made me happy to see. As he helped her up the steps to the front door, I met them halfway and took her other arm. She wore an outfit almost identical to the one from last night, except this time she was in white from head to toe, from her hair wrap all the way down to her tiny white shoes. Although she looked weary, her deep feelings for Rafa were unmistakable.

"Good Morning, Doña Delfina," I said. "Thank you for coming today. Welcome." She turned and took my hand in hers, which was strangely comforting.

"*Preciosa*, I know you have your doubts, but you'll see."

At her request, Rafa and I took her through the grounds while Sandro stayed by the car. It occurred to me that he might be her bodyguard as well as her driver, which of course made me wonder why she would need one. I guess if everyone knows you're wealthy, you need protection, but in my case, very few people even had the faintest clue.

I walked her through the boathouse first, then the garden, and finally to the tiny little guesthouse behind the pool. It was used for storage now, and it had been so long since I'd been down here, I'd almost forgotten about it. I rarely came out here at all, but our gardener did a great job of keeping everything pristine. Inside, however, the guesthouse was a total mess. Even so, Doña Delfina stuck her head in the door and nodded in the affirmative.

"It's clean." *Esta limpiesita.* I turned to Rafa, knowing the little house was a total disaster.

"She means there's good energy here," he explained.

In the main house, Delfina was not as happy. Right at the entrance to the foyer she began to sigh. "Sadness." *Tristeza.* She walked around a little bit and asked us for the coconut.

She held it in her hands and said a prayer over it in a language I couldn't understand. "I'm ready," she finally said.

"Sweetheart, she wants to follow us around the house, but you have to take her through every room. She can't miss anything, not even a closet. I'll walk with her, and you lead us."

I led them through every room of the house, and unlike anyone else that had ever seen Boxwood for the first time, Delfina said nothing. If she was impressed, she didn't show it. She recited prayer after prayer while holding the coconut in both hands as we took the long walk through every single part of the house, including Kieran's wing. I hadn't seen it for a while, but I was amused to note that as always, it was immaculate. He'd be home from Asia soon, and I hoped that he and Rafa would like each other, but my brother was always so stressed out from work his moods were pretty much unpredictable. Delfina spent the most time in my bedroom, where she and Rafa exchanged a few words I couldn't make out, but when they were done they seemed satisfied.

Finally we made it back to where we started, and Rafa opened the front door for Doña Delfina without her having to ask. She set the coconut down carefully in an out of the way spot on the driveway. "Careful with that," she warned. "Rafa, you know what to do." He bowed his head respectfully and helped her back inside. "Now the bath. Get the dove."

"She wants you to have an herbal bath, Amada." said Rafa. "Can we use one of the bathrooms down here so that she doesn't have to go up the stairs again? I'll clean the tub after we're done."

"Me? She wants to give *me* a bath?" I started to panic a little, wondering exactly what type of strange ritual this would entail.

"No, she wants to *prepare* a bath for you."

"Rafa—"

"Sweetheart, it won't hurt anything. Do you have any idea how long people have to wait for her help? Years sometimes. Please let her." I couldn't believe a trained medical doctor was so adamant about this nonsense, but, as he said, it wouldn't hurt.

"Alright," I said. "There's a bathroom right here. But the bird is not going in the water with me, is it?"

"Of course not!"

Rafa went to get the rest of the bags Octavio had dropped off with the dove, and I took Doña Delfina to the downstairs guest bath, a bright and spacious marbled washroom with a deep claw foot tub. She walked so slowly that by the time we made it, Rafa was back with the supplies, including the dove.

"Perfect," said Doña Delfina, presumably referring to the all-white color scheme. I was starting to understand just how significant the color white was to them.

"You have to take off your clothes," said Rafa to me.

"Right now?" Surely he didn't mean with her in the room, too.

"Yes, sweetheart. She's going to pray over you before you get in the water, and then the dove will carry away all the things that are weighing you down. It's a cleansing." *Es una limpieza.*

"You don't want to?" asked Doña Delfina, surprised.

I didn't know what to say because I didn't want to hurt anyone's feelings, but all of this was so strange.

"She doesn't understand why." said Rafa, apologetically. "Maybe we should wait."

"She shouldn't do anything she doesn't want to do. However, my time is quickly coming to an end. You can do it for her later, but if you want my help, you should accept it now."

"What is it, Madrina?" he asked, taken aback. "Maybe I can help you."

"No, my son. That's it." *No, mi hijo. Asi es.*

Rafa embraced Doña Delfina and gave her a kiss on the cheek as he held back his tears. My heart broke for him. He wasn't even thinking about the bath anymore, but I began to remove my clothes, hoping she would still be willing to do it.

"Good," said Doña Delfina to me.

With his mind elsewhere, Rafa began to fill the tub with tap water and coconut water. When I was completely undressed, Delfina went to the cage and picked up the cooing dove. Surprisingly, the bird didn't struggle and was very relaxed in the elderly woman's gentle hands. Delfina brought the dove close to me, and starting at the top of my head, traced the outline of my body with the dove while reciting a prayer. The dove never touched me, but she went down one side of my body with it and up the other, then put the bird back in the cage. I looked over at Rafa, who was on his knees beside the tub, head down, devastated.

"Step in," she said, pointing at the tub. Rafa helped me sit down while Doña Delfina pulled a bouquet of fresh herbs out of her pocket. "No black nightshade. I know you don't like it." *Sin la yerba mora. Se que no te gusta.* Rafa nodded his approval, and after another prayer, she untied the bouquet and scattered the stems and leaves in the bathwater.

"The flowers." He handed her the bouquet of white orchids, and as she threw the petals in the water, she prayed again. Finally, she took a handful of water and sprinkled it over the top of my head. That was it. Whatever I had been expecting, it wasn't something as simple as this. The water smelled divine from the herbs and flower petals, and I already felt quite relaxed and light.

"Feel good?" Rafa asked, leaning over the edge of the tub, his eyes red and wet. "It's good for your sunburn, too."

"Very nice, but are you ok?" I didn't like the way he broke down, and I was frustrated that I couldn't get out and comfort him.

"Yes, I'll be alright. We're going to go outside and release the dove. You only have to be in here a couple of minutes, but you have to air dry, so wait for me." He kissed me on the cheek and took the cage out of the bathroom.

"Enjoy it while you can, my dear." *Disfruta ahora que puedes, cariño.* "You'll feel the effects soon. See you Tuesday," said Doña Delfina.

"Thank you." I wondered what was happening on Tuesday, and as nice as it turned out to be, I hoped it didn't involve any more baths. *Enjoy it while you can.* I'd heard that somewhere before.

As I settled into the water, I could see Delfina and Rafa in the foyer talking about something, and judging from his mannerisms, I knew Rafa was upset. She let him say what he wanted, but then when she spoke, he said nothing. After about a minute, he put his arm around her and walked her in the direction of the front door without further conversation. I was worried until he came back inside, but whatever Delfina said to him had helped because he seemed much better.

"What did she say?" I asked.

"She explained what's going on with her health." He didn't seem to want to talk about it, so I didn't ask anything else.

"Did you let that poor bird go?"

"Yes, but I have to get rid of the coconut later. It can't break open while it's in our possession." His eyes were full of mischief, as if he knew exactly what I was thinking.

"*Of course* we can't break the coconut. What about the Voodoo doll?" I couldn't help it. It was just all so absurd.

"It's under your bed in a very dirty sex position," he said, kissing my shoulder.

"Excellent. So can I get out out of here please?"

* * *

We ended up out back on the covered patio, and though I'd suggested to Rafa that we go lie out by the pool to dry off, he didn't want me in the sun, so he pulled two lounge chairs close together and we stretched out in the shade facing the bay. It was a busy morning, and more than a few yachts passed us on their way out to the Atlantic. I dried quickly, but it was so lovely outside that we lounged a little longer. Rafa held my hand as we enjoyed the ocean breeze and the beautiful vista.

"So what's the plan for today?" he asked, flicking his thumb across the palm of my hand.

"Well, I need to unpack all those suitcases, go grocery shopping, and help you get settled." I smiled at him and squeezed his hand.

"Settled? Where?"

"Here, handsome."

"Amada, we've been over that."

"Why not?" I sat up and faced him. "We did the cleansing so that you would feel comfortable, didn't we?"

"No, we did the cleansing so that I wouldn't worry about you while you're living here. You need positive energy around so you don't fall into bad habits." He arched an eyebrow.

"I don't see why you would want to be anywhere else."

"I am not going to move in with my rich girlfriend and lounge by the pool all day," he said, looking away from me out to the water. "I have to work and support myself. You're a highly intelligent woman, Amada. How can you not understand something so simple?"

I didn't answer. I certainly didn't want to get in another epic fight over the same thing again, especially now that at least I had him here in town. When I thought he was gone forever, I was in hell, so I gave in about the living arrangements.

"Then I guess the question is, what's *your* plan?"

"Well, I have to buy a car, preferably today or tomorrow."

"Rafa, there are five cars downstairs that never—"

"Let me finish. I have to buy a car. Then, starting tonight, I'll be working for Doña Delfina again. I'll live in one of the staff apartments over the restaurant, like I did before, but I'll still come see you all the time, and you'll come see me. Every day."

"You're going to be working at a nightclub? Interesting." My mind's eye flashed back to all the young, beautiful women I saw last night, and there was no doubt every one of them would want Rafa. Jealousy cracked through me like a whip, but as I went to get out of the chair, he held my arm tightly enough so that I couldn't leave.

"Amada, I don't want anyone else."

"But why does it have to be there? You can work anywhere. Let me get you a job at the hospital. Kieran knows—"

"I promised Doña Delfina. She has metastatic breast cancer, and she needs me around until it's time. I have to help her get her affairs in order."

"Oh," I said, feeling terribly guilty. "How long does she have?"

"It depends. She's in pain and can barely get around anymore. She doesn't trust doctors, so she wasn't diagnosed until it was too late." He sighed and looked back out over the water. "I remember so many older people in Cuba being the same way. Their logic is that if you see a doctor for something minor, you're looking for problems where none exist, and then you'll end up with a real problem. You go in with a sore elbow and come out with a brain tumor. My mother used to talk like that, too. She would say, "Careful with those doctors, they'll end up killing you." *Cuidado con esos médicos, que al fin y al cabo te matan.*

"Anyway, she's refused any treatment but she doesn't want to die in a hospital. It took a lot for her to come today, but she wants to make sure I'm alright once she's gone, and she knows that involves you. She told me she chose you for me, whatever that means." He started to choke up.

"I was so alone and scared in that hospital bed, Amada, and she was the only one who stepped in and took care of me until I was well. Do you realize she was dying while she was nursing me back to health? I have to be there for her now. You can understand that, can't you?"

"Yes, I can." I said softy, realizing how deeply connected they were. I went over to his chair and lay down on top of him, and once I buried my face in the nape of his neck, his body relaxed underneath me. Our breathing synchronized, and in minutes we were asleep.

Only about an hour had passed when Rafa began to run his rough, warm hands up and down my naked back, letting me know what was on his mind by gently pushing my pelvis down into his.

"I want to make love to you," he whispered. The sound of his voice in my ear always made me shiver, just like the first night we met.

"Out here?" I asked, already aroused. It didn't take much when I was around Rafa. A look from him was enough.

"No, the sun." His energy was quiet and intense, more so than usual, but even so he kissed me before sitting us both up and bundling me in his arms. Effortlessly he carried me upstairs to my room and set me down in the center of the bed. I was still groggy and relaxed from our time outside in the gentle warm breeze, and as my eyes and body adjusted to the cool darkness of the bedroom, I could see that Rafa was no longer the grief-stricken man from earlier. There had been a shift, and though he was impossible to read at times, it was clear that among other things, he was very hungry for me now.

I'd been lying naked with him for the last hour, but it was only at this moment, under his austere gaze, that I began to sense a power imbalance between us. It was clearly intentional on his part, and he sported such a strange expression that I didn't know whether I should go to him or wait for him to come to me. He stared at me from the center of the room and it made me feel shy, so I curled up and waited. Then, he began.

"We have a few things to discuss first." He took off his shoes and socks, and then unbuttoned his shirt at the wrists and down the center. Throwing it off, he stood before me arms crossed and half-naked, looking like a Greek statue. He was hard everywhere, even his face.

"Later, I plan to cook for you, help you straighten up the house, maybe give you a massage and probably take plenty of orders from you, because we both know you've got me wrapped around your finger. But I want you to remember one thing." Slowly he unbuckled his belt and tossed it aside, then dropped his pants and stepped out of them. He was painfully erect, and judging by the way he unveiled himself, he wanted me to have a good look.

"You will not control me, Amada. I let you have your way because I choose to, not because you can force me. But it can't be like that all the time." He rested his hand on the base of his penis as if he were holding up an imaginary towel, which made it difficult for me to concentrate on what he was saying. "You can't have *this* and call all the shots, because it doesn't work that way in our bed. You will not have a tantrum or invent an emotionally draining argument every time we disagree. I cannot satisfy you as a man if I allow you to emasculate me. Do you understand that both things do not go together?" He let his hand drop to his side and walked toward the bed. "I'm talking to you, Amada. Are you listening or paying attention to something else? This is the last time I want to have this conversation."

"I'm listening."

"Look up here, then," he said, tilting my chin upwards.

"I want you in my mouth." I made a move in that direction, already anticipating the feel of him on my tongue, but he took a step back.

"I'm so sorry, but I'm not ready yet. You're going to have to wait." He raised his eyebrows and stared right back at me. I sat back on the bed, thrown for a loop. Not two feet away from me was something I wanted, and he wouldn't let me have it. There had to be some truth to what he was saying, because I really was having trouble processing it.

"It looks like you're starting to get it. Are you?" he asked, coming closer.

"I understand, Rafa, but the way you withhold things is so hard to tolerate sometimes."

"You do the same. Look how much you know about me, Amada, and how little I know about you. Have I tried to force you to open up by getting angry or making you feel guilty?"

"No." He had a point. He'd been very patient in that regard.

"That's right. Because I'm *waiting* until you're ready." He sat on the edge of the bed.

"You can't get angry with me because I won't live with you in a house that isn't mine, or take money from you that isn't mine. I'm not really thrilled about making love on a bed that isn't mine, either, but you indulged me today, so I'm going to make an exception. When I'm ready to buy a house in cash, which shouldn't be too far off, then you can move in with me. Until then, you can't try to control where I live and work because of petty jealousy."

"It's not petty!" I said, pulling the blanket over me, feeling the sudden need to be covered. "I know how women think. You should have heard the way Sharon talked about you, like you were a piece of meat, and that's the type that'll be around every night."

He found this really funny and started laughing. "Amada, the difference is, I decide who I go with. Not them. If I say you have nothing to worry about, then you don't. Otherwise, it would make me a liar, wouldn't it?"

"That reminds me, what did you say to Sharon when you turned her down? She was furious when she figured out we'd been together."

"I told her I wasn't feeling well and said maybe tomorrow. When I'm not interested, I either say I'm sick or I've had too much to drink. Problem solved. I know what to do."

"It's not always that simple. Look at how much trouble that girl in Haiti caused you because she wouldn't take no for an answer."

"That's true. But she didn't get her way, did she? Look, I can't have an argument with you every time I have to go to work. What if I have to travel on Doña Delfina's behalf like I've done before? Will you *allow* me to do that, or are we going to have a big fight about it? I want to indulge you, but you have to learn to be patient about certain things. You can't go into a tailspin when I have to be away." He slipped his hand under the blanket to caress the side of my breast. I closed my eyes and leaned in, my anger subsiding. Rafa always knew exactly how to touch me. It wasn't fair; I was powerless when he used his hands on me.

"So, after we take care of your immediate needs, you're going to prove to me that this won't be a recurring issue by being very patient for a few days while I'm occupied at the restaurant."

He paused to see if I would protest, but I said nothing—in spite of the fact that my heart fell. What the hell was he planning on doing without me? I closed my eyes and kept listening, just to see what more nonsense he was going to dream up.

"I'll pick you up Tuesday night and bring you to the club, where Doña Delfina wants to do something special for us called a binding. If you don't want to do it, that's fine. I'll bring you up to my apartment and we'll have a nice evening just the two of us. In the meantime, I'll do everything I need to do for myself and Doña Delfina, and while

I'm busy over there, I'm asking you not to drink alcohol or lie around in a dark house. I want you to spend time doing positive things that make you happy."

"I have an idea of what to do." I couldn't believe how he thought he could just decide everything. It was inconceivable that he wanted to actually go out and find a place to live when I was literally begging him to stay with me. *My apartment.*

"Good. It should be easier now that Doña Delfina was here. I can feel a difference."

"Really? The energy doesn't feel that great to me." Not nice, but I knew I was going to turn into a world class bitch in about half a second, and there was nothing I could do about it. At this point, I was a runaway train.

"It definitely is," he said, and even though I know he noticed the change in my mood, he continued with his agenda anyway. "But this house is way too big. If you insist on staying here, you should remodel so that you have a normal size living area and then do something else with the rest of the square footage. You could live on the ground floor and build an incredible personal library upstairs. Then again, I'm sure your brother would have his own opinions, too. I don't know," he shrugged.

"Interesting idea, but I like big things," I said crudely, totally dismissing him. I really didn't process much after he said he was leaving, so I turned my attention to the only thing about him that wasn't pissing me off, which was his erect penis. I was tired of playing stupid games, and I'll be damned if he thought I was going to wait around for him like a dog he'd ordered to sit and stay. I might be impatient, but his arrogance was really remarkable. He was going out of his way to show me that he intended to come and go as he pleased.

"Amada, did you hear anything I said?" Of course I had, but I couldn't take my eyes off him, either. In spite of myself I was highly aroused, and he did certainly love to show his body off. Rafa was many wonderful things, but he was also outrageously handsome, and he knew it. If I've never heard no, then he's never heard it either, at least not from a woman. I had to shut this down. I was going to have him completely or not at all, and there was no way I was going to sit home and wonder how many women were crawling all over him every night. Time to play hard ball.

"I heard you, Rafa. You need space and time to yourself. Don't worry, I have other options." I crawled over to the edge of the bed and opened my nightstand drawer, revealing an arsenal of sex toys. "I'll be fine."

Rafa's mouth fell open. He went straight to the drawer and started rifling through its contents. "Unbelievable," he said. "What is all this shit?"

"Let's see, which one reminds me most of you?" I pushed everything around until I found the biggest one, my favorite pink rabbit. "Oh yes, this one is great." I held it up so that we could both admire it. "You don't mind, do you?" I said. "Since I'm not really into this lecture, you can just run along to work now and I'll get started."

At first Rafa was aghast and stared at me like he couldn't believe what was coming out of my mouth. It was satisfying to get a rise out of him, but as the shock wore off, something darker emerged and the gloves came off.

"'Ladies don't do that, huh?" He clenched his jaw and narrowed his eyes, which went from me to the drawer and back again.

"Not in front of anyone," I said, hoping I hadn't blushed. The idea of touching ourselves in front of one another turned me on beyond belief, but I was too angry with him right now to let him know. Even so, I think he picked up on my thoughts.

"Well, I do mind. Put that stupid thing down, get on your knees, and take what you really want."

"Oh, now I can have it? But I thought you said I have to learn to wait. What did you think I would be doing all alone then?" I brought the tip of the vibrator to my mouth and flicked my tongue at it in the most perverse way I could think of. I'd bet money he'd never seen a woman lick a sex toy, because he was speechless.

I could tell he was also livid. Even on a good day he'd hate anything designed to take his place, but in this context he was especially revolted. I made a mental note to relocate my stash soon or it'd be gone for sure. "I told you to put it away," he continued, simmering with fury. "You have the real thing right in front of you, and I guarantee it's a hell of a lot better."

I looked down at him, shrugged my shoulders and made eye contact. Very slowly I brought the plastic phallus to my mouth, took it all the way in and sucked like it was the most delicious popsicle I'd ever tasted, making a nice show by adding plenty of sound effects to go along with it. Fanning my long, red fingernails along the shaft, I took it out and smiled sweetly at Rafa.

"The real thing is better," I admitted, wistfully looking down at his erection. "Maybe while I'm waiting I can find some of that, too."

That was it. That was the comment that enraged him like nothing I've ever seen before. He smacked the toy out of my hand and jumped on me, pinning me to the bed. Placing both of my arms above my head, he held them together with one hand and kept me in position as he used his own strong legs to keep me snugly beneath him. I struggled, but it was no use. He was far stronger and used it to his advantage.

"Easy," he warned. We locked eyes, knowing it was the moment of truth. Either one of us could take it too far and that would be it. It would be interesting to see who'd back down first, because I wasn't sure how this could possibly end well. We were both just too mad.

Given my behavior, I thought he might become even more hostile now that he had me completely at his mercy, but he didn't. He could have done any number of things to really make me go ballistic, but instead he calmly watched the rise and fall of my breasts as I struggled to catch my breath and compose myself. I turned my head away, still unhappy and unwilling to engage on his terms, and then I closed my eyes because I had no idea what to do next. That was when he brought my arms down under his legs as he edged his way up my body, and at that point I probably could have pushed him off, but I had to admit that the way he had me pinned down was very erotic. I opened my eyes and saw that he'd arranged himself so that his knees were on either side of my arms and his testicles dangled over my chest.

He arched downward so that I could see his face, which I glad to note had softened, and as he weaved his hand through the hair at the top of my head and grabbed a handful, a glimmer of tenderness emerged. He gently tilted my head back so that my neck was fully extended and my nose and chin pointed upward. As he gazed down at me, in very measured increments he angled his pelvis in the direction of my mouth, and with his free hand, he took his penis and held it so that it was about an inch from my lips.

"Open."

Rafa spoke with his usual authority, but I read in his eyes that it was a question. If I yielded, it represented more than a simple truce between us. It signified my acknowledgement of him as he was, dominant and stubborn, and his acceptance of me and all my girlish whims and insecurities. It meant that above all else, we would be there for one another no matter how much we quarreled. And for obvious reasons, it was also an expression of mutual trust.

I brought my hands up to his hard, round buttocks and traced his contours with my fingernails, then took a breath and parted my lips ever so slightly until there was enough space for him to fit. The truth was that I desired him more than I had even realized myself. I went crazy when he denied me, because I wanted him so desperately that it hurt. It was in that moment I realized I loved him.

"I know," he said. "Show me," he pleaded, as he placed the tip of his penis just beyond my lips. I flicked the head, using my tongue to consume the salty little bead of extract crowning the tip, savoring his taste. Emboldened, I maneuvered his pelvis toward me by guiding him from behind with my fingertips, essentially directing all of his power with the barest whisper of a touch. Little by little, I took every inch of him until he was up against the back of my throat. Surprisingly I didn't gag, but my movements were so restricted that everything was in his control. He remained in place for a few seconds, savoring the view of himself buried in my mouth. Spellbound, he caressed the side of my face and traced the outline of my lips with his free hand. Finally satisfied, I pursed my lips and flattened my tongue against the underside of his shaft so that he felt strong pressure as he pulled out. He moaned my name in a way that I'd never heard before, a broken mix of longing and pain, and I waited for him to find my mouth again, but once was enough. Shaken, he climbed off and immediately put distance between us by sitting at the foot of the bed, with his back to me and his head in his hands.

"I know you didn't mean it," he said quietly, "but don't ever threaten me with that again." Without letting me see his face, he grabbed his clothes off the floor and walked out, and when I heard the front door slam shut downstairs, I dove under the comforter and cried.

CHAPTER EIGHT

woke up after dark to the sound of voices downstairs, and because I heard people and laughter, I thought I must be dreaming. Now, fully awake in the darkness of my bedroom, I realized there really were other people in the house, so I put on a robe and stood at the landing to see what was going on. Kieran wasn't supposed to be back until next week, but it had to be him.

I went down as quietly as I could to make sure I wouldn't stumble into one of his formal dinner parties wearing nothing but a dressing gown and smudged mascara. I peeked around the corner and saw my brother, his driver, and a tall, handsome man in a navy suit walking back and forth, shuttling suitcase after suitcase into the house. I heard them both erupt into laughter together at some shared joke, my heart exploding with happiness at the sight of my brother. He always seemed so alone and melancholy, like me, and I couldn't remember him being any other way. But tonight, he was different.

"Kieran!" I called out from behind the sliding foyer doors, hoping I wouldn't attract the attention of the other man. His bespoke suit looked just as expensive, which could only mean he was a business associate. I probably should have stayed upstairs, but I hadn't seen my brother for two months and missed him quite a bit.

"Amanda!" My brother smiled when he saw me and tugged on his companion's sleeve. "She's here, come on." As they both came closer, I first noticed how carefree my brother looked, and then how tall and handsome his smiling companion was. "Amanda, come out here and meet Ken."

Knowing what I must look like, I stayed behind the door and shook my head no, but Kieran's expression was so jubilant that I had to smile back. "I'm in a robe, I can't. I just wanted to say hello." I waved and turned to leave, but my brother jogged over, caught me by the arm and gave me a hug. "I'm so glad you're home," I said. He looked great, though his dark blond hair had grown a little longer than he usually wore it. In fact, he looked a lot more relaxed in a lot of ways. I don't remember the last time I saw him wear a suit without a vest or a tie. He looked so good, I had to wonder what exactly he'd been doing in Japan.

"Are you OK?" He noticed something was off, but I couldn't bear to ruin his nice evening.

"I'm fine. I just got back myself and I've been sleeping for the last eight hours. I still have to wake up." I don't think he believed me, but since Ken had come close enough to hear our conversation, he let it go. My brother's new friend was sporty, lean and attractive, his Midwestern wholesomeness a perfect compliment to Kieran's edgier cosmopolitan look.

"Amanda, this is Ken Daniels."

"Kieran, look how I'm dressed," I whispered, mortified.

"That doesn't matter." Kieran put his hand on Ken's shoulder. "He's family."

Ken stepped closer, smiled and extended his hand. "I've heard so much about you, Amanda." I took it, slightly embarrassed, but then forgetting everything when an image of Rafa's thumb on my palm flashed through my mind.

"Family?" I said, studying the stylish man before me. Did we have some distant relation I didn't remember? Kieran took Ken's left hand in his own, and held them out for me to see their matching platinum wedding bands.

I sucked in my breath and covered my mouth as I looked at them both. "You're married?" There could be no other explanation, but how was it possible that I didn't even know my own brother was gay until this very moment? To call this unexpected would be an understatement to say the least. "Kieran, I didn't know—"

"Neither did I." He and Ken exchanged a knowing glance. "Well, it's complicated, but let's just say once I met Ken, everything made sense." Overcome with emotion, I embraced them both and wept again for the second time today. Life can be so difficult for so long, and then one day everything changes. "I think this calls for a celebration," said Kieran. "I'll go down and get a bottle."

They'd married last night in Las Vegas in a spur of the moment ceremony at the Bellagio, and over one of Kieran's finest bottles of Bordeaux, the happy newlyweds told me the story of how they met. Shortly after his arrival in Tokyo two months ago, my brother started getting his morning coffee in the packed Starbucks around the corner from his hotel every day at seven o'clock. The baristas always had a terrible time understanding Kieran's name, so when they called him, Kieran wouldn't understand and miss his coffee. After about a week, Kieran changed his strategy.

"Every day I made up a name I knew I couldn't miss, like Shakespeare or Ben Franklin—"

"So you can imagine, I'm in this packed Starbucks every morning at seven for a week listening to orders for Abraham Lincoln and Albert Einstein," added Ken, finishing my brother's sentence, "but I can't see who's going up to get these drinks. I'm thinking, either there are some big dead celebrities in this place, or it's another American with a great sense of humor, but either way, I'm finding out. So the next day, when they called out coffee for Napoleon at exactly seven again, I made sure I was waiting by the counter. And there he was, the little tyrant."

I sat across from them, laughing along and marveling at the change in my brother and the loving, intimate body language between them. For so many years I'd watched my brother bury himself in his work, for him the easiest way to distract himself from the sad things that had happened in our lives. Losing our family had weighed very heavily upon both of us, and we'd each coped in the best way we could. For Kieran that meant endless business trips, a negligible social life and constant worry about me and my state of mind. For the first time since my parents died, Kieran was actually happy, and I knew it was because he had found true love with Ken.

"When I picked up my coffee, Ken said, 'Well hello there, Emperor. You look great for your age. Can I have your autograph?'

Kieran took a sip of wine and smiled from ear to ear, remembering the moment. "Everything changed after that."

"I fell in love with him in Rome." Ken gazed at my brother with an expression of pure devotion. "It took Kieran a little while longer to see us as more than friends, but that was fine."

"Ken, you picked out the lace Valentino, didn't you?" I asked.

"How did you know?" The corners of his mouth turned upward into a satisfied grin. "I get invited to the fashion shows in Italy through work, so I talked Kieran into flying out with me. It was a such a romantic evening," said Ken. "There's nothing like Rome at night." He finally tore his eyes away from Kieran and turned his attention back to me. "Did you like it?"

The man who bought that dress was madly in love, Rafa had said.

I began to tear up at the thought of Rafa. My brother and Ken exchanged a concerned glance as they set their wine glasses down and leaned in toward me. "I love it," I choked out between sobs. "It's very special."

"I knew something was wrong," whispered Kieran.

"Honey, tell us," said Ken.

"I'm not going to be a wet blanket because this is your night, but I'll tell you so that you're not worried, and then we're not talking about it again." I dabbed at a tear in the corner of my eye.

"Oh no," said Kieran. "Are you sick?" Ken held my brother's hand in case he had to brace for something awful.

"No, nothing like that." I looked at them both and said it out loud. "I fell in love, too. On the ship."

"Thank God," said Kieran, sitting back, as Ken put his arm around his shoulders.

"He's been obsessed with the idea that something terrible will happen now that we're so happy," explained Ken, patting my brother's back. He was really cute. I could see why Kieran was smitten.

I told them about Rafa and they literally were on the edge of their seats as I filled them in on what had been going on. They were particularly interested in his association with Santería.

"Well, that explains the coconut in the driveway," said Ken, his hand now on my brother's knee.

"Oh, it didn't break did it?" Rafa would be beside himself. With the way he'd left, I wasn't surprised he'd forgotten to take it with him.

"No," said Ken. "You know, recently there have been all sorts of interesting constitutional law cases regarding Santería and freedom to practice it as a religion. The Santería community must be very powerful here in Miami, because they just never lose in court. It's a fascinating legal topic." I thought back to how many judges and lawyers there were in Doña Delfina's waiting room. Considering her client list, it wasn't surprising.

"Stop pretending to be a serious lawyer," teased my brother. "He practices entertainment law out in Los Angeles. Tour riders and non-disclosure agreements. You should see the bizarre demands."

"Hey!" Ken playfully smacked my brother's thigh. "I *am* a serious lawyer, thank you very much!" I just adored Ken, and I loved them both together. I was so grateful my brother had found someone so wonderful, and I told them so.

We chatted a while longer about Japan and Ken's life out in California when the discussion turned to the future. Ken and Kieran raised the subject carefully, as if they'd already had a conversation about it themselves.

"Amanda, Ken's practice is out in California, and he has three kids from his first marriage."

"You do?" I asked. "Do you have any photos?"

"Are you kidding?" Ken pulled out his phone and showed me at least a dozen photos of his kids, Marc, 12, Jessica, 9, and Ethan, 5, who were absolutely adorable.

"Kieran, you have stepchildren now! You're a stepdad! Wait, that means I'm a step-aunt!" Things just kept getting better and better. I could see why Kieran was worried the other shoe would drop. It was too good to be true.

"I know," he said, puffing up with pride. "I met them on the way home. They're fantastic."

"He's already spoiled them rotten," teased Ken.

"Careful with that, Kieran. Rafa thinks I'm spoiled and he can't stand it."

"Amanda," said Ken, "as beautiful as you are, that man will come crawling back in a hurry, I assure you."

"Oh, he thinks you're a dead ringer for that actress."

"Who?"

"You know, the one who sings on the piano in that movie," said Kieran. "I guess I can see it," he said squinting and turning his head to the left a little.

Ken nodded in the affirmative, crossed his legs and took another sip of wine. "Yep."

"Amanda, maybe I should have called last week, but I wanted you to meet Ken first, in person. It's a lot to tell someone over the phone."

"How could you think I'd be anything but thrilled for you?"

"I didn't," said Kieran. "But it just seemed better to wait and come see you."

"See me?" I asked. "Aren't you staying?"

An awkward silence hung in the air between us. Clearly there was something they still hadn't told me yet. My brother rubbed his hands together.

"Well, Ken's life is on the west coast. He has his practice and his kids. We want to live in both places, but I'm going to be spending a lot of time out there, at least for now. Plus some of the usual business travel—"

'But not as much—" interjected Ken.

"Not as much," agreed Kieran, squeezing his husband's hand.

"Oh. That's understandable." I couldn't hide my disappointment, but what else could he do? Ken looked just as upset about it as my brother.

"We'll stay here when we visit if you like, but you keep the house, and of course I'll still take care of the business. Eventually you might consider having a home base over there, too. You could even live with us."

"Stop, it's not—"

"Amanda, we've been each other's only family for a long time, and we've been through a lot. Don't think for a second I would ever leave you alone." There it was again, the same undue concern for me that had been a constant source of stress for him, but before his mood could plummet, I put his mind at ease right away.

"Kieran, I know you would never forget about me, and trust me, if I did feel lonely, I'd move out to LA, but for now I'm fine here." I made sure he heard me by looking directly at him, then at Ken, then back at him. "But the house is too big for me, and Rafa doesn't like it. Anyway, that's if he ever comes back. We had quite an argument today."

"He'll be back. Mark my words," interjected Ken. "You're a ten, honey."

"Really? Your sister-in-law?" joked Kieran. Ken shrugged and finished his wine.

I had to laugh, but then I thought about how ugly it had gotten between us today, mostly because of me. "Kieran, let's just see how everything plays out. I love you both for wanting to include me."

Kieran came over and gave me a hug. "You are my baby sister and I will always love you and take care of you." Feeling my shoulder blades through the thin robe, he remarked, "She's lost weight since I've been gone. We have to make sure she eats. She's all bones."

After we polished off the bottle of wine, I stayed downstairs while Kieran gave Ken a tour of the house. I knew I'd have to excuse myself soon and give them some alone time, but I'd slept all day and had no idea what to do now. I put away the wine glasses and was about to start dragging my still unpacked luggage upstairs when my phone rang. It was Rafa.

"Hello?" Unsure of his mood, I didn't want to appear too excited and show my hand just yet. He'd been so adamant about not speaking until Tuesday that he could have been calling just to break it off, and my stomach turned at the thought, but it was an unfamiliar voice on the other end of the line that spoke to me in English.

"Eh, hello, can I talk to Dr. Amanda Rose?"

"Speaking." I started to panic. Why would someone else have Rafa's phone?

"This is Sandro. I work—worked—for Doña Delfina." His voice cracked and he took a moment to clear his throat. "She passed away tonight, about an hour ago."

"Tonight?" It couldn't be.

"She had a heart attack." He covered the phone for a second, and got back on the line, sniffling.

"Sandro, I'm so sorry." I walked back to the couch and sat down.

"I wanted to let you know that Rafa is here and he's not taking it well."

"What's he doing?"

"He was with her when she passed and now he won't leave her side. I mean, you know, he's going to have to, but no one wants to go in there."

That didn't sound good at all. My poor Rafa.

"Sandro, I want to come, but he and I had a very bad argument today, and I don't think he wants to see me. I might make it worse." I looked in the mirror and touched my neck where he'd left the mark. It was gone now.

"He told me." Thinking about what had happened, I turned bright red. I hoped he hadn't been too specific. "He said he'd been very disrespectful to you and he didn't think you would ever speak to him again, but he definitely wasn't angry. Um, I don't want to overstep my bounds, but I think you're the only person he would talk to, so if you could put that aside for now, we would all be very grateful."

"Of course I'll help. Whatever you need."

"Can I come pick you up in ten minutes?"

"Leave now."

I went upstairs and was about to take a right at the top of the stairs to my side of the house when I thought I heard Kieran and Ken on the other side. I turned in the direction of Kieran's room, praying I wouldn't stumble upon anything intimate.

"Kieran!" I called out, wanting to give them plenty of notice.

"In my bedroom!" They were still laughing and having fun, and it sounded like maybe they'd opened a second bottle.

I knocked on his bedroom door and my brother answered in an open robe and pajama bottoms, looking like he was ready to party. I'd only ever seen him in sweats to go to sleep.

"I'm sorry to bother you, but I wanted to let you know I'm going out and I'm not sure when I'll be back. I'm going to see Rafa."

"Did you work it out?" he asked. I caught a glimpse of Ken in the bed under the covers.

"Not yet."

"Ken and I are staying until tomorrow night and we'd really like to meet him before we go to back to Los Angeles."

"I'll see if I can get him to come home with me tonight, but I don't know if he will."

"Do you need us to take you?" Ken, called out from across the room, obviously listening to our conversation. "It's too late for you to be driving around by yourself alone."

My brother moved aside so that I could speak directly to him. "No, a car is coming."

"Wear an outfit that'll rock his world," said Ken. "Sex it up!"

"Be careful," said Kieran. "Call if you need us."

"Hey," I said, lowering my voice. "Ken is *wonderful*."

"I know." He glanced over his shoulder at his new husband. "I'm so lucky."

In fewer than ten minutes I had thrown on a fitted black turtleneck, a black pencil skirt and black pumps, and was already waiting downstairs in the living room when the Mercedes pulled into the driveway. I made it outside so quickly that Sandro barely had time to get out of the car. He didn't look great, so I gave him a hug and let him know again how sorry I was. Though he appreciated my condolences, he stressed that he was fine, and his only concern was for Rafa.

Sandro got me into the car quickly, and as he was about to shut the door, he spotted the coconut in the driveway.

"You want me to take care of that?"

"I'm not sure where it's supposed to go. All I know is that it can't break."

"I know what to do."

He sped down the empty freeway and went through a couple of red lights without blinking an eye, driving like he was part of a presidential motorcade, with no regard for stoplights or traffic signs.

The only thing he yielded to were other motorists, and at one in the morning, we didn't pass too many.

"Do you always drive like this, Sandro?" Maybe he was more upset than he wanted to admit, and I didn't want to end up in a horrible accident, especially tonight.

"Always," he said in the mirror. "We have to."

"Don't you worry about getting pulled over?"

He smiled. "That wouldn't happen."

We arrived at The Copper Crown in record time, and unlike the other night, the parking lot was deserted.

"Where is everyone?" I didn't see a soul outside, which was eerie.

"We're closed Sundays and Mondays." He pulled right up to the front door and turned around.

"He doesn't know you're coming, but I'll wait close by until *you* let me know what to do. Not him," he said, and pointed at me. "You." With that, he got out and opened the door. As he helped me out of the car he added, "If you can keep him out of here until tomorrow, that would be best. He doesn't need to see her being taken away."

I followed Sandro through the anteroom of the dark, empty club, and instead of going all the way to the back as before, he pushed open a door to that led to a concrete stairwell. Unlike the club, which was dark and exotic, the stairwell and the floor it opened up to was well-lit and inviting. The upper level consisted of one central corridor with several doors off to each side. We walked about fifty feet until we came to a set of double doors all the way in the back.

"That's mine," he said pointing to the single door to the left. "This used to be a motel, so when Doña Delfina bought the building, she kept a floor of rooms up here for herself and for staff." He bowed his head, as if even saying her name was difficult. "She was a smart lady."

He inserted a key into one of the double doors and let us into the living area of the suite. The room was filled with familiar faces as well as two paramedics and two police officers in uniform. Most of them were drinking coffee and speaking quietly, but there was a collective sigh of relief when I entered. Carlos and Javier came right over, gave me a kiss on the cheek and thanked me for coming.

"Follow me," said Sandro, wanting me to keep moving. "Please just try to get him out." He stopped at what I presumed was the bedroom door and put his hand on the knob. "I'll be right here."

As soon as I stepped in, I saw her. Doña Delfina lay peacefully on her bed in a pretty long-sleeved white nightgown, hands folded and eyes closed. She looked like she was sleeping, and someone, probably Rafa, had arranged long stemmed white roses along the foot of her bed.

Rafa sat beside her on a wooden rocking chair, head in his hands, exactly as he had been earlier before he'd left me. I took the desk chair and set it down right next to him. He must not have heard me come in because he looked surprised to see me. I hesitated, wondering if he would be angry with me for coming. I prepared myself for the cold shoulder when he stood up, expressionless.

The first thing I noticed were his glassy, bloodshot eyes. He could never be anything but beautiful, but it was by far the worst shape I'd ever seen him in. My heart broke, and when I reached for him, he took my hand and kissed it as he liked to do.

"Sit with me." I hesitated, knowing that everyone was waiting for us. "I know they want me to go. Just one more minute, and I'll say goodbye."

I sat down next to him, and he spoke to me as he looked at her. "This was her rocking chair, and she sat in it night after night when I was sick. She prayed over me, fed me pumpkin soup, and told me funny stories. One day I asked her why she was so good to me, and she said it was because we were connected. She said, 'I know I'm not your mother, but I'm your mother's mother.' She always spoke in riddles like that.

"Amada, tonight she told me she left me *everything*. This is all mine now." He looked around the room, visibly moved by her generosity. "Doña Delfina wanted to take care of me even after she was gone. She's changed everything for me again."

"She loved you." It seemed like he was going to break down, so I squeezed his hand so that he would look at me. "Yes, she's gone, but you're not alone. I'm your family, too. You're part of me now, and even if you reject me, it won't change the way I feel." He bowed his head and listened as I clasped his hand in both of mine.

"You're a queen," he said, "and look at what a vulgar thing I did to you today because I lost my temper. I can't stop thinking about it. I'm not worthy of you." We sat in silence for a moment and I considered whether I could finally tell him everything. I didn't know if the words would come out, but for him, I would try.

"My son's name was William." Rafa looked up and turned toward me. "He was five when he died. We knew he wasn't a typical child, but when they told us he might be autistic, we didn't believe it. We were hoping he'd grow out of it, but still we took every precaution with his safety because his behavior was so unpredictable. Then, around Thanksgiving four years ago, I had to attend a conference, and it was his father's turn to have him, so they went to visit my son's grandmother. I'd warned her to keep all the doors locked because William had a tendency to run off, and she did, but one day he followed her out to the garage. He pressed the button and slid out underneath the door before she could catch him." I realized I'd never said the words out loud until now, and I began to sob. "He was hit by a neighbor's car and didn't make it."

Rafa embraced me, wanting to take my pain onto himself. "Amada," he said. "I can't even begin to imagine what you've been living with."

I wiped my eyes, angry at myself for crying again, but it was good to share the burden. "Everything fell apart after that. I quit my job right away and was depressed for a long time. My brother suffered right along with me and did everything he could to get me through it, but there's nothing that can stop the pain that comes from losing your child. Nothing. I drank a lot. Then after a few years, I started traveling and that helped. But it wasn't until I met you that I was able to see the beauty in life again. So when you say you're not worthy, you just don't realize what you mean to me. You saved me. You're my life and my family now. I love you."

Rafa kissed my mouth, then each of my eyes, and then spoke into my ear as he liked to do. "I love you, too, Amada. I meant it the first night and I've wanted to tell you so many times since then. I don't know why I've been afraid to say it, but I'm not afraid anymore." Still holding my hand, he looked at me with those beautiful blue eyes and said it again. "I love you." *Te amo*.

"Rafa, can we please go home?" I asked. "I'm sick without you. Nothing is right unless you're there. I promise we'll figure it out so that it works for both of us, but for now, just come with me, please."

He glanced at Doña Delfina one more time, then back at me.

"Yes, you're my home, Amada," he said, finally ready to go.

Rafa and I came out of the bedroom hand in hand, and the people who'd been waiting on us rushed in. The crowd in the living area had doubled, and I imagined that many people would come over the next few days to pay their respects. Almost everyone in the room patted Rafa on the back or shook his hand on the way out, but when Sandro gestured to me, I led Rafa as quickly as possible out the front door. He'd had enough for one night.

We walked back out through the club and made our way to the front circle drive where the sedan was waiting. This time, Rafa opened the door for me and Sandro got right in the driver's seat.

"Back to the house?" Sandro asked me in Spanish, as he put the car in gear. I noticed that he was perfectly bilingual as so many people were in Miami. He switched effortlessly from English to Spanish, and I decided that Rafa would be able to do the same within a year.

"Yes," I said, turning to Rafa. "Should we get your things before we leave?"

"Done," said Sandro.

He put the car in drive, and in less than a minute we were back on the freeway to Boxwood. It was a relief to be with Rafa again, and I knew everything would be fine now that he'd let me take care of him. As we practically flew past the Miami cityscape, for the first time I noticed what he was wearing.

"All white?" I asked.

"Her dying wish. I'm a *santero* now." He put his hand between my knees, and because my pencil skirt was so tight, thankfully there wasn't room left for him to do much more. "I can't believe what I'm thinking, Amada, but even now, after this terrible day, I still need you more than I need to breathe." As sexy as it was to hear him say that, I knew Sandro was listening to every word, so I simply put my hand on his thigh and stayed quiet.

"Boss," said Sandro, "you want me to stop and pick up any groceries?" He and Rafa exchanged a knowing glance in the rearview mirror.

"Good idea," said Rafa, slowly inching up my skirt, and I tried to keep him still, but he would not be stopped. Shaking my head, I darted my eyes in the direction of the front seat, but Rafa just shrugged.

By the time the Mercedes pulled into a secluded overlook by the ocean, Rafa had my skirt halfway up my thighs. He was all hands, like a horny teenager, and it reminded me of being seventeen years old in the back seat of my boyfriend's car. In spite of the somber night we'd had, I couldn't help but smile as he snaked his way under my top and caressed my breasts. "What is this?" he whispered in my ear, intrigued by the unusual shape of my bra.

"I wasn't sure what I'd have to do to get your attention, so I came prepared."

He traced his fingers along the scalloped lace edge. "Sandro, groceries."

"Anything specific?" he asked, putting the car in park.

"Get some rice, picadillo ingredients, a loaf of bread, butter, Bustelo, sugar and a *cafetera*."

"Got it," said Sandro, unbuckling his seatbelt. "Back in ten."

"Twenty. And put on some Zeppelin."

Sandro turned on the satellite radio and made a quick exit. Before the door had even shut, Rafa unbuckled my seatbelt and pulled me over so that I was sitting sideways on his lap. He kissed and touched me all over, and I wrapped my arms around his neck as he caressed my legs and let myself get lost in his kiss and in the music. Nothing in this world could be sexier than listening to Jimmy Page work his magic on the guitar while Rafa worked his magic on my body. Nothing.

Rafa went higher and followed the seam of my stockings up under the back of my skirt, gliding his fingers past the lace top and the garter in search of my panties, but when he found nothing but bare skin, he let out a groan and pushed his tongue in my mouth so hard that I almost fell off his lap. He put his hands in my hair and broke our kiss to look at me.

"You," he panted. He might have been trying to say something, but I was in a state and didn't let him finish. I took my top off to expose the shelf bra I'd worn just for him, dying to feel his mouth anywhere on my skin, and when he saw my nipples peeking out over the top of the demi cups, he lost it. He took one roughly in his mouth and bit down, while using his fingers on the other to pinch me hard. I'd never been bitten on the breast like that, but the pain quickly turned into a pleasure so intense I thought I might climax right then and there. I clenched my legs together and arched my back, and resisting the strong urge to bite him back, I dug my fingernails into the top of his shoulder instead. He shouted an obscenity I didn't understand, and I watched with detached fascination as the bloodstain began to travel along the top of his white collar.

"I need you inside me," I begged, wondering how many of the twenty minutes were left as I writhed in his lap. "Please, Rafa."

Needing no further invitation, Rafa grabbed me by the hips and turned me away from him so that we were front to back, and although I knew there was no other way to do it in the car, I wished I could see his face. He yanked my skirt up past my thighs and within moments his pants were around his ankles and he was inside me. I moaned as he wrapped both arms around my chest and pulled me tight, nestling his face between my shoulder blades.

Rafa moved for both of us, grinding himself into me with ease. He filled me up so completely that I became aware of nothing but us, and the feeling of his skin on my skin deep inside my body took on a life of its own. We had ceased to be in control from the moment he entered me, and now our energy was far more potent as one than as two.

His hands were everywhere tonight, on my neck, in my mouth, and especially on my belly. The shelf bra must have made him borderline delirious because he wouldn't leave my breasts alone, kneading and giving them far more attention than he ever had before.

"I want to see your face," I said, sucking on his fingers. "Kiss me."

In one swift motion he maneuvered us both out, leaned me up against the side of the Mercedes facing the ocean, and kissed me wildly, pinning me against the car with what felt like all his strength. Whenever he was out of his mind with desire like this, it made me appreciate just how much he held back for my pleasure, because if I hadn't specifically asked to be able to see him, I knew he'd already have me bent over, his favorite way to have me.

Naturally, I ended up off my feet with my legs wrapped around his hips, the headlights of each car bathing us in light as they came around the curve not twenty feet away so that we were plainly visible to any driver who took his eyes off the road.

"People can see us," I gasped.

In response, he placed one arm underneath me and used the other to pull me so close that I almost couldn't breathe. Unable to resist, I simply gave in, forgetting about the cars, the highway, Sandro and everything else in the world except Rafa inside me and the sound of the ocean below. I yielded and let him lead us, my pelvis softening and widening in accord with my full surrender.

"That's it, baby. Now I'm in all the way," he said, thrusting with almost distressing urgency. He felt how I'd opened to him completely and it made him savage, his instinct to dominate only heightened by my submission. I thought of the sweet Rafa who kissed my hand and taught me about medicine and rubbed my feet, then looked at the undeniably alpha male who at this moment was fucking me within an inch of my life. It was incredible they both were one in the same.

"Say it again," he barked, his body rolling inside mine.

"I love you, Rafa."

He moaned and shifted so that he hit a spot inside me that could only be described as an epicenter of pleasure. Going far beyond anything I could ever find by myself, Rafa touched me in a physical and spiritual haven only he was privy to. It was his special place inside me, where only he had access. His presence there triggered the start of an orgasm, but inexplicably I curled up and tried to push him away. I still didn't understand why I always had this urge, but Rafa had once said it was fear. He wouldn't allow it.

"Don't," he rasped. "Together."

"Rafa!" I cried, and we exploded in sync, our spirits now indistinguishable from our bodies, and as our joy peaked, Rafa bit my neck and kept his mouth there, sucking gently. Closing my eyes, I ran my hands all over his back, aware that he was completely inside me now, forever, in every possible sense. There was only us.

"Goddamit," he said, out of breath. He ran his hand through his hair and rested his forehead against mine, a semblance of his sweet self shining through again.

"I know," I said, laying my head on his shoulder.

We'd barely recovered when there was a noise just beyond the clearing. "Is it him?" I asked, quickly covering up. My eyes fixed on the lights of a yacht in the distance.

"No," he said, gently sliding out of me and looking down at something on himself. "He won't come back until I call. It's been forty minutes, sweetheart."

The splash of red across Rafa's collar caught my attention this time, and now that I was fully lucid, I was horrified. I reached out to see what I'd done, angry at myself for not caring about it earlier. "Oh, you're bleeding."

"So are you," he said. I followed his eyes and saw a trace of bright red blood on his penis.

"I must have just started! I'm so sorry!" I would have stopped him if I'd realized, but I hoped he wasn't unreasonably squeamish about it like some men were.

"Sorry for what? Being a woman?" Still out of breath, he laughed and zipped his pants right back up. "Anyway, it's barely a drop."

"Don't you want to wipe it off?"

"Didn't you wait a whole day to wash me off?" he asked devilishly, making me blush as I pulled down my skirt and pushed my breasts back into my tiny bra.

"Still, if I'd known—"

"Amada, stop apologizing," he said, and shot me a concerned look as if it really bothered him. "A doctor would say your orgasm brought it on. A Santero would say that blood is life, and because we both bled tonight, we've been reborn. Together. Either way, it's beautiful."

Still uncomfortable, I didn't answer, so he brushed the side of my face with the back of his hand, and said thoughtfully, "You really are such a lady."

We got back in the car and Rafa texted Sandro, who'd been somewhere close by entertaining himself. I'd barely gotten my top on when we heard the trunk open and shut, and as soon as he got in the front seat and looked in the rearview mirror, Sandro's eyes fixed on Rafa's neck like a hawk.

"Boss! You need a Band-Aid or something?" Sandro reached inside his jacket pocket and pulled out a handkerchief, and as he turned around to hand it to Rafa, I could see that he was trying not to laugh.

We made it back to the house in minutes, and Sandro helped us get Rafa's bag and the groceries as far as the foyer. Rafa noticed Kieran and Ken's Louis Vuitton luggage all over the place but turned his attention back to Sandro.

"Rafa, I got a call while you were listening to Led Zeppelin." I had to give him credit for being so professional, but among three adults I was surprised he managed to keep a straight face. "Someone important asked to see you tomorrow. I told him you would be busy making arrangements, but he asked for a favor. His oldest son is in a lot of trouble. Drugs." He leaned over and whispered a name in Rafa's ear.

"Three o'clock."

"I'll be here at two." With that, Sandro said good night to us both and left.

"Who?" I asked.

"A congressman." Gesturing toward all the luggage, he asked, "Is your brother back?"

"He is," I said, nuzzling his neck. "He met someone in Japan and got married last night! I have a brother-in-law now."

"It's *cuñada*, with an a," he said, running his hands along the back of my skirt.

"No, I mean *cuñado*. A man."

"Oh. I see."

"He's wonderful. I can't wait for you to meet them both in the morning." Then I remembered the rest of it. "They leave tomorrow night, and then Kieran's moving to Los Angeles to be with his husband."

"I'm sorry about that, mamita." said Rafa, sensing my disappointment. "But I'm here with you now." Then, smiling, he ran his hands along the garters under my skirt. "I like these," he purred.

"Want to come with me and clean up?" I raised my eyebrows and glanced at his pants.

"Nope," he said. "I'll wash my hands down here and start cooking. I'm starving, and you must be, too." He took off his shirt and gave it to me. "But since it's a mile up to that room, you can throw that in *our* laundry basket for me though, please." I admired his physique as always, and I couldn't wait to watch him cook shirtless.

"You don't want to take a shower?"

"I took a shower a few hours ago."

"Well, I mean because of—"

"Amada," he said in a low, measured tone, "to be honest, I like knowing it's there, and the way you're acting is making me like it even more. I'll take care of it later."

"I'll be right back then," I said, still uneasy, but bizarrely turned on again by the deep tenor of his voice.

"Actually, wait a second," he said, reaching for my shirt. "Before you change, let me see that bra in the light."

* * *

We spent the next hour making Cuban picadillo in the kitchen. First, he washed some uncooked rice by scrubbing it between his hands until the water ran clear, explaining how washing the rice had always been his job in his mother's kitchen. After setting the pot of rice to cook on the stove, he made something with onions and peppers called a *sofrito*, added ground beef, a splash of sherry and a handful of raisins, then let it all simmer for a while in a very small amount of tomato sauce.

In less than fifteen minutes he'd plated the meat over rice and we were eating together at the kitchen table, and to Rafa's delight I ate far more than I should have of his delicious food. I particularly loved the raisins, which I'd never had in a savory dish, because they made every bite slightly sweet and extra delicious. Rafa agreed and told me a story about how he always used to save them for the end, until the day his brother came by and stole them all. After that, he made sure to always enjoy the best part of his meal first.

"Never put off for tomorrow what you can enjoy today, mamita," he said, blinking slowly as his eyes went down my body and back up again.

"I love it when you tell me stories," I said. I pierced the last plump raisin on my plate with my fork and brought it to his lips, in awe of how he opened his mouth and accepted it as if it were the most natural thing in the world.

"I love it when you feed me," he said, almost to himself.

When we were done cleaning the kitchen together, he said we'd have Cuban coffee and toast when we woke up. He promised I'd enjoy it, and I had no doubt I would. I watched as he wiped off the counter and started the dishwasher, trying to remember where my coffee cups were. I spotted them on the very top shelf of a tall cabinet and stood on my tiptoes to try and pull two out for the morning. Still a few inches out of my reach, I was just about to go drag a chair into the kitchen when Rafa's strong hands locked around my waist and lifted me up with ease.

Up in our bedroom, Rafa finally got around to showering and changing into his regular sleeping attire, a soft pair of cotton boxers, when I had an idea, so I went down the hall to my office and pulled a big leather-bound edition of a book I hadn't read since college. I found my book light and went back to the bedroom, pleasantly surprised to find him still awake.

"Hey," I said quietly, slipping under the covers beside him. "I thought I could read a little of this to you every night. In English."

"What is it?" he said, tilting the spine of the book in the direction of the light.

"Miguel de Cervantes," he read aloud. "*Don Quijote de la Mancha.*" His beautiful blue eyes went back up to mine. "You remembered."

"Ready?"

He turned on his side and faced me. "Ready."

"*In a village of La Mancha, the name of which I have no desire to recall, there lived not so long ago ...*"

CHAPTER NINE

In the morning I opened my eyes to total darkness except for the light streaming into the crack between the cream colored drapes. For one brief moment, my heart sank just as it did every morning once I became fully conscious of the ennui that had slowly seeped into my mind and discolored everything around me. But today, it was the opposite. I shut off the alarm and leaned back into something sharp, so I reached behind me to find the ten pound book I'd been reading when I fell asleep. That's right, it was *Don Quijote*, and Rafa had been with me, arms crossed, on his side, watching my mouth as I read to him. I don't remember anything after that, but it had been like a dream. I hesitated, afraid to turn around and find no one there, but when his hand found mine, my fears fell away.

"Good morning, my queen," said Rafa, his voice scratchy and dry. *Buenos dias, mi reina.* I smiled, not really because of his many terms of endearment for me, but simply because I loved the sound of his voice. He moved the book aside and in one swift motion pulled me into him. He was hard everywhere, and I wondered what it would be like to fall asleep on his chest if he got fat and soft. It would be divine either way.

"How did you sleep?" I asked, pushing my bottom into his erection.

"Better than I have in a very long time." He nuzzled my neck and slipped a hand into my robe. He began to stroke my breasts with the lovely feather light touch he knew I enjoyed. "I feel rested." *Descansé.* "And you?"

"The same." I turned to face my Rafa, still so sleepy, but handsome like no other man could ever be. His usually gelled and groomed hair was an unruly mess, which made him all the more adorable. It was nice to know that there was one thing about him that wasn't perfect.

"Take this off," he said, trying to undo the loosely knotted tie at my waist.

"Say it in English, and I'll take it off."

"You would deny me pleasure because of my shortcomings? That's just cruel."

"We can't, Rafa," I whispered, kissing his forehead. "I'm bleeding. For at least another two days."

"Oh, *that* again," he sighed. "I told you I don't care."

"Well, I do."

"Because of the sheets?" he asked, still trying to coordinate himself enough to open the knot. "Let's go in the shower."

"No, it's not that. I don't even like buying tampons at the store."

"Oh, wow, you really are uptight about it then," he said, giving up on the knot, still half asleep. "Well, I'll buy them for you." Then, he closed his eyes and started to laugh. "Anyway, tonight I'll get you so worked up you'll let me do anything." I'm not sure if he even meant to say it out loud, but it was exactly how I imagined Rafa's mind would work. He opened one eye and added, "Maybe we'll have to switch to anal sex once a month."

I sat up, tense. "No way."

He burst out in laughter and pulled me back down to the bed, showering me with little bites and kisses all over my neck and chest. "I know, Amada, but you make it so easy, I can't help it."

"Do you like it?" I asked.

Rafa studied me for a minute, clearly wondering if this was casual conversation or if I was leading up to something. "I've never done it and have never really had a desire to." He groaned and came closer, wrapping his leg around me. "But I've thought about it with you."

"You thought about it the day we were out on the balcony."

"Yes, and many times after that." He kissed me on the forehead and rubbed my thigh, then gave it a little squeeze.

"So it's safe?"

"We'd have to be careful about certain things."

"Like what?" I propped myself up on my elbow and stared down at Rafa. "You know, Kieran has only been with women up until a few months ago. I wonder if he's aware of the things you're talking about. Are most people?" Rafa rolled onto his back and thought about my question, probably debating how technical to get with his answer.

"In my experience, no. I don't think the majority of people are as cautious as they could be, but keep in mind you don't know for sure how experienced he is unless you ask, and you might be surprised." Rafa took my hand and held it in his. "You shouldn't worry. He's a grown man, and I doubt he wants to discuss it with his sister. Just be happy he's in love, and let him handle the rest."

"Believe me, I'm thrilled, but I still think you should talk to Kieran," I said. "Actually, I'm kind of interested, too. I think we both need *the talk*." I couldn't help but giggle at the thought of Rafa as a medical professor in front of a whiteboard, pointing at all sorts of charts and diagrams.

"Wait a minute," he said, sitting up. "If he ever comes to me on his own and asks, then fine, but I'm certainly not going to approach him, and don't bring my name into it if you start asking nosy questions. I want us to get along, and I have as much interest in his sex life as I assume he has in mine. None." But then he changed from stern to playful in an instant, a knowing smile creeping across his face. "And I'll give you more than just a talk right now if you keep it up."

"No, thank you," I sighed, feigning boredom. "I'm uptight, remember?"

"I shouldn't have said that," he said, kissing the bridge of my nose. Now we were on our sides, face to face. "You're just proper. Until you're underneath me."

"My hang ups about blood must seem ridiculous to you."

"If it matters to you, it matters to me," he whispered in my ear. "But blood is powerful and sacred, the halfway point between body and spirit. I don't know why you'd think I wouldn't want to touch yours. If I were bleeding, would you recoil from me?" His tone changed and I started to realize he was aroused, so I began to think about how I could make him happy, but his mind was already there. "One thing you might like," he said, touching my face, "is oral sex."

"We already do that, handsome."

"Not everywhere." He closed his eyes, presumably imagining us in that position, then kissed me, his tongue moving in odd ways, as if trying to show me what it would be like. I blushed at the thought, yet it turned me on immeasurably.

"As soon as you let me anywhere near your beautiful ass," he panted, "I'm going to lay you on your stomach, tuck a pillow under your hips and show you."

"Are you sure, doctor?" He arched an eyebrow. "Don't think I haven't noticed all the hand washing. I think you're a little germ phobic." I meant it as a joke, but apparently my comment was more accurate than I anticipated.

"Maybe," he said. He rolled onto his back again and tucked an arm under his head.

"What's wrong?" I asked.

"I *am* afraid of sickness. I'll never forget what it's like to walk into a field hospital at the beginning of a shift. God, the smell. During an epidemic it's packed with nothing but cholera beds, and every single one is occupied with a patient in extreme distress."

"What's a cholera bed?" I asked.

"It's a plastic sheet with a hole in it and a bucket underneath. That's the deluxe accommodation. When you run out of those wooden cots, it's the ground." He shifted uncomfortably, his body language betraying how deeply troubling the memories were to him.

"Oh my God, Rafa," I said, looking into his eyes. I'd never fully understand what he'd been through. My face must have fallen because he immediately put his hand under my chin and gave me a big smile.

"Hey, that's why I don't like to talk about it with you. Out of necessity, I've had a lot of practice disconnecting emotionally, but you haven't."

"You can tell me," I said, wanting to relieve his burden somehow.

"No, I can't. But I just want you to understand why I am the way I am, that's all. I'm probably too cautious, but when you've seen so much needless suffering, it's difficult to be cavalier. Amada, you have to start taking care of yourself. Just trust me when I tell you I know what I'm talking about. Good health is precious."

"I will," I said, feeling overwhelming respect for him. I caressed the back of his head and put my cheek on his, something I did when I was feeling particularly close to him.

"You're a good man," I said, breathing in his scent. "You must have looked like an angel in white to all those sick people."

"Green," he said, with a little laugh. "Ugly, dirty green scrubs." He started to rub his cheek against mine. "I'm not what you think. I was so arrogant when I was younger. I fought a lot, and I have a horrible temper when I'm upset or scared. I'm no angel."

"That's called being human," I said.

"I love you," he breathed. He rotated his hips so that I could feel his arousal. "Please, don't worry about all that and let me touch you."

"I have a better idea. How about we work on your English so that you can get back to doing what you do best?" I asked, stroking the side of his face. "Well, second best."

I glided my fingertips down his neck and over his chest, tracing his nipple and following the small little curls of chest hair all the way to the waist band of his white boxers. I slipped my hand inside and found him, warm and inviting.

"This is your first special language lesson," I said in English, "and if you do well, there will be more just like this." I swirled the little bead of moisture at the tip with my finger. "Do you understand?"

"Yes, *profesora*, " he said, speaking to me in English now. He pulled off his boxers and rolled onto his back, now fully erect.

"Professor," I said, absentmindedly brushing my fingertips up and down his smooth phallus. "In English there is no distinction between a male or a female teacher. A woman is also addressed as 'professor.'"

"Yes, professor," he hummed. I didn't think it was possible for Rafa to get any sexier, but his Spanish accent in English was so seductive. I'd heard it the first night, but now that I was used to speaking to him in Spanish, I really noticed the nuances of his speech. For whatever reason, his voice seemed even deeper.

I continued to touch him at a leisurely pace, propping myself up as I contemplated his flawless body. We both watched as my hand went up and down his length, then locked eyes.

"In English, how many women have you had sex with, Rafa?"

He hesitated, so I released him. He groaned and caught my wrist before I could pull away completely and placed my hand back where it had been. "Seven, with you. Only with my girlfriends."

I resumed stroking him and watched as he closed his eyes and his expression relaxed again. He put his arms behind his head and sighed. "Repeat after me," I said. "'Seven *including* you.'"

"Seven. Including. You." He was careful to pronounce every syllable, making each word sound like a separate sentence.

"Now the most important question. Were any of them prettier than me?" He smiled, the corners of his eyes crinkling in the most adorable way.

"No. You are not pretty. You are beautiful."

"Very good. Whether it's true or not," I said, leaning in, "that's the right answer."

"Yes, I know this." Rafa laughed and then rested his hand on my arm and left it there. "But is the truth." As his lover, I adored his sexy accent and savored the compliment, but as a teacher, I made a mental note to explain the parts of speech and insist he stop rolling the letter r in English. This was a lovely new level of intimacy for us, as I knew how self conscious he was, yet he still let me see him at his most vulnerable.

"Did you love all your girlfriends?" I wasn't sure I wanted the answer to this one. I reached underneath and followed his curves to the flat spot that always made him moan.

He hesitated again, but this time I could tell it was because he was trying to find the right words, so I didn't stop. "Care, yes. Love, no."

"Did you tell them you loved them?"

He licked his lips, remembering and struggling to find the right words. "I said, *te quiero*, not *te amo*. Is different. I say *te amo* to you."

"I understand," I said, still teasing him with my fingertips. "When did you fall in love with me?"

"When I saw you at the table," he said slowly, trying to string the words together properly. "You were ... *elegante*. Elegant. I wanted to kiss you and... *acercarme?*"

"Get closer," I answered.

"I wanted to get closer. I wished ... you were my wife."

With those simple words the floor fell out from under me, and I recognized that I was no longer in control of his body or even my own. "That's enough for now," I whispered, and promptly took him in my mouth, desperate to be closer to him. I barely got to taste him before he exploded, lovingly cradling my head in his hands as he gave and I received.

* * *

We changed and made it downstairs by eleven, just in time to catch my brother and Ken. With all the shades and drapes open, the house was light and bright, illuminated by the sunshine reflected off the water and the marble floors. Rafa went right to the kitchen and started making coffee, while I sat down at the counter and watched him.

"This," he said pointing to the silver pot on the stove, "is called a *cafetera*." He turned several knobs on our big Viking range like a pro and unscrewed the pot, revealing its inner chambers. "The water goes here, and the espresso goes here," he said. "I make the best coffee you will ever taste, by the way. In medical school, even the guys who wanted to fight me would never turn it down."

"Why would anyone want to do that?"

"Some of them thought I was after their women." He spoke casually, but it seemed like it bothered him more than he was willing to let on. "If saying 'hello' and 'good morning' is flirting, then I guess I was."

"Did any of them ever try?" My heart ached for young Rafa, forced to fend for himself in a way that I could never fully understand.

"One of them did once, and then never again. Where I grew up, you learn to fight very young." He noticed the expression on my face and added, "Forget about it, sweetheart. Don't think about ugly things." *Olvidate de eso, mi vida. No pienses en cosas feas.*

He filled the pot with water and espresso and put it on the stove, leaving the lid open. While he kept an eye on the coffee, he sliced the Cuban bread lengthwise and slathered it with butter. "As soon as the coffee starts coming up into the reservoir, I take it off the heat and let it finish, but first, I stir a few drops into about ten teaspoons of sugar to make the foam. Then I pour the hot coffee over it so that it's smooth and extra sweet."

"That sounds complicated. Wait, are you trying to teach me how to do this?"

"No, Julia Child," he laughed, "you're going to have to use a Keurig." He put the bread in the oven and came around to my side of the counter.

"Rafa! I can cook a little."

"Sweetheart, your kitchen has never been used."

I sighed and looked him up and down. He'd thrown on a tight navy tank top and dark khaki shorts, and he looked so good, I decided that blue was most definitely his color. "I'd rather assist my handsome man, to be honest." Reading my thoughts, he came closer.

"Well, that's fine with me. That way you have plenty of energy for more important things," he said, giving me the first real kiss of the morning. As he stood between my legs, he held my chin and neck with an open hand and swirled his tongue in my mouth. He was about to slide his other hand into the back of my pants when we heard Kieran and Ken come down the stairs. I had my back to them, but clearly Ken saw us first.

"What do we have here?" he bellowed. "I spy two lovebirds!"

"Ken's still drunk," called my brother after him. "Pay no attention."

I looked over my shoulder and saw Ken bound down the last few steps and practically run over to us. Kieran, usually a cool character, didn't waste much time either. They looked rested and full of energy, and judging by the way they were dressed, I assumed Kieran planned on spending the day out on the boat. I wanted to give them my full attention, but it was quite a task to pull away from Rafa, who was already aroused again and ready to pounce. Somehow I managed to compose myself and stand to greet Ken properly, but not before Rafa could give my breasts a quick squeeze. "I can't wait to suck on these later," he whispered, just before Ken was within earshot.

"Good morning, Ken! I'd like you to meet my boyfriend, Rafa," I said in English. To Rafa I said in Spanish, "Rafa, I'd like to introduce Ken, my brother-in-law." *Rafa, te presento a Ken, mi cuñado.* They shook hands, and as Kieran approached, I said simply, "And my brother, Kieran." *Y mi hermano, Kieran.*

"A pleasure," said my brother in Spanish, shaking Rafa's hand.

"You speak Spanish as well as your sister. I'm impressed." Noting the cool confidence in his voice and demeanor, I marveled at how Rafa could switch so quickly from sex fiend to polite gentleman when I was sure it was still written all over my face.

"Well, I ought to, we learned from—"

"Kieran," I interrupted. "Rafa isn't interested in that."

"Yes, I am. What?" he asked, intrigued.

"So," said Kieran to me, "Teresa and Isaura are a big secret?"

"Well," I said, sitting back down on the stool, slightly annoyed with Kieran. "Rafa already suspects I grew up with a silver spoon in my mouth, but go right ahead and confirm it."

"Our nannies," said Kieran without a second thought. I knew he had even less of an understanding of how different our upbringing had been than I did, and I didn't want Rafa to see that side of him until they knew each other better. "Rafa, what are you cooking? It never smells like food in this house."

We spent the next hour drinking coffee and eating breakfast together at the kitchen table. The 'toast' was was like garlic bread without the garlic, and like everything Rafa made, it was delicious.

"This coffee," said Ken, licking his lips. "It's espresso, you said? The espresso at Starbucks does not taste like this." Ken's Spanish was much more basic than mine or Kieran's, but working in LA he'd had to pick it up, so he was able to carry on a conversation with us.

"Rafa is an extraordinary cook," I boasted. "Name it, he can make it." Turning to Rafa, I said, "Remember the oysters and pearls you made me? One of the women at my table said she'd eaten the same dish at French Laundry in Napa."

"That's serious gastronomy," remarked Kieran, impressed. "You know, I love a good Bordeaux. Do you know anything about French wine? Actually, Rafa, have you ever made Boeuf Bourguignon?"

"Yes, many times," said Rafa, sipping his coffee. "But the traditional French method takes three days. If you give me some notice next time you come home, I'll make it."

Kieran's face lit up as he accepted Rafa's gracious offer, and as they began discussing the particulars of my brother's favorite dish, Ken and I took the opportunity to check in with each other.

"Wow," he whispered, nodding his head. "That man is smoking hot! Oh my God, don't tell Kieran I said that! Damn, and he cooks, too."

"I know."

"I assume the bedroom situation is acceptable?"

"It is so good, Ken, that if it is in fact possible to be fucked to death, then that is how I am going to die." I looked at him as he let his mouth drop open. "Excuse my French."

"Oh, hell no," Ken blurted out, as he set his cup of coffee down more roughly in the saucer than intended, causing Rafa and Kieran to briefly look over. We smiled in their direction, but when they resumed their conversation, Ken looked me dead in the eye. "Listen to me very carefully, new sister-in-law. Lock. It. Down. Do not leave unattended. He is way too fine to take any chances."

"Believe me, I know," I said, putting my hand on his arm. "That's what our fight was about."

"You must keep me abreast of this situation."

"Here," I said, handing him my phone. "Put your number in."

"What's this?" said Kieran in English, clearly amused by our fast friendship. My brother was sharp as a tack and never missed a thing, especially when it came to me. "Cutting me out of the loop already?"

"Oh, stop it, honey," said Ken, tapping keys on my phone. "Would you rather we didn't like each other?"

"No," said Kieran, "it makes me very happy to see the two people I love most in the world spend time together."

We continued to chat about food and bedroom situations until Rafa's phone rang and he excused himself to take the call in the kitchen. With him out of earshot, I took the opportunity to speak to Kieran and Ken privately.

"Listen, I wanted to ask you both for some advice. Someone close to Rafa just passed away and left him a lot of cash and some businesses. Coming from a communist country, he's never really had money before, so I'm not sure if he understands how to manage it." I cringed inwardly, realizing I'd talked to Rafa about Kieran's sex life, and now I was discussing Rafa's finances with Kieran. Rafa had been right to call me nosy.

Both Ken and Kieran went from jovial to dead serious in a second. I caught a glimpse of how they must appear to others in their professional lives, two sharks not to be messed with. "How much are we talking about?" asked Kieran.

"Millions."

"First, he has to hire an attorney who understands business and estate law very well to handle the transfer of assets," said Ken. "I can guide him until he finds counsel here, but I'm not licensed in Florida."

"He also needs to hire a personal CFO to monitor payroll, budgeting, cash flow and, most importantly, to make sure the taxes are taken care of properly," added Kieran. "If you want, I'll do that for him until he gets set up locally." Glancing at Ken to confirm, he added, "Look, if we need to take some time off and come back to help you, we will." Ken nodded right along with him.

"I'll let you know, but I think he already has a network of trustworthy people here in Miami. I just want to run everything past you, if you don't mind." I had no idea where Ken had earned his degree, but my brother had graduated top of his class at Harvard Business School, and there is no one in the world I'd trust more with my money, even if he weren't my brother. In less than a decade, Kieran had doubled our net worth, so I knew Rafa couldn't be in better hands.

"Well, if he's the man you're going to end up with, you can rest assured no one is going to steal from you on our watch," said Kieran, sitting back, overprotective as always.

"No," added Ken. "I think not."

Rafa returned to the table, but his mood had changed, so I assumed it had to have been a call about Doña Delfina.

"Are you alright, Rafa?" I asked, setting down my coffee. The three of us looked at him, waiting for him to say something. "Honey, you're scaring me. What's wrong?"

"Fidel Castro is dead." He looked at all three of us, one by one. "Finally."

Confused, Ken and Kieran started to flip through their phones. "I didn't get any news alerts, did you?"

"It hasn't been announced yet," said Rafa emerging from what I presumed to be a mild case of shock. "They'll announce it at midnight. That was Sandro. The Congressman coming to see me today had to reschedule because of it. Everyone is scrambling to see what happens next."

"That's good news, isn't it?" I went to Rafa and put my arms around him. He was so overcome with joy, I knew he would have broken down in tears if Ken and my brother hadn't been there.

"It's amazing news. It means so much to all of us there and here that he's finally gone. They can't show their true feelings in Cuba, but believe me, it's a historic moment we've all been dreaming about for a long time. I only wish Doña Delfina had lived to see it. We have to celebrate tonight when they announce it. Miami is going to go crazy!" He picked me up, spun me around, and gave a me a big kiss on the lips.

I hugged him again and whispered in his ear. "I'm so happy for you."

"Does this change your plans at all, Rafa?" That was Kieran, always thinking of me.

"Not one bit. My home is here in Miami with my Amada. Nothing changes that. But it does mean that maybe soon I can take her to Cuba and show her around."

"What did you call her?" asked Ken with a half-smile.

"Amada," he said without the slightest hesitation. "Because she's my love."

"Oh my God," said Ken, putting his arm around my brother's shoulders. "That's so romantic. Should we tell them what you call me—"

"No, we shouldn't," laughed Kieran.

"So," I said to Rafa, "does that mean you have the rest of the day to spend with me now?"

"Why, yes it does. What did you have in mind?" he asked, dropping his voice.

"Oh, it's getting a little hot in here," said Ken, just after I gave him a wink and mouthed 'told you.'

"In all seriousness," said Rafa, "we have to be at The Copper Crown tonight by nine o'clock for our celebration in honor of Doña Delfina, and then around midnight, we'll break out the champagne and have a big party when Fidel Castro's death is announced. She gave me very specific instructions about her memorial service, but she was adamant that it should be a happy occasion. Most of her famous clients wanted to come perform, so I chose her favorite and she'll be on stage tonight as well. Then at sunrise tomorrow, a very small group will attend the burial at an undisclosed location, and after that, we close for two weeks. I have to meet with the attorneys, make some staff changes, update the menu and the decor, then have a grand re-opening." He squeezed my hand and smiled. "So yes, I definitely think we should take some time today if we can."

"Tomorrow morning seems so soon," I said. "Can things really happen that fast?"

"They have to," said Rafa. "She was a santera, so she can't be cremated and her body isn't safe until it goes back into the earth. The location of her grave cannot be public information, so the burial itself can only happen in the presence of her most trusted loved ones. Her body is being protected by armed guards until then, so the sooner, the better."

"Armed guards! If she's already passed, why wouldn't she be safe?" asked Ken.

"Look, I know how all this must sound to people who've never been around Santería before, but it's believed that people can work very powerful, dark magic with the bones of a deceased Santería priest or priestess. Her body would be desecrated if we didn't protect it. I know it's very morbid, but that's why."

"Well, damn," said Ken, taking a seat.

"You know," said Rafa, "there was always a strong rumor in Cuba that Fidel Castro was a santero. People will be watching very closely to see what happens with the body. If that's the case, then the true location of his remains will never be revealed. Can you imagine what would happen?"

"Do you believe he was?" I asked.

"Well, I think someone who's gotten away with what he has for more than fifty years had to have some kind of deal with the Devil himself, and that's not Santería, so no." Rafa sat down in the chair beside Ken and pulled me on his lap without a second thought, just the way he had at The Copper Crown. He picked up his last piece of bread and offered it to me, then scarfed it down. "What a week," he said thoughtfully.

"Rafa, I do have a question," began Kieran, speaking in Spanish again. "As a medical doctor, that means you're a scientist. How is it that you can also believe in Santería?"

"It's no different than a scientist who is a Christian, or a urologist who is also an ordained Rabbi. It's true that the majority of scientists are atheists, but there are still some people of faith. We simply believe that the living and the dead are connected, and they can have a positive or negative impact on our lives depending on what their intentions are and how we treat them. If we're lucky, they can guide and protect us during times of uncertainty. That's all. Practitioners of Santería also believe in the unequalled healing power of Nature. I strongly ascribe to that aspect myself, and I think there are many diseases that will eventually be cured when we synthesize the right combination of plants that are already growing all over the planet. All of our most potent drugs come from plants; think of opium and cocaine, for example." He jostled me slightly, as he sat forward, inspired.

"I know a famous *Osainista*—someone who works with medicinal plants—who lives in the jungles of Costa Rica, and I've convinced him to write down all of his cures and sacred knowledge. I'm hoping one day he'll share it with me, and that I can pass it on to the right people who'll know what to do with it. There are those who say he's hundreds of years old and can cure anything. That's pure science, not magic."

"What about the animal sacrifice we hear about in the news?" Kieran arched an eyebrow, as if in apology.

"Kieran! You don't think I'd be with someone who participates in that, do you?" I hopped off Rafa's lap, feeling tense.

"Amada, it's fine. This is why I think it's important to talk about it," said Rafa, pulling me right back down where he liked me. "There are so many misconceptions."

"I have to be honest," said Ken, "I'm really curious about it, too."

"It's very simple. Historically, an animal you would normally eat is slaughtered, like a chicken or a lamb, and everyone else involved in the ceremony eats the animal. The animal must be treated humanely. Sometimes the animal is not consumed and it's just the blood that's needed. Blood has a very special significance in Santeria." Rafa shot a glance at me and continued. "There are different reasons for animal sacrifice and different ways to carry it out, but in most cases it's presented as an offering in exchange for a favor from the Orishas. However, today I believe there's no need to sacrifice an animal. What I would request is something of personal value. In your case, Kieran, you might offer a rare bottle of Bordeaux, for example."

"Have you ever done it before, Rafa?" asked Ken, leaning forward.

"I've seen it done in Cuba, when I was younger. But keep in mind I used to watch my grandmother kill and prepare chickens all the time as well. In the Cuban countryside, everyone has to know how, or you don't eat. It's normal and necessary." He smiled and added, "No French Laundry in Cuba, I'm afraid."

"But what about those cases where they've found people—" began Kieran.

"That's not Santería. That's the worst kind of Haitian Voodoo. I would never have anything to do with that. It's very evil. You know, my grandmother once told me the story of how she became friends with a little girl in her town when they were both about eight years old. The other child was the granddaughter of a *houngan*, a Voodoo priest, and when my great-grandmother saw them talking, she walked up to my grandmother and slapped her across the face before dragging her away. Years later, my grandmother said her mother told her she did it because there was a rumor that Haitian Voodoo practitioners were stealing children to sacrifice." To me, Rafa added, "That's the kind of evil magic Doña Delfina said I brought back with me from Haiti that made me so sick."

Rafa straightened his back and shifted in the chair, and figuring he had to be uncomfortable with me sitting on him so long, I went to get up, but once again he extended his arm over my lap to let me know he wanted me to stay put.

"I know that in the age of technology and your world of yachts and private planes all of this must seem ridiculously primitive, but my only response to that is to ask you to remember how most of the world lives, what little they have access to, and how faith helps them survive even the most horrendous circumstances. For centuries, and even today in desperately poor countries, food, animals and blood are the only things of real value people can offer in exchange for desperately needed help. It's not bloodlust. I can't even begin to tell you the unspeakable things the medical community believed in less than a hundred years ago, but they've modernized, and I intend on doing the same.

"I also don't want it to be a secretive practice anymore, because it doesn't need to be. The days of religious persecution, in the way that it once existed, is no longer a threat, and ignorance only breeds contempt and fear. Santería is just one of many ways to believe in something greater than ourselves and help others. Some people say it's all in the mind, and I don't argue, but I personally believe the people who loved us in life don't just die and disappear as if they never existed. They change forms, but they still want to watch over us and make sure we're safe and happy, just as they did when they were with us, and we should do the same for them. For me, it's a comfort. It means that even if you're alone, someone who loves you is never far away." Glancing up at me with his hypnotic blue eyes, he added, "It also means that we should enjoy physical pleasures while we can. In fact, the *muertos* love to come back every once in a while and—" He stopped abruptly, obviously censoring himself around a friendly but skeptical group. "Well, it's just like your favorite poem, Amada."

My body responded to Rafa again, and horrified at the idea of losing even the slightest bit of composure in front of my brother, I hopped off his lap and asked Kieran what they were doing today. Rafa let me go this time, giving me a little wink as I arranged myself casually beside his chair. After a measured pause, my brother set aside his intellectual curiosity and accepted that the conversation was over for now.

"We're going out on the boat," he said, "and we'd love it if you'd join us."

"Don't you two want to be alone?" I asked. "It's your honeymoon."

"That's right," said Rafa. "Congratulations."

Ken and Kieran beamed as they showed him their rings and insisted we come along.

"Come on," said Ken. "We ordered a ton of food and we'll be back by five or six at the latest. Besides, Kieran says there's four staterooms on board. Plenty of privacy if needed."

"Can't you stay one more day?" I begged. "That way you can come to Rafa's party tonight."

"I wish we could, but it's Ken's son's birthday tomorrow. We can't miss it." Turning to Rafa, Kieran mused, "I have to say, I like talking to you. I do hope you'll spend the day with us."

Kieran and Ken went out back to board the boat while Rafa and I went upstairs and grabbed some essentials. He sat on the bed and called Sandro and several vendors to place orders for tonight's event, and I heard him leave a message for a friend he clearly liked named Sal. I threw in several changes of clothes for each of us, a couple of swimsuits, and our phone chargers. I really couldn't think of anything else, since there was already food, water and linens aboard.

"Sunscreen, sunglasses and a hat, mamita," said Rafa, looking up briefly from his phone call. "You're not baking in the sun again. Dramamine, too, if you have any."

In less than ten minutes we were out back at the dock boarding the *Coy Mistress*. She was a gorgeous seventy-seven foot 2017 Riviera Enclosed Flybridge yacht that my brother had custom ordered. She'd only been delivered a few months ago, but he'd already taken her out several times, and even though the cost to maintain her was ridiculous, Kieran loved her. He ordered the largest yacht the neighborhood association would allow, otherwise he would have had to keep her at the country club marina.

"You named her," said Rafa as we boarded, his hand caressing my behind. "Is your brother driving?"

"No, he pays a professional captain and his crew to maintain her and take us out. You won't even see them on such a short trip. We're just going to Key Largo and back."

"I have no words," he began, as he surveyed the boat. It was utterly decadent, and even I could see that. My brother had exquisite taste in all things, and his new yacht was no exception. On the lowest level, she featured a state of the art engine room and four fully fitted bathrooms and cabins, two with four bunkbeds each, the queen size stateroom, and the king size stateroom. On the main level was a medium sized aft deck, a well-appointed U-shaped gourmet kitchen, one outdoor dining area, one indoor dining area, a living room large enough to entertain a dozen people or more, and a larger forward sundeck, all surrounded by spectacular 360 degree views of the ocean.

A teak spiral staircase led to the third level, the location of a very comfortable bridge with two leather captain's chairs, a seating area for at least six people, another small alfresco aft deck, a small outdoor eating space, and a even a twin bed sized couch beside the control panel in which a captain and a small crew could command the yacht in complete comfort and privacy. All of the floors and woodwork were clear-stained teak throughout, and she boasted the highest quality bourbon-colored quartz counters in the kitchen and all bathrooms. Each bedroom was carpeted and outfitted with the best mattresses and linens money could buy; Kieran had truly spared no expense, and it showed.

I didn't realize how much I would adore the boat, but now I thought that if he eventually decided to take her with him to Los Angeles, I'd have to consider ordering another one for us. I turned my attention back to Rafa, who was completely bowled over, and as he stood outside on the sundeck and gazed out on the glassy, calm waters of the ocean, he reflected, "This is a five million dollar yacht, Amada."

"Let it go," I said, wrapping my arms around him from behind. A brief distance sprang up between us that could only be fixed by the feel of his skin on mine. "Please, let's enjoy each other for one beautiful day without any guilt or sadness."

"You're right," he said, pulling me around and kissing me on the lips. "I'm very lucky to be here with you, and today there's nothing to think about except being together."

CHAPTER TEN

he idea that Amada owned a yacht was strange enough, but it wasn't until I stepped aboard and saw it up close that the hair stood on my arms. The equally spectacular house had been difficult for me to understand, but eventually I came to view it as her security blanket, hard and cold as it was. She'd never known anything different, and to her it was simply home. I'd only seen it in photographs, but I imagined that Boxwood was Amada's own little Versailles, a sanctuary that deconstructed was nothing more than a gilded cage, an island unto itself that kept her away from everything she feared but also everything she most desired. For as long as she wanted me there with her, we'd find the warmth we needed in each other, but the boat was a fantasy come to life, an illusion that only wealth of epic proportions could conjure. It was then I realized Amada and her brother weren't just rich, they were billionaires. It frightened me to my core because I knew she'd never need me for anything, and if she wanted, she could disappear and put endless walls and miles of ocean between us as easily as she could snap her fingers. Even as an old woman, young, handsome men would still want her for what she could give them, while I would have to stand aside, everything I had to offer long gone. My Amada had real power, far more than I, and if she wanted to disappear from my life one day, there wouldn't be a damn thing I could do about it.

Her arms slipped around my waist and her face pressed against my back, a welcome sensation considering I was in a serious panic. I'd never let her know, of course, but seeing this yacht had thrown me off balance again. She would always be richer, more desirable, more intellectual, and more sophisticated, and the day she realized the laughable inequality between us, I might have to suffer a loss I didn't know if I could recover from. She had a dagger pointed right at my heart, and it was too late to do anything about it because I was already incapable of saving myself.

The captain and the two crew members he'd brought along stayed on the upper deck while the four of us lounged on the large forward sundeck. The yacht was traveling at a leisurely speed, allowing us to enjoy a very relaxed, scenic journey, and as the Miami skyline receded in the background, Ken and Amada went to pour the four of us some wine. Kieran jumped at the opportunity to speak to me alone, and I wasn't surprised. I knew it was coming sooner or later.

"Rafa, I already like you more than most people, but I'm suspicious of everybody. I want you to know I'm having you background checked by my team, and if I find any inconsistencies between what you've told my sister and what comes up, we're going to have to address it."

"Do what you have to," I nodded, respecting his instinct to protect his family. "Feel free to ask me anything you want to know." I'd expected as much from a smart man like Kieran, and I couldn't hold it against him, because I'd do the exact same thing in his position.

"Quickly, identify every bone in the hand," he said.

"*Falanges distales, falanges medias, falanges proximales, metacarpianos* and *carpianos*," I said, pointing as I spoke. "Don't bother asking for it English, because I don't know, but most anatomical terms come from Latin, so it's probably similar."

"OK, you passed," he said, a wide grin on his face. "That sounds about right."

"It's right." I said, breathing in the crisp salt air. "Pretty funny."

"I'd think you'd be offended."

"No. I get it. It's just that your sister quizzed me like that, too," I laughed. "You two are very much alike."

"Yeah, people tell us that." He leaned back and closed his eyes, but continued talking. "I bet you've seen some serious shit if you were one of those traveling humanitarian doctors."

"It's bad enough when people become sick due to a lack of food or clean water, but it's really hard to stomach when you see atrocities people commit during war or in the name of religion. I remember my colleague had to sedate me the first time I saw a mass grave. The absolute worst was when I had to care for a woman who was burned alive because she'd been accused of being a witch. She was in agony for four days and then died."

"Goddamn," he said, opening his eyes. "Don't ever tell Amanda about things like that."

"I would *never*."

"Do you know about what happened a few years ago?" he asked.

"It took her a while to share it with me, but yes."

"It was a long, hard road to come back from that, and she almost didn't. Don't ever be cruel to her," said Kieran. "She couldn't take it. Losing her son almost killed her, and it almost killed me to watch her drown in grief. This family is overdue for some happiness."

"Your sister," I said, sitting forward, "is the most beautiful, delicate, precious thing I have ever laid my eyes on, and I'm fully aware she's way out of my league. If anything were to happen, I assure you it would be because she breaks it off. I'm deeply in love, and the only reason I haven't brought up marriage is because of your family's enormous wealth. I don't ever want anyone to think I'm after that."

"Prenup," said Kieran. "Ken signed one." He put his hand out and I took it. "All I want is to protect her. You can understand that, can't you?"

"I wouldn't have it any other way," I said. We were shaking hands just as Ken and Amada returned with four glasses of white wine.

"Hey," said Ken, passing over the chardonnay. "Did we miss anything juicy?"

"White?" asked Kieran, unable to hide his disappointment.

"You'll be fine," said Ken, settling down beside his adoring husband.

"What were you guys talking about?" asked Amada, her sweet face opening up into a big smile. "You're right, Kieran, it is nice watching the people you love spend time together."

We spent the next thirty minutes or so drinking wine and talking about Tokyo and all the other places they'd visited recently.

Unfortunately, I didn't have much to contribute that would be pleasant, so I just listened. In the middle of the conversation, Amada went back into the kitchen and brought out a platter of cold cuts and cheese that she placed in the middle of the table. Absentmindedly, she started feeding me bits of meat like I was her little dog, and I found it so relaxing that after a few bites and nips at her fingers, I laid my head on her lap and shut my eyes. "Are you wearing sunscreen?" I asked groggily.

"Yes, doctor." I was out as soon as they switched back into English, falling asleep to the sound of the ocean waves and the exquisite sensation of her soft fingertips as she softly scratched behind my ears and all over my scalp.

I awoke some time later when I heard Ken say, "by the way, the captain and his crew have signed a very detailed non-disclosure agreement, so feel free to be as uninhibited as you like."

"Yeah, that and the fact that he always brings those two cute crew members with him and never comes down," said Kieran jovially. "I bet they have their own little three-way up there. Doubt he's watching us." I loved the way Amanda's body rocked with laughter.

Ken leaned in close and whispered in English, "We'll be on the back deck, so that means unless you want an eyeful, you stay up front or go down below for a while, *tu comprends?*"

"*Oui,*" she said.

I waited until they'd cleared out to open my eyes and look up at her. She'd put on her hat and sunglasses and looked like she was about to fall asleep herself. Between the cool breeze and the soft motion of the boat, it really was difficult not to just drift off, but there was no way I was going to let her do that again. In fact, I made a mental note to check on Kieran and Ken later in case they fell asleep bare-assed in the sun, too.

"Bed," I said, kissing her thigh.

Two of the bedrooms were very nice but only contained small bunkbeds, however the master suite and junior master were spectacular. She led us to the queen size stateroom and tossed her hat on the couch next to the bag she'd packed for us.

"How long was I asleep?" I asked her, grinding my pelvis into her from behind as we stood beside the bed. I wanted her so badly, but I knew she wouldn't have me yet.

"Almost two hours. I had to go to the bathroom, but I didn't want to wake you. Hold on." She went into the lavatory and shut the door. "I thought you said you rested last night."

"I did," I said, checking out the small but luxuriously appointed cabin. Even the dresser and nightstands were crafted from the same high quality teak found in the public areas of the ship, and the carpet was uncharacteristically thick and soft.

"Rafa?"

"What, sweetheart?"

"Can you go in the bag and get me a—" She paused mid-sentence, so I waited, but she didn't finish.

"A what?" I said, rifling around to see what she might want. I took a box out of the bag and went toward the bathroom. "A tampon?"

"Yes, sorry." Her voice was so uncharacteristically small and awkward that it concerned me.

"You have to stop with that," I sighed, handing it to her.

She didn't answer, and within a few minutes we were on the bed together spooning. As beautiful as it was outside, it was nice to be in the cool shade for a while, and considering the long night we had ahead of us, I didn't feel guilty about taking another little nap. She was completely relaxed in my arms, so I spoke softly in her ear the way I knew she liked.

"Amada, what is it really about?" I was prepared to wait all night for the answer to my question.

"My ex."

Oh, now we had it. "What happened?"

"Brent was one of those men who had to be perfect all the time. He would fluff a throw pillow a certain way, and if he came back into the room and it was different, he'd want to know who messed it up."

"People like that are impossible," I groaned, reminded of a particular roommate.

"Yep. Everything had to be just so. Material things and aesthetics were more important than comfort and people. No one was good enough to sit on his custom made furniture, and if you prepared him a sandwich, he'd find five things wrong with it. According to him, I could never pick out the right clothes for myself, and he wouldn't even hold the baby if he was in a nice suit. He was just cold."

"Sounds like a psychiatric issue," I said, thinking specifically of Narcissistic Personality Disorder.

"He made such a big deal when I had my period. Nothing ever happened and he never saw anything, but he still wouldn't come near me, and by that I mean he literally wouldn't even sleep in the same room. He said it was disgusting, and that any man who claimed otherwise was lying. I've never had anyone kiss me—intimately—until you."

"Amada." I stroked her hair, thinking it one of the saddest things I'd ever heard. "I'm sorry for your sake, but I'll be honest. I'm happy to be the only one."

"Me too," she said, sounding far away, lost in her memories.

"Anything else I should know?"

"No, not really. It was all just a bunch of stupid little things. I remember he also had a thing about seeing my long hair in the bathroom, so he was always trying to get me to cut it off. He was relentless about it, really. At one point I seriously thought he was going to do it while I was sleeping—or worse—so I started locking my door at night."

I was aghast at what she was telling me, because this man truly sounded like some kind of serial killer. "Amada, how did you meet this creep, and why did you put up with it? Was he your first boyfriend?"

"He was Kieran's college buddy. I was only twenty-two and a virgin, and I got pregnant after only having sex with him a couple of times. He had some of those tendencies before, but after the baby he became unbearable. I think he felt like I'd trapped him, but I never asked him for a cent or for marriage or anything else. I only put up with it because of William. I hired a great nanny to watch the baby while I was at school, and we didn't have to struggle at all, so I don't understand why he was so miserable. It could have been wonderful.

I was young, so I thought I had to stay with him, that it would be an unforgivable failure if I didn't."

Once she mentioned her son, I knew it was time to change the subject quickly, but I had to let her know it wasn't her fault. A total misogynist had been putting that toxic garbage in her head for years and she'd never known anything different. No wonder she thought I'd be the same.

"It should have been a wonderful time for you, and I'm sorry that it wasn't. Amada, that behavior is abnormal." She stroked my arm and moved even closer to me, which was the loveliest feeling in the world. I wrapped my body around her and pulled her in as tightly as I could.

"I can assure you that everything about you turns me on to the point where it's physically painful sometimes." I stroked the back of her head and inhaled the scent of her coconut shampoo. "If I saw your hair in the bathroom, I'd start thinking about you naked and it would make me very happy. I love seeing it draped all over my body when we make love, especially when you have me in your mouth—"

She let out a breathy moan, picturing it.

"Yes, baby," I whispered, my voice low. "I love looking down and seeing your lips around me, hair everywhere. It makes me hard. Feel that?"

"I do." She pressed up against me, but instead of her body, this time her mind opened up and she began to recite poetry, a quirk of hers I adored.

She put my arm about her waist,

And made her smooth white shoulder bare,

And all her yellow hair displaced,

And, stooping, made my cheek lie there,

And spread, o'er all, her yellow hair,

Murmuring how she loved me —

"Another favorite, professor? "What's it called?"

"*Porphyria's Lover.*"

"It's beautiful."

"Not quite," she said with a giggle. "He strangles her with her own hair."

"Jesus," I said, shaking off the image. "I never knew poetry could be so dark."

"Like life."

My sweet Amada been lonely for so long that my heart broke for her. I sighed as I rocked us both back and forth and held her tight, loving every last inch of her.

"Do you have your phone there on the table?"

"Yes, why?" she asked, reaching for it.

"Put on some soft music, mamita." She found a 1940s station and turned it down low.

"This OK?"

"Perfect. Sounds like Tommy Dorsey. My grandmother liked him." I instantly relaxed, and so did she.

"I had no idea you liked to fall asleep to music."

"I usually don't," I said.

* * *

It didn't take long before I drifted off and dreamed I was in Cuba at the Hotel Nacional dancing with my Amada to Glen Miller's "Moonlight Serenade." There were at least a hundred couples on the crowded dance floor, but I only had eyes for my Amada, the most beautiful lady of all. She was nothing less than ravishing in her floor length, beaded red dress, and as I spun her around the terrazzo dance floor, she threw her head back and laughed, giddy like a schoolgirl. I reached out and touched her beautiful golden hair, now sculpted into the long, glossy waves of the era.

"Amada, we're here," I said, pulling her toward me. "Look around." I pointed to every exquisite feature of the art deco ballroom, spellbound by it all, from the frosted crystal lighting fixtures, to the carved stucco walls, all the way down to the geometric patterns on the gold lipped coffee cups. "That's *El Malecón*, out there, past the balcony," I said, gesturing toward the ocean. "Look at all the bronze on those elevator doors. Amada, look at the chandelier above us," I exclaimed, unable to contain my excitement. We gazed at the work of art hanging above our heads, a colossal three-tiered structure of concentric circles, wrought iron and etched glass. "We've stepped back in time."

A flash of something familiar caught my eye, and I saw my mother across the room as I remembered her. I tried to get her to look at me, but she wouldn't take her eyes off her partner, a tall, dark man I didn't recognize. She felt distant, so I gave up, but he turned his blue eyes in my direction and blinked. I wondered if it could it be Miguel as a grown man. *No*, said a voice in my head, it was the love of my mother's life, Lázaro, my father.

I turned my attention back to my Amada, who was no longer in my arms but dancing with Kieran beside me. "Stay close," I warned, as she blew me a kiss and let her handsomely dressed brother guide her across the floor. In her place, I found myself dancing with a new partner.

"Dr. De Leon," said the girl, a young, lithe woman with white skin and eyes of pure carbon. "Do you remember me?" While she seemed familiar, I couldn't place her right away. She couldn't have been older than twenty-one but had a very mature presence that was in direct contrast to her coquettish expression. I noticed that she was blushing, only one of many charming things about her.

"I'm sure we've met before," I said, as I gave her a little turn and caught her again. "Give me a hint. I certainly remember your beautiful eyes."

"You attended a performance of *Les Sylphides* at the University of Caracas and cared for me when I broke my ankle." She turned her head to the side and smiled, as if recalling a pleasant memory.

"Yes, you're the ballerina!" The night we'd met she'd been in full costume and makeup, an ethereal vision in white. She'd looked so different for her performance, but her eyes and voice were exactly the same. "You had such a pretty name."

"When I fell, they called for a doctor and you came back stage. You were so dashing in your dark suit and tie. You asked my name and told me you knew it hurt, but that it would be better soon. Someone brought you scissors and you cut off my slipper and stocking, and then you told them I had to go to the hospital. I cried because I wanted to keep dancing, but you said "No, Filomena. Tonight is our night.'"

"Of course I remember now. I spoke to your father over the telephone, and then we went to the hospital together."

"Yes, and your girlfriend said you shouldn't go, but you took me anyway. You waited with me until my family arrived."

"That's right," I said, the memories of that night rushing back. "It was only a couple of blocks away, but we had to go in a cab because you couldn't stand."

"You carried me all the way into the hospital, and everyone stared at us. It was so romantic." She blushed again, unable to look me in the eye. "I kept the handkerchief you gave me for years. I never did find a man who could compare to you."

"You were a vision," I said, remembering the crown of feathers in her hair. "What are you doing here?"

"I've been waiting to dance with you for a long time, Dr. De Leon," she said, expertly following my lead, "and now I can."

"Are you dead?" I asked. *Eres una muerta?*

"Yes," she said matter of factly. "I starved to death."

"What happened?" I asked, shocked. "Your father was rich. He offered me money."

"Oh, nothing like that. I did it to myself." She gave a little quickstep as we passed Kieran and Amada again, who gave me a look that let me know she was ready to go. "This ballroom is divine."

"You're a wonderful dancer, Filomena."

"Listen carefully, Dr. De Leon," she said, suddenly somber and unsmiling. "Tonight you'll have a visitor named Achille. He'll come to you as a friend, but he's a bad man desperate for you to stay out of his way. Achille is vain, so he won't like you from the moment he sees you. Keep in mind that his deepest desire is to make his father proud, and this is what motivates him to seek money and power by any means necessary. Achille's black magic is strong because his *muertos* are unhappy troublemakers, but he has no love."

Somehow I knew she wanted me to give her another twirl and a low dip, so I complied, marveling at how her graceful dancers' body arched perfectly over my arm. As she came back up in one elegant, sweeping motion, she added, "Keep your men and your woman close to you because there will be chaos. Fidel sold his soul, you know, and now the Devil is coming back to collect."

"You want to protect me," I said, moved by her generosity. "What sort of gifts will please you?" Again, she blushed before she made her request. Instinctively I realized she'd died a virgin, or perhaps it was more likely she communicated it to me in some unspoken way.

"It makes me happy when you come and dance with me, and I especially like to see you in a suit and tie, just like that night," she said, bashfully fingering the lapel of the tuxedo I had only just realized I was wearing. "I'm not your madrina and we're not related by blood, so remember that I can only speak to you in your dreams, but I'll be watching over you. In fact, it's one of my favorite things to do," she said with a giggle.

"I'm honored," I said with a bow, as the dance ended. "Thank you."

"Remember, Dr. De Leon," she said, fading away into the crowd, "love is everything."

* * *

Amada and I got up just as the boat was pulling into the dock behind Boxwood, arriving just before six as promised. I emerged from sleep lucid and clear-headed, my vision nothing like the chaotic, disordered dreams typical of the subconscious when it does nothing more than express its countless anxieties and desires. It was more like a deep meditative state, tangible and real. Doña Delfina had told me to expect almost all of my spirit guides or *muertos* to come to me in a dream or in a waking dream-like state, and to always pay attention to what they were saying, no matter how confused I might become. She'd prepared me well, explaining that I could only hear her voice in my ear, as she'd been the closest to me in life as my madrina. It might not sound like her, but she was the only one who could speak to me that way at any time, and I would know it was her.

We were lucky that we'd had time together, because it had allowed us to make plans for the future. It gave me great satisfaction to know I had her blessing and that she approved of everything I was going to do. For that, as well as everything else she had been to me in life, I'd be forever in her debt. She said someone special had been her madrina, and she expected me to follow tradition and take on a godchild or *ahijado* when the time was right. She'd laughed that she'd lived to be so old because it took that long for me to find my way to her. We'd talked about so many things on her deathbed that when Amada came in to Doña Delfina's bedroom, I still had very little sense of time and place. However, that night I emerged a changed man with a greater sense of purpose than I'd ever felt in my life, and Amada was the most significant part of it.

Amada turned to face me in the bed and stroked my hair. "We slept all afternoon, handsome." Her green eyes were wide and bright, full of life, and I was overcome with such emotion in that particular moment that all I wanted was to be inside her, but I kept my promise.

"We did, but you'll be glad later," I said. "It's going to be a late night."

"What did you dream? You were smiling."

"I dreamed I was in Cuba, dancing with you. My mother and my father were there, too." I'd tell her about Filomena later, at the right time and in the right context. I was excited to have met a spirit guide, but I didn't want Amada to think I was dreaming about other women.

"That sounds lovely," she said. "Maybe one day soon we can."

We disembarked easily, and while Kieran and Ken rushed upstairs to pack up, I stayed downstairs and made another pot of coffee. As I stood at the counter, I looked out across the grounds to the gargantuan vessel that was nothing more than a toy to Amada and her brother, and I marveled at the absurdity of stepping off a yacht and walking a hundred yards to the back door of the house. I thought of the brave men and women who crossed the Florida straits in little more than a floating tin can, fighting for their lives and their children's lives, sometimes only to be turned back to face a punishment worse than death. If anything was a dream, it had to be this life. Nothing made any sense, and nothing was fair. It was, without a doubt, the luck of the draw.

"More?" asked Amada, rousing me out of my thoughts as she passed through the kitchen to the back stairs. "I couldn't have any this late. Won't it keep you up?" As I appreciated her exceptionally tight backside, it took a moment to realize she meant the coffee.

"In this case," I said, removing the pot from the stove, "that wouldn't be a bad thing, but no." She grabbed the handrail and tried to lug the big bag upstairs, but it was easily half her bodyweight. It was cute how she tried to drag it up behind her. "Leave it there, mamita. I'll bring it up in a minute."

I poured myself a cup and sipped the sweet, dark brew, sighing with pleasure. Nothing smelled or tasted quite like Cuban coffee. "I drink it all day, even late at night. My mother used to put *cafe con leche* in my baby bottle," I said absently.

"You're kidding," she said, now halfway up the stairs, pulling her top off to reveal a barely there pink bra.

"No, I'm not. The taste of coffee is my earliest memory."

I watched her petite, shapely legs take each step gracefully, amazed by how something so simple could turn me on beyond comprehension, excited simply by how her perfect calf muscles flexed with each movement.

"Amada, I want those sexy legs around my neck," I said, taking another sip. She responded to something in my tone and in return teased me by unhooking the back of her bra and wiggling out of it. It was a lovely sight, but then I remembered we weren't alone. I put the cup back in the saucer and cocked my head to the side. "What are you doing? They're still here. Cover up."

"I don't think so," she said, and let the bra drop, giving me only the briefest glimpse of her bare breasts as she disappeared out of view. "Why don't you come make me?"

I don't remember going up the stairs, but I must have taken the steps three at a time because in a split second I was rounding the corner into our bedroom. She had stripped down to her lacy pink G-string and stood at the big bay window watching as the crew unloaded the boat. I came up behind her, pushed her long hair aside and rubbed her shoulders.

"What, mamita?" I whispered. I knew she wanted me, but I wasn't sure what she would allow me to do. Normally I would have just acted on instinct, which was to bend her over and take her right here, but after what she'd shared, I didn't want to push.

"I don't know," she whimpered, placing her palms on the glass and arching her back.

"I do," I said, deepening my strokes. I focused on the area between her shoulder blades where women tend to carry tension, and she moaned with pleasure. "Your mind says no, but your body says yes. You're uncomfortable."

"Yes," she moaned, dropping her head down.

"You know, it's a blessing and a curse to be so attracted to each other." I began to nuzzle her back and then stopped, reasoning that it wasn't the best idea. "I can already tell that when we can't be together, it's going to be hell."

"Don't stop," she whispered.

"Amada," I said, resuming my massage. "There's foreplay and then there's torture." I laughed, but I meant it. "We should just wait until we can do everything we want to do." Obviously this little hang-up of hers wouldn't last much longer, but the decision had to come from her. There was just no way we could stay away from one another so long.

"Do something, please." She leaned her head back on my shoulder and brought my hands to her breasts. I massaged the muscles just above, then let my right hand glide down her abdomen to the swell of her belly. Predictably, her body stiffened.

"How about if I just touch you over the fabric?" I murmured in her ear, gently grazing her clitoris. "Nowhere else."

"Yes," she hummed, responding to my touch. "I need you."

"Sit," I said, and went down to the floor with her. I spread my legs and let her nestle into me, so that she leaned against my chest as we both faced the open window. I took off my shirt so that I could enjoy the feel of her skin on mine.

"You can relax," I said, placing a hand on her knee. "I know where you want me to stop." She rested her legs against mine, a shift in position that allowed me to stroke the inside of her thigh with my left hand and slowly touch her with my right. I began to make love to her with my two fingers, steadily bringing them up, down and around her most sensitive spot.

"Mm, Rafa, that's perfect." Her excitement surged, which always gave me enormous pleasure.

"Let me see if you're being truthful." I placed my left hand over the middle of her chest, reveling in every flutter of excitement as I continued to lightly scratch and tease between her legs. "You are. Your heart is racing."

"Harder," she begged, grabbing my knees.

"That won't help." Keeping the same rhythm, I lewdly licked the nape of her neck and shifted to the other side, feeling my erection stiffen between us both. "What you want is for me to crush you with my weight and suffocate you with deep, rough kisses, so that we both lose every last bit of control." I nipped at her skin, flattening my tongue as I glided my mouth slowly across her shoulder to the top of her arm. She shivered, mumbling something incoherent. "I'm right, aren't I?"

"Oh yes," she gasped, as I continued to tease her with both hands. I cupped her breast and used the same feather-light touch on her nipple, and by the way her breathing changed I thought she might be close, but it was hard to tell without being able to feel her from the inside.

"You'll have a little orgasm for me now, but just to hold you over until you let me give you a deep one. The kind that comes from here." I put my hand on her abdomen and thought about how good it would feel to finally empty myself inside her, then moved it up to her neck and squeezed just a bit, seeking to dominate her any way I could. She parted her lips and took two of my fingers in her mouth, sucking and biting, leaning forward as she whimpered.

I knew she was close when she put her hands on the outside of my thighs and began to squeeze, digging her nails into my skin. It was inexplicable, but I loved when she bit me, and I would have never allowed any other woman to do it, but I relished it with my Amada. It made me crazy to know she wanted me that much, so I took my fingers out of her mouth, gently brought her face to mine and kissed her.

"Amada," I said, completely lost in her flesh. "I love you. We're meant to be, and I knew it the second I laid eyes on you. I would do anything for you." I don't know if it was because of my words or our kiss, but as she looked over her shoulder and met my eyes, I knew something had changed. All her inhibitions fell away and in their place was nothing but appetite and longing.

"Rafa, I can't be near you and not—" She turned around and put her legs over mine. Wrapping her arms around my neck, she pressed against me and kissed me softly, as only she could. I responded, our bodies in perfect sync, demanding one another with an intensity that bordered on insanity. This woman could absolutely make me mad, cause me to make terrible decisions, ruin me. I knew then that nothing had meaning unless she was there to define it. I took her by the hips and pulled her into me, no longer thinking rationally, only feeling.

"I want you so much I'm in agony," I said. "But I was wrong. With you, torture is better than nothing. I would stay like this forever if it was the only way to have you."

"Rafa—" she said, wrapping herself around me and lifting herself onto my pelvis. All of her softness was on top of me now, and it was only then that I realized that my hands had gone under her panties and pushed the scrap of fabric separating us halfway down.

"Sorry, I didn't mean to," I said with a sigh, pulling her underwear back up.

"Do it," she said, arching so that I could slip them off.

I knew that she had to be just as turned on as I was, if not more, but I still couldn't help but feel that proceeding would be taking advantage of her. She'd clearly stated what she wanted earlier, and this was not it. We were as high off one another as if we'd taken a drug, and she wasn't thinking clearly. I barely had the willpower to stop, but I wouldn't allow her to look back on anything between us with regret.

"No, Amada, if you want me now, you do it," I said, finding her eyes. "You have to be comfortable."

She sat back and pulled her legs into her body, rising gracefully using my shoulders to steady herself. She took a step back and stood above me with a look of love in her eyes that was at once hypnotic and compelling. There was no way any man in this world could look at her and not want her desperately. It just wasn't possible. I wanted to encourage her, but instead I leaned back on my elbows and waited patiently to see what she would do next. I really thought she was ready, but to my surprise she closed her eyes, took a deep breath and said, "I can't. It feels so wrong to be apart from you, but something won't let me."

I stood up and resolved that if it was the last thing I did, I was going to erase those terrible memories from her mind. I put my hand on her neck and worked my fingers into her hair, giving it a slight tug at the nape as she moaned with pleasure. I kissed her and whispered in her ear. "Don't worry."

I took her hand and led her to the full length mirror in the bathroom, positioning her in front of myself, and as we looked at our reflection, I said, "You are the most beautiful woman I've ever seen, Amada." I took her hands in mine and placed them on her belly, rubbing her hands and forearms as I spoke. "Your face is feminine and sweet, but you're so sophisticated that sometimes I'm afraid I'll say the wrong thing and sound like a *guajiro*. Do you know what that is?"

"No, handsome," she said, relaxing.

"It what they call a Cuban man from the countryside. In English, you might say 'hillbilly.'"

"You're a highly educated man, Rafa. You're far from a hillbilly."

"Compared to you, I am. I don't know much about the civilized world. Now that I'm in a new country, I have to relearn almost everything, but who I am and where I come from will never change." I decided to share something very intimate, to show her that I was willing to reveal my vulnerabilities as well.

"I know you speak to me in Spanish so I don't feel stupid." Her mouth dropped and she tried to turn to me, but I wouldn't let her.

"Don't argue," I commanded, letting go of her hands. I took a chance and slipped my own just under the waistband of her underwear, going no further. "I worship you," I said, rubbing her hips. "I love how you look when you're in a beautiful gown, hair up, looking at every man in the room like they're beneath you, because they are, and trust me, they all know it. I've told you before that you scare men to death." I took her hair and twisted it up off her neck.

"Not you," she said.

"I was willing to risk complete humiliation. I had to try, because I knew you were special," I said, letting her hair fall around her shoulders. I heard her breath hitch as I brought my hands to the spot just above her pubic bone and stroked her skin, softly at first, then harder.

"When you didn't reject me, I thought, I have to give this woman the best night of her life, because it's all I have to offer."

"Oh, it was the best night ever," she murmured. "But you're so much more."

"I want you to understand your value, Amada. What he said wasn't true, it was just a way of taking away your power, and he could have degraded you a million different ways, but that just happened to be what he chose. He made you feel badly about yourself to control you. It's textbook narcissism, and if he ever crosses my path, I'll make him get on his knees and apologize. I swear I will." That got a smile out of her, and I gladly returned it. What I wouldn't give to get my hands on that little prick.

"I love you," she said.

"This body, these perfect curves, they're every man's dream. Look at yourself." She did, then watched with interest as I brought my finger to my mouth, licked it, and very slowly brought it back down under her panties. If she objected, she had plenty of time to let me know, but she said nothing.

"This is my job," I whispered into her ear as I began to stroke her again. "I can't let you out of the house like this." Without the fabric between us I was able to fully manipulate her so that she was on the edge in less than a minute. "It's too dangerous. Other men will sense you're unsatisfied, and we can't have that."

"How?" she asked breathlessly.

"We just know," I said rubbing harder, as she reached back to grab my hair and squirmed against my hard on. "It's in the way a woman walks and how much she touches herself. We can sense it a mile away, and we're drawn to it." She sighed and trembled in my arms, and just as I was anticipating watching every detail of her face as she came under the bright lights of the bathroom mirror, a knock came at the door. Although I didn't stop what I was doing, she went still and listened.

"Amanda, honey bunch," came Ken's voice through the door, in English, which caused me to tune him out. "I'm so sorry, but the bags are in the car and we're heading out now. You don't have to come out, but we can't miss that flight. I'll talk to you soon."

"Ken, wait," she called. "I have to say goodbye," she whispered apologetically. "I don't know when I'll see my brother again."

I arched my brows at her in the mirror, and when she nodded, I reluctantly let go. As she threw her robe on and went to door, I unzipped my shorts to give myself some much needed breathing room. "Keep in mind we won't have a minute to ourselves until tomorrow."

"Are you sure we can't finish up after they leave?" she said with a little pout as she stood in the center of the bedroom, looking every bit the seductress.

It was difficult to say no to her when she looked at me like that, but in this case, I had to. "No, mamita, tonight of all nights we cannot be late," I said, adjusting myself. "I also need to pick up a suit on the way."

"I'll help you with that. What do you want me to wear?" she asked, her hand on the doorknob.

"Anything you want, except tonight it can't be black." I reluctantly leaned against the doorway, somehow already exhausted despite the plentiful amount of sleep I'd had. Perhaps it was the tremendous sense of responsibility I felt toward Doña Delfina's legacy, the people who worked for her and the people who needed her help. But at the core of everything was Amada and my instinctive need to keep her safe and happy no matter what.

"Do me a favor, though," I added. "Don't look too good, or you might kill me." I meant it. My love and my desire for her was so strong that I feared one day it might be my undoing.

CHAPTER ELEVEN

I called my personal shopper at Saks and had her team pull about a dozen ready to wear suits for Rafa, and when we arrived at 7:30, a wide selection of suits, shirts, ties and shoes had been laid out for us in a dressing room. By 8:15 we had Rafa in the one I liked best, plus another five suits in the back of my Ferrari.

"I love this color on you, handsome," I said, stroking his thigh as he drove us to the restaurant. Rafa looked good in anything, but he really could wear the hell out of a high end suit. I'd gone right for a navy blue Tom Ford, but when he went to try it on, I made him promise he wouldn't look at the price until we made our choices. He'd stepped out of the dressing room wearing the vest, but we both agreed it looked phenomenal without it. Three piece suits, in my opinion, were for old men, and I explained to Rafa he should avoid them. Deferring to me about anything related to clothing, he allowed me to dress him however I liked. I knew he loved my taste, even if he took issue with the exorbitant cost on principle.

It was no surprise that I caught a couple of women gawking at Rafa from across the store, and I resigned myself to the fact that this would never change, and I'd better get used to it. However, if my personal shopper Laura had similar feelings, she knew better than to make it obvious. My business was far too valuable to her bottom line to be anything less than professional, and I appreciated it. I had her put six Tom Ford suits on my account to the tune of thirty-five thousand dollars, a sum which I was able to keep from Rafa until we got in the car. I told him it would be faster to let them bill my account, and then he could reimburse me. He was so preoccupied with tonight's event he let me handle everything and didn't ask too many questions until we got in the car.

I particularly liked the navy suit because it perfectly comple-mented his eyes as well my vintage Halston, a long sleeved, V-neck crimson gown with a tasteful front slit. I'd gone into my special closet specifically looking for something with covered shoulders, and though it was demure enough to wear to a serious event, I knew Rafa would like the color and body-conscious fabric. I put my hair up the way he liked and chose a crimson lipstick in the exact shade of the dress. Paired with my 18K gold and diamond Rolex and teardrop diamond earrings, I hoped I would make a good impression on his behalf. As usual, Rafa could barely take his eyes off me.

"Amada, I told you not to look too good, but you didn't listen." His hungry eyes traveled from my gold stiletto sandals all the way up to my red lips. "I'll spend all my time keeping the men away from you." It wasn't just a compliment because I could hear the trace of anxiety in his voice. He was genuinely worried about other men, oblivious to the fact that no one could ever capture my attention the way he had.

"Don't be silly," I said. "Oh, I almost forgot. I brought this for you to wear tonight, until you get a chance to buy your own." I reached in the back seat and grabbed the large black box out from under one of the bags. "It was my father's watch." I took it out and handed it to Rafa. "I'd love to give it to you, but I know you'd never accept it," I said wistfully. Without a word, Rafa held out his left wrist and let me snap the 18K gold Presidential Rolex in place. It fit him perfectly, and I must have been smiling because I saw that he was beaming back.

"I'm honored to wear your father's watch tonight, Amada. Thank you," he said. He stared at me a minute, then focused on the road as the city lights flickered along the angles of his face.

"Amada, I don't want your money to come between us. It scares me." I waited for more, but that was it.

"Why would it?"

"Please don't take this the wrong way, but it's obscene. The cars. The yacht. Amada, your house is a castle. If we stay there, you're going to have to at least let me pay for the monthly expenses, but I was thinking that now I can buy a normal-sized house in Little Havana for us. I'll miss the water, but it'd be so much more manageable. What do you think?" he asked, eyes still on the road.

It felt like he'd overturned a cold bucket of water on me. A lump started to form in my throat, and I was about to launch into a series of questions and protests when something came over me and I went with a different tack.

"I don't," I said in English, pissed.

"What do you mean?" he asked. His blue eyes finally turned and burned into me, demanding clarification.

"Look," I continued in English, "you've got bigger things to think about, so I'll keep this short and sweet: get over it." I uncrossed and crossed my legs as I turned my body in the direction of the passenger window. The cityscape was alive with color and light, our home a truly unique place without equal. "This is Miami. You're going to be dealing with very rich people, and please don't take this the wrong way, as you say, but you'll need to look like them to get any respect. Right or wrong, that's how it works here. You're not a waiter, you're not a missionary, you're a high-profile businessman in a world-class city. Just get off your moral high horse, buy what I tell you to buy, and then focus on your business."

I saw his jaw drop in the reflection of the glass and had to suppress a grin. I knew it sounded harsh, but it was for his own good. "You'll thank me later when you walk in that restaurant and see what everyone's wearing. A Rolex to that crowd is nothing; all those powerful Cubans and their wives have been here for years and dress like heads of state. You'll see. By the way, our beautiful house is in a trust that pays for everything, I never see a bill, ever, so I'm not leaving, and neither are you. When you start entertaining business associates, you'll appreciate it more."

"Holy shit. What in the hell has gotten into you? Why are you speaking to me like that? And in English!" He was without a doubt shocked at my brutal honesty, and I didn't know why I had the urge to be so bitchy, but I was tired of having to apologize for my money all the time. It was becoming tiresome, and it was as unfair as expecting him to apologize for having been poor.

"English is easier." I shot him a look. "By the way, the suits were five thousand each," I added, as I picked a piece of imaginary lint off my dress. "I'd like to give them to you as a gift, but I'm sure you'd just give them back like everything else, which honestly is getting a little old. As far as the car, use the Ferrari as long as you want, or if it's more your style, go buy a used pickup truck or call an Uber. Whatever. I'm tired of all this accounting."

"Are you kidding me?" he said, fuming. "Spoiled rotten is not even the word. Delusional is more like it." He turned into the parking lot of The Copper Crown, which as I predicted was full of Mercedes and Bentleys, not to mention an army of personal security teams. "Well, if we're going to be this blunt with each other, then I should confess that you're making me reconsider how tolerant I've been of your anxieties as well. In fact, my patience has suddenly run out." He put the car in park and turned my face toward him, his ice blue eyes on fire. "Look at me. No more bullshit. This morning when I get home, I expect to find you waiting for me naked in bed, and then I'm going to do whatever I please regardless of what's going on under that dress."

"We'll see if I feel like it," I quipped, as the valet opened my door. The truth was that as always, I was extremely turned on, but tonight I didn't want him to know.

"You will," he said under his breath, offering his arm to me like a complete gentleman and smiling for the cameras.

Even the parking lot full of luxury cars and photographers didn't prepare us for the opulent crowd inside. As I predicted, the most important people in Miami were in attendance and they were of course dressed to the nines. The club was now a sea of exotic flowers, luxurious textiles and shimmering lights, and in addition to the many of the people I'd already met, Rafa introduced me to an endless procession of local celebrities, athletes and politicians. One mega-famous singer had in fact taken over the VIP area, holding court behind a wall of personal security. Sandro met us at the door and followed us as we spent at least thirty minutes greeting people on our way to the back of the club for the sit-down dinner.

"Were all of these people Doña Delfina's personal friends?" I leaned into his ear but still had to raise my voice so that he could hear me over the crowd and orchestra.

"Yes," he said. "Every single person here has been a client or dear friend for many years." He squeezed my hand and pointed to the big screen at the stage. Pictures of Doña Delfina at every stage of her life scrolled across the monitor, including images of her with the rich and famous from all walks of life.

"What exactly did she do for them?" I wasn't sure I wanted to know the details, but it was impossible not to be curious. She clearly had been very loved and respected.

"She offered them guidance and protection."

Rafa continued walking ahead and I followed behind until we reached our table at the front. Women shot Rafa subtle and sometimes not so subtle glances as we passed by, which was more because he looked like a Tom Ford model than because he was the host. I'd chosen the perfect label for Rafa, an intelligent designer for an intelligent man.

The eighteen piece Cuban orchestra lit up the back wall, but instead of the usual lively music I recognized, it was something more somber. "I like this music, Rafa. What is it?"

"I think it's from *Buena Vista Social Club*. It was her favorite. Nice isn't it?" Seeing him emotional again, I regretted the things I'd said in the car, but before I could apologize, several people swooped in to shake his hand. He introduced me to everyone as his girlfriend, which for many people was an unexpected surprise.

"Amada, have a seat," said Rafa, motioning to an empty chair. "I have to give a little speech and then I'll be right back." Like everything else in the space, the table setting was gorgeous. I feasted on every detail, from the abundant flower arrangements to the floating candles, but the place settings took my breath away. Rafa had chosen one of my favorite patterns, Lenox British Colonial Tradewinds, a Robin egg blue and gold fine bone china featuring a high seas nautical theme of palm trees and antique sailing ships.

Before he left, he greeted and then introduced me to the three women already seated at the table drinking *mojitos*, Lidia, Raquel, and Silvia. Lidia and Raquel were married to Oscar Garcia and Carlos Betancourt, whom I'd met playing cards, and Silvia, he explained, was married to Dr. Rogelio Machado, the Chief of Staff at Miami's most prestigious teaching hospital. They all stood and gave me a big hug and kiss on the cheek, which in my circles was strange, but I knew that among Latins a kiss on the cheek was a typical greeting. All of the women were distinguished and very friendly, accepting me as part of the group right away. Lidia, with her jet black hair and perfectly arched eyebrows reminded me of old Hollywood glamour. Like the other two, she was talkative and not at all embarrassed to ask questions.

"It's so nice to finally meet you. There's been a lot of talk about Rafa's new girlfriend," Lidia said in English, finishing her *mojito*. She raised two fingers in the air in the direction of a waiter.

"There has?" I asked. "I hope people are saying nice things!"

"Yes, definitely," said Raquel, Carlos' wife. The exact opposite of Lidia, Raquel had a sweet, motherly demeanor I instantly liked. "Everyone is just so curious about who finally caught his eye. Let's just say the women are not shy about pursuing him."

"Oh." My insecurities reared up again as I pictured all the young, beautiful women who would be flirting with Rafa every day. It must have been obvious what I was thinking.

"Raquel!" snapped Lidia, raising her eyebrows at her friend. "Look what you did."

"Sweetie, I'm so sorry!" Raquel leaned forward and scrambled to find the right words. "I just meant that he has a lot of options, and he chose you, so you must be very special to him."

"Are you kidding? *A lot of options?*" Lidia gave her the side-eye, which made me laugh. "Don't listen to Raquel. She literally has no tact. The other day she told me I gained weight, *but it looked good.*" Lidia made some kind of guttural sound that couldn't be mistaken for anything but absolute disgust.

"It's true," giggled Raquel good-naturedly. "I'm always putting my foot in my mouth!"

"Well, even though he's calling you his girlfriend, he's going out of his way to introduce you to everyone with the same respect you give your wife, so that's very telling," said Silvia. "He obviously wants everyone to know you're practically married and therefore very taken. Typical possessive Cuban man. He's so handsome, Amanda. You won the lottery." *Te ganaste la loteria.* Lidia and Raquel exchanged a glance that suggested Rafa's good looks had been the topic of conversation more than once.

All three women spoke perfect English, but occasionally they threw in a little bit of Spanish here and there, especially when making a joke. They asked lots of questions about me, and I learned that Lidia and the petite, lively Raquel both lived in Coral Gables, while Silvia spent most of her time with her daughter and grandchildren in New York City. We had a great time chatting and I thought it would be nice to invite them and their husbands over for drinks this weekend, so we exchanged numbers and resolved to meet up on Friday.

As the waiter brought Lidia's *mojito* over and set the other one down in front of me, the orchestra finished their song. The band leader briefly introduced Rafa as the godson of Doña Delfina, Dr. Rafael De Leon, and he was welcomed in the form of a standing ovation. I was thoroughly impressed by his poise in front of the expectant crowd, completely in command of the space and everyone in it. The suit I'd chosen for him was impeccable and complemented his chiseled features perfectly, which made me think about how wonderful he'd look in something custom. I made a mental note to order a few made to measure suits and a tux directly from Tom Ford soon. And hide the receipt.

"I'd like to thank all of you for coming here tonight in honor of Doña Delfina Beatríz Ramirez," began Rafa. He was a charismatic public speaker, looking out over the audience as he spoke evenly and confidently about Doña Delfina's life and many accomplishments, not the least of which was funding several orphanages in Miami and rural Cuba, as well as an artists' enclave in Little Havana.

"As you all know, Doña Delfina was a great believer in her people, and in enriching the human experience through art, brotherhood and love. At her insistence, tonight must be a happy occasion, a celebration of her life. Many of you will take the stage later to share your good memories, but before I leave you tonight, I want everyone to rest assured that I will honor her legacy exactly as she wished. We discussed at length what my responsibilities to our community would be, and with her blessing I will carry on her work, modernizing in accordance with twenty-first century medicine and technology. We will continue to fund important humanitarian and cultural endeavors, and most importantly, it is my goal to bring our spiritual beliefs out of the shadows, where ignorance and fear only breed contempt. I will openly promote and educate others about our highly ethical and moral practices, which we all know is so inexorably tied to our very distinguished Cuban heritage, both here and there. As Cubans we've had to be very strong the last half-century, and it's now time for unification. We are one, and it is our duty to ensure that our nation and people flourish culturally, economically, and politically. During this vulnerable time in transition, we must protect ourselves from those who would use us and do us harm for their own gain." The crowd began to make noise, but he continued. "It is time for us not only to rejoin the world, but also to make important contributions to humanity in every field. This is our Renaissance." The room went wild, erupting in a long series of cheers, and Rafa waited patiently until he could continue.

"After our evening comes to a close, The Copper Crown will close for refurbishments and reopen in two weeks as *Madrina's*, in honor of our beloved Doña Delfina. We will continue to be open to the public as an upscale nightclub featuring live music and five star Cuban cuisine, but for the first time, we will also offer a members-only cigar room and salon that I know you will enjoy. I look forward to seeing you all at the grand opening. Finally, before dinner is served and we welcome The Honorable Oscar García to the stage, I want to let you know that we have a very special surprise for you around 11:30." Rafa paused and stepped back from the microphone for a moment, cleared his throat and then continued, his voice laced with emotion. "You'll know soon why it's a historic night for many reasons, and I'm overjoyed to be able to share it here with you, among my cherished brothers and sisters. Thank you."

The crowd gave Rafa a standing ovation, and if our table hadn't been so close to the front, I don't think he would have been able to get through the crowd for quite a while. Everyone was buzzing with excitement, not only because of Rafa's inspirational speech, but also because of the surprise he'd promised. After a few minutes of accepting more congratulations and endless pats on the back, he found his way to our table. He stood next to me behind an empty chair and put his hand on the back of my neck, but he didn't sit down.

"You were fantastic, Rafa," I said. I motioned for him to lean in close. "I don't know what got into me in the car. I'm so sorry."

"I'm sorry, too," he said, giving me a peck on the lips. Coming closer, he surreptitiously flicked my ear with his tongue and whispered, "But we still have a date later." I nodded, thinking I'd love nothing more.

Soon, Carlos and Oscar found their way back to the table and greeted us with enthusiasm. Unfortunately, Silvia's husband, whom I'd been looking forward to meeting, was on call at the hospital all night and sent his regards. We chatted a while, but the men refused to sit down and instead insisted on a pit stop at the bar before going back to working the room with Rafa in tow.

"Stay together," said Rafa, as they disappeared into the crowd. "Sandro is right over there." He pointed in the direction of the nearby bar where Sandro occupied two full spaces. Everyone else was crammed in elbow to elbow, but no one dared invade Sandro's space. Already looking in our direction, he pulled the cigar out of his mouth and made a hand gesture that loosely resembled a salute.

Shortly after the men left, dinner was served. Lidia said not to expect them back for a while, as they would be having fun gossiping with all their friends.

"They're worse than we are."

We went ahead and started dinner just the four of us, an elevated Cuban menu of steak and onion, sweet plantains called *maduros*, and a mix of black beans and rice I think they called *moros*.

"Mm, this is good," said Lidia, enjoying the beans and rice. "They definitely added sugar. I put it in mine."

"You have to," said Silvia.

"You know that trick, right?" said Lidia to me, asking the question in a way that people do when they think they already know the answer.

"I don't cook," I admitted.

"Cuban food or any food?" said Lidia, setting down her fork.

"Any food."

"Really?" she said, looking at the other two women knowingly.

"Sweetie, even if you have a career and can afford a chef, you have to cook for your husband. These old school Cubans expect it and act like little babies if you don't feed them all day long. Even if you hate it, you *have* to. To them, it's love."

"He says he doesn't care," I protested.

"You have so much to learn. He cares." Lidia pointed her fork at me.

"Has he made any 'funny' remarks about you not cooking?' asked Silvia.

"Well, he called me Julia Child one day and told me to get a Keurig so that I can make his coffee." They all rolled their eyes and erupted in laughter.

"I'm sorry, but he's not joking. We'll get you some cooking lessons, and you'll pick it up in no time," said Silvia. They conferred for a minute amongst each other, trying to figure out whose mother or grandmother could come over and teach me. Maybe they'd call a Cuban chef, they said, but then rejected the idea because it wouldn't feel like home cooking. "If you want to keep him fat and happy at home," continued Silvia, "that's the way it is. Cuban men make wonderful husbands. They're very devoted, very passionate, but they require a lot of babying, like lapdogs. We call that being *ñoño*. Rafa is no different, trust me. He's young, but he just got here. Deep down, he still thinks the old fashioned way."

"Don't make *him* too fat, though," said Raquel, without thinking. "That would be a damn shame."

"Easy, tiger," said Silvia. "He's her man now."

"Sorry, Amanda, I would never say that in front of Carlos, but I do still have eyes!" We all had to laugh at her honesty, especially me, because she was obviously incapable of not blurting out the first thing that came to her mind. I imagined it could be annoying, but on the other hand, Raquel was the type who could be trusted.

"Take our advice," said Lidia, "and learn to cook before some little flirt starts bringing him food at work." She put her fork down and crossed her arms defensively, which made me wonder if something like this hadn't happened to her already.

"*Ay*, Lidia," laughed Raquel. "That's exactly what my mother used to say." She lowered her voice and looked around, as if she was about to the say the worst thing in the world. "Except she would say *puta*." They erupted in fits of giggles, but I didn't get the joke.

"Well, we just met her," said Lidia, gesturing toward me. "I don't want her to get the wrong idea about us, but that's what I meant!" Whispering, she put her hand beside her mouth and explained, "*Puta* means whore."

These three, especially Lidia and Raquel, were a complete hoot. Though they were a few years older than me, Lidia and Raquel were still quite a bit younger than Oscar and Carlos, so I wondered if they were second wives. Regardless, they were hilarious and lively, and they definitely could give me some much needed insight into Rafa's cultural quirks. I loved being around people with a great sense of humor, and it was clear this group liked to laugh and have fun.

We happily ate dinner and chatted about other things they thought I should know about their favorite subject, Cuban men, until it was almost time for Lidia's husband to share his memories of Doña Delfina. Before he began speaking, I took the opportunity to go to the ladies room and snuck off quietly to the rear of the building where I thought I'd seen the restrooms.

I'd almost made it back to the dining room when a hand found my shoulder from behind. Thinking it was Rafa, I turned around to find myself face to face with a tall, good-looking man in his late twenties. With bright amber eyes and glowing skin the color of goldstone, he was so attractive I thought he might have been one of the many models or entertainers attending the event this evening, but he touched me with such familiarity that I assumed we had to know each other somehow.

"Hello, Dr. Rose," he said in English, extending his hand. "My name is Achille Desmarais." His black suit, I noticed, was unmistakably bespoke, and if I had to guess, I'd say it was made by one of the finest tailors on Savile Row. I took his hand and admired his striking presence. I didn't think I'd ever forget a lovely French accent like his, but I'd taught so many students and not all of them had made a lasting impression. It was embarrassing when I couldn't remember someone, but it happened sometimes.

"Hello," I said, trying to place him. "Have we met?"

"No, I've never been so fortunate. Doña Delfina and I were acquainted, so I've been looking forward to introducing myself to you and Dr. De Leon. It sounds like he wants to make a lot of changes." His smile was polite, yet something about him read cold, and because looking into his eyes made me feel peculiar, I focused on his red and blue pocket square instead.

"Rafa's right there in the other room." I took a step in the direction of the dining area. "Let me introduce you."

"Wait," he said, putting his hand politely on my elbow. Are you feeling alright? You look pale."

"I'm fine." I gave him a half-hearted smile, and though I tried not to look at him again, I was compelled to do just that. Everything went quiet and felt peaceful.

"Maybe things are a little stressful now," he said evenly.

"Yes," I agreed in spite of myself.

"You know, you can always leave."

"I can leave?" I asked, more confused than ever.

"You're free. When it gets to be too much, just look elsewhere."

"Amada!" Rafa's sharp voice broke my concentration, bringing with it an awareness of surroundings that had momentarily fallen away. Achille awkwardly released my arm, but not before Rafa saw that he'd been touching me. Sandro was right behind him, and then the room flooded with at least six men, two of whom I knew worked for Rafa under Sandro. The other four must have been a private security detail for another VIP. Rafa, in spite of all his intellectual and humanitarian inclinations, looked like he was possessed by a demon.

"Everything's fine. I just went to the ladies room and then started chatting with Mr.—" Still foggy, I couldn't remember his name.

"Desmarais. Achille Desmarais." He gave Rafa an icy smile and attempted to shake his hand, but Rafa was having none of it. It was painful to watch the exchange between the two men, and like a pack of wolves, Sandro and the others circled us as soon as they sensed Rafa's mistrust. Every set of male eyes in the room fixed on Achille, and not in a good way.

"Why are you back here talking to my wife?" hissed Rafa, in a tone I'd never heard from him before. He was on the verge of losing his temper, which in a normally good-natured man is even more frightening to witness.

"No, you misunderstand," replied Achille in near perfect Spanish. "It's nothing like that. I was actually looking for you, Dr. De Leon." He gazed into my eyes so intently it was as if he was trying to draw me in, pulling me toward him somehow. "Tell him, Amanda."

Achille's presumptuous familiarity and commanding tone triggered something feral in Rafa, who likely would have struck him if Sandro hadn't stepped in between them.

"You know better, bro," said Sandro in English. Though Sandro towered over him, it was hard not to notice that Achille held his own, completely unafraid.

"Cubans," he said, smoothing down one of his sleeves. "So predictable." He looked back up at Rafa and let his face fall back into its natural hard state. "Let's talk."

"Sal, take Amada back to our table and stay with her." Rafa didn't take his eyes off Achille for a second, even to look at me, and seeing him behave that way scared me beyond words. It reminded me of the guard dogs my father had when Kieran and I were children; when threatened, they would remain crouched even as they moved around and kept their eyes fixed on the target. My father explained that even though it looked awkward, it was so they could leap up and attack at any moment. It had scared me how the dogs could be so loving with our family, yet turn into snarling, fanged beasts during their practices with the trainer. I recognized the same abrupt metamorphosis happening now in my sweet, loving Rafa. His fearsome protective instincts had just kicked in, and if he were to get hurt because of me, I don't know what I would do.

"Rafa, please—"

"Do as I say," he snapped.

A very sweet-looking young man stepped out from behind the others and approached us with caution, clearly aware of Rafa's explosive state. "Shall we?" Even though I could feel him willing me to do so, I didn't look back at Achille and took Sal's arm instead.

I was a nervous wreck until Rafa returned to the table about fifteen minutes later. Sal excused himself to go off and find his girlfriend, Lisa, who he said was probably already three sheets to the wind. Rafa put his hand on my neck before he sat down beside me, but there was no trace of the man I'd seen in the back hallway, enraged and dangerous, and if there had been a physical altercation, there was no sign of it.

"Are you mad at me?" I asked. Somehow, it seemed like my fault.

"No, of course not," he said evenly. "He was trying to get my attention through you, and he succeeded."

Even though everyone had finished dinner, a waiter brought a fresh plate of food and set it down in front of Rafa. He ate heartily as if nothing out of the ordinary had happened and talked to Carlos and Oscar, who'd finally sat down to eat themselves. Silvia commented on Rafa's healthy appetite, obviously trying to make a point, and the women all gave me knowing looks which I had no choice but to grudgingly acknowledge. We spent the next hour and a half chatting and tasting all the sweets from the dessert bar as we listened to the moving tributes to Doña Delfina, whose memorial service had turned out beautifully.

Finally, as a special homage, a very famous Latin pop star took the stage and sang Doña Delfina's favorite songs, the Cuban folk song *Guantanamera* and Celia Cruz' version of *Quimbara*. Apparently it was an open secret that Doña Delfina had been instrumental in her rise to worldwide fame, so she'd been expected to attend, but she'd also generously insisted on giving an electrifying performance that brought the crowd to its feet. "Doña Delfina," she said into the microphone, "you made dreams come true. We love you, now and forever."

At around 11:30, when the big screen went to black and then switched to live television, Rafa turned toward the stage and held my hand tightly in his lap, breathless with excitement. The crowd went silent as Raul Castro spoke live from Havana, behind a desk littered with framed photographs of Communist icons Josef Stalin and Vladimir Lenin, and reported that "today ... at 10:29 pm, the commander in chief of the Cuban Revolution, Fidel Castro Ruz, has died."

I can't say whether it was because people were in shock or because it simply took that long to fully decode the words, but it was only after several beats that the eerie silence erupted into a roar that could only be described as more joyful than every New Year's Eve, every victory cry, and every winning moment in the history of time all rolled into one. Each person in the room leaped to their feet and kissed and hugged their friends and loved ones, deeply entrenched in the significance of this night in a way that only they could understand. Even as an American, it was impossible not to be moved to tears upon witnessing the flood of emotion ripping through every Cuban in exile, a diaspora of misplaced souls openly weeping for their past and now their future.

We spent the early hours of the morning drinking champagne and listening to stories about the Cuban Revolution and its profound impact, and as everyone became happier and drunker, the more open they became. Even Rafa and I had several rum and cokes, *Cuba Libres* as they were called, to celebrate with everyone else. By three in the morning, emotions were running high. Everyone had cried more than once about loved ones they'd lost because of Castro's regime, not to mention generations of fractured families that now wouldn't even recognize each other after fifty years. So much damage had been done, some thought it could never be fully righted.

"I wonder if now the change will be fast or slow," wondered Carlos aloud, his arm protectively around his wife.

"More importantly," said Oscar, "what kind of change? Don't assume it will be for the better. We have to make sure it turns the right way. It's going to be the Wild West for a while. Everyone is going to try to claim a piece."

I started to feel a little drunk, so I leaned against Rafa as he continued to talk to the people who came to our table. Silvia had left hours ago, but Lidia and Raquel were wrecked and talked their husbands into leaving around four. We all kissed and hugged and confirmed that we'd see them Friday, and as soon as Rafa made sure they had a driver, he sent them on their way. Rafa, whom I'd never seen anything but sober, had a slightly different air about him. His breath smelled of alcohol and cigars, and he was much less talkative than usual, but considering how emotional the evening had been for him, it wasn't surprising.

"Let's have one dance before the band leaves," he said. Out on the floor we swayed to a slow, seductive Cuban son, one of only three or four other couples also lost in their own world. Rafa held me so close I had to wrap my arms around his neck and put my head on his shoulder. Our bodies were moving in a way that I wasn't sure was entirely appropriate, but he had no qualms about putting his hands all over my backside as he kissed me with abandon, so I didn't concern myself either. I rubbed the back of his neck and pulled on his hair the way I sometimes did when we were making love, a suggestive act to which I knew would he would have a strong response. Accordingly, he moaned and swirled his hips in tune with the music, pressing my pelvis into his and not caring in the least that we were in a public place. Momentarily embarrassed, I looked around and was relieved to see that no one was watching because they were either too drunk or too tired.

"Even if a thousand people were watching," he said in my ear, "it wouldn't stop me."

"Doctor," I laughed, "are you drunk?"

"A little," he confessed. "I'll be fine in half an hour. You can tell?"

"Of course," I said. "You're too quiet. What are you thinking about?"

"I can't tell you." He squeezed my backside again so hard that I jumped, letting his hand settle right between my legs from behind.

"Rafa!" I squirmed so that he'd move, but he left it right there.

"You'll get upset. I'll tell you later, when I'm inside you. You can't get mad at me then." He chuckled to himself, obviously lost in some indecent memory of us. We finished dancing to the last song just like that, in complete silence, wrapped up in each other's arms.

Sandro drove me home around five so that Rafa could attend to Doña Delfina's burial with a select group. As Rafa had explained earlier, it was a secretive operation that he said I needn't concern myself with. Out of necessity it would be over quickly, and he said he'd be home by seven. Sandro walked me to the door, and instead of saying goodnight, he surprised me by saying he'd be right outside until Rafa got home.

"That's ridiculous, Sandro," I exclaimed in English. "You must be exhausted. Why can't you go home?" I stood in the doorway, annoyed that Rafa would keep Sandro from his family for foolish reasons.

"It's my job," he said simply, peering inside. "You have my number, or you can just call out if you need me. If I notice anything strange, I'll be right in." I wondered how that would happen if he didn't have a key, but decided not to ask.

"Well, then come inside and have coffee at least." I put my hand on my hip and stepped aside, expecting him to accept my invitation. It seemed as if he was about to agree when he thought better of it.

"No, Rafa said outside." He raised his eyebrows a little, and it was enough to catch his drift. He didn't want to have to spell it out, but it was obvious Rafa had a jealous streak Sandro wanted no part of. "Thanks anyway, though. Goodnight."

I was going to go upstairs and go to bed to wait for Rafa just as he had instructed earlier, but when I sat down on the fluffy white chaise in the living room to take off my shoes, I decided I was too tired to go up. I tucked a throw pillow under my head and stretched out so that I could see the black Mercedes in the circle drive on the other side of the three huge glass windows facing the front of the house and closed my eyes. Soon the sun would be up, and it would be so bright I'd have to move upstairs anyway. Rafa had a point about the location of our bedroom, I thought as I drifted off to sleep. *Maybe we should switch to one down here...*

I had no idea how much time had passed when I woke up later to the sound of the front door opening and closing, but the room had flooded with sunshine as it did every morning. I didn't have to look to know Rafa was standing over me, and I waited for him to say something, but he didn't speak. When I realized he must be staring, I opened my eyes and looked up, but I wasn't prepared for what I saw, which was Rafa utterly exhausted, disheveled and somber. He'd taken off his jacket and tie and unbuttoned his collar, but other than that he was fully dressed and excruciatingly gorgeous.

"How did it go?" I asked, still half asleep.

"I told you to be naked in our bed." He spoke slowly, deliberately, which made me wonder how much more he'd had to drink since he sent me home with Sandro.

"Where's the car?" If the Ferrari was still at the restaurant, then he'd been too drunk drive home. I craned my neck in the direction of the picture window. Bingo. Circle drive empty.

"You have thirty seconds to go in there," he said, nodding toward the guest bath off the foyer where I'd taken my cleansing bath, "and take care of whatever you need to."

"It's not an issue any more," I said, feeling more awake. "What's wrong? You said you weren't mad."

"I'm not," he said, blue eyes flashing. He unbuttoned his shirt all the way down as he spoke to me, then shrugged it off and tossed it aside. I never tired of admiring his chiseled physique, one of the many reasons my body always submitted to him even when my mind didn't want to. "Get undressed."

I sat up, but didn't do anything else. He was in a strange mood, and I wasn't sure if I liked it. We were in some kind of standoff again, and it would be interesting to see who would win this one, as the energy was noticeably different between us from when we'd parted only a few hours ago.

"No," I said, returning his piercing stare. "You're not acting like yourself. Sleep down here." I tried to get up and go around him, but he grabbed my arm and held me in place.

"You must be out of your damn mind." He laughed and kissed me so hard I thought we would both fall to the ground, but he held me up with ease. My first instinct was to push him away, but then, as always, I yielded to the deep longing for him that was always buzzing just beneath the surface. When he felt me kiss him back, he let go.

"It's not my fault!" I said. "He followed *me*."

"He approached because you were open to it." I noticed the dark circles under his eyes and wondered why he'd been drinking when he normally hated alcohol. It certainly didn't have a good effect on him. I couldn't believe he was suggesting I led Achille on.

"Are you serious?" I asked.

"You were so cold to me in the car. You could have kept walking, but you stopped and listened to him." He looked me up and down like he didn't even recognize me. "He called you *by your name* in front of me. What made him think he could do that?"

"Hell if I know!" He had me by both elbows now, and he was so close I could smell the rum he'd been drinking after I left.

"You haven't let me make love to you for days," he spat with disgust. "I let us both walk out of this house unsatisfied and disconnected, and look what happened. There has to be more to it than what that weirdo used to say to you. You'd better figure that shit out, because it's not happening again."

"You're right, maybe it won't happen again. At all!" I jerked my arms away and was just as surprised as he was when I slipped out of his grip. I tried to leave the room but he was too fast, and before I knew it he had me bent over the back of the couch I'd been sleeping on. With very little effort he held me in place with his body to remind me I was physically powerless if he wanted me to be. As time passed, I was learning about his many quirks, especially that there was no walking away from him during an argument, so instead of compliantly waiting for him to let me go, I decided to dish it right back in my own way.

"The master of seduction indeed. How romantic," I quipped. I'd noticed his recent predilection for taking me from behind, though I hadn't wanted to mention it in case it was just a personal preference. Everything between us felt incredible, but I did prefer to look at him when we were making love, and I wondered why it wasn't the same with him. There was a long, awkward pause, and I thought he wasn't going to answer me, but then his voice cracked, breaking the silence.

"I'm sorry, mamita. It's just that when I look at you when we make love, all I can think about is getting you pregnant." He took all of his weight off me, defeated. "Don't be angry." He pulled me up by the waist, turned me around and hugged me. Kissing me on the cheek, he said it again, and judging by the panicked look on his face, he'd expected me to react badly to his confession. Perhaps I should have been more surprised, but I suspect that somewhere deep down in my subconscious I'd known it all along. I slipped my hands around his back, enjoying his sweet kisses and taking pleasure in his soft, warm skin.

"Is that what you were thinking about when we were dancing?"

"Yes," he said, nuzzling the nape of my neck.

"I'm not angry, Rafa. Maybe that's why I've been scared to have sex with you lately. I might have picked up on your thoughts and had some of my own as well. I can't believe I'm even considering—just don't be angry with me, either."

"Please don't ever say you're scared to have sex with me. I can't think of anything worse. If I get you pregnant, it'll be because we both decide together. We're very connected, Amada, in ways I don't think even we realize." He brought my hand to his lips, kissed it, and was about to say something, but changed his mind. Instead, he looked at me with his tired blue eyes. "Life can be hard. I think we should just give each other a break sometimes and leave it at that." And with those simple words, it was over. Rafa took my hand and led me out of the room, but not before stopping abruptly in the doorway. He went to the plant I'd brought inside last night and glared at it.

"What's wrong?" I asked.

"What is that ugly thing?" He leaned in and really looked at it from top to bottom, revolted.

"Oh, it was by the front door last night, but there was no card."

"It's a black slipper orchid," he said, taking a step back. "I haven't seen one of these in a long time."

"It's purple." I squinted. "I brought it inside before we went to the party."

"It's from *him*." Rafa stiffened, suddenly tense the way he was when he first came home. He reached into his pocket for his phone and sent a quick text message, then picked up the plant and went out the front door. I watched him walk it all the way down the driveway and toss it over the gate. "Sal will come get it," he said, as he came back inside and turned the deadbolt.

"Rafa, no one can get in here past the guards." We'd never once had an unannounced visitor to our house thanks to the top notch off-duty police officers employed by the homeowner's association. Their salaries were outrageous, but residents insisted on round-the-clock law enforcement. However, in spite of the heavy police presence he'd seen with his own eyes, Rafa looked doubtful.

"I want to clear out that guest house for our own live-in security. Maybe we should get some dogs." Dogs didn't actually sound like a bad idea. I'd love to have German Shepherds again, and Rafa could handle them.

"Do you know what he wants?"

"Something I'm not going to give him. That plant is an instrument of malevolence, and it's why we argued before the party and just now in here." He stopped and thought for a moment, replaying the evening's events back in his mind. "It's how he knew you'd be receptive enough to talk to him last night. He wants me to know he can get close to you."

"I remember a little of what he said to me now. He said that when things became stressful, I should remember that I'm free to leave." It sounded awful out loud, and Rafa actually cringed when I told him.

Furious again, he asked me to repeat everything Achille had said, word for word. "That son of a bitch. You stay away from him, and don't bring anything else inside the house unless you buy it from the store yourself." He kissed me and added, "We always sleep together in the same bed, no matter what. Nothing comes between us. Promise me."

"I do, Rafa. I promise."

Upstairs in our bedroom, he stood by the foot of our bed and watched as I took the pin out of my hair and let it fall down around my shoulders. I found the side zipper of my gown and pulled it down, leaning forward so that the delicate fabric would easily slip down my shoulders and glide down to the floor. I stepped out of the dress and then my nude colored G-string, so that when I went to him I was wearing nothing but my jewelry and gold stiletto sandals. In spite of his unmistakable arousal, he was patient enough to let me scatter soft kisses across his chest, but when I began to play with the dusting of hair across his belly, he reached his limit and dropped down to his knees.

Rafa licked my tensed, clenched thighs, but when he pushed right into my sex with his fingers, the sensation was so unexpected and intense that I had to grab his hair and put one of my legs over his shoulders to keep steady. Now opened up to him, he devoured me with abandon, savoring every inch of flesh he'd been denied, desperate and unashamed to feed hungrily. To my amazement, he managed to gracefully pull me down to the floor by the hips so that I was sitting on his face, and I protested, mortified by the sheer obscenity of something I never imagined I'd do.

"Rafa, no," I said, trying to lift my pelvis, but his hands were like clamps around my hips, bonding me to him. Knowing I needed reassurance, he lifted me off himself with ease. "I've missed your taste," he said. "Let me."

I did as he said, feeling strangely euphoric as I slowly relaxed my thigh muscles and steadied myself against the footboard. I could feel that he had me mostly supported with his arms, moving me at will, his lips and tongue at an angle that created sensations I'd never imagined were possible.

"Oh my God, Rafa, I've never felt anything like this before," I panted. "Rafa, I love you, I do, I love you so much." He replied by thrusting his tongue in even deeper, twisting and rolling it in such an intricate dance that I couldn't even begin to visualize what he must be doing. It wasn't long before I began to feel warmth spread across my body, first down my arms, to my forearms and wrists, and then finally in my chest and between my legs. In spite of my self-consciousness, I began to moan and thrust my hips, so he loosened his grip a little, giving me the opportunity to move on my own accord. Instinctively I started to crawl up on to the bed, over his head, not wanting to climax astride him, but when he realized what I was doing, he pulled me back. I knew then he wanted exactly what I was most afraid of, so I let go. I shouted out his name again, and as I went over, he drank from me until there was nothing left.

We were an amalgam, so physically and emotionally fused that he was truly in the climax with me, a bizarre altering of both our consciousness that was like stepping into the same dream together. The physical act of love, I now understood, was every bit as powerful as the spiritual connection, yet Rafa had known this about us from the beginning. He'd just taught me never to exile him from my body again, no matter what.

I was collapsed against the footboard when Rafa slid out from under me, slipped off my shoes and lifted me onto the bed. I curled up, still reeling from whatever magic he'd just conjured, but when I started to miss him I opened my eyes and saw him across the room, standing naked in the doorway of the bathroom as he wiped his face with a hand towel. He tossed it aside, on top of the pants he'd left on the floor, and came to me.

"Amada," he sighed, slipping into the bed. "You're right here next to me, but I'm still lovesick. It's never enough." He filled me from behind with no further comment or preamble, as if that was the way our bodies should be by default. Arms and legs entwined, I moaned softly as Rafa whispered *te amo* in my ear and made love to me for a long time.

CHAPTER TWELVE

We had just under two weeks together before the grand reopening of Madrina's, and there were way too many things to do, but we'd have to try. I spent almost every waking moment with Amada, taking care of all the household and business details that had to wait during Doña Delfina's funeral and burial. We took care of mundane tasks like stocking the kitchen with food and cleaning out the guest house, but because we were together, they were fun. Amada read to me every night from *Don Quijote*, which I loved, but when she insisted I read to her, I was a little less enthusiastic. Still, I did my best and tried not to feel self-conscious. She was a fantastic teacher, explaining exactly why certain words sound like they do, and how their linguistic origin influences meaning and pronunciation.

First, she showed me a diagram showing how Western languages evolved, then explained how closely related Spanish and French are because they're both Romance languages. Any word in English with a French origin would likely very easy for me to understand, she said, but the ones that were Germanic in origin I'd just have to memorize. The word *helmet*, for example comes from the German word *helm* and is nothing like the French and Spanish words for helmet, *casque* and *casco*. That would be a difficult word for me to figure out, she warned, but something like the word *intelligent* is identical in French and therefore the Spanish cognate *inteligente*.

She looked so sexy during my English lessons that I was tempted to point out that rule also applied to the word *sexo*, but I thought better of it and kept my mouth shut. There was a time and place to come on to her, which was pretty much all the time, but not while she was teaching. I reasoned that it was just like when patients flirted with me, which I loathed for many reasons, so I made sure to remain respectful toward her while we were in her office. She showed me other tricks that could help me in a pinch, such as how words ending in *-tion* often end in *-cion* in Spanish. To learn everything I needed to know, we'd have to speak to each other in English at least part of the day, she said, to which I reluctantly agreed. Finally, she demanded that by our next lesson I'd have registered for the USMLE Step 1 and bring proof of registration to 'class.'

"You're tough, Professor," I said in English. "How do you know what the USMLE is?"

"I made it my business to know," she said. "I already downloaded sample items. We have to see what this test looks like if I'm going to prepare you for it. You know the information, you just have to be able to read the questions, correct?"

"Yes, but they're long, and then the second part of the test later will require me to speak to patients in English. That's hard. If you came to me as a patient and told me your wrist hurt, I wouldn't be able to communicate with you at all. I have to be able to take a history and write notes. Everyone says it's horrible. Very few foreign doctors ever get past that part."

"So how did you and the other physicians get along in Haiti if you can't speak French?"

"You just make do in an emergency, but most of the time we used translators to communicate with patients."

"Interesting. Trust me, Rafa. Schedule part one for twelve months from now and you'll be ready. We'll worry about the other sections one at a time, and don't concern yourself with what other people say; they didn't have *me* as their coach. My Ph.D. qualifying exam was three solid days of nothing but essay questions. Do you know how many novels and poems there are just in the area of Eighteenth-century English literature alone?"

"I'm sure I don't."

"Here's volume one." She pulled a book called *The Norton Anthology* from the shelf behind her, set it on the desk and opened it. It was at least four inches thick with pages so thin they felt like rice paper. "I had to be prepared for any question on hundreds of texts, Rafa, and I did it. It's certainly not as important as what you do, but I know how to prepare for a beast of an exam. Lucky for us, in this case your weakness is my strength, and if you let me push hard, you'll be fully bilingual by this time next year."

"Thank you, Amada. I believe you." Her confidence was quite remarkable. When she was in her element, she was dominant and aggressive, and I loved to see her this way. It turned me on in fact, and I could see it was going to be difficult keeping my teacher fantasies in check. It amused me to think that she probably had no idea how many college-aged men had sat in her classes so innocently by day, but then thought about her with great enthusiasm at night. It was better she didn't know, actually.

"Don't thank me, Rafa. We're a team." She sighed and leaned forward, the front of her robe dangerously slack.

"Can you just do me one favor?" I asked.

"Of course." She took off her reading glasses and smiled. "Anything for you, handsome. I know you need a work space of your own, so I've already ordered furniture for your study. I'm giving you the room down the hall. You're going to love it."

"That sounds wonderful, Amada. But it's not that. When you want me to pay attention, don't wear that robe."

*　*　*

I tried to buy a car, but Amada wouldn't hear of it. She stressed how 'wasteful' it would be for me to let the other four cars sit and rot while I went out and bought another. Using words that she knew would bother me like 'decadent' and 'sinful,' she successfully convinced me to use one of her cars for now. I told her I would buy the Range Rover from her, but she refused, insisting she had no idea where the titles were.

"You really want me to feel like a kept man, don't you?" I had no idea how we were ever going to get around this, so I tried to make light of it for now. "I hope it doesn't affect our sex life."

One of our first errands together was to the medical supply store, where I went crazy looking at the warehouse full of every item imaginable. I'd heard about these places from other doctors and I thought they'd been exaggerating, but sure enough, the quantity and quality of medical equipment was staggering. My mind raced as I thought about how I could buy and donate as many supplies as I could.

"Rafa, you look like you've seen a ghost," said Amada.

"No, I just can't believe it. If you only knew how little we had out in the field. Even gloves were scarce."

I walked around like a kid in a candy store, marveling at the masks, gauze, ointments, catheters and pristine German steel surgical instruments that sold for about four hundred dollars each.

"What are these things?" asked Amada, holding up a pair of bandage scissors.

"They're for cutting off a dressing," I said, dragging it against the palm of my hand. "The blunt tip slides safely against the skin."

"What about this?" she asked, holding up a different kind.

"Tenaculum forceps. It's what your doctor used to hold your cervix in position while inserting the IUD."

"Ugh! It has teeth!" She put them down in disgust. "Please, just the thought of it nauseates me."

"What does?" I dug through a deep bin of enormous adhesive bandages. Damn, these were awesome. "The clamping of an internal organ?"

"I don't know." She rolled her eyes and turned away. "Just don't tell me any more."

"So squeamish." I laughed and gave her a little pinch on the rear. "You asked."

As we browsed up and down the aisles, Amada inquired casually, "Do you know how to take it out?"

"The IUD? Why?" She'd be the type to hide a health issue, so I immediately became concerned. "Are you having a problem? Pain? Bleeding?"

"No," she said, fingering a nebulizer mask.

"I'm not going to assume anything," I said, choosing my words carefully, "but obviously we're on the same page. We both have reasons to be cautious, but things change. Circumstances change."

I gave her a kiss and a hug, silently thanking my beloved Madrina as I brought Amada in close. My instinct told me Doña Delfina's cleansing had the intended effect, liberating her of heavy energies that shouldn't be around. When the time was right, I'd teach her how to honor the dead properly so that they were happy. Amada was finally ready to move forward, and for that I'd be eternally grateful.

"I'm thrilled you want it out," I whispered in her ear, "but unless there's some kind of emergency, let's have an OB/GYN remove in the proper setting. There could be complications. I'll go with you. It'll be fine."

"Why?" she asked, clearly annoyed at my suggestion. "It's easy. There are dozens of videos on YouTube—"

"YouTube?" I laughed. "I *hope* you're joking. This is just about your dislike of doctors, which you have to get over. You should be going at least once a year anyway, which I know you're not." I was about to ask how she managed a pregnancy and Cesarean section without anyone touching her, but thankfully I caught myself before making the epic blunder.

"Amada, if something happens, say you break your leg one day, are you going to refuse to go to an emergency room? What if I had a seizure and refused treatment? How would that make you feel?" I started to become upset at the thought of something happening to her and stupidly focused on the bin of thermometers I'd happened upon. "You are sadly mistaken if you think I'm going to watch another person I love—"

When I finally took a breath and turned around, she was white as a sheet.

"Amada, are you alright?" I took her hand in mine and found it clammy and cold as ice. "Do you need to sit down?"

"No," she said. "It's just all of this. The smell of alcohol. It reminds me of a hospital." She wrinkled up her nose and closed her eyes. "Can we get out of here?"

For obvious reasons we wrapped up our visit, and thankfully I'd already found a great stethoscope, a high quality blood pressure cuff, an otoscope, and ophthalmoscope, all things that would be useful just to keep around the house if nothing else. I'd been watching Amada carefully, and as soon as we changed the topic she'd been fine, but I knew that sooner or later I'd have to figure out what was at the root of her issue. If it had anything to do with her son, maybe I could get a better sense from Kieran and help her work through it.

On the way out, the attractive young woman at the register stole a few glances at me as she rang up the merchandise, which didn't escape Amada's notice. Sliding the paper sack across the counter, the girl asked, "Are you a doctor? Where do you practice?'

I was about to answer when Amada snatched the bag away and intertwined her arm in mine. Never having seen her so openly jealous, I was fascinated. The girls in my old neighborhood would have been on the floor fighting already, but Amada was another breed. She tilted her head to the side and smiled sweetly before turning on her heel, pulling me along with her.

"Sorry, sweetie. He's not a plastic surgeon."

* * *

Feeling guilty for upsetting her, I spent the rest of the day baking her favorite syrupy Capuchino cakes, submitting to double English lessons, and giving her a back massage in front of the fireplace that led to very relaxed lovemaking as I spooned her from behind. After we'd finished, we lay side by side on the silk rug and lounged for a while, luxuriating in all the sensations around and between us. I held her hand and remembered the moment I first saw her, an untouchable lady who, according to Freud, I instantly recognized as my deepest unfulfilled wish.

"What makes you happy?" she asked, reading my thoughts. The way the shadows from the fire danced along the curves of her body was one of the most erotic things I'd ever seen.

"Being inside you. Making love to you. When you tell me you love me." *Sentirme dentro de ti. Hacerte el amor. Cuando me dices que me amas.*

"What else?" Her green eyes glimmered like diamonds in the warm, incandescent light.

"I don't know. I've never really thought about it."

"*Caracol* pastries," she prompted. "Cuban coffee. Beautiful, exotic things. The Arts. Making friends and meeting new people. Fixing."

"Fixing?" I asked.

"You like to solve problems, especially when it helps other people. You also love this house because it's beautiful, but you feel guilty, so you won't admit it to yourself. I see the way you look out at that water. You're intensely spiritual, and you love sex because you love life."

"Is that so?" I asked.

"And you're a philanthropist at heart. You're the type to fund a public museum instead of hoarding a private art collection. You're a good man, Rafa, and I'm learning how to be a better person by watching you."

"I disagree." I took her hand and held it. "To me, you're already perfect. You love to learn. You're curious about everything. You're a wonderful teacher. You're cautious, but you do want friends." I stroked her palm with my thumb. "Even when I tried to push you away, you still cared and wanted to help me. More than once." A lump began to form in my throat, so I paused until it passed.

"I like that you're reserved with most people. It's dignified. I feel like I have a queen on my arm when you're with me. You have such beautiful manners, such poise. I'm learning so much by watching you, too. But when we're alone," I said, suppressing a groan, "you are the most loving and sexually open person I've ever known. I enjoy sex, yes, but it's our sex that makes me wild. Sex with you."

Later that night in bed, as she fed us Capuchino cake while I struggled through my chapter of *Don Quijote*, I was drunk with happiness. I stopped to ask her more questions than usual just because I wanted to hear her talk. About anything.

"English is so damn hard," I complained. "In Spanish everything is written the way it sounds."

"You have a point, but let's just be glad neither of us has to learn Japanese. Imagine trying to learn to speak and read *that* language. I had to drop a Japanese class in college because my average was a seventeen. Out of a hundred. And I had one of the highest averages in the class, too. You'd like Russian, though. It's surprisingly easy."

"I know," I said. "I had to take it in elementary school, but I forgot it all."

"Oh, how interesting," she said, as she took off her eyeglasses and brought the plastic tip to her plump lips. "I'd like to hear more about that sometime."

"Of course, sweetheart. Just remind me." I continued to read but quickly came upon another word that gave me trouble. "What's this word?" I asked, completely mangling the pronunciation.

"Modesty. Put emphasis on the first syllable as if there were an accent over the o." I visualized the accent as she suggested and managed to pronounce it properly. "Good. It means humble. The opposite of lying around half-naked and distracting me with your body." She let herself steal a glance and then looked away, very endearing considering all of the incredibly intimate things we'd already shared. I continued to read, feeling strange and excited all at once.

"And this word?" I asked, pointing impulsively to the middle of the page.

"Matrimony," she said. "Same thing, accent on the first syllable. It means—you know what it means, Rafa. *Matrimonio.*"

"Tell me more." Amada looked at me sideways, not getting it yet.

"Well," she said stretching out, "it's from the Latin *matrimonium,* so it'll be the same in Spanish. We talked about that, remember?" Tonight she wore her favorite robe in lilac. She must have two dozen of the same robe in every color, I mused, thinking she'd probably like a silk kimono. They were everywhere in Cuba, but I had yet to see one here. Her little idiosyncrasies were beyond charming.

"You're right. It's so obvious." I agreed. "What else?" I bet she could talk about the etymology of a word for an hour, and maybe I'd get her to. I suppressed a smile at the thought.

"Let's see, the base comes from *matrem,* which means mother, and then the suffix *monium,* I'm not sure but I would guess it means something like being in the state of, like pandemonium means being in the state of chaos. But that last part is a guess. Do you want me to find out for sure?"

"Yes, definitely get back to me on that," I nodded seriously. I set the book down. "But for now, what do you think of that word? Is it a good word?"

"What do you mean?" she asked. I took her left hand in mine and stroked her ring finger. Finally, after what seemed like an unreasonably long time, a look of recognition shot across her face. "Oh, yes, it's a very good word."

"Amada," I began, "in my mind, you're already my wife."

"You've said it before," she whispered. She looked down at my hands, which I'd placed around her waist.

"I have?" I untied her robe and drew her close, wanting to feel her skin on mine. "If I had my way, I'd marry you tonight, but your brother wants to make sure you're protected and I promised him we'd do things properly."

"The brother who ran off to Las Vegas and got married without telling anyone?"

"I don't blame him. I wish I had a brother or sister who loves me as much as he loves you. Truthfully, I agree. It's important for me to be accepted by your family, and I never want there to be any question. Family is everything."

"So, what are you saying?" She put her cheek against mine the same way she did the first night we met. Her heart felt like it was going to burst out of her chest.

"When you're ready, Amada, will you marry me?"

"Yes," she whispered in my ear. "Oh, yes. I love you so much, Rafa."

I kissed the side of her face until I could get her to look at me, which she always found it difficult to do. I kissed her the way I always did, yet somehow it was deeper, more full of love than ever before. I reluctantly broke away and opened the same nightstand drawer that had once contained those awful sex toys, because earlier when I was looking for a place for the ring, I was delighted to find it empty and decided to put it there. I opened the box and presented it to her, a large emerald cut diamond ring set in platinum flanked by two tapered baguettes, and I had the matching band set aside for the wedding day. She gasped and hugged me again, delirious with excitement. "I love it," she said, over and over.

"I saw it and bought it on the spot. It reminded me of you." I hadn't even been looking for a ring, but when I saw it, I knew it had to be hers. It was elegant and sophisticated, a ring fit for my queen. I slipped it on her finger, and naturally it looked even more beautiful. She put her delicate hand on my chest and kept it there for a while, admiring it.

"I can't stop looking at it, Rafa. It's gorgeous. How do you know me so well?"

"Because you're everything I've ever wanted," I said.

We made love again, but this this time there was a whole different energy I couldn't really define. This woman was going to be my wife, and every part of her body was now mine to cherish and honor as only a husband can. *My wife's breasts*, I thought as I caressed her from behind.

She offered me her body in a way she knew I liked, on her hands and knees, so I took her like that, but after a short while I pulled out and put her on her back to that I could get on top, which was her favorite. Predictably, she started to get excited and bit my shoulder, which I'd grown to crave, and when I went to enter her, she placed her left hand over her sex, the ring glistening between her legs in the soft light of our bedroom. "What do you want, Rafa?" she asked. "Tell me."

"You," I said with a wry smile. Judging by her level of excitement, I had a pretty good idea of what she wanted me to say, but I played dumb. Let her have fun trying to use my own unscrupulous methods on me. The truth was I'd never used explicit language around women because it had always seemed disrespectful, but, then again, I'd never been in love.

"Oh no, that's not enough," she said. "What part of me do you want? Say it." Glad she felt safe enough to try something out of the ordinary, I decided I'd go as far as she'd let me. If she responded with disgust at any point, it might ruin a special evening, but at least then we'd learn where our limits were.

"Your mind?" I teased, hovering above her.

"Rafa," she begged. I smiled and pushed her hair behind her ear, running my fingers down her neck to distract myself from feeling emotionally overwhelmed. I swallowed hard. There was no question I'd give her anything she desired, but I didn't want to her to see a different side of me and not like it.

"I know what you want. Are you sure?" I cautioned, leaning in. "If I accidentally say something a little too vulgar, you're not going to get mad at me, are you? I'm not even sure if I'm forgiven for upsetting you this afternoon."

"If it's too much, I'll tell you," she said, nuzzling my neck. "I won't get mad."

"Good," I said, trusting her. "Well, since you asked, I think I'm in the mood to eat my wife's pussy." I looked directly into her eyes and waited for a reaction, but I took her silence as a good sign, so I moved her hand aside and kissed it. I paused and took a moment to admire her, brazenly holding her open and contemplating her in a way that was so intimate I even surprised myself.

"Open your legs for your husband, mamita. I want to look at you for a while." She hesitated, so I put a hand on her knee and guided her so that she was comfortable but spread wide.

I took my time caressing her vulva with an open hand, then slipped a finger inside. I continued to talk to her, watching as she squirmed. "So pretty. So soft. No one gets to kiss you here but me. Only I know what you taste like."

"Only you."

"I love to run my tongue along the slit of your pussy. Do you like it when I do that?" I withdrew my finger and lightly caressed her on the outside, simulating the movement.

"Yes," she said. "I think about it when I touch myself."

"Do you?" I ran my fingertips along the sensitive skin of her inner thighs. "When does this happen?" A while ago I'd gotten the feeling she was turned on by the idea of being watched but was still too shy to ask for it. Maybe tonight would be the night.

"When you're not here and I miss you."

"Oh, baby, you have to let me see," I groaned. "Do you call out my name when you make yourself come?" I leaned in and gave her a peck on the lips, then licked the curve of her breasts as she ran her fingers through my hair. It drove me wild to imagine what she must look like on her bed, alone, eyes closed, legs spread, fingers slick, thinking of me.

"Yes, I really do," she gasped, then looked up at me with a mix of excitement and coyness. "Would you let me watch you?" she whispered.

"Watch me what?"

"*Rafa.*" My lady couldn't say it. She was struggling to express her desires with me, of all people. We couldn't have that.

"This?" I asked, stroking myself. "You want me to make myself come in front of you? Of course, I'd do anything to make you happy." I waited for an answer, but she only stole a glance and then averted her eyes.

"It's alright to look, mamita. We're in love." I wanted to teach her how to keep her eyes on me, but she didn't seem ready, so I stopped and put both hands on the outside of her thighs until she felt comfortable enough to turn back. I'd find another way that was softer, less aggressive. "How does your favorite poem begin again?"

"*Had we but world enough, and time,*" she began, a faint smile across her lips, "*This coyness, lady, were no crime.*"

"There's nothing to be embarrassed about with me." Wanting to give her something to look forward to, I had an idea. "It'll be one of my gifts to you on our wedding night. I promise, you'll enjoy it." I caressed the side of her face with the back of my hand, reveling in her sweet femininity.

"What if I'm shy again?"

"You'll let me know you're ready." I thought carefully about what would be easiest for her. "I'll wait for you to ask me to show you how much I love you."

"And then what will you do?" she panted. I closed my eyes for just a moment and imagined Amada in her bridal lingerie.

"I'll sit you up against the headboard, legs spread, and enjoy the view of your beautiful pussy as I undress. When I'm naked, I'll dip my fingers inside you to get them wet."

"Rafa—" She reached out to touch me, wanting me closer, but I kept still, not wanting to spoil the moment. Stroking my arm, her chest rose and fell like a scared rabbit's.

"Then I'll lie back between your legs and take my hard cock in my hand, stroking slowly at first, then faster as I think about us, maybe the night you were in the tub and I had to pretend I wasn't dying to fuck you."

"Then what?" she asked, her voice a thin whisper, her lips parted and dry.

"You'll watch over my shoulder until I come. And if you want—" Her eyes wide, I hesitated, wondering if it was too much.

"Yes?"

"You can clean me off with your tongue."

Amada gasped, but before she had time to react, I intertwined my hands with hers and dove down between her legs, thinking of nothing but how much I adored her as I made love to her with my mouth. When I knew she was close and I was about to burst, I came up and used her hand to wipe my face, making sure she saw exactly how much of herself was all over me. I was usually more discreet, but tonight was different. It was time for us to open up and begin to test the limits of our intimacy, if there were any, because I wanted my wife to be my best friend, too. Above all else, we had to be each other's sanctuary.

I know she was taken aback by seeing herself all over me, but this time she didn't look away, even when I brought her hand to her mouth so that she could taste herself. She hesitated but did as I asked, and when she looked up for approval, I nodded. "Now you understand why I can't get enough."

Never breaking eye contact, I inserted two fingers inside her and gave her an internal massage while putting pressure on her abdomen from the outside to intensify the sensation. I knew it had to feel very good by the way she clutched at my arm and gasped.

"Oh, God," she moaned. She brought her legs together and squeezed my arm, but I pushed them apart again.

"Hm, you're so swollen inside," I said. I kept going until she started grabbing at the sheets and then at my wrist over my watch.

"What are you *doing*?" she moaned.

"I'm rubbing my wife's G-spot. I could give you an orgasm this way, but I think I'd rather feel you come around my cock." I applied particularly strong pressure and made her rise off the bed a little.

"I think you're ready to be fucked," I said, meeting her eyes.

"Yes, Rafa," she said. She was so worked up she was struggling to speak, which I took as a compliment.

"Tell me. Do you want to come this way or do you want me to fuck you?" I continued to finger her while using my free hand to caress her chest and belly. I waited patiently, deciding that I would give her as much time as she needed to find the courage to speak openly, occupying myself by thinking about what kind of pendant I'd like to see dangling between her breasts.

"I want my husband to fuck me," she said finally, then took my hand off her collarbone, licked it and then bit down hard on the fleshiest part. With my hand still across her mouth and cheek, I licked the fingers of my other hand clean, then positioned myself over her.

Eager to please, I said everything that came to mind between deep kisses and gentle bites on her neck. "Amada, you'll never want for anything in this bed. I was put on this Earth to please you." I placed her hand on the base of my engorged penis. "Feel what you do to me. No one can make me this hard but my wife." I stroked the inside of her thigh and continued to talk, hoping it wouldn't be too much, but the uncertainty made it very hot for me, too.

"You need your husband's come inside you, don't you?"

"I do." She was so aroused she could barely speak, and really, so was I.

"Good, because that's where I'm going to put it every night. Relax your pelvis and keep your legs spread for me so that I can go deep." I told her to put her arms around my shoulders and checked one last time that she wet and ready, then entered her slowly, using long, measured strokes I knew would ignite every nerve ending inside her.

"Deeper," she begged, so I leaned back, put my arms under her legs and held her by the hips as I continued my slow, deep thrusts.

"If you want more of me than that, you're going to have to let me get behind you," I said, noting with satisfaction that in this position I was still able to reach the A-spot beside her cervix at the finish of every stroke, just like I had the night we made love by the ocean.

"No, this is perfect," she said, stroking my arms. "I want to see you."

"Then keep your eyes on me, mamita," I said. "I'm right here, fucking you."

I made love to her with as much vigor and passion as I thought she could endure, taking the time to push and grind into her hips with the satisfaction of knowing I'd be on her mind tomorrow when she felt the inevitable ache between her legs. She was all curves and softness underneath me, and when we found our steady, perfect rhythm, it was beyond divine. I looked down and saw that Amada had put one of her delicate hands on my chest, her long thin, fingers and French-tipped nails spread out across my skin like a silk fan. Contemplating her sweet face, I recalled a time when I never dreamed I could be with a woman like her.

* * *

I had just celebrated my nineteenth birthday and was walking home from a bar with a couple of friends at two in the morning. It was warm and breezy as it usually is in Havana, and as we turned the corner of San Ignacio and Empedrado, she saw me and called out. *"Pssst. ¡Oye! ¡Ojos azules!"*

We stopped in our tracks, drunk as skunks and barely aware of where we were and what we were doing. My friends Mateo and Samuel were even drunker than I was and burst out laughing at the sound of her voice.

"Who's there?" said Mateo, badly slurring his words. "Is that Patrizia and her horny sister?" He called out with the complete intellectual disconnect of every man who's ever had way too much to drink and knows he's doomed to pass out or throw his guts up, whichever comes first.

"Shut up, stupid!" I said, my voice a low hiss. "You're going to get us arrested."

Samuel came up behind me and pushed me in the direction of the darkened apartment building. "That's Patrizia and Jacinta's house." He slapped me on the back and whistled under his breath. "Let's go."

Somehow we managed to make it up three flights of stairs without killing ourselves, and we found Patrizia and Jacinta were waiting for us at the top floor, obviously blotto themselves. We went inside the dim, sparsely furnished apartment that usually smelled of pork fat but tonight smelled of cigarette smoke and cheap alcohol. The peeling paint was particularly bad in this building, and to make matters worse, it looked like no one had swept the floor in months.

"Where's your aunt?" asked Samuel, flopping down on the couch. Jacinta sat down next to him holding a cracked drinking glass full of rum while Mateo laid himself out on the grimy floor, already half asleep.

"With her boyfriend." Patrizia came and stood next to me. Her frosted pink lipstick and skimpy tank top reminded me of the *jineteras* that approached tourists in Old Havana, and I wondered whether sooner or later this apparently unintentional look wouldn't become a job requirement.

"Why weren't you in class today?" I asked.

"I'm not going back to school. It's boring, don't you think?" She took my hand and led me to the other end of the couch where Samuel and Jacinta had already started making out. His hands were exceptionally busy under her tiny denim skirt, so I turned away from them and laid my head back to rest a second. Thankfully I'd shown some restraint tonight and hadn't gone off the rails like Mateo.

"Yeah, I guess so," I said, not in the mood to argue with someone drunker than me.

"What are you going to do? Don't you want to get married soon?"

"Married?" I practically choked on the word. "No, I'm going to be a doctor."

"Sure you are," she said, snorting.

Before I realized what was happening, she'd climbed on top of me and had shoved her tongue in my mouth, but I maneuvered her back onto the couch at once, thoroughly repulsed. It wasn't the first time she'd tried to get me to have sex with her, but tonight she was especially aggressive. She tried again, and when she put her hand on my chest, my eyes zeroed in on her chipped nails and thick fingers.

"Patrizia, no."

"Why not?" she said. Her dark eyes narrowed. "Don't you like me?"

I was sobering up quickly and starting to realize what a mistake it had been to come up to the apartment, but I was stuck now, because Mateo was practically a dead body and Samuel was balls deep in Jacinta, who was beginning to moan a little too loud not to attract attention.

"I'm too drunk. Let's just hang out."

"Maybe what they say about you is true," she said.

"And what's that?" I waited expectantly for her reply, but I knew what was coming. I could never win. She brought her hand close to her face and started absentmindedly flicking off more bits of blue nail polish.

"That you're gay. All the guys think so. They say if you put on some eyeliner and mascara your eyes would be prettier than a girl's." She started cackling at the thought. "Luis said they're going to hold you down one day and do it."

"Really?" I asked, turning to her. "Well, do me a favor and tell Luis I'd like to see him try, because after I kick his ass, I'll take his mother up on her offer and fuck the shit out of her in every room of their house, starting with his."

"I'll tell him," she laughed. "I'd love to see that, but they know better, especially after last time. Such idiots."

I got up and tried my hardest not to look in the direction of Jacinta's bare ass moving up and down on Samuel. "I'm going," I said over my shoulder.

"You alright?" I asked, leaning over Mateo. "You want to leave with me?"

"No," he said, coming out of his stupor a little. "I think I'm about to get lucky."

"Maybe," I said, eyeing Patrizia. "But I wouldn't call it lucky. Use a rubber."

I wasn't even halfway out the door when I saw her straddle Mateo. She looked up, obviously not the least bit embarrassed to be acting like a common whore.

"Hey," said Patrizia. "I saw that picture in your locker. You like blondes. What if I dyed my hair like that Irma Truman?"

"Who?" Then I realized who she meant. "That's not who it is, and no thanks."

"My God, you're so stuck up," she laughed, unbuttoning Mateo's pants. "Have fun jerking off by yourself, Rafa."

* * *

"Rafa?"

It was Amada, bringing me back to a very welcome reality.

"I'm close." She tugged at my neck with both hands trying to pull me in closer.

"Not yet, my queen." *Todavía no, mi reina.*

I stopped thrusting, rolled over on to my side and made sure we were both comfortable while I continued with manual stimulation. I pulled her head into my chest and slipped my hand between her legs, using long, lazy strokes just to keep her idling as we caught our breath for a few minutes in a quiet embrace. I wanted to make sure it was particularly good for her on our special night, but soon it became clear she was too far gone to keep at bay and wouldn't settle down. It wasn't long before she started to kiss and touch me all over, putting her hands on my face and kissing me with such hunger that I completely lost track of what I was doing and climbed back on top of her.

"I'm on fire," she gasped.

"Another minute. You can do it." I kissed her again, teasing her with the tip of my cock.

"Don't do that to me now. You'll make me cry. I can't take it," she moaned, trying to move me.

"No, baby, I know you need me inside you right away. You can't stay still can you?" I was poised above her, trying to make her wait one last second or two.

"I ache inside," she whispered. "Rafa, I'm begging you." When she started to shake, I nearly lost it.

"I will, sweetheart," I said, struggling to control my own body. "You're going to come soon, but first I want to teach you something you're going to like." I entered her again, propping myself up on my arms to give her space. Her breath hitched and her hips relaxed and opened wide for me as if I'd managed to take the edge off by being inside her most of the way.

"Oh, yes," she said. "Thank you."

"Squeeze me with your pussy as hard as you can. Don't use your thighs, just the muscles you have inside. Do you understand?"

She did it beautifully, and I tried to keep a neutral expression to see if she liked it, but when I saw her toss her head from side to side, I knew she was loving it, too.

"That's it. Hold it for me as long as you can."

"Why does that feel so good?" Amada panted and writhed like a woman possessed, and she licked my chest and nipples with an abandon that was so hot it was an absolute miracle I didn't climax right then and there.

"Because you're making love to your husband's cock from the inside." I leaned in and barely grazed her lips with mine, being sure to use just the tip of my tongue to lick the outside of her mouth before leaning back into position. While she was still clenching around me, I slowly withdrew from her, astounded at how tight she could make herself. It was an exquisite, ethereal sensation that made me shiver.

"Look at me, Amada." I said. She tried to do as I asked but looked away and then back a few times, and as I searched her eyes, I felt such love that I found it difficult to continue talking. I resolved to teach her how to maintain eye contact during our lovemaking because I craved it with her like never before.

"Now I want you to release those muscles and push out as I go in." I slid back inside her at a snail's pace, watching as she concentrated. "More, baby. Open up more, just for me."

"Like that?" she asked. It took her a minute to figure it out, but she got it.

"Just like that, mamita. Do you feel what's happening? Your pussy is opening for me on the way in, and milking me on the way out."

"God—" She threw her head back, uttering some words in English I didn't understand. She gripped my arms tightly, digging in.

"I know, me too." It was by far the most intimate moment we'd ever shared, and I tried to etch every detail into my mind, knowing it was one of many we'd experience together over a lifetime.

"Deeper, Rafa," she said.

"Not yet, sweetheart. Soon." I gave her another peck on the lips and tried to keep my voice from trembling as I spoke to her, but I don't think I quite managed. "Two more strokes. Squeeze tight on the first and open up for me on the second. We're not going to last very long."

I lowered my body onto hers and withdrew slowly as she tightened up, exquisitely aware of her all around me. "Perfect, mamita. Oh, that's *so good*."

"Now open," I said, pushing in again. Approaching the end of her, I lowered my voice and gave her one last direction, even though I was drowning in pleasure myself. A little bead of sweat trickled through my hair at my temple and down the side of my face, then fell off me and landed on her chest.

"Look at me," I commanded. She obeyed, our eyes locked. "Contract your muscles right after I thrust, and that's when you're going to come, *hard*. Let your body do whatever it wants. It doesn't matter what happens. Hold on to me and try to look in my eyes as long as you can. Ready?"

I pushed myself up inside her as far as I could go, all at once. "I love you," I said. Without further direction, she tightened up exactly as I told her to, and that was it.

"Rafa!" she cried. She kept the eye contact longer than I expected, so I knew exactly when it hit her, and as she clutched me with her arms and legs and scratched at my back, she told me she loved me, too. I savored every second of her well-deserved orgasm right along with her.

"That's it, baby," I whispered. Feeling the changes in her body as she climaxed was all it took to send me reeling with her, the familiar hot rush that coursed through me and completed in my wife a bliss like no other. Every cell in my body drove me to leave part of myself inside her, and when our eyes met again, I couldn't help but think of how I'd like to see her full and round. To hell with it, maybe I *would* just pull that damn thing out. I rested my cheek on the top of her head and stayed in place, remaining inside her until I slipped out.

Now completely spent, I rolled over expecting her to fall asleep on top of me, but before she allowed herself to drift off in my arms, my intelligent lover was overcome by curiosity.

"Rafa, what was that? Why did it feel so good?"

"I told you." I smiled, thinking of what I'd said on the spur of the moment. "Isn't my answer plausible?"

"Come on," she said. I didn't want to ruin the mystery, but I knew she'd either get it from me or just go look it up.

"It's a technique called *pompoir*. You have quite a few muscles—specifically two major muscle groups —that make up your pelvic floor. When you contract them, blood flows to the area, triggering all kinds of atypical sensations, and those are the same muscles that involuntarily contract when you have an orgasm, so when you do it yourself, it's a very nice way of getting the process started for both of us. The stronger those muscles are, the more you can do, but yours are damn strong already."

I stopped short of discussing the less appealing advantages of a strong pelvic floor, because there are some things you don't want to hear about in bed, no matter how curious you are about the human body. Besides, I was far too relaxed to keep talking. For the first time, all I wanted was to lie with her in silence, but when I realized my sweet girl had been quiet for a while, I looked down and tried to make out whether her eyes were open or closed.

"Hey, are you still awake?"

"Yes," she said, snuggling up against me. She ran her fingertips along the ridges of my abdominal muscles, going over one particular spot a few times.

"What's this muscle called? I love it."

"Oh, do you? Good, but it's not a muscle. It's a ligament. *El ligamento inguinal.*"

"One more thing," she said, pulling the covers up to her chin, which I knew meant she was down for the count. "What's the psychology behind the—the way you were talking to me? It was perfect."

"Forget it. I just went from sexual magician to science nerd in thirty seconds because you have to understand how everything works. I know when to do it, and when not to, and that's all you need to know." I rubbed her back, feeling heavy and lethargic. "Mystery, Amada."

"Fine." She put her head on my chest and stretched her arm and leg across my body. Her voice began to drift off, and her breathing started to slow.

"My husband," she murmured.

"Forever, mamita." I kissed the top of her head, knowing I was the luckiest man in the world.

CHAPTER THIRTEEN

mada and I had just welcomed Lidia, Oscar, Raquel and Carlos to Boxwood when she couldn't keep it in a second longer and waved her left hand in the air.

"Is that an *engagement* ring?" squealed Lidia, bringing Amada's hand right up to her face.

"Let me see!" said Raquel. "Look at that gorgeous rock! Congratulations you two!"

"Come on, let's text Silvia and Rogelio a photo!" said Lidia. "She'll be beside herself she missed this."

After countless hugs and kisses, Oscar, Carlos and I went out to the lanai to smoke cigars while the women stayed inside to talk. It was dusk and we had about fifteen minutes before we had to leave for dinner.

"Well done," said Carlos, leaning back in his chair. *Te la comiste.* "Look at this view." He was right. I never tired of looking at the bay that surrounded the house. I'd learned that it was such a great tool for meditation that I'd ordered several water features installed in the restaurant, which was coming along nicely.

"Things are working out well," said Oscar. *Estas acabando.* "Lidia really likes Amanda. They both do. She says they're going to get into a lot of trouble together."

"I don't doubt that," I said, puffing on the Montecristo Carlos had brought over.

"Speaking of trouble," said Carlos, "I heard there was a problem the other night. Some man approached Amanda. What the hell happened?"

"Yeah, I was going to tell you about that." I flicked some ashes into the large glass ashtray on the table between us. "Have you ever heard of a man named Achille Desmarais?"

They looked at each other and shook their heads. If anyone had a legal problem in Miami, they'd know about it, which meant Desmarais had to be based in Haiti. I told them how I'd found him cornering Amada in a dark hallway in the back of the restaurant and how he'd left the plant outside. Before I could even get the words out, they both agreed that the orchid had to have been black magic or *brujería*.

"We brought him back to the office, and after I threatened to cut his balls off if he ever went near Amada again, he told me that he wanted to be my friend, and all he asked was that I allow him access to this kid I have working at Madrina's now."

"What's so special about him?" asked Oscar.

"He's been messed up on drugs for a long time. His father has tried every rehab in the country but it never works, so he brought him to me. I've got the kid cleaning toilets and meditating with me every day, but I can see he was in deep. He's a tough case."

"Why does this Demarais need your permission to talk to the kid?"

"Because his father is a congressman planning to run for president. He has two bodyguards that never leave his side."

"He's worried his son is going to create a scandal," observed Carlos.

"Yes, but also because his dealer finds him wherever they send him. They don't want anyone getting close to him."

"Is this who I think it is?" Oscar leaned in, fascinated.

"Yes. *Him.*"

"Oh, shit. He's Cuban!"

"That's why he trusts us. That kid is my responsibility now and he's going to get better. I told Demarais to fuck off and I kicked him out, but he didn't seem too scared. Yet. We're going to have to change that."

"What do you think Demarais wants?" asked Carlos. "To kidnap him for money?"

"Well, he wouldn't tell me, but I had Sandro ask around and it turns out Demarais is a very well-known drug dealer. He's got to be the one feeding him the drugs, so he's been playing the long game.

Word is he wants to be the first to establish a direct route from Peru through Cuba to Miami, but he's not the only one." I took another puff of the Montecristo. "My hometown, Playa Larga would be the first city in Cuba on that route. It's going to become another Medellin if this cocksucker has his way."

"But everyone knows you can't get drugs through Cuba. Castro didn't tolerate it."

"Well, the bastard is gone now, and things are going to change fast." I took another puff. "You said it yourself, Oscar. It's the Wild West."

"Demarais wants to trade the kid's life for a politically sanctioned pass through Cuba," observed Carlos. "Son of a bitch."

"Looks that way. Not to mention that Demarais is associated with one of the most notorious Voodoo practitioners in Port-Au-Prince. They say that's how Desmarais' family made their money, under the protection of a notorious priest named Agwe."

"They're probably into that ass backward animal sacrifice," said Carlos.

"It's not just *animal* sacrifice, from what Sandro tells me," I said.

"Listen Rafa, from the cases I've heard, I can tell you that some of the people who practice Voodoo here in Miami go away for doing some horrible things. Drugs. Human trafficking. Prostitution. Murder. The poverty they have over there leads to some seriously depraved shit. Hell, I don't have to tell you, of all people. You have to be very careful."

"I know," I said, thinking of Amada. I pointed to the guest house. "Sandro is going to turn it into a guard house and keep a couple of guys here day and night to watch over Amada." I watched as Carlos and Oscar puffed on their Montecristos. "If Demarais tries to hurt her, I'm going to the electric chair because I *will* kill him."

"Take it easy and do what you have to do to protect your family," said Oscar, patting my arm. "Don't worry about anything like that."

* * *

On the way to the French restaurant we'd chosen for dinner, I had Oscar and Carlos follow me to Madrina's so that I could check in and see how everything was going. I wanted to see the fountains that had been installed, the oils that were supposed to go up, and check on the remodeling of the back salon which would now be an oak paneled members-only area with cigar lockers and Chesterfield sofas. Most importantly, I wanted to check on the kid and make sure he was alright.

I parked Amada's Ferrari in the back because of the construction and debris along the front, which I was also changing a little, mostly for security purposes. It was all costing just under a million dollars, but Kieran and the CPA he'd recommended assured me it was a good investment. I'd never dreamed of having the kind of net worth Doña Delfina left behind, but I still thought like a poor man. As far as I was concerned, the money could disappear as quickly as it came, so I wasn't about to spend unwisely on anything.

"Rafa, everything looks great out here already," said Amada. "I love the new entrance! The big double doors in the front look so much better than the little side door." My sweet girl had worn red again for me tonight, which I appreciated very much. The high slit up the side of her dress was driving me mad.

"Hey, forget about that and give me a kiss," I said, reaching for her. "Those legs, mamita. Damn."

Inside, the six of us toured all the areas under construction. I was delighted that the fountains had gone in, and although they weren't running yet, they were every bit as beautiful as I hoped they'd be.

"Rafa! I love this one!" said Amada. She stood in front of the sixteen foot tall bronze statue of a ballerina in fifth position, whose skirt would be formed by jets of water when it was running. Lidia and Raquel came to stand beside us, fascinated.

"Rafa, all of the fountains are exquisite, but this one is breathtaking," said Lidia.

"Does it have a special significance?" asked Raquel.

"It does," I said. "It reminds me of someone I knew a long time ago."

"A girlfriend?" asked Amada, arching an eyebrow.

"No, nothing like that, baby. I'll tell you the story soon."

We toured the members only section, which was still being fitted with custom cabinetry and the special trophy bar I'd ordered. When the accent lighting was installed, and the uber-masculine furnishings arrived, it was going to be spectacular.

"This is what I'm talking about," said Carlos, slapping me on the back. "My new home!"

"Excuse me," said Raquel, playfully smacking him with her Chanel bag. "No, it's not."

In the restaurant, I saw the dozen large oils on canvas I'd commissioned. They'd been carefully placed along the walls, presumably to be hung tomorrow. Doña Delfina had been a long time supporter of an artists' enclave in Little Havana that she called *El Taller* or The Workshop, and though all of the artists there were unbelievably talented, there was one young man there who was on another level. Alonsito Reyes or *Piraña,* as he signed his paintings, had come to her at the age of seventeen for a dishwashing job after having been arrested for spraying graffiti all over Little Havana, but when Doña Delfina realized how talented he was, she promptly moved him into the artists' residence and encouraged him to paint. He'd done two of the paintings himself: the one of her, which was the largest, and another of the Orisha called Babalú-Ayé. Rather than a literal representation, I'd told him a little about what Babalú-Ayé represents—health and sickness, among other things—and asked him to do something modern and artistic for the main salon. The result was breathtaking, a blue hued Cubist-inspired allegory of life and death as arresting as any Picasso. The other paintings, which I'd asked him to supervise, were all done by different artists in various styles, each more spectacular than the next.

"Rafa, they're unbelievable," said Amada. "This is real art. These paintings could sell for a lot of money. I'm bowled over."

"I am too," I said. "It's more than I could have imagined. This is what Doña Delfina had the foresight to cultivate."

We looked at all of the paintings and could have easily stayed there for hours, but when we were interrupted by Sal, Lisa, and my newest employee, Alex, getting ready to lock up, we realized just how late it was.

"Hey, we have to go" said Oscar, glancing at his Rolex. "I don't want to lose the reservation."

I hadn't seen Lisa since the ship, but I knew in that time she'd become Sal's girlfriend and come to work for me with him. I was glad to have her as I knew that, like Sal, she could be trusted. I gave her a big hug and introduced her to everyone. "Nice suit," she whispered in English as she leaned in to embrace me. I winked at her and asked Amada to tell her I was glad she was here. I was happy for them both that they'd become a couple, but especially for her, because now she was far away from those animals on the ship that would never leave her alone. When I introduced her to Amada, I was pleased that there wasn't the least bit of jealousy on Lisa's part, probably because she'd found a satisfying relationship with Sal. Amada seemed to like Lisa right away and told her to call her if she needed to get away from the restaurant and hang out with another woman. Not wanting to ruin a potentially nice friendship, I'd have to think carefully about whether it was a good idea to fill Amada in on Lisa's former crush.

"Sal," I said, "how's our newest fry cook doing?" I put my hand on Alex's shoulder. He was thin and pale, but I had to say he was looking better every day. He still didn't talk much and mostly kept his eyes down around other people, but that didn't stop me from trying to build his self-esteem by involving him in as many things around the restaurant as possible. It was hard to believe he'd had every advantage in life and still couldn't conduct himself in a developmentally appropriate manner among a small gathering of people, a testament to the utterly devastating effects of hard core drugs on a young mind. As usual, his two bodyguards had followed him discreetly into the room and seated themselves in a corner away from the group.

"Everyone, this is Alex. He's new, and he's doing a great job." Our group greeted him enthusiastically, especially Amada, who seemed taken by his shyness and vulnerability. I looked at Carlos and Oscar, then gestured to the two bodyguards in the corner. Their eyes went to the stern-looking men, whose demeanor and reserve made them no less intimidating than federal agents or Secret Service. Even Oscar, who sometimes had to be under the protection of a marshal when presiding over high profile cases, seemed shocked by such heavy security.

Once I was satisfied that everything was in order, we headed out to dinner, but as the others made their way back outside, I grabbed Sal and hung back a second.

"Hey, you two comfortable in the apartment upstairs?" I asked. "Do you have everything you need?"

"Are you kidding? It's the Ritz compared to the ship. We're great."

"Good," I said. "Listen, Sandro has a family thing, so I need you over at the house tomorrow night around seven o'clock. I have to come here and spend some time with Alex, and I don't want Amada to be alone. She'd probably like it if you brought Lisa, too."

"Sure, no problem," said Sal. "Hey, is that what I think it is on your lady's finger?" he said with a grin. I told him all about Amada, my English lessons and the proposal. "Yo, congratulations." He gave me a big hug, sincerely happy for me.

"Sal, what did I tell you about saying 'yo'? Have you applied to UM yet?"

***

We'd all had a magnificent dinner at the Palme d'Or at The Biltmore, and as a special surprise Lidia and Raquel ordered a gorgeous strawberry and champagne flavored cake and several bottles of Dom Perignon to celebrate our engagement. It had been a wonderful evening among good friends, and we'd gotten home late, tipsy, and in the mood for love, so Amada and I stripped down inside the house, grabbed a few towels and headed out to the pool for a dip.

"Make sure there's nothing in the water, Rafa. I'll die if there's a snake in there!" She wouldn't come in until I swam all around and looked for alligators, snakes and rodents. When she was satisfied that I'd looked over every square inch of the pool, she finally tiptoed in.

"Get in here," I said, pulling her in by the waist. I cornered her over by the edge and kissed her till she was dizzy, but when she put her legs around my hips I had no choice but to playfully slip out of her hold.

"It's not good for you." I dove under the water and nipped at her thighs until she pulled me up by the hair. "I'll make love to you after we rinse off."

We spent a little while relaxing in the water, kissing and touching each other as we talked about our evening and then the remodel, which must have reminded her of the fountain.

"Rafa," she said thoughtfully, "tell me about the ballerina fountain."

I thought about how to best approach a sensitive subject and then decided there was no good way. I just decided to be as direct and honest as possible.

"Amada, I've told you that a big part of Santería is our connection to the dead. Do you remember that?"

"Yes, you talked about it when Kieran and Ken were here."

"Well, I have a spirit guide named Filomena. She was a Venezuelan ballerina, and I met her many years ago when I attended the ballet in Caracas and she broke her ankle during the performance. She died a few years later, and now she comes to me in my dreams."

"Did you have an affair with her?" Even though I didn't want her to be jealous, I thought it was a good sign that she was more interested in the relationship than the fact that I had *muertos* who came to me.

"No! Of course not. I just took her to the hospital that night and I never saw her again. Apparently she never forgot me, though."

"No woman could ever forget you, handsome." She ran her fingers across my eyelids and lips as she often did. "Is she the only one?"

"So far, yes. Delfina said as I get older I'll meet more." I noticed the look on her face and wanted to make sure she understood. "Amada, I've always been very intuitive, but when I meditate, especially around moving water, I can tune in to other things. Thankfully it's not like my brother, but I suppose you could call it something like lucid dreaming. Some people might say I'm simply tapping into my own subconscious, but sometimes I have experiences that I'm certain don't come from within myself. You know, Delfina told me that after many, many years, she was able to project herself to other places. Isn't that amazing?"

"It's not what you're talking about," she said, "but I have dreams about my parents, and it's always the same. They come back from their trip, and Kieran and I ask what took them so long. It's like they were never dead, just on a long journey." She looked down, a little sad. "Kieran thinks it's unresolved grief because I refused to go to the funeral and I've never been to their grave. I'd really like to stop having those dreams after all these years."

"You know, we can work on that together. I can help you resolve some of those things or get the information you need so that you can move on." I was about to ask her if she ever dreamed of her son when we heard a noise just beyond the pool deck. I looked in the direction of the thick hedge and saw a squat, big-eyed creature jump out onto the concrete and sit dangerously close to the edge of the pool. Fascinated, we both stared at it but didn't move, so it came even closer and let out a loud croak.

"Yuck, Rafa, that frog is going to jump in," said Amada, climbing out of the pool.

"That's not a frog, that's a toad." *Eso no es una rana, es un sapo.* "Funny, my mother was terrified of them, but I think they're kind of cool." I swam right up to it and looked into its glassy eyes.

"Ew!" screamed Amada, "Gross! Come on, let's go inside!"

* * *

The next day we woke around noon, still wrapped around each other in virtually the same position we'd made love in. I heard footsteps in the house and shot up, unaccustomed to the sound of anyone in our space besides us.

"It's just the house cleaners," mumbled Amada, still face down in the pillow. "Hear the vacuum? It's fine. They come twice a week and do the whole house. We weren't home the last couple of times they came."

We slept another hour until they'd left and then went downstairs for breakfast. I got the coffee going while Amada talked to Ken on the phone, who apparently wanted to be involved in planning the wedding. I gathered that Amada and Ken had some sort of inside sexual joke because she was giggling uncontrollably while stealing sexy glances at me. I put a glass of orange juice in front of Amada, but she pushed it away and mouthed 'Diet Coke.' Tapping my finger on the counter, I moved it right back, refusing to leave until she started drinking.

"You need potassium," I said.

'Hold on, Ken, Rafa wants me to drink something," she said in English, taking a sip, and I was delighted that whatever Ken said on the other end of the line made her howl with laughter.

"Here," I said, handing her a bowl of dried black beans. "Pick out the ones that are broken. Normally we soak them overnight, but we should have enough time since we're eating them much later today." She nodded and kept talking to Ken as she swirled her hand around the bowl like she was mixing a cake.

"Like this, sweetheart," I said, showing her how to examine a handful at a time. She rolled her eyes, but I just pointed at the bowl and motioned for her to get going. "Sorry, but she who does not cook peels potatoes and picks through black beans." I swatted her on the rear and went back to preparing the mojo marinade for the steaks.

We had breakfast out on the lanai and then I managed to get her downstairs to Kieran's gym, where we worked out for an hour and a half. I lifted weights and had her walk on the treadmill for an hour, which she tolerated well enough. On the way back upstairs, we went through the art gallery, which was empty save for some display cases and expensive lighting fixtures.

"You know," said Amada, "I wouldn't mind putting some oils up in here. We've never gotten around to doing anything with this room. Do you think that amazing artist would paint something for us?"

"Piraña? I'm sure he would," I said. "What did you have in mind?"

"How about a nude of us together?" she asked, totally serious. "Something erotic. But that one would have to go in the bedroom."

"I don't think so," I said. "He's twenty years old. Do really think I'm going to let him see you naked?"

"What if it's just my back and your front?"

"No. Don't waste your breath," I said. "That will never happen." There was nothing in the world that would persuade me to let her pose for another man, no matter how talented he might be.

"Well, what if I'm covered and you're nude?" She kissed my lips and placed her hand seductively on my penis over my sweatpants. "How about that? Please."

"Amada, why?"

"Look at your body, Rafa. I want to capture you in all your glory now," she said. "That way when we're old and you run out of your little blue pills, I have something to pleasure myself to."

"Well, when you make it sound so enticing, how can I possibly say no," I laughed.

"See, I know exactly how to talk to you."

"I'll consider it." The more I thought about it, the more I actually liked the idea. I pictured how beautiful she looked when she was lying on the bed waiting for me to undress and come to her. Now *that* was a painting I'd love to have.

* * *

By the time Sal arrived at seven o'clock, Amada was already wrapped around me with that look in her eye, reluctant to let me go.

"Do you really have to?" she asked, playing with a button on my shirt. "I'll make it worth your while if you cancel."

"Baby, there's no question about that," I said, rubbing her lower back, "but I promised Alex's father I would be personally involved in his recovery. He likes boxing, so we're going to watch a fight on television from eight to ten or so and then I'll be home. Trust me, this kid needs to occupy his mind with something other than getting high."

"Yeah, he's nice. I can survive without you for two hours."

When I opened the door for Sal, I was surprised to see him standing on the porch alone, looking a little less than happy. "Where's Lisa?"

"We had a fight."

"About what?" I asked, standing aside so he could come in.

"I don't know. She's bored, I think." Sal looked around in complete fascination. "Rafa, what the hell is this place?"

"I know. It's unreal. Amada will show you around."

"Hi, Sal," said Amada in English, coming up behind me. "Where's Lisa?"

"I've got to go, mamita," I said, giving her a peck on the lips. "Hey, make yourself useful." I slapped Sal on the back and headed out to the restaurant, already running late.

* * *

Traffic was hell, so I arrived a few minutes after the start of the match, but Alex was already changed out of his uniform and watching it on the big television in the upstairs communal space. His two guards were sitting at the table in the back playing cards, though I noticed they were different men. I'd intentionally given him the smallest apartment, a studio the size of a dorm room so that he would be more likely to spend time in the shared spaces, and it seemed to be working. I sat down beside him and to my delight he excitedly began to fill me in on what I'd missed and offered me the snacks he'd set out. Between each round we talked about his favorite fighter, Mike Tyson, who he surprisingly knew a lot about.

"Maybe you should take up boxing," I suggested. "There's a lot more to it than people realize." Boxing lessons had certainly had helped me get out of a few tough situations. I'm not sure what would have become of me if one the neighborhood fighters hadn't taken me under his wing and shown me how to quickly take someone down.

"Nah, my Dad would never let me. It's too rough." He looked down, visibly uncomfortable.

"You know, Alex," I said, popping some chips in my mouth, "I know you were born and raised in Miami, but your Spanish is perfect. Usually that's not the case with the generation that's born here. How is that?"

We were distracted for a moment by a vicious uppercut thrown by one of the boxers. "See that right there? Mike Tyson invented that move! Right hook to the body, then right uppercut to the head!" After he rewound the punch and watched it two or three times, Alex remembered my question.

"Sorry, you asked about my Spanish. It's because my grandmother would pretend not to understand me if I spoke to her in English, so I had no choice."

"Pretend, huh?" I had to laugh because it sounded exactly like a Cuban grandmother.

"I know she understood plenty from watching her with other people." He looked down and started rifling through the bowl of peanuts. "She's gone now."

"You loved your grandmother, Alex?"

"Yeah. She was my best friend. She used to say that we were exactly alike, and that when I was older I'd see just how much. I catch myself saying and doing things just like her all the time. It's pretty funny. She was right."

"Did you start using after she died?"

"I was fourteen."

"Your parents are busy people, aren't they?"

"Yeah."

We continued to watch the boxing match, and when Alex took a bathroom break between rounds, I sent Amada a quick text. Expecting a fast reply as usual, I left my phone on the coffee table and kept checking it. While I was scrolling through the news waiting for a reply, Lisa came out of her apartment wearing a pair of short shorts and a tank top and sat down on a wing chair across from me.

"Hey, I thought I heard your voice," she said in English. "What's this?" She pointed to the TV and then gathered her hair at the nape and twisted it so it was off her neck. The low cut top sank dangerously low on her breasts, and instead of pulling it back up she left it there.

"Boxing," I said simply. I couldn't say much else to her when I didn't have a translator, though usually I understood most of what she said.

She crossed her legs in a way that made me wonder if this was just a friendly visit or something else. Thankfully she adjusted her top and folded her legs under her body when Alex came back and sat down in his spot.

"Oh, we have company?" he said, less than excited. Something about their body language toward each other was awkward, and I think Lisa noticed his lack of enthusiasm but clearly didn't care.

"Alex, can you ask her in English to text Sal? Tell her I want him to call me."

I sent Amada another text, but I imagined they were somewhere in the house far from their phones. Yet another thing I disliked about that enormous place.

Neither of us heard from Sal or Amada for a good hour, but since we'd been distracted by a very entertaining fight, I hadn't dwelled on it too much. I also caught Lisa looking at me way too many times, which I knew was going to be big trouble. Sal's feelings were part of the equation, and what was an innocent crush on the ship now felt deceptive and calculating on her part, which really rubbed me the wrong way. Thanks to Lisa's antics and a very good fight, I'd been far too focused on trivial matters to notice how much time had passed.

When the fight was over, I looked at my watch. It was ten thirty and I hadn't heard from either of them since I'd left the house. Now I was really getting worried. Alex had said goodnight and was getting ready to go back to his room when I stood up, swatted his shoulder and told him it had been fun to hang out.

"Yeah, it was, Rafa. Do it again sometime?"

"Absolutely," I said, and as he turned to walk away, shoulders hunched, I called after him. "You're doing great, Alex. I've got a lot of plans for you." He gave me a little thumbs up and went back to his room, the two guards already right behind him. I decided I liked the kid, and I knew he could do well if someone bothered to spend time with him and help him find himself.

I was hoping to make a quick exit, but it soon became evident that Lisa had no intention of returning to her room. Quite the opposite actually, as she'd fully stretched out, her shapely legs draped provocatively over the back of the chair. I wondered what exactly she was trying to do, especially without Sal here.

"Please, call Sal," I said in Spanish, too frustrated to try to remember the words in English. "He's not answering." I called Amada and paced by the window while the phone rang, already knowing something was wrong, but it was worse than I could have ever imagined.

CHAPTER FOURTEEN

*I*t didn't take long for Sal and I to become friends. I'd wanted to spend some time with Lisa, too, but Sal was a lot of fun by himself. He was obviously a smart, motivated kid who looked up to Rafa in many ways. He reminded me of the brightest students in my class, who always wanted to know more and asked endless questions. Rafa, he said, was the father figure he'd never had.

"Everyone looks up to Rafa," said Sal. "It's amazing. He cares about everyone so much, especially the ones who need the most help. You'd think a dude like him would be a jerk, the way women throw themselves—"

"I'll bet," I said, arching an eyebrow.

"Sorry," he said, trying to backtrack. "I just mean he's a really good guy who never takes advantage of anyone, even though it would be so easy. People are drawn to him. I swear he could be president one day," he said.

"You have to be born here, I think," I said.

"Well, maybe not president of this country, but of something."

After we talked for a while, I took Sal on a leisurely tour of the house, and as an architecture student he pointed out things about Boxwood I'd never considered before, such as the unusual shape of the roof and the high ratio of balconies to rooms. The house had been exquisitely constructed and maintained, he said, a prime example of the Mediterranean revival style. He was particularly fascinated by its arches and highly ornate keystones.

"Amanda," he said, barely able to contain his excitement, "would you let me use this house as the subject of my thesis?"

"Of course," I said, glad to see his mood lifting. "I'd be honored. You know, Rafa wants to sell it. He thinks it's too big."

"No!" said Sal, horrified. "Let me talk to him. This house is special."

We'd spent so much time chatting and walking the house that we decided to scrap our original plan to play cards and decided to just watch television in the family room until Rafa got back. I offered to make sandwiches, but Sal wouldn't hear of it and insisted I relax and let him take care of the snacks. He'd been in charge of the cocktails and tapas menu on the ship and said he had quite a few go to recipes I'd love, so I told him to make himself at home in the kitchen. True to his word, it took no time at all for Sal to pull together an appetizer platter worthy of a five star restaurant.

"You can tell Rafa's in charge back there," he said, bounding into the living room with a tray in one hand and a bottle of wine in another. "Two trash cans, a stack of bleached towels on every counter, no sponges anywhere and an empty knife block."

"I didn't notice any of that." I said, craning my neck to get a look at the beautifully arranged hors d'oeuvres. Sal had made a small Spanish omelet, grilled chorizo medallions, bacon wrapped dates drizzled in honey and some sort of fresh green dipping sauce for the shrimp cocktail Rafa had left in the fridge. "What's wrong with sponges and knife blocks?"

"Hates 'em. Says they aren't hygienic." Sal pointed to the smoked Gouda and prosciutto on mini toasts I hadn't noticed yet. "Try one of those."

"Everything looks delicious," I said, putting an assortment on my plate. "Which wine did you pick?"

"Just a California pinot you had in the pantry."

"Oh," I said, popping a date in my mouth. "Don't you like Bordeaux?"

"Of course, who doesn't?" he laughed, getting ready to open the bottle.

"Wait," I said. "Go downstairs and pick out a nice one. Do you remember where the cellar is?"

"Really?" said Sal, dropping the domestic wine like a hot potato.

"Yes, whichever one you want. I'm sure Rafa just had that one in there for cooking."

"If you insist," he said with a smile. "Be right back."

I opened the Netflix app and scrolled through my recommendations, which hadn't updated since before I'd gone on the cruise and met Rafa. I couldn't help but notice how dark my movie choices had been, like *Melancholia,* the last film I'd downloaded. I'd had a lot to drink that night and barely remembered anything about the story except the little wire circle, the depressed girl and its apocalyptic ending. Tonight everything offered to me on my homepage seemed unbearably gloomy, so I typed 'romantic comedy' in the search box and began scrolling.

I was just in the middle of watching a preview for the new Sandra Bullock movie when the front door swung wide open. Expecting Rafa to come around from the other side, I dropped the remote and turned in the direction of the foyer, calling out. Unless I'd lost track of time, it seemed a little early for him to be home.

"Hey, handsome, you're back—"

But it wasn't Rafa who entered the foyer and shut the door behind him. It was Achille Demarais, the man I'd met at Delfina's memorial service. First his eyes went first to the back of the house, then to his right in the direction of the living room where Sal and I had settled in for the night. Never having witnessed an almost complete stranger simply walk into my house, I was speechless. I probably should have been afraid and tried to get away, but for whatever reason I remained in my seat, motionless, fascinated by him. Though most people were dwarfed by the volume ceilings and tall wooden doors, Achille still looked imposing, his commanding figure in just the right proportion to the room. Like the other night, he wore a dark suit that fit so perfectly it had to have been custom made.

"Amanda," he said, as if surprised to see me in my own home. "I'm so sorry to disturb you. I'm looking for Dr. De Leon."

"He's not here," I said, rising slowly from my chair, wishing Sal would come back. "How did you get in?"

"It was unlocked. I thought I heard someone say come in. If I was mistaken I do apologize." He put his hand on the doorknob as if to let himself out.

"No, it's fine," I said, realizing now that it had been a misunderstanding, but still it was so unlike Rafa to leave the door unlocked. "Come in and wait. He'll be home soon. Let me call him." I offered Achille a seat in the living room and glanced at my phone, noting there had been a few missed calls and texts. I knew Rafa wouldn't be happy Achille was here, but it seemed unnecessarily rude to ask him to leave, and truthfully his company wasn't unpleasant. We sat across from one another, the awkwardness quickly evaporating.

"No, please don't," he said, more of a command than a request. "I can't stay long. I wasn't expecting to find you here, but I must say it's a pleasant surprise. I just flew in from Europe and thought I'd check in with Rafa on some business matters. He's very difficult to reach."

"Where in Europe?" I asked. I found myself mirroring his body language and quickly shifted in the chair, covering my bare feet with my skirt. "I go a few times a year."

"Geneva." He casually fingered his silk tie as if he were thinking about taking it off. "I went to school in Switzerland, so it seems there's always a party or wedding to attend. Some of my best friends still live there."

"How nice. Switzerland is beautiful."

"Speaking of beautiful scenery, is this your house? What a spectacular property." Achille crossed his legs and made himself comfortable in the wing chair, his manner so charming and graceful that it was difficult to remember why Rafa disliked him so much. For a moment our eyes met, and his lingered until I looked away.

"It is," I said, my gaze cast downward, settling on the food. "Would you care for a canape and some wine?" I asked, gesturing to Sal's tray.

"No, thank you," he said, without so much as a glance in that direction. "You know, I bet we have a lot in common. I have a house about this size in Haiti, right on the water at the top of a cliff. Very scenic. I try to get back as much as I can to check on my horses. Do you ride?"

"No," I said, intrigued. "I've always been too afraid."

"Understandably so," he said, smiling. "My favorite horse is a black stallion named Diablo, but he's thrown me a few times. I should stop riding him, but he's so much fun."

"I bet he's beautiful," I said. "Spirited creatures always are."

"I couldn't agree more," said Achille, his eyes on me again, lasting just one beat too long. I started to relax as romantic images of a couple riding horseback on an exotic beach invaded my brain, the man on a black stallion and the woman close behind on a brown mare. Like watching a movie, the images grew larger and clearer until the figures came into view and I realized that it was us, Achille and me. After a few moments Achille brought his stallion to a slow gallop beside my mare and pulled on her reins until both animals came to a complete stop. He dismounted and came around to me, the Caribbean sun casting its bright, hued light across his honey-colored skin. Gazing down at Achille, I took his outstretched hand and slipped easily off my horse into his arms. With amber eyes aglow, Achille licked his pillowy lips and leaned in to kiss me, murmuring, *Maintenant tu es mienne." Now you are mine.*

"What's going on here?" It was Sal, who had just returned from the wine cellar. As if aware of some danger that had eluded my consciousness, his playful demeanor from earlier was markedly different now, senses heightened. I saw his eyes dart from Achille to the phone on the table, as if wondering whether he should try to grab it.

"Amanda, why didn't you tell me you were entertaining?" said Achille. "It seems I've interrupted your party," he said, rising.

"Rafa's not here," said Sal, eyeing Achille with distaste. Still holding the wine bottle by the neck, he asked, "Was he expecting you?"

Achille ignored Sal's question and turned his attention back to me. "Amanda, I can't tell you how much I've enjoyed chatting with you, but I really should be going. Please give your fiancée my regards and ask him to call me. I have a proposition for him."

"Of course," I said, still reeling from the vision of us on the horses. Achille grinned as if he could read my mind, which of course was impossible. Deeply disturbed that I'd thought about kissing another man when I was so deeply in love with Rafa, I was at least thankful no one would ever know. Eager to shake off the strange feelings that Achille stirred in me, I was just about to walk him to the door when my phone vibrated on the coffee table and Rafa's name popped up on the screen.

"It's him," I said, reaching for the phone. I pressed the green button and was just about to bring the phone to my ear when Achille held out his hand.

"May I?" he asked. "I really do need to ask him a question."

"Certainly," I said, giving him my phone without a second thought. I was finding it very difficult to say no to any of Achille's requests, big or small.

"Thank you," he said, pointing to the door. "I'll leave it on the bench outside. Always a pleasure, Amanda." He extended a warm greeting to Rafa just before stepping out on to the loggia and closing the door behind him to take the call.

CHAPTER FIFTEEN

"*R*afa, my friend! It's Achille," he said.

My heart leaped into my throat, and I have no doubt I went white as a ghost because Lisa noticed the change in my expression and sat right up.

"What the *fuck* are you doing with my wife's phone?" I snarled.

"Relax," he said, his French accent even more pronounced in Spanish than it was in English. "Everything's fine."

My mind raced, thinking of every possible scenario. Had he kidnapped her? What had he done to her already? I was falling apart inside, but I knew I couldn't show an ounce of weakness to this bastard. "If you've touched her, you're dead. Do you hear me?"

"Come on. No need for threats. We've just been sitting in the living room having a nice conversation. She's charming, but you know that."

They were still at the house. The only other person in the room was Lisa, and I had no expedient way of telling her to call 911 or why, so I took off downstairs and tried to get to the Ferrari as fast as I could.

"Is Sal alright?" I asked through gritted teeth.

"Yes, of course. How's my buddy, Alex?" he asked, his voice dripping with sarcasm. "I'd really like to pay him a visit soon."

"I don't know who you're talking about," I said, which probably wasn't the best idea, but all I could think about was how frightened my Amada must be. I made it out to the car in record time and started the engine, not caring if Desmarais heard it.

"Yes, you fucking do, asshole!" he yelled into the phone. "This is your last chance. Next time, I put her on a boat and take her to Haiti with me. I promise you *no one* will find her there, so pay attention.

"My associate Luc will come have a drink with you tomorrow night at nine. You'll invite him in and ask Alex to join you. That's all I need. If you have police waiting, or you refuse him entrance, this exquisite beauty and I are going to get to know each other very well."

"Let me talk to my wife." I swung into traffic and gunned the engine of the Ferrari, narrowly avoiding two cars and a truck. Angry drivers blared their horns at me as I floored it, completely disregarding every red light and vehicle in my way.

"She's not your wife yet, you liar," said Demarais, sickeningly calm once again. "You can slow down you know. I'll be gone way before you get here."

"You'd better be," I threatened, but he only laughed.

"Oh, one last thing," he said. "Next time she wants you to fuck her in the pool, don't be such a pussy. She won't have to ask *me* twice." The line went dead, and then it hit me. He'd been watching us. He heard us talking. And he'd seen me kiss and touch Amada all over, and he *liked* what he saw.

By the time I flew inside the house, Amada and Sal were in the kitchen. Sal stood on one side of the counter while Amada sat on the other side, looking down into a glass of wine.

"Rafa," she said. She smiled when she saw me but didn't seem entirely there. She had to be in shock.

"Oh my God, baby, are you alright? Did he hurt you?" I hugged her and then looked her over. She was still wearing the same clothes from earlier and didn't seem any different.

"She's fine," said Sal.

"I am, Rafa," she said simply. "There's nothing to be upset about." I noticed the glazed look in her eyes again, almost as if she'd awakened from a nap. She was too calm, I thought, but wanting more detail, I motioned for Sal to follow me into the dining room.

"What the fuck happened? How are you both so calm?"

Sal told me how he'd come up from the cellar to find Achille in the living room flirting with Amada. "I remembered how you almost killed this dude the night of the party, so I knew he wasn't supposed to be here. We have home invasions in Colombia all the time, so I kept pretty calm. I was just wishing he would take what he wanted, money or whatever, and leave. But when I saw he wasn't looking around or interested in the house, it occurred to me that she's so rich, maybe what he wanted to take was *her.* That's when I started to get fucking nervous. Damn, Rafa, get some dogs. She said the door was unlocked and he walked right in."

"No fucking way that door was unlocked!" I snapped, losing my temper. Poor Sal deserved none of this, but I was beside myself.

"Man, that dude is suave. You should have seen him stroll out of here with the suit and the accent, like a GQ model or some shit. He was really hitting on her, Rafa. When I walked in he was staring at her like he was about to—I'm not sure what would have happened if she'd been here alone."

"Sal—what the fuck!" I bellowed.

"I know, man." Sal put his hand on my shoulder and spoke softly. "Calm down or you're going to upset her."

"Alright," I said, grateful for his self-possession. In his position, I don't know that I could have maintained my cool. "No gun?"

"He might have had one, but he didn't take it out."

I was speechless and felt like I'd been punched in the stomach, so I sank down into a chair at the dining room table. Sal went back into the kitchen with Amada, but I wanted to pull myself together a little more before I went to her. I sat in the chair and waited until I could think clearly, going over the night's events in my mind over and over. *What if Sal hadn't been here?*

Still in somewhat of a daze, I decided to call Oscar and tell him what happened. I'd barely gotten half the story out before he said he was coming right over, but I assured him it wasn't necessary.

"Oscar, what should I do? Contact the police and file a report?" There was a long pause, so I asked again. "Oscar? Are you there?"

"Technically he didn't do anything illegal that would be worth their time. All they'll do is make you miserable asking a million questions to put in a file somewhere. It won't be to your benefit." His voice was low and tempered.

"So then don't?"

"No," he said. "Ultimately it might be better if there's no paper trail leading back to you."

I went back outside and shut off the engine and closed car the door, thankful I'd been clear-headed enough to at least put the Ferrari in park before running into the house. I checked the front door for damage or tampering and found nothing out of the ordinary. I was a meticulous person, always careful with things, and distrustful of almost everyone. He had gotten in somehow, but it wasn't because I had forgotten to lock the door. That much I knew.

In the kitchen I hugged and kissed my Amada again. She seemed to be snapping out of it somewhat, and so did Sal. I was still in a fog myself and didn't know what else to do, so I pulled out the meat from this morning and turned on the grill.

"What's that?" asked Sal.

"Mojo steak." Always a great team in the kitchen, Sal caught the towel I tossed in his direction and threw it over his shoulder, ready to cook. He spotted the beans soaking in the bowl on the counter and went in the pantry to find a stock pot while I took out a knife and started chopping the pepper and onion, and when the vegetables hit the hot pan and sizzled, their distinctive comforting aroma spread throughout the kitchen.

"Ah, there's nothing like the smell of onions and peppers," said Sal, crossing behind me with an enormous Dutch oven.

"So, what kind of dogs are we getting, Rafa?" asked Amada. "German Shepherds?"

"Hey, what about Rottweilers?" Sal turned on the water at the stove and let the pot fill while he rinsed the beans in a colander at the sink. "Those dogs are badass. They'll fuck someone's shit up." He nodded with conviction. "Rottweilers."

"If Amada wants German Shepherds, then that's what it has to be." I eyed her from across the kitchen, still aware of a strange lethargy she hadn't been able to shake off yet.

"Hey, don't get me wrong," he said over his shoulder. "I like 'em, too. German Shepherds are damn nice dogs. Smart as hell."

"Hey, buddy." I leaned away from the splash as he shook out the water, a pool of jet forming in the bottom of the sink. "I owe you. Thanks."

"Get outta here. You don't owe me shit," he said, darting around me with the colander. At the stove he turned the knob to high, dumped the beans into the deep pot, and covered it with the lid, pausing only to peek at the water level one more time.

"I know what we need," he said, wiping his hands on the towel. "Where's the bar? I'm getting us all a shot."

"I agree. It's the big cabinet in the living room," said Amada. "Am I allowed, Daddy?" I knew she was trying to flirt and lighten my mood, but I was still too shaken to even think about it.

"Damn," said Sal, looking at her, then at me. "I don't know if I need to be hearing about all *that*." He went off to find the liquor, and though I knew it was time to stir the peppers and onions, I went to my Amada instead.

"Were you scared?" I held her face in my hands and made her look at me.

"At first," said Amada weakly, "but it wasn't like that. He thought someone told him to come in."

"What?" None of this made sense, and I wasn't sure what to make of her obvious confusion. I hadn't discussed Achille in any great detail with Amada because I hadn't wanted to frighten her, but I'd clearly warned her to stay away from him. I couldn't figure out why she'd invited him inside when she knew I wanted him as far away from us as possible. She finally met my eyes, her expression a mix of anxiety and excitement, and it was then that I recognized a hint of something I'd seen many times before, the residue of *brujería* or witchcraft.

"He wants you, Amada, and he's using something powerful. It's hypnosis or magic, or both. I can't tell yet," I said, my heart breaking apart into pieces.

"Rafa," she pleaded, "I would never—"

"I know, mamita. It's not your fault."

I held her close, fully driven by instinct to protect the woman who would soon be my wife and the mother of my children. Anything that came between us and our family would have to perish, and for the first time I was as compelled to extinguish life as I was to preserve it, my heart hardening to the world as it softened for my Amada.

ACKNOWLEDGEMENTS

Preceding all others, I'd like to thank Omnific Publishing for their professionalism and skilled management of the complex publishing process. In a capricious and often illusory industry, Omnific stands well above the rest, a giant in the making. Special thanks to Elizabeth Riley, Ph.D., whose erudite yet artistic editing style is the perfect elixir for nervous writers, the most demanding and fragile souls on earth. Last but certainly not least, I would like to express my gratitude for this beautiful nation called America, our cherished home, and then send a message of support to the Cuban people both here and there, who have bravely persevered in spite of it all.

ABOUT THE AUTHOR

Kim is a first generation Cuban American who grew up with a Spanish-speaking family that loved to tell stories, play cards and talk late into the night. One of her earliest memories is the day her grandmother casually swiped a poisonous banana spider off her shoulder, prompting Kim to ask why she wasn't afraid of bugs. "The outhouse scorpions in Cuba never bothered me much," she said. "Neither did the snakes or spiders. Just the toads." Ultimately her grandmother's long, fantastic tales of colorful characters and life in early twentieth-century Cuba fed Kim's imagination and sparked a lifetime love of storytelling. Accordingly, as a writer, Kim finds herself drawn to themes of love, language, diversity, diaspora, and adventure.

9 781623 422554